The Soldier Gets His Girl

JANE POLLER

By Jane Poller

Crimson Creek

The Soldier Gets His Girl
The Sheriff Gets His Girl
The Songwriter Gets His Girl
The Surgeon Gets His Girl
The Mechanic Gets His Girl
The Ranger Gets His Girl
The Cowboy Gets His Girl

Vinci Books

vinci-books.com

Published by Vinci Books Ltd in 2026

1

Copyright © Jane Poller 2021

The author has asserted their moral right to be identified as the author of this work in accordance with the Copyright, Designs and Patents Act 1988. This work is a work of fiction. Names, characters, places and incidents are the product of the author's imagination or are used fictitiously. Any resemblance to actual persons, living or dead, places and incidents is entirely coincidental.

All rights reserved. No part of this publication may be copied, reproduced, distributed, stored in any retrieval system, or transmitted in any form or by any means, including photocopying, recording, or other electronic or mechanical methods, nor used as a source for any form of machine learning including AI datasets, without the prior written permission of the publisher.

The publisher and the author have made every effort to obtain permissions for any third party material used in this book and to comply with copyright law. Any queries in this respect should be brought to the attention of the publisher and any omissions will be corrected in future editions.

A CIP catalogue record for this book is available from the British Library.

Paperback ISBN: 9781036707934

The EU GPSR authorised representative is Logos Europe, 9 rue Nicolas Poussion, 17000 La Rochelle, France
contact@logoseurope.eu

Chapter One

The scent of flour and cinnamon surrounded her before soft hands covered her eyes from behind. A light, tinkling voice said, "Guess who?"

Cindy didn't even have to guess.

"Maryanne."

"No fooling you, is there." Her sister chuckled as she rounded the bench and sat beside Cindy. "You ready for work?"

"Yep, just waiting on you." Cindy eyed her sister. An orange t-shirt with a smiling black pumpkin stretched over her chest and hung off one shoulder, showing her orange bra strap. Beside the pumpkin was a steaming cup that said *I'm a latte to handle.*

"Nice shirt," Cindy said with a nod. Compared to her own dark purple scrubs, her sister always seemed perfectly put together. The candy corn earrings, black choker, and black skinny jeans really put the look all together, and Cindy sighed wistfully.

"How can you wear those all day?" Cindy asked,

pointing at the high heeled, black open-toed shoes. Her baby sister always knew what she wanted and charged after it with abandon. If someone tried to convince her to do something else, she'd dig in her heels and do it anyway. She knew better than to tell her to wear something more practical while at the bakery.

"What, these? They're the most comfortable pair I own. You should try them on."

She kicked them off as Cindy shook her head. "Nah, I'm okay."

She looked at her sneakers, the epitome of comfort. Though comfortable, they still pinched her toes at the end of the day. She sighed as the timer on her phone went off. She silenced it and gathered her purse from her feet.

"James! Owen! I'm heading to work!" Cindy called to the boys on the playground.

Maryanne jumped up and strode with confidence toward the playground equipment. "I'll get them and meet you at the parking lot."

Cindy stood and stretched, looking for the oldest.

She smiled as her lanky boy ran over from the soccer field. Her brown-haired little boy wasn't so little anymore. He was only twelve, but already taller than her. But then again, she was barely five feet, so that wasn't saying much.

She smoothed the escaped curls back into her braid as she waited for him. "Good practice tonight?" she asked Cody with a smile.

He nodded and grinned, his teeth still too big for his mouth. "Yep. All good. Coach says I need to work on cardio at home."

She frowned, thinking out loud as they turned to the parking lot. "Okay, we can figure that out. I don't want you running in the neighborhood, though. It's not safe enough."

He rolled his hazel eyes, whining, "Mom, we live in like, the smallest town ever. There's only a few thousand people here! No one is going to do anything."

Maryanne and the other boys caught up to them at the fork in the sidewalk. They were talking a mile a minute, the two boys vying for their Aunt Maryanne's attention.

"Old habits die hard, though. Living in Houston, caution was ingrained into us," she reminded Cody.

Maryanne said something so low Cindy couldn't hear, then James fell back to walk with Cindy and Cody, tucking his little hand into hers.

Maryanne took off running, and Owen yelled, "Hey, that's cheating!" Then he raced after her, their laughter ringing in the air.

Cody sighed, "I know, Mom. But this isn't Houston. It's Crimson Creek, where nothing ever happens and everyone's happy."

Cindy grinned as they reached the SUV. Cindy was still helping James inside her SUV when Maryanne's little red car drove past, Owen smiling and waving from the backseat. Moving here had been the right choice, even though it was in the middle of nowhere. It was her hometown, a sanctuary that she was so glad to provide for her boys. They chatted about homework and their plans for the weekend before she dropped them off at their apartment with Maryanne.

She kissed them all before hopping back into her SUV to head to work. Every weekend, her heart broke a little as she had to leave them with her mom or her sister. Those few precious moments at the park during Cody's soccer practice were a balm to her soul and made her feel like maybe she wasn't totally failing as a single mom.

Working the weekend shift at the hospital was hard, but

worth the money. Cindy rounded the corner of the hallway of the hospital, humming *Walking on Sunshine*, bobbing her head, and trying not to think of the full moon tonight on a Friday night.

She shook off thoughts of missing so much in her boys' lives. It was going to be a great but busy weekend shift, then she'd go home and snuggle them.

Then on Monday, she'd start all over again with her second job as a physical therapy assistant. Juggling work seven days a week and the boys' school events was still better than the six years of hell they'd lived through. Moving here had been the right decision. She pushed thoughts of her ex-husband out of her mind too as she approached the nurse's station.

Resuming her song, she smiled and greeted Carrie. "Evening! How's it going tonight? You ready to get out of here?"

"God, so ready. I don't envy you the night shift. The full moon already has us busy as bees." Carrie bounced on her feet and leaned in to whisper, "But they just brought up a hunk from the ER. Girl, I am so jealous you get to take care of him. He's delicious, even rolling in on a gurney and hurtin'!" She passed off his chart, and Cindy skimmed it as they caught up on their lives from the past week.

"Kidney stone? Ouch." She wrinkled her nose as she turned to head into the room. The door opened, and she chatted with the two ER nurses before they left.

She entered the room and stopped. Normally, she'd be checking his IV, his chart, and the readouts from the ER. But Carrie had definitely been telling the truth about the hunk.

His jet-black hair was longer on top and short on the

sides. It looked like he'd been running his fingers through it a lot today.

Her heart skipped a beat as she glanced over his face. The nurse in her noted he was breathing deeply and methodically through the pain.

The woman in her noted the cleft in his chin and the crooked nose. He had high cheekbones and a five o'clock shadow on a firm jaw that was clenched in pain.

He wore a plain black t-shirt that stretched tightly over his chest. She sighed, catching sight of the huge biceps as he clenched his fists.

His icy blue eyes popped open at the sound of her sigh and captured her gaze. Her breath stuttered as he stared at her without blinking, then she straightened her spine and stepped toward him.

"Ma'am." His voice was deep and sent a tingle up her spine. But the pain clear in the tight, growly words sent her into action.

She cleared her throat with a smile. "Hello, Andrew. I'll be your nurse this weekend, if you're here that long. I hear you have a kidney stone?"

He nodded and closed his eyes again. "That's what they tell me. Had a CT scan already to confirm. And call me Andy."

"Nice to meet you, Andy. I'm Cindy. We'll wait for the CT results. Then the doctor will go over your treatment plan. On a scale of zero to ten, what's your pain level?"

"About an eight, I reckon, but I've had worse." He waved to his left foot, sticking out of the sheet.

He was wearing blue basketball shorts and his thighs looked like they could crush a man. They were so big.

She blinked at the running prosthesis attached below his

knee. How had she missed that when she walked in? Geez, some nurse she was.

"What happened there?" she asked, as she leaned over to check his IV. Hell, he smelled good. A combination of leather and wood smoke tickled her nose. She inhaled deeply.

"IED hit the Humvee in Afghanistan seventeen months ago." He clenched his teeth, her eyes dilating slightly with the pain.

"Thank you for your service," she said softly. "My father was in the Army for twenty-three years. What branch are you in?"

"Was... They kicked me out."

"Oh," she frowned, turning to the computer at his bedside and typing away. "I'm sorry."

He sighed and rubbed his eyes. "Not your fault. If I'd been injured twelve years ago when I first joined, I might have been able to switch my MOS and stay in."

"Twelve years? So, was it a medical retirement?" She checked the machines, then documented the information.

"Yeah," he said, seeming to melt into the bed in defeat.

"That's gotta be tough. Twelve years is a long time. Where all were you stationed? We moved a lot with the Army. The longest we were ever in one place was Fort Hood."

"Hood was my last duty station. You know what they say about Fort Hood, don't you?"

She grinned back. "Oh yeah. To leave, you either die or retire. So, I guess you got lucky, even with the bum leg. Medical retirement beats dead, doesn't it?"

He blinked rapidly, and his forehead wrinkled. "I guess it does."

She smiled and patted his arm. Jerking her hand back at

the spark of electricity that shot through her, she walked around the end of the bed to take his blood pressure. Her face heated, but hopefully her caramel complexion would keep him from noticing the blush. Still, she'd keep up a steady stream of conversation to distract him from the pain and her own awkwardness.

"We were stationed in several other places, but my favorites were the ones with trees. How about you? What was your favorite duty station?" She monitored the blood pressure machine and waited for it to stop testing him.

He groaned and clutched his side. "I was at Campbell first. The Land Between the Lakes was my favorite area. It was peaceful there."

She nodded and charted the results of the machine. "Peace is underrated. The world needs more peaceful places for sure."

He just grunted, so she continued. "The medication in your IV should kick in any minute now. You can rest until the doctor gets here, if you'd like." She unwrapped the blood pressure cuff, inhaling his earthy scent once more.

He licked his lips as though thirsty. "Can you talk to me until he gets here? You're a wonderful distraction from the pain."

She smiled and nodded, grabbing the plastic up of water with a straw from his bedside table and holding it to his lips to drink. "Sure thing. I haven't been to the Land Between the Lakes, but I grew up vacationing in the Arkansas Ozarks. I love the mountains! And trees. It's why I was so happy to move back here."

He stopped drinking and laid his head back on the bed with a wince. "How long have you lived here?" he wheezed.

She put the cup back on the table as she talked. "My grandmother lived in this part of Texas, so we came up and joined her about five years ago. She lost a foot to diabetes, so I'm quite familiar with prosthetics. Helping take care of her is actually why I became a nurse... How are your physical therapies going?"

He turned pale and whispered, "Been doing them on my own for the past week, since I moved into my house." He clutched his stomach and groaned, and she knew exactly what that body language meant.

She grabbed the bowl beside his bed in time for him to throw up. She crooned to him softly, telling him it was going to be all right.

When he'd finished, she hummed *Let it Go* while she cleaned up and grabbed him a wet cloth. She wiped his face, and he reached up, taking the cloth gently from her.

His lips twitched in a shaky smile. "Thank you, but I got it. Is that the cartoon movie? We watched that in Iraq." He wiped his face, and she grabbed the cup of water again.

Holding it to his lips, she couldn't help but notice how full they were. Perfect for kissing. *Wait, what the hell am I thinking? He just threw up! I shouldn't be thinking about kissing him!*

"It's a 'girly movie' according to my oldest, but he still watches it with us on movie night. My sister lives in town and loves the girly movies. She may be an adult, but not with Disney princess movies." She put the cup back on the table as he seemed to finally relax.

"Your oldest?" His eyes fluttered slowly, his eyes glazing over.

"I have three boys, twelve, ten, and four. Looks like the meds are kicking in. You rest until the doctor gets here," she said.

She felt pulled to him by an invisible string. It was more intense than how she normally ached to stop the pain of a patient. She left the door cracked when she left, not really wanting to go too far away from him. She snorted. What was wrong with her? Yeah, she could stare at his handsome face all night. But she'd never been drawn to a patient before. Or any man, really, since her ex.

She kept thinking of him as she checked the other patients on the floor, then went to the nurse's station. Movement from the corner of her eye caused Cindy to look up from charting at the computer. Dr. Jensen shuffled down the hallway. The sweet, old man's bushy white hair stuck up every which way. Probably should have retired by now, but she'd gotten to know him well when her grandmother had been a patient of his.

She sat back in her chair and smiled as he rounded into the nurse's station. "You pulled the short straw this weekend, huh?"

He cleaned his glasses on his shirt and shrugged. "Just another full moon weekend. Amanda sent some fried chicken, so I at least have that to look forward to."

He grabbed the chart from beside her desk, giving it a quick read. Groaning echoed through the hall, and a chill went down her spine. She jumped up and sped after the doctor into Andy's room.

He was tangled up in the sheets. Sweat poured off him as he moaned, his eyes closed. She grabbed the washrag and wiped his forehead, shushing him.

"No," he groaned, "No! You can't take it. No, I need it. It's fine! It's fine!" He shouted louder and louder with every sentence. Dr. Jensen was trying to untie his legs from the sheets.

"Shh. It's alright," Cindy crooned softly. His enormous arms grabbed her and pulled her half on top of him.

"No," he said, burying his head in the crook of her neck. Her curly hair had come mostly undone from her braid and spread over them. She gasped as his nose touched the soft spot where her neck met her shoulder.

"No, don't go. Don't leave me," he groaned.

She pushed off his chest, trying to sit up, certain that her weight was hurting his kidney stone. But he simply wrapped his arms around her tighter. She huffed and shifted sideways on him, drawing her knees up onto the side of the bed.

Feet hanging off the bed, her entire chest was on top of him, trapped in his arms. Dr. Jensen had gotten the sheets untangled and pulled away from his legs, muttering the whole time as he began to test Andy's groin and stomach.

"Yep, time to pass that kidney stone. Just a few minutes more," the doctor said.

"Andy, wake up," she said, trying to speak strongly, but hearing the wobble in her voice. He jerked back against the bed, and she pushed on his chest to see his face.

His bright blue eyes stared over her shoulder, unseeing.

"Andy," she mumbled, wiping his forehead with the washcloth. He sucked in a breath like a drowning man. The move pressed her breasts even tighter against his chest. It was like a chain reaction, making her gasp in response. It'd been years since a man held her.

Then Dr. Jensen spoke up with a strict, no-nonsense tone of voice that reminded her of how her dad used to talk when he went into military mode. "Andy, Andy, wake up. You need to pass this kidney stone NOW."

She saw Andy's gaze snap around, then lock onto her. He looked confused as he tried to place her, but his eyes were clearer.

"I'm Cindy, your nurse. You're in the hospital, and you need to pee to push this kidney stone. Do you hear me?"

The Soldier Gets His Girl

His arms wrapped tighter around her as he whispered, "Yes, just—just don't leave me."

She nodded. "I won't. But listen to the doctor. You need to push, alright? You can do this."

He nodded, then buried his face in her neck again. His groans grew louder as his arms tightened.

She held onto his shoulder and wiped his forehead with her other hand. She couldn't move, even if she wanted to, could barely use her arms.

His breathing sped up, and she tried to get him to take a deep breath. He roared, squeezing her enough that her back popped.

But it must have been when he finally passed the kidney stone, because she heard a soft *plink* before he slowly let his arms relax. He breathed in deeply at her neck before letting her go completely and leaning back, panting.

She stood on wobbly legs, staring into his eyes. She was breathing as deeply as he was, but it wasn't from pain. Her cheeks burned as she glanced at Dr. Jensen as she climbed off the bed.

He handed her the cup with the stone in it. He rolled up the now soiled top sheet and disposed of it in the receptacle. Cindy glanced down and noted that his basketball shorts were still clean.

"Well done! You can stay in your clothes if you want, Andy. I kept it contained," Dr. Jensen said as he washed his hands. "You should be feeling better soon. Your CT scan only showed the one kidney stone, and that was it. You'll need to stay overnight for observation, but you can probably go home in the morning."

Andy nodded shakily. "Thank you."

"If you need me, I'll be down the hall. Just holler,

alright?" Dr. Jensen said as he grabbed the cup from her and walked out the door.

Cindy stood frozen, her gaze locked on Andy's. They both still breathed heavily. Even through the haze of pain, she saw awareness in his eyes.

She breathed deeply, glancing around in panic. Her eyes lit on the cup of ice water from earlier. She helped him drink. Putting it back, she checked his IVs.

"Well, you didn't bust an IV, so that's good."

He smiled wryly. "I'm sorry about earlier. I hope I didn't hurt you."

"No, no. It's fine. I've had worse in this hospital, trust me. I'm just glad that you got the job done so quickly!"

He rubbed his side softly. "Yeah, it doesn't seem like it's been quick. It's been hurting for weeks now."

"My friend Holly is really into natural medicine and such. We like to compare notes, so to speak. Her great-aunt got kidney stones after her house burned down."

She put the cup back on the table and turned the computer on to chart the incident as she continued talking. "Her aunt was scared to death of what would happen next. And that's what caused her kidney stone. Are you scared of something like that?"

She wondered if he had more than physical pain.

He looked across the room for a few minutes, staring unseeing. She thought he wasn't going to answer. So, she grabbed clean sheets and blankets.

After she'd made the bed and tucked the blankets around him, she turned to leave.

His soft voice stopped her at the foot of his bed. "I guess I'm afraid of what comes next. I've been gone for nearly two years. I didn't expect... Well, now that I'm retired? I don't know what to do."

She glanced at him as his eyes fluttered slowly. She grabbed the washcloth and smoothed the frown line between his forehead. The tension in his shoulders visibly released.

"Thank you," he whispered.

It made her heart flip over to know that she was helping. She started to reply but stopped. He was asleep, the deep snoring breath making her shoulders finally relax. He needed to sleep, especially after tonight's adventure in the hospital.

Chapter Two

The rest of the night shift was just as busy. The full moon finally waned around one in the morning, and the floor finally chilled out enough for her to breathe through the rest of her shift. Before she went to the quiet room for her required scheduled sleep, she found herself outside his room.

She grabbed the breakfast tray from the chart and pushed the door open. "Good morning! How are you feeling today?"

He pushed the button on the bed to sit up, grimacing and rubbing his jaw. Covered in a five o'clock shadow, he looked gruff and a real man's man. Her dad would've liked him.

"I'm fine. Are you alright? I didn't squeeze you too tight, did I?" His voice was so deep, it made her stomach quiver.

She placed the tray on the rolling desk and pulled it to him, ignoring the attraction. It wasn't like she could or would do anything about it.

She smiled brightly and waved a hand. "Oh, I'm alright

too. Don't worry about it. Happens all the time around here. Were you having a nightmare about when they took your leg? My dad used to have nightmares."

He frowned and looked down at the tray, reaching for the fork. Typical guy to ignore a tough question.

She sighed and shrugged. "If you're not fine, you're not fine. No need to gloss over it. I'm a nurse. You can be honest."

He looked up, still frowning. But she refused to break eye contact, crossing her arms. He finally took a big breath and cocked one eyebrow up. "Fine. I'm not fine, but I'll be fine, okay?"

She nodded, "Sure. Fine." Her lips twitched, then a giggle escaped. He blinked before a chuckle escaped, making him clutch at his side.

"Oh, no laughing. Laughing is *not* fine!" he gasped.

Cindy laughed loudly but reached over to rub her hand across his forehead to feel for a temperature. She just wanted an excuse to touch him. "Oh, you poor thing. I'm sorry!"

He snorted as he grabbed her hand, holding it for a second too long. Butterflies danced in her stomach. "No, you're not. You're enjoying this."

She felt her face soften as she smiled again, cradling her hand when he released it. "Ha! You're right. I'm not that sorry. You should smile and laugh more, though. It's good for the soul."

He smiled at her. "Yes, ma'am. Whatever you say."

Dr. Jensen came into the room as Andy began eating his eggs and bacon. "Well, good morning! How's our fair patient today?"

"Fine, doctor," he said.

Cindy laughed too loudly, then fake coughed to cover it.

She caught Andy's eyes, and he winked. She turned and fiddled with the computer.

"Well, it looks like you can discharge within the hour. I can't let you drive yourself home, though. You'll need a ride."

Andy threw his head back against the bed and groaned. She hurried to his side, thinking he was in pain. But he said, "Can I stay here until I can drive myself?"

"Do you not have anyone?" Her chest lurched with the need to take care of him.

He grimaced. "No, it's not that. It's just... my aunt can be a bit much. And if she comes, then she'll smother me next week. I thought this first week home had been rough with her hovering..."

Clicking in the hallway echoed throughout the room, followed by a soft voice. She frowned as Andy froze, his eyes wide.

Suzie, one of the older women at church who still tried to be hip and fashionable, walked through the door. A friend of Cindy's mom, she didn't even glance at Cindy or Dr. Jensen as her poodle skirt swished from side to side.

"There you are!" she said, rushing to the bedside. "You weren't at home this morning, so I used that Find My Friends app, and it said you were here. What's going on?"

Cindy glanced between Andy and Suzie. Suzie's blond and gray hair was pulled back in a ponytail, accentuating the fine lines around her eyes. She didn't act like an older woman; she seemed to bounce and glow with energy.

When she moved to town, Suzie had been one of the church ladies who'd welcomed her. She'd been gone for almost two years but had been at the ladies' meeting at church earlier this month.

Suddenly, it clicked in her head like a puzzle.

phone, and Cindy's brows rose as she stepped into the hallway with it to go over the details.

Andy sighed and shifted on the bed. "Sorry about her. I told you she could be a bit much."

Dr. Jensen said, "Nothing we're not used to, son. I grew up with her." The doctor chuckled and went to the door. "I'm going to go finish up the paperwork. I'll be right back for your signature. Cindy, you can unhook him."

Cindy nodded, turning to him as they were left alone. "You alright?" She pulled out his IVs.

He sighed and nodded, "I'm fine."

She giggled. He smirked at her. That smirk haunted her as she went to sleep in the quiet room at the hospital.

On Sunday night, she wearily pushed through her apartment door. The sounds of splashing and little laughter echoed through the small space.

"Hey, sis! How was work?" Maryanne asked, ducking her head out of the kitchen. Cindy closed the door and kicked off her shoes.

"Not too bad," she replied, stepping into the kitchen and leaning against the cabinets as her sister finished stirring dinner on the stove.

Maryanne knew the weekends were brutal, but there was no point in complaining about it. She slept at the hospital on her mandatory rests for the forty-eight-hour shift. Missing her boys on the weekends was the worst.

"Oh, come on. It was a full moon. You don't have to lie to me. I'm your favorite sister."

Cindy chuckled. "You're my only sister. But seriously, the hospital was fine." Her cheeks widened in a grin. She seriously hadn't been able to say that word all weekend without thinking of Andy.

"Whoa, what's that smile for? Something good happen

at work?" Maryanne plated up some pasta. The noise in the bathroom grew louder, and Cindy sighed and stepped toward the entrance.

Maryanne's hand on her arm stopped her. "I'll get it. You sit and eat. You look like you're about to drop."

Cindy grabbed a plate and sat at the table, enjoying the warm garlic bread. Homemade food after hospital cafeteria food all weekend just hit differently. What would be good under normal circumstances became the most amazing meal she'd ever eaten every Sunday night.

Maryanne came back into the kitchen, wiping her wet hands on her black leggings.

Cindy shoveled another bite of alfredo into her mouth. "God, sis, you have no idea how good this tastes. Thanks for always helping. I—I don't know what I'd do without you and Mom."

Maryanne sat at the table with a plate, the sparkles on the orange pumpkin on her oversized shirt winking in the fluorescent light above.

"Don't mention it. You know we'd do anything for you. That's what family is for, right? And we have a lot of fun with the boys. They're no trouble at all."

"Speaking of, are they getting ready for bed?"

"They probably got more water on the floor than on themselves. But hey, It's better than nothing." Maryanne lifted the fork.

"How was the soccer game this weekend?"

"Oh, it was good! Cody had this really cool block in the last part of it. I got it on video! Here." She fiddled with her phone, then handed it over.

Cindy's heart lurched as she watched him check his opponent and sweep the ball right out from under him. The need to be there for him threatened to overwhelm her.

The Soldier Gets His Girl

Cody joined them in the kitchen. "Hey, bud! Good game! Auntie M showed me the video of that block."

"Yeah, it was pretty sick," he said, as he grabbed a glass of water and leaned against the counter. He crossed his ankles and grinned so big it took over his entire face.

"Dude didn't even see it coming! Coach said I did good and might move up to JV next year. Wouldn't that be cool? I'd get to play against the eighth and ninth graders!"

"That'd be amazing!" Cindy jumped up to hug him.

He gave her a quick hug back before ducking back down the hall. Owen came running in, his socks sliding on the tile.

He hit her right in the legs and nearly knocked her down. "Whoa there! What's the hurry?"

"Mama, Mama, Mama! I have a loose tooth! Look!" he said, sticking his still wet finger into his mouth and wiggling his front bottom tooth. Her heart skipped a beat. *No! He couldn't be big enough to lose teeth already, could he?*

"What? Oh wow!" she said, bending down to get a closer look.

She overly dramatized looking down the hallway, before lowering her voice to a whisper, "I think you might lose that tooth before your brothers lost theirs. They didn't lose their first tooth until they were five!"

He grinned and whooped loudly, rushing down the hall to tell his brothers that he was going to beat them in the first tooth competition.

"They're growing up so fast," Cindy said, sitting back down at the table. She pushed the plate away and laid her head down with a groan. Maryanne picked up the plate and cleaned up.

"Yeah, but it's alright. Look how amazing they're doing. They may be loud and typical boys... but they're respectful and pay more attention than most adults. You're doing an outstanding job with them," Maryanne said, drying the last dish.

Cindy checked her phone emails and sighed.

"No interviews?"

Cindy shook her head. "I don't get it. Both Decatur and Denton hospitals have openings I qualify for. I've applied and there's been no word!"

"Yeah, but when do the jobs close?"

She frowned, "One closed last week, and another closes this week. The third... I'm not sure. I can't remember."

"Well, they either, have internal candidates that they were going to promote or they were waiting for the positions to close. You're going to be fine!"

"I just want to be home more. I'm so tired of missing out, M. I want to be home when they're home, go to soccer games, and be part of losing teeth!" Cindy swiped a tear out of her eye.

Maryanne drew her into a hug, the kind only sisters give.

"I know you want to be here. And they know that too. You'll get the job, don't worry. It's going to be fine."

Cindy chuckled at the word and squeezed her sister one more time before she headed home for the night. Monday started her PTA patients for the week. She already needed a day off.

Chapter Three

"I can't believe I let you talk me into this. I'm already sore!" Landry complained as they walked through the parking lot outside the gym. Andy took great pride in smoking Landry in cardio, especially with his recent hospital stay. Dark eyes and a sweet smile haunted him at the oddest moments, but he didn't want anything to do with any doctors or nurses.

Andy wiped his face with a small towel and slung his gym bag over his shoulder. "Me? You're the one who wanted to go to the bar!"

"Yeah, because I have to. My brothers would kill me if I didn't." Landry sighed and ran his fingers through his still wet hair. The gym had been good for them both, but he wasn't so sure the bar would be.

Andy teased. "*Have* to go to the bar? Not want to? You getting tired of the bar scene?"

Landry punched him lightly in the shoulder before they split to go around the classic blue Ford. It was Landry's pride and joy, a keepsake from his grandpa that he'd kept in pristine shape for years. "Not so much getting tired of it as thinking there's something more out there. Weekends are supposed to be relaxing and fun."

"And playing at the bar with your brothers isn't relaxing or fun anymore?" Andy asked as he shut the door to the truck.

Landry's grin flashed white in the glow of the parking lot lights as he turned on the truck. It was only half hour's drive to the bar, which would give Andy a chance to get off his aching leg.

"Nah, it's fun enough. Can't and shouldn't complain, really. Not even Mom complains about it anymore. Ten years of playing in that bar almost every Friday and Saturday, and we've never once missed church on Sunday morning. We promised her, and we've stuck to our word." Landry's thumbs tapped a rhythm in time to the soft country music echoing through the cab of the truck.

"Aunt Suzie is already after me to go to church, but I can't handle all the little old ladies and their questions." Andy adjusted his prosthetic to scratch at a sore spot.

Landry glanced down at the floorboard. "You can't even tell, with your jeans on and that boot. Is the boot foot better than the one you were wearing yesterday or the one at the gym?"

Andy sat back on the seat and tried to stretch out more. "They're about the same as far as comfort level goes. The one I wore at the gym was the same one as yesterday. It's better for cardio and quick movements. Wearing a shoe or boot with this one is more restrictive. I feel like I limp more with it, but I've been told that it's all in my head."

"Well, I'll be watching you dance from the stage, so I'll tell you if it's noticeable." Landry's sly grin flashed in the lights from a passing car.

"Gee, thanks." Andy's voice dripped sarcasm as he shifted on the seat.

"What else are best friends for? Shootin' it straight and being a wing man is in the job description."

Landry was right. They'd been best friends for decades. He'd been the first one to visit when Andy had moved back to town just over a week or two ago. Andy looked out the passenger side window into the darkness, the trip home from the airport replaying in his head.

Andy groaned as Aunt Suzie pulled the truck up to the cabin. He kept ignoring her as she kept up a steady stream of chatter.

When the truck came to a stop, he pried his eyes open and rubbed them with the heel of his palms.

"We've kept it maintained so you won't have anything to worry about. You remember Herman?"

Andy shook his head as she pulled the keys out of the ignition and looked at him. She smiled and continued. "That's alright. He's checked on the cabin once a week while we were traveling and helping you. Have I told you how excited I am that you're home for good?"

He rolled his eyes and opened the passenger door as she kept talking.

"It makes my heart so happy. It could've been so much worse. I don't know what I would've done if you'd... if you'd..." she stuttered and he looked back across the bench seat. The fear flashing in her eyes made him pause and turn back to her on the seat.

He patted her on the arm. "I know," he said. "But I'm fine, and I'm home, so no need to worry. Can we go inside now? Is Uncle Mike bringing lunch?" He pushed the door and slowly stepped down onto the dirt drive. All the travel had left a dull, steady ache in his leg.

"Lunch should be already inside," Aunt Suzie said, closing the driver's door behind her and rounding the front of the truck.

He stared at the long, low wooden house. What had once been his oasis in the woods now seemed an icy prison.

Gathering his courage for this new life, he shut the door and limped to the cabin. "Leave the bags. I'll get them out after lunch."

Aunt Suzie bounced alongside him as they walked. "I'm so happy you're home, Andy. I've talked to the ladies at church, and we'll be starting a meal train soon."

"Wait," he frowned as he stopped on the front porch. "I don't want a bunch of strangers coming around. I can't... It's too soon." His gaze darted around the porch of the cabin before looking down the shaded dirt driveway, half expecting the little old church ladies to descend on him any minute.

Aunt Suzie sighed, "I figured." She opened the door ahead of him, and he limped inside.

The lights flipped on and a male voice boomed, "Surprise!"

Andy's chest twisted, and he dove behind the couch. He covered his head, listening to the silence as his heart raced. Blinking, his eyes adjusted as he realized what had happened.

A little blond curly-headed three-year-old came tearing down the hall yelling, "Prize!" Sitting up slowly, he peeked around the side of the couch. He hated surprises. His nostrils flared in frustration and embarrassment. Working hard to even out his breathing, he sat there until Mandy popped her head around the couch.

"Found you! Now I hide," she sang before skipping off back down the short hallway. Her smile and easy-going nature settled some of the frustration, and he sighed. This was just his life now, and he better get used to it.

He moved to his knees. Using the back of the couch, he pulled himself up onto his right foot. Waiting a few seconds, his heart not nearly slowed down enough, he stood.

"Andy! Are you ok?" Aunt Suzie squeaked as she jumped toward him from the doorway. He nearly fell backward as he flinched away from her. She stopped in her tracks with a stricken look on her face.

Then she spun toward the kitchen. "How about some food? We have a week of meals already in the fridge, but Mike made steak for lunch. He should have all the fixin's in the stove to keep warm. Just let me grab them..."

She kept mumbling to herself as she fluttered around the kitchen, her blond bun bobbing at the base of her skull.

Placing his full weight on both feet, he turned toward his Uncle Mike who shrugged sheepishly. "Sorry about the surprise. I should've known better."

"Don't worry about it. I have to get used to it, right? This is the civilian world." Andy's lips pursed. Not that he'd ever asked for this world. But that wasn't Uncle Mike's fault.

Uncle Mike walked slowly toward him and reached for a hug. Andy forced himself to stand still and pat his uncle on the back.

"It's good to have you home, son." His eyes glistened in the light with unshed tears.

Andy nodded as he trudged toward the kitchen. "It's good to be back." It was the right thing to say, and he did love this cabin. It was always good to be back here. He just never expected to land here permanently so soon.

"Better not sit down yet. You heard Mandy. You're supposed to go find her. Check the quilt chest in your closet. She likes it in there with her little lantern."

He shuffled past the kitchen on the right and the living room on the left to the hallway. When he reached his bedroom, his brows rose. There were some unauthorized updates to his room and the connecting bathroom. He'd only bought the old hunting cabin from Uncle Mike a few years ago.

Andy had joined them and his cousins every year as a kid and the memories here were all happy ones. Andy rubbed at the tightness in his chest. He hadn't planned on living here yet. He'd wanted to do the repairs and updates himself, with his buddy Landry.

A giggle from the closet had him peeking in. The lid of the quilt chest was barely open and light shone out from inside it. She'd definitely grown in the past year, if she could climb in there by herself. Seeing her *in the hospital and rehab center wasn't the same as seeing her in his cabin.*

"Oh Mandy? Come out, come out, wherever you are," he sing-songed in her favorite voice. Another giggle floated through the air, making him smile fully for the first time in months. He dragged the lid up, and his smile grew.

"Found you!"

Mandy giggled again. She was mostly laying down on a quilt in the bottom of the chest, a pink princess lantern beside her making her eyes bright and clear as she smiled at him. She had Sarah's eyes. Some of the tightness around his chest loosened.

"You found me, Unca Andy!"

"I sure did, princess. You ready to eat?" He reached down to lift her out. He paused, kneeling on his left knee to get more leverage.

Why couldn't things be simple anymore? If he wanted to lift something, he had to actually think about it. Lifting like normal didn't work anymore. He swung her up and grunted before he put her down on her feet.

She giggled again and pointed to the chest, "Light." He grabbed the lantern and handed it to her. She took off skipping out the door, swinging her lantern in her chubby little arm. He pushed himself to his feet and followed her out of the walk-in closet.

The light from the window landed on the silver prosthetic of his foot, bouncing light across the bedroom. It was a curved piece of metal for running and attached about halfway down his left shin.

He snorted. Calling it a foot was a joke. It was seven inches of carbon fiberglass, but it was a big milestone.

Getting this foot meant he had hit an Activity Level 4 in record time. He had worked his butt off in therapies and in the gym to maintain and increase muscle tone.

Reaching it had been his only goal for months. It meant he could go home and get back to normal.

But there was no more normal. The invisible weight pressed onto his chest once again.

A horn blared, bringing him out of the memory. He turned his head to glance at Landry.

"Fucking deer are everywhere. Can't wait for deer season this year," Landry grumbled, making Andy smile. His friend had shown up at the cabin the very next day, and they'd talked about everything and nothing for hours. He was also the only one who'd made the trip to the military hospital when Andy had been stuck there for months.

"Did I ever thank you for coming to see me in January? You're the best, you know." Andy's matter-of-fact tone rang with truth, but he kept it lighthearted.

"I know I am. I'm the best wing man around, remember?" Landry laughed. He was always good for a laugh.

Andy shook his head. "Well, I don't need a wing man right now. I don't think I could handle a woman. I'll barely be able to face the crowd tonight. Did I tell you that Aunt Suzie drug me to the mall a few months ago? She dressed Mandy up for some event. There were tons of people…"

Andy shivered, the cloying press of bodies, the smell of body odor and too much perfume had been a terrible mix with the loud chattering crowd.

"Got too close, did they? But hey. She loves you like a son. She wouldn't have made your Uncle Mike stay in Virginia practically all year to help you recover if she didn't. I rather pity your uncle sometimes. Being stuck in that RV with your Aunt Suzie and an energetic toddler?"

Andy chuckled, surprised already by how much he'd laughed since being home the past few days. "The man is definitely a saint."

They pulled into the parking lot of the Electric Cowboy. Turning off the truck, they could already hear the music spilling out the doors. A bouncer took cover charges at the front door of the large, over-sized barn.

"Don't worry about him. You're in the band tonight," Landry said as they got out of the truck. Andy forced himself to breathe deeply and evenly. He could do this.

"What am I supposed to be doing with the band tonight?" Andy smoothed his sweaty palms down his jeans as they reached the door.

"Hey, Hank! This is Andy. He's just returned from the sand pit and is helping with the band tonight," Landry said, shaking the bouncer's hand.

Hank tipped his hat and said gruffly, "Welcome home. Go right on in. Still quiet but it'll pick up."

Landry grinned at the ladies in line by the door, "I'm looking forward to it!"

They waltzed inside. But Andy automatically stepped to the left. He waited for his eyes to adjust to the light.

Landry scanned the room and waved at his brothers already on stage. "I'm going to go set up. You need anything, man? Want to hang out by the stage?"

Andy shook his head, his breathing evening out in time with the music playing from the jukebox in the corner. "I'll head over to the bar first. Quieter there."

Landry glanced at the bar and started towards it. "Hey, I see Nick. Come on, I'll introduce you."

His legs carried him toward the bar, but he couldn't tell if it was graceful or awkward. The loud music already overwhelmed him. Thankfully, the lights were dim but not blinking.

By the counter, it was quieter. Landry approached a hulking, short-haired blond man with a neatly trimmed beard. He shook Landry's hand, his biceps bulging out of his plain green t-shirt.

"Nick! Good to see you, man. This is Andy, the guy I told you about at poker this week. Andy, this is Nick. He's a vet too," Landry said. Andy reached forward and shook the man's hand.

"Nice to meet you," he said, as Landry gave them a thumbs up before swaggering towards the stage.

"Likewise," Nick said. "Welcome home. Heard you've had a rough year. Grab a stool, and I'll buy you a beer." He flagged down the bartender.

"Thank you. What branch were you in?" Andy tried to deflect the questions from himself.

"Marines for six years. Got me through college and then some. You?" Nick drained the beer he'd been nursing and swapped it for the new one.

"Army for twelve. Deployed?" Andy took a drink of his own.

Nick nodded, "Twice. You?"

"Three and a half," Andy grimaced. They swapped deployment stories and jobs, and it eased some of Andy's loneliness. The military was a brotherhood, and he didn't know where he'd find that kind of ready-made family now that he was out.

"How long have you been out?" Andy asked before sipping his drink.

Nick rubbed his beard thoughtfully. "Three years maybe? You never truly leave it behind… You grow up around here?"

Andy nodded, "Sort of. Spent summers here. I don't recognize you. You from one of the surrounding towns?"

Nick nodded, and they chatted about moving to small towns until Landry's brother, Gunner, did a mic check. Then they turned around on their stools.

Andy's gaze scanned the crowd, which had grown

considerably in the past few minutes he'd been there. The bar behind them stretched half-way down the room. To the left near the door was the side-room with the pool tables. The dance floor in front of them led to the stage on the right. To the right of the stage was the little hallway to the bathrooms.

"All right, all you cool cats and kittens. We're going to get feisty and kick off our Friday night right. Y'all ready to get this party started?" Gunner asked into the microphone.

People were already moving onto the dance floor as they struck up the tune to Miley Cyrus' *Can't Be Tamed*. Andy cocked his head to the side and chuckled.

"Seriously? This isn't a cowboy song," he said to Nick.

Nick nodded and grinned, "Yeah, but sometimes they grandfather her in because of her dad. Tonight is a themed night about lions, tigers, and taming the wild. I overheard them talking about it at poker night. Hey, you'll join us this week, right?"

Andy shrugged, "When is it? I've heard it mentioned but don't know the details."

"Tuesday at eight at Landry and Parker's. They'll grill out, and it's BYOB," he said, tipping his beer up to drink.

Chapter Four

Turning to set it down on the bar behind him, Nick leaned a little too far toward the dark-haired girl on the stool beside him. She almost tumbled to the floor, but he caught her with a gentle hand to her elbow. Her friend on the stool next to her gasped as the first woman's drink sloshed.

"Oh, I'm so sorry, ladies. Can I buy you a drink to make up for it?" he flashed a grin, teeth shining through his blond beard.

Both women grinned and nodded as Nick raised his arm for the bartender, flexing his bicep.

Andy laughed. This guy was smooth. He scanned the room, seeing it was almost half full now as another song started to play.

"Hey, Andy. Meet Martha and Jo. Ladies, this is Andy," Nick said as the two women slid off their stools and stood in front of theirs. Martha, the dark-haired one in the mini skirt and boots, was already stroking Nick's arm. She stopped to shake hands.

Jo was blond, taller than most, and her jeans were practically painted on, they were so tight. He shook her hand and said, "Nice to meet you. Would you like a drink?"

She raised a bottle and smiled. "I'm good. Thanks though. Want to dance after I drain it?"

He nodded, knowing he had to join civilian life eventually. "Sure. You from around here?"

She shook her head. "Nope. Just visiting Martha. We were college roommates, and we get together a few times a year. You?"

"Just moved back to town, actually." The pressure built in his chest. Why didn't they give classes on small talk?

A new song started, and Nick carried the conversation between the three of them. Andy slowly scanned the room again. It was getting crowded now, and his shirt felt too tight.

Just as his heart picked up speed, Jo leaned around him and grazed her arm along his bicep as she placed her beer on the counter. She smelled like cigarette smoke but the cut of her red plaid shirt revealed the deepest cleavage he'd seen in a while. His eyes noticed but the rest of his body didn't care, too consumed with the rising panic.

He blinked as she grabbed his hand and tugged him toward the dance floor with a shout, "Come on! I like this song."

It only took him a few minutes to remember the fast dance steps. He mentally patted himself on the back. He didn't think he stumbled too much, but it still smarted when Jo switched partners halfway through the song.

Another woman quickly took her place, though. A petite brunette, she was cute with her little dimples, but she didn't pique his interest either. Maybe because the walls were closing in.

Three songs later and as many dance partners left him

winded and fighting the panic. His heart was pumping faster than it had at the gym.

He pushed towards the bar, but it was packed without a bit of breathing room. Glancing to the stage, he saw Landry grinning, singing, and strumming his guitar.

Andy wound his way through the crowd to the front door. The blast of cool night air hit him in the face, but it didn't slow down the beat of his racing heart. The line to get in was longer. He nodded at Hank on his way out.

He mentally catalogued his surroundings, but his mind was already sinking back into the bunker half a world away.

Stumbling towards Landry's truck, he realized he was stranded. He was supposed to drive Landry's truck home, but he hadn't actually gotten the keys.

Maybe the visor, he thought as a flash of light blinded him. A squeal of tires drowned out the music behind him. He threw his hands up to cover his head, and something hard slammed into his hip.

Then he was falling. *Aunt Suzie is going to go ape shit*, he thought before crashing to the gravel drive and losing consciousness.

"I'm telling you, I'm fine. There's no need for this," Andy grumbled, as they strapped him Onto the gurney. Hank stood beside him with arms crossed over his chest.

"Standard procedure, man. Boss has to cover their ass from a lawsuit. Not that this happens often. Or actually, ever. But just go get checked out, alright?"

Andy's leg and hip pulsed in pain. He clenched his jaw as a woman's voice rose above the music. "Which hospital? I'll meet you there. I have to know that he's ok."

The closed-in feeling had just grown worse because of this little run-in. Andy shook his head and fisted the bed as the paramedics lifted him into the ambulance. "Fine, just get me out of here."

The ride to the hospital was quiet with soft music playing in the background. Andy frowned. He couldn't hear the words. Was it hearing loss? It wouldn't surprise him, with what he'd gone through the past few deployments. The paramedic asked him questions and took his vitals.

Rolling into the ER, he caught sight of two women pacing the lobby. One was young, probably still in her twenties, but the grey hair made her appear older. The other was tall with dark auburn hair and blue eyes that widened in surprise when they met his own.

"Lola? Lola Rogers?" He frowned, brows lifting in surprise. "What are you doing here?"

Lola gasped as she got a good look at him. "Andy Reynolds? Oh man, I didn't know she'd hit *you*! Suzie is going to freak!"

She pulled her phone out of her pocket before he could reach out or say anything to stop her. She turned toward the corner to make her phone call.

He groaned as they pushed him through to a room beside the entrance doors. The little grey-haired woman followed them, gushing apologies.

"I'm so, so sorry. I'm not used to driving her big old truck. Not used to driving at all. Especially at night. But they've been pushing me to drive again, and it seemed a nice night for it. Oh man, oh man, oh man. Are you okay? Is he okay?"

She directed the last one to the paramedics as they tried to ease out the door, but she used her tiny frame to block it pretty effectively. The two EMS guys glanced at each other and nodded.

"He'll be a bit bruised up, but overall should be alright. Nothing broken. Doc will need to check the leg. Probably won't need surgery though," one of them said, before they both slipped out the door.

The woman turned to him, hands raised and eyes wide. "Surgery! Oh my God! What's wrong with your leg? Does it hurt? What kind of surgery would you need if it's not broken?" She tripped over her own questions, and his anxiety climbed.

A nurse in navy scrubs strode into the room and stopped in surprise. "Holly? What are you doing here?"

It was her voice that jolted him from the panic. He raked his eyes over her frame, and it clicked in his brain. The weight of her petite body on top of his had perfectly balanced out the pain from the kidney stone last weekend.

It's her! The nurse from last weekend! What was her name?

"I'm here too!" Lola said, pushing the nurse further into the room.

The nurse was dark eyed. Her smooth and perfectly arched dark brows rose in shock, and her full lips were in an adorable O shape. When she licked them, his heart skipped a beat again but for an entirely different reason.

Oh hell. Perfectly arched brows? I'm mooning over her eyebrows, for crying out loud! Maybe he hit his head when he fell, and that's why he lost consciousness.

She walked around the gurney and strapped on a blood pressure cuff. Her long black hair was braided but curls had already escaped. He remembered her hair falling over his face, burying his nose in her neck. The smell of her skin, the feel of her had been an anchor he'd desperately needed.

He inhaled deeply. That smell had haunted him for the

past week. *Is it shampoo? Or is it her?* His fingers twitched as she took a flashlight and checked his pupils.

He wanted to push the stray curl behind her ear. *Good God, what is wrong with me? I didn't want to touch the girls at the bar. Why is she any different?*

His mind blanked with her standing so close. *What do I say?* Taking a shaky breath, he said, "Hello again."

She smiled at him, and he blinked rapidly as his heart tripped. It was a shame that she hadn't been smiling the entire time.

"Hello again yourself," she whispered. Time paused as their eyes met and something shifted in his heart. The blood pressure machine beeped and gave her the reading, causing her to frown again.

"Your blood pressure is elevated. I hear you got hit by a truck?" She eyed the two women in confusion.

The grey-haired woman raised her hand timidly. "That was me. I was too nervous. I told y'all I couldn't do it. It's too soon."

The nurse and Lola flocked to her side for a group hug.

"Nonsense," Lola said. "We pushed you, and we'd do it again because you need it. But next time, we'll practice in the daylight and not in a crowded area, hmm?" Lola leaned back and grinned down at... had the nurse called her Holly?

"You guys know each other?" he drawled from the bed. Three pairs of eyes whipped in his direction with varying expressions. But his gaze couldn't leave the nurse. The hairs on his neck stood up as she drew closer.

"Of course. It's a small town, or have you forgotten?" Lola asked, taking charge like always. "Holly leads our weekly yoga classes, which we make sure Cindy here never misses. She *needs* to de-stress."

She had a name! He smiled in victory, breathing her name like a prayer. "Cindy."

Her eyes softened at his voice. "Andy," she said, reaching for his hand to put the blood pressure cuff on. When their hands clasped, the vice around his heart released a bit. It was like she had poured cold water from her hand up his arm to his chest.

He breathed deeply, inhaling her spicy scent. *Cinnamon? Nutmeg? What is it?*

She blinked rapidly and put the cuff on quickly. She started the machine, then shied away toward the ladies, talking faster than she had before.

"Let's get you charted up. Holly, will you go write your contact and insurance information for him to have later? Andy, do you need to call anyone?"

"Already done that. Suzie's on her way," Lola smirked as she met his gaze. He winced.

They all three glanced at him in sympathy. It would have been comical if it weren't scarily true. His aunt was a bit much.

"Speak of the devil," he muttered as a high-pitched voice echoed outside the room.

Cindy chuckled, and his eyes snapped to her. She was covering her sweet little bow-shaped mouth with her hand, but her eyes met his. They glittered with mirth.

His aunt stopped in the doorway and gasped before rushing to his side. Her blond ponytail swayed with every step, and her pencil skirt and Van Halen t-shirt made her seem like a rock-and-roll version of a fifties housewife.

She gripped his cheeks and leaned over him, saying loudly, "Andy! Are you okay? What happened?"

He pried her fingers from his face, but instead of being annoyed, he just grinned. There was something about

Cindy's reaction that put him at peace. Aunt Suzie didn't quite bother him like she did before. He squeezed her hands and pulled them away from his face. "I'm fine. Got bumped, fell down, and blacked out."

Lola snorted and crossed her arms. "Oh sure, he just got bumped and fell down."

Holly twisted her hands together, and Aunt Suzie opened her mouth to probably try to boss them all.

Cindy strode to the side of the bed and removed the blood pressure cuff, then typed on the bedside computer. "We're about to do a concussion protocol and run a CT scan. You'll all need to wait outside so we can get that started."

"But I just got here! I can stay. I'm family," Aunt Suzie said, patting her hair and nodding fiercely.

Cindy smiled and shook her head. "You are family. The absolute best aunt in the world, from what he was telling us. But you'll still need to wait outside."

Suzie teared up and gazed at him, her eyes wide. "You said that? Aww!"

She threw herself into his arms, and he patted her back, frowning hard at Cindy. The corners of his mouth wobbled as he saw her cover her mouth, her cheeks lifting with her grin as she chuckled. Suzie was too busy talking to notice, but he heard her. His hearing must be alright after all.

"Alright, you two can come tell me exactly what happened while the nurse does her thing." She pulled both Holly and Lola out the door. Lola grinned and waved, but Holly looked lost and apologetic.

He let out a long, exasperated sigh as the room finally fell silent. As she went through the concussion protocol questions, his mind wandered to thoughts of her. He couldn't stop thinking of ways to touch her again, even though he tried to focus on her words.

This was frustrating. Here he was acting like a randy teenager, trying to just touch her hand. He groaned.

She leaned over him again. "What hurts?"

"Everything," he choked out. No way was he telling her where it ached most.

"Need more specifics, big guy. Your head? Kidney stones back? Does your side hurt from the truck or the fall? Your leg?" She once again flashed the light in his eyes.

He tried to catch her gaze but saw stars from the light instead. He heard the door open. As his eyes focused again, his jaw dropped.

"Kendall?" Andy's eyes widened in surprise as he saw his long-time friend approaching. "What are you doing here, man? I thought you were still at Fort Rucker?"

Kendall reached out and shook Andy's hand with a firm grip. "Hey, Andy. Moved here about six months ago. Hit thirteen years and just… had enough. How about you? You get the card I sent to Walter Reed?"

"Yeah, I appreciate it, man. Thank you. Thought I'd left the hospital visits behind when I moved here, but I've only been home two weeks, and this makes the second ER trip."

Kendall checked the computer and typed as he talked. "Not going to lie. When I saw your name pop up in the system tonight, I looked into your file. You've had a rough go of it."

Andy snorted. "Got that right. I'm already ready to get the hell out of here."

Kendall just chuckled and stepped away from the computer. "We'll check your head first and run the CT scan, then we'll check the hardware, see if there's damage from the hit and run."

Kendall grinned and winked, and Cindy giggled. The sound echoed in the small room, and it seemed to brighten with the warmth of her laugh. The comforting sound relieved some of the weight on his shoulders.

Andy grinned and shifted on the bed. "Yeah, right. Those two didn't run. They would have ridden in the ambulance if they could've. Did you see Aunt Suzie in the hallway?"

Kendall grimaced and looked sheepishly at Cindy and the chart. "Actually, I heard her in the waiting room and went around the long way to get to your room. So no, not yet."

Andy laughed as Cindy giggled, the joy of it lifting Andy's spirits and making the weight of his injuries momentarily fade away. Being in the same room as Cindy, hearing her laugh, and seeing her face light up with a smile was definitely worth the hospital visit.

Chapter Five

Cindy glanced from Kendall to Andy and back again. "You guys obviously know each other well."

Kendall nodded as he flipped open the chart and made a notation. "Yep," he said. "We went to basic training together."

"Then we were stationed at our first duty station together at Fort Campbell. How long were we there?" Andy rubbed his jaw.

Man, he had a strong jaw. The dark stubble was more than a five o'clock shadow. She wondered how abrasive it would feel against her skin.

She spun around and started fiddling with the drawers, looking for a distraction. *Good God, what is wrong with me?*

Sure, he was handsome in that dark, rugged man kind of way. He was a big man too, nearly overwhelming the ER bed. Spying the hospital gowns in the drawer, she grabbed one.

"Three years and a deployment," Kendall said. "Then I went to Bragg and back to Benning."

"I went from Campbell to Germany to Hood," Andy said.

She handed him the gown. "Can you put this on so we can take you to for the CT scan?" He frowned as he took it. The brush of their fingers sent a shock up her arm. She tucked a stray hair behind her ear as she walked to the door.

Kendall patted him on the shoulder before he sat up. "It'll help us assess where the truck hit you and your leg too. Just open the door when you're ready, and Cindy will wheel you down to the CT scan," he said, before he shut the door softly behind them.

They could still hear the three women talking—okay, mostly Suzie talking—down the hall.

She followed Kendall to the nurse's station. "Do you know what happened to his leg? Have you kept in touch with him?"

Kendall nodded with a frown, peering over his shoulder toward the room where Andy was. He lowered his voice. "Yeah, below the knee amputation. Don't know the details. He spent over a year at Walter Reed and rehab, though."

She blinked at Kendall as she thought of Andy. His legs filled out the jeans perfectly. His thighs bulged with muscles and his cowboy boots were covered by the jeans. It was a more rugged look than the basketball shorts of last week. She'd seen the prosthetic then, but hadn't pried into the details.

She opened the computer program, thinking of all the church ladies had said about him. "Well, he's doing well with it. The way everyone's talking, I thought it was a not so visible injury like yours."

It was Kendall's turn to pull away from her as he scowled. "What do you know about that?"

The Soldier Gets His Girl

Cindy shrugged, assessing him with a critical eye. "What? Girls talk, and Holly is your sister. She was the one who hit Andy, by the way."

"I thought that was her voice," Kendall groaned, rubbing his eyes. "It's too early in the shift for this. Let me know if he needs anything. As soon as they send in the CT results, I'll be back to talk with him." With a turn on his heel, he strode back down the hallway, past Andy's room.

The cafeteria was in the middle of the hospital. One side was the ER, but Cindy raised a brow as Kendall retreated. He was avoiding Suzie again, going in that direction. Smart man. Suzie was nice as could be, but she steamrolled people. The other church ladies had been more relaxed with her gone this past year.

The door to Andy's room creaked open. A lump formed in her throat as she took in the sight of him standing in the doorway. His muscular frame filled the entire space, and she could feel his raw masculinity radiating towards her. She had thought his biceps looked impressive in his t-shirt earlier, but now they seemed ready to burst through the flimsy fabric of the gown.

His blue eyes bore into hers, full of intensity and something almost predatory. She could see the slight twitch of his jaw as he clenched it, trying to contain whatever emotions were brewing within him. Her skin prickled with goosebumps under his intense gaze, as if his eyes were physically touching her.

The intensity of their gaze was like a bolt of lightning, striking her chest and taking her breath away. She tried to maintain her composure, but her smile felt fragile and forced, like a delicate flower wilting in a storm.

"Ready to roll? You'll have to sit in the wheelchair."

He pushed his left leg forward. "Do I have to take this off?"

She rolled the wheelchair to him. The foot looked like a regular foot, but the part that attached to his leg was about four inches of an American flag pattern.

"No, you'll need to leave it in the room."

He sighed as she pushed the wheelchair into the room, stopping to lock the wheels beside the bed.

When he walked toward her, the look in his eyes made her wary. His blue eyes reminded her of the wolf James had printed out for his science project. His gaze was definitely predatory.

His proximity was both thrilling and terrifying. The scent of leather and cologne wafted towards her, mixing with a hint of sweat and the faint whiff of aftershave. How long had it been since a man had smelled so enticing? Before she got pregnant with James, probably.

He slid past her a little closely before sitting in the wheelchair and leaning forward to pull off the leg. She stood spellbound behind him. His back was smooth and tan where the hospital gown had slipped open. Her gaze slid downward and caught sight of navy blue boxer briefs.

She snapped around the wheelchair, her heart pounding. She took a moment to compose herself, reminding herself that this was just Andy, a war-wounded soldier she'd just met a week ago. "That's a different one than last weekend. How many do you have?"

He slowly peeled the liner down his left leg and sat it on the bed with the prosthesis. Massaging his leg and scratching the stump, he sighed in relief.

"Better?" She unlocked the wheels, her chest aching for the pain he must've gone through.

He sat back in the chair and put his foot on the footrest.

The Soldier Gets His Girl

"Hmm. I have four of them. One for the gym, one for shoes, one for running, and a backup."

"Do you go to the gym and workout a lot?" She wheeled him backward through the door and into the hall.

"Every day."

She turned a corner in the hall and leaned forward to keep talking with him, the spicy scent of him filling her soul. "Keeping up the energy levels will help maintain that Level 4 you were talking about last week."

Her nose neared his dark hair. It was almost as black as her own, but she saw some salt and pepper strands near his temples. It matched the more salt and pepper scruff he had on his chin.

And damn it, he smelled good too! Couldn't he have smelled like sweat or something from that club? She needed a distraction and quick.

"Let's do some more concussion protocol questions as we go, shall we? When did you move back to town?"

"Flew in a week and a half ago," he said. His voice was deep and made the hair on her arms stand up.

"And you were already at the Electric Cowboy a few days later? Wow, nothing keeps you down, does it?"

"What do you mean?" He looked over his shoulder, his eyes squinting in the hospital lights. They captivated her. She nearly ran into the wall and quickly snapped her gaze away.

"Well, isn't flying exhausting? And moving? When we moved, I swear it took me a month to set everything up. If I were you, I'd probably be curled up in front of the fire or taking a bubble bath instead." She blushed as she pictured him in a bubble bath.

He chuckled, saying, "I don't do baths. Although I did

have a hot tub installed. I got pretty used to having one when I was at rehab and the gym in Virginia."

"How long were you there?"

"Almost fifteen months."

"Are you happy to be home?" She wheeled him toward the CT machine. She moved around to grab his arm but he'd already pushed up out of the wheelchair, balancing on his right foot.

Then he placed a hand on the CT bed and sat. She moved the wheelchair out of the way as he laid down.

"Yes, and no. I own my house, but I've only visited for the past decade. It's like a vacation house, not really a home. And I'm not so happy that Aunt Suzie comes over most mornings to smother me." He sounded so forlorn, she grinned as she tucked in the edges of his hospital gown. Her fingers tingled at him being so close, at almost touching him.

"Your aunt is something else, but she has your best interests at heart. Now, if you were in the hospital and rehab for so long, do you remember how the CT scan works? Do you want me to explain it?" She stared down at him, rubbing her fingers together to keep from touching him.

He shook his head and grinned up at her, his blue eyes twinkling in the light. "I'll be fine."

She walked toward the small room that operated the machine, saying over her shoulder, "Get comfy. If you're snoring when I come back, don't worry. I won't tell anyone."

He chuckled as the machine whirled on, the noise a low hum. She watched his top half slide into the machine.

Only his lower half was visible. His thighs were definitely bigger than hers, and that was saying something.

Three kids had done a number on her thighs. But at least she still had her booty. She wondered if he was an ass or boob man.

Whoa! Hold up a minute. What was she thinking? She didn't fantasize about men! She stepped out of the room, telling the technician she'd be right back. Once in the hallway, she called Maryanne.

"Hello?" came her sister's sleepy voice. Cindy frowned and looked at her watch.

"Hey, didn't mean to wake you," she said. "Just wanted to check on the boys."

"It's fine. Got them all in bed by like nine-thirty," Maryanne said.

The sound of rustling sheets came through the phone. "What's going on? You never call from the hospital."

Cindy sighed, "Nothing. Everything is fine. It's all fine. He's fine. I mean, I'm good. Just wanted to check in."

Cindy slapped her forehead and winced, hoping her sister didn't catch that slip of the tongue. But she smiled, thinking of the conversation about him being fine last weekend.

"What? Who's fine?" Her sister was a player. Talking to her would help.

Cindy rubbed her temple. "Remember how the ladies at church said Suzie's nephew was coming back home? Well, I met him last weekend, and now he's here this weekend too."

"Ah, that explains the missed text from Lola. I'm catching up on the group chat now. And he's fine? As in, fine fine?" Her voice rose in surprise.

Cindy smiled, her stomach flipping from nerves. "Yes, he's fine. Ask Lola what happened, but Maryanne, the guy is *built*. I mean, jaw dropping, can't think, gave me goose bumps when we shook hands kind of *built*."

"Oh, hell yeah! Finally!" Maryanne said with a giggle. "It's been forever since you've been interested in someone. You're way overdue, sis."

"Oh hush, there's a difference between finding him attractive and doing anything about it. I wanted to step out and take a breath for a minute while he's getting his CT scan," Cindy said, cracking the door and checking on him through the technician's window.

Maryanne sighed through the phone line. "Cin, I love you. You take care of everyone and their brother. And their pet squirrel. And their kids." They both chuckled, remembering when Cody brought home the neighbor's pet squirrel with a broken leg, and he'd asked her to bandage it up.

Her sister continued. "You are the most self-sacrificing woman. You haven't had fun in years. Everyone needs a break now and then. Isn't that why we drag you to Holly's yoga on Thursdays?"

Cindy frowned, never liking when they poked at her to get out of her comfort zone. "Yeah, but that's different."

"All I'm saying is if there's an attraction, flirt a little. It won't kill you, for crying out loud." Maryanne yawned on the phone.

Cindy snorted and rubbed her forehead. "No, but it could be embarrassing. What man signs on for three kids? Not to mention, relationships take time."

It was Maryanne's turn to snort. "Who said anything about a relationship? I'd be happy if you just got laid."

Cindy blushed, but she couldn't help but laugh at her outspoken sister. "Yeah, not going to happen. But I'm still glad I called. Thanks for answering. I think I can go face him now without doing something stupid."

"Alright, I'm going back to sleep. And I'll be looking forward to that meal train next week way more than normal. Can't wait to meet the man who's finally gotten your attention." Cindy could almost hear the grin on Maryanne's face as they hung up. Then she groaned. The meal train from the church! She'd signed up for Tuesday.

She'd get to see him again, in a place that was decidedly *not* the hospital. He'd cancelled the physical therapy appointment she'd set up for him this past week. She hadn't pressed him on it, but she'd bring it up on Tuesday when she saw him again. She wouldn't mention Tuesday to him either, though. She didn't want to appear too eager.

She groaned and took a deep breath, mentally preparing herself to face him again.

Chapter Six

Cindy opened the door and slipped back inside to join CT tech. A few minutes later, the technician gave her the thumbs up and pushed the button to slide him out of the CT scanner. She grabbed the wheelchair and took a deep breath before opening the door and strolling toward him. She smiled at the soft snoring.

That machine either put people to sleep or caused a huge panic attack, even though most scans only took a few minutes. She locked the wheels in place and touched his right bicep to wake him.

His left hand reached over and slapped her hand down onto his arm hard, pinning it to his skin. She gasped as her eyes met his. His hand on hers was like a vise, but it sent shock waves of awareness through her body.

He blinked in confusion and looked around. Slowly, he removed his hand and pushed up on his elbows. He frowned at her, mumbling, "Shit, I'm sorry about that. Got disoriented." He sat up and rubbed a hand down his face.

"That's ok," she said brightly, hovering as he stood and

hopped to the wheelchair. "I warned you about falling asleep. But at least the snoring wasn't the worst I've ever heard either."

He gave her the stink eye, and she laughed. She covered her mouth as she unlocked the wheels.

His face softened into a smile. "You should laugh more often."

She smiled wider, her cheeks growing warm. "Thanks, but we rarely get a reason to laugh in here." She wheeled him out the door and down the hall.

"Then why do it?"

"Like, why did I become a nurse?"

When he nodded, she said, "My grandma had diabetes. I had to take care of her a lot. I enjoy taking care of people."

He nodded and crossed his arms as they rolled down the hallway. She pried her eyes off his biceps so she could steer.

"That makes sense. She's the one you talked about last week? The one who lost her foot?"

"Yep. Why did you join the Army?" She could visibly see him tense up as he shifted in the chair.

After a few seconds, he uncrossed his arms and shrugged, gripping his hands in his lap. "Wasn't much choice. I grew up here, but my mom sent me to military school when I got into some trouble in ninth grade."

"Ahh," she said. "Did you enjoy it at least?"

They were almost back to the ER room when he answered her. "Parts of it, but not really."

She locked the wheels beside the bed. "So, a decade doing something you didn't enjoy?"

He stood up with a grunt and sat on the bed beside his prosthesis. He stared at it with a frown, then his pale blue eyes met hers. His solemn expression about broke her heart.

She could only imagine what he had been through, both physically and emotionally. She took a deep breath, steeling herself for any hard memories or emotions he might bring up. But his pale blue eyes met hers again, and she saw something different in them this time—vulnerability.

"I guess that's exactly what happened," he said with a sigh.

Pressure built in her chest at the lost look. The need to see him smile again propelled her closer, and she laid a hand on his forearm.

"Well, it all led you to here. While I'm not happy to see you in the hospital two weekends in a row, you're fine. It's going to be fine."

He let out a small chuckle and winked. "Yeah, it'll be fine, but I seem to be making a habit of the hospital lately."

She gave him a warm smile and squeezed his arm reassuringly, the feel of his forearm sending a tingle of awareness up her own arm. "Well, who knows, maybe your next adventure will be finding something you love to do."

Amusement sparkled in his pale blue eyes. "Maybe I will," he said with a grin, his brows raised in surprise.

"After all," she teased, "you never know what life has in store for you. Sometimes life takes us down unexpected paths, but they can lead to beautiful things if you take them," she said softly, thinking of her kids and their move here.

He chuckled again and shook his head, staring at his stump. "You're right. Losing the leg was an unexpected path for sure." His calm smile and charming wit made her heart flutter, and she wanted to spend more time with him.

She imagined the pain and struggle he must have gone through to come to terms with his amputation. She stroked

The Soldier Gets His Girl

his arm with her thumb. He didn't pull away, but put his hand over hers and squeezed her hand lightly.

He looked up, catching her gaze with his deep, blue penetrating stare. "And I didn't expect to meet you, either. You're right. Life can lead us to so many beautiful things."

His words trailed off, and she sucked in a quick breath, her cheeks heating from his compliment. The way he looked at her, she knew he didn't mean she was a thing, an object to be possessed. That was what her ex-husband had been like. With Andy, she felt seen and heard, not objectified.

Suzie walked in the door. "There you are! How long for the CT results?"

Cindy stepped back, dropping her hand from his arm, and unlocked the wheels to roll it out the door. Suzie stepped aside, eying her suspiciously.

Cindy smiled, her cheeks still hot. "Half an hour, maybe more. Dr. Kendall will bring them. Andy, you can put the prosthetic back on if you like. Your choice. Do you need anything else? I'm going to run to the cafeteria and can pick up some juice, coffee, tea?"

Suzie crossed her arms and glanced between the two of them, nodding. "Let me get him settled, then I'll go to the cafeteria and join you."

Cindy nodded, rubbing her fingers on the wheelchair as she pushed it to the door. They still tingled from touching him. "Sure, I'll see you there. Andy?" She looked back at him, her soul craving his presence and not really wanting to leave him.

His blue gaze met hers, and he smiled softly. "No, I'm good. Nothing for me, thanks." Then he reached for the liner and looked away to slip it over his shin.

Cindy pushed the wheelchair down the hall and spied

Lola and Holly. Holly was wringing her hands again, and Lola was rubbing her temples.

Cindy smiled, "Hey, do y'all want to grab a cup of coffee or something? Looks like you could use it."

Lola jumped up, grumbling, "God, yes. And tell Holly that he's okay. She's driving me nuts worrying about it. She even drove Suzie away."

Holly jumped up and clenched her fists, squaring up with Lola. It was comical, really. Holly looked like a teenage girl with her short stature and slight frame. She wore a grey yoga sweater and black tights that complimented her striking silver hair.

But Lola towered over her. At nearly six feet with curves for days, her red hair was swept up in a ponytail like always. She wore her signature cowboy boots, dark jeans, and green plaid pearl snap shirt. Cindy was thankful that her boots were relatively clean, and she didn't smell like her ranch.

She put her arms around them as they walked. "He really is fine. Haven't seen a scratch on him," Cindy said to Holly with a smile.

Her friend's green eyes peered into Cindy's own intently. "For real? You're not just saying that because of patient confidentiality or anything?"

Cindy snorted. "What confidentiality? Y'all stormed the ER and now that Suzie's here, it's probably already all over town. Last weekend, she found him in the hospital around eight am, and by nine am, I'd already gotten three texts from church ladies asking what he looked like. Plus, I might have called Maryanne too. One of y'all will have to fill her in."

Lola's eyebrows lowered with a frown. "Why'd you call her? It's like midnight! The woman has to be up at three."

Cindy let go of Holly, guilt stabbing her as she

shrugged, refusing to meet their gaze as they arrived at the cafeteria's door. Their feet shuffled on the linoleum floors, scuffed and worn from constant use. The smell of freshly brewed coffee mixed with antiseptic cleaner sent her away from them to the drink bar.

She grabbed a coffee and a seat as Holly and Lola bickered. The two acted like sisters, their voices mixing with the murmured conversations and clinking of silverware from the two groups on the opposite side of the room.

Holly and Lola sat across from her, Holly with a bowl of fruit. At the break in their conversation, Cindy asked, "What are y'all taking for the meal train for Andy?"

Holly brightened, and Lola stole a grape from her tray. "I'm going to make some lettuce wraps and some California rolls."

Lola snorted as she bit into a chip, "The man grew up here. In north Texas in the middle of nowhere. He won't want sushi, darlin'."

Holly frowned at her and slapped the table. "Hey! I'm making shredded chicken California rolls, not sushi ones. Everyone loves chicken. Right?"

Cindy was quick to nod and smile. "Oh absolutely. What are you making, Lola?"

Lola rolled her eyes and said, "Beats me. Granny will probably make two dishes, one for her to take and one for me. I've not had time to cook since Mama got sick."

Cindy patted her on the arm in sympathy. Whatever she made Andy, she'd double it and take half to Lola's place.

Suzie strolled in and smiled at the girls like a Cheshire cat. She already had a water bottle in her hand, so she claimed the fourth seat at their little table.

"There you are. Got the patient settled in to wait?" Cindy asked with a smile.

"Yes, he shooed me away. He's probably tired of me hovering, which I don't blame him for. I thought being home would help us all get back to normal. This wasn't exactly how I pictured his homecoming," Suzie said ruefully.

Holly murmured, "I can imagine. I'm still fuzzy on the details. You were gone for so long to help him."

Suzie's shoulders drooped as she played with the label on the water bottle. "When he was first injured last year, I about had a heart attack; it was very hard on us all, especially with the holidays. He's made so much progress, not just physically. We had a beach day a few weeks ago. He even swam in the ocean and splashed around with Mandy."

"That's great!" Holly said.

"It is. But now he's home and been in the hospital twice already. I'm not sure what's best for him at this point…"

"He's fine," Cindy said, trying to reassure the woman. Her lips quivered at the joke. But she didn't seem to hear as she stared at her water.

Cindy saw Holly and Lola glance at each other as the silence stretched. Cindy sighed, once more stepping in to help soothe emotions and hurts.

"He's worked hard to get to the level of independence he's at, right? Two hospital visits are just a drop in the bucket compared to fifteen months of hospitals and rehab. He really will be alright, Suzie. Moving is stressful, and things will settle down. Don't rush trying to find a new normal. It'll happen when it happens."

Suzie sniffed and wrinkled her nose, her smile watery and wobbly.

Lola shifted uncomfortably at the display of emotion. "Well, if you're sure he's okay, we'll be going now. I gotta be up early for chores, anyway." She jumped up from the table and collected her trash.

Holly reached out and squeezed Suzie's hand. "And you call me, night or day, if he or you need anything at all, okay? I'm so, so sorry."

Suzie patted Holly's hand before they left. "Accidents happen, dear. It's just life."

When they disappeared around the corner, Suzie snorted and straightened her spine. "I just bet she wants a call in the middle of the night. I'm not dumb. Andy's a catch, and she's probably after him."

Cindy snorted coffee out her nose in surprise. She quickly grabbed napkins out of the dispenser on the table and cleaned up her mess as she coughed. Suzie crossed her arms and narrowed her eyes.

Once she'd thrown away the dirty napkins and returned to the table, she sat down again and pasted on a brittle smile. Cindy clenched her hands tightly as they shook. She did not do confrontation, but she had to defend her friend.

"I know you've been gone, and Holly and Dr. Kendall are new in town. But she's not some hussy stranger. She's grieving and the sweetest woman you'll ever meet. Maybe you should get to know her before passing judgement."

Cindy's face burned hot and her hands shook at the confrontation. She didn't normally stand up to people. That was Maryanne's thing. But she would not let her talk about Holly.

Suzie squinted and tilted her head to the side. "Oh yeah? And what about you? Don't think I didn't see you touching him earlier on the arm. I'm not blind. The man is still healing. He doesn't need a booty call or a relationship. And he certainly doesn't need to be anyone's baby daddy or sugar daddy or whatever you kids are calling it these days. A mom like you should have more decorum."

Cindy blinked and burst out laughing. She laughed so hard the cafeteria worker peered around the cut-out window to stare at them before popping back inside.

She laughed until tears rolled down her face. Reaching for another napkin from the dispenser, she wiped her face. God, this was embarrassing. She had to get out of here.

"Oh, Suzie. How we have missed you around here. You honestly think he'd be interested in someone like me? Ha! And even if he was, a mom *like me* doesn't have the time. So you can keep your precious nephew." She smiled as she stood up and threw her trash away.

She patted Suzie on the back as she walked out the room. "Goodness, I needed that laugh tonight. Thanks, Suzie! I'll see you later when he's ready to discharge and go home!" She gave a brief wave and left.

The fake smile she'd thrown at Suzie fell sharply as she walked down the hall, her head held high. She was so tired of people judging her because she had three kids without a dad.

Sure, Andy was hot. But she hadn't dated in the five years she'd lived in town, and she wasn't about to start. Building her reputation as a good, moral woman had taken time. No man was worth tearing it down.

Chapter Seven

Cindy pulled her SUV up to the cabin and parked. She wiped her sweaty palms on her thighs and breathed. It was a cute little place with a porch swing. Trees rustled in the breeze, providing shade and making the entire place look cozy.

She smiled wistfully. Someday she'd have a cozy home. She stepped out of the vehicle and popped open the trunk. Footsteps sounded behind her, and she turned her head. Andy jogged down the dirt lane.

He was dripping sweat in the hot October sun and his broad, bare chest shone in the late morning light. She swallowed hard as her heart beat in time to his footsteps.

Even when he started slowed to a walk, her heart still beat too fast. The closer he came, the hotter the sun felt beating down on her back.

His prosthesis glimmered in the sun, a silver curved running one, but she barely noticed. Her eyes were riveted on his broad shoulders, the tattoos flowing down one shoulder. She forced her eyes to his face.

He smiled when he drew near, and her heart tripped completely before she thought to smile back.

Raising his hand, he raked the dripping sweat through his dark hair. "Hey, Cindy. What are you doing here?"

Cindy followed the trail of his hand through his hair, wishing she did that. She snapped her gaze back to his blue eyes and said, "Meal train from the church. Hope you like fried chicken."

He grunted, his grin spreading wider. "What man doesn't? Can I help you carry anything?"

She nodded as he stepped closer. Her feet froze in place as he reached around her, close enough to smell the scent of sweat, leather, and something else she couldn't place. He grabbed one of the aluminum foil disposable dishes and stepped back.

She reached for the warming bag to lift it out. As she stepped back, he reached up to push the lift close button, and his biceps rippled. She swallowed hard and stepped further away, turning from him completely to walk toward the front door.

"I appreciate you bringing it all the way out here. I told Aunt Suzie not to do the meal train thing," he said as he quickly out strode her to open the door.

She stepped past him through the door and caught that scent again. *Stupid butterflies in my stomach need to go away,* she thought.

As she stepped inside, the spacious living room greeted her with its simple yet elegant decor. A plush couch and two recliners were arranged around a warm fireplace, and above it hung a large TV that seemed almost out of place in this cozy setting.

"It's not a problem," she blurted out, eager to make herself useful as she looked around.

Her attention caught on the expansive window to her right, offering a stunning view of the surrounding wooded landscape. The light filtering through the sheer curtains danced across the hardwood floors, inviting her to step closer. And as she did, she noticed the spacious dining table set by the window, surrounded by natural light. Beyond it lay an open kitchen, complete with an eat-in island and gleaming stainless steel appliances.

She walked to the gray slate kitchen island and set down the bag to take the dishes out.

"I also appreciated your help last weekend. And the weekend before. You're a pretty exceptional nurse." His smile lit up the room, and she was drawn closer to him like a moth to the flame.

Her face burned as she smiled. She couldn't help it, really. He smiled, and it made her face automatically want to smile too. Maybe it was his superpower or something.

"Thanks, but I was simply doing my job," she said. She cocked her head to the side, her eyes raking down his glistening chest and up again. "It's good to see you smiling and not in pain. Where do you want the food?"

"I can eat it now, but only if you'll eat with me. It gets lonely out here by myself. I finally convinced Aunt Suzie to stop coming over every day, but the quiet is getting to me. Don't tell her I said that, though!"

He made an exaggerated puppy dog face. She laughed and made a motion of zipping her lips.

Realizing he was still shirtless, he said, "Sorry about this. Let me go grab a shirt. Can you stay and eat?"

His blue eyes looked so hopeful, she nodded before she'd even thought about what he'd said. "Sure, but you don't have to put on a shirt for me. I mean, it's fine the way it is. Unless... umm... you'd feel more comfortable with one."

Her face really heated now. She glanced at him with wide eyes open in horror only to see him grin so big a dimple appeared on one cheek.

His eyes twinkled as he replied, "Sure, I can leave it off. Consider the eye candy payment for the excellent food." He winked as he walked to the sink to wash his hands.

She groaned. "No, that's not what I meant! Ugh, whatever. Put one on. Leave it off. Just... whatever, ok?" She put her face in her hands. *Had she even made sense? Dear Lord, he's going to think I'm a moron. Or horny. Or a horny moron. Oh my god.*

He chuckled as he set plates and forks at the island. "I suppose I can put one on if it'll make *you* more comfortable."

She nodded quickly, looking away from him to make her plate. "That might be a good idea. I don't know that I can have a decent conversation without it." She gasped in surprise. *Did I seriously just say that out loud?*

"I mean... oh god..." She shook her head as he belted out a laugh so loud he put a hand on his abs, which were almost a six pack but not quite, and her fingers twitched. What would his skin feel like?

"Yes!" she squeaked. "Put on a shirt." He laughed and went around the island to the living room, and she turned quickly to wash her hands, hoping it'd give her a few moments to calm down.

"Alright, calm down. It's all fine." He laughed again, and she chuckled at their inside joke as she dried her hands.

He grabbed the shirt laying on the recliner and slipped it on. She watched his muscles move and then blinked as she took in the black jogging shorts with the grey t-shirt. She read the shirt. A laugh burst out, and she covered her mouth with her hand.

"Seriously? *My leg is in my other pants*? Who gave you that shirt?" She held back a snort of laughter. God, that would've been embarrassing.

He grinned as he began fixing his own plate. "Jake got it for me for Christmas last year. Have you met my cousin Jake? Do you say grace?"

She nodded as she put down the fork again. Bowing her head, she waited for him to speak. When he didn't, she glanced up. He was looking at her so earnestly, head tilted as if he was trying to puzzle her out. His intense gaze made her heart speed up.

He smiled when she looked up at him, then flipped his hand open. She smiled softly and placed her hand in his before bowing her head again. A tingle shot up her arm at his touch.

"Lord, thanks for making Cindy giggle. And thanks for this exceptional food. Amen," he said. Then he slowly let go of her hand and reached for his fork.

She hopped up, her hand tingling. "Drink?" She walked to the fridge. His touch left her mouth dry.

She tried to play it cool as she stood and walked to the fridge, her mouth suddenly dry and her heart racing with anticipation. "Drink?"

"Water, please," he said, clearing his throat. The gruff sound caused a shiver to race up her spine as she inspected the fridge. She grabbed two bottles of water and smiled at the leftover containers, the clear top making the contents visible.

"Is this a sushi roll?" she asked, closing the door and handing him a bottle.

"Yeah, Holly and Lola brought it by yesterday along with a casserole. Holly apologized again and made sure I was alright."

Cindy grinned and arched a brow. "And the California

roll? How was it? Lola badgered her into using chicken, but she was nervous about the recipe."

He blinked at her, brows raised. "They're chicken? I was afraid it was sushi, so I left it in the fridge! I figured if I let it go bad, then I could throw it away with a guilt-free conscious."

She laughed again and leaned toward him on the barstool. "She didn't tell you they were chicken? Oh man. Yes, they're supposed to be chicken. I'll look at them before I leave and verify, though."

He shrugged and took a bite of the salad he'd put on his plate. "I can figure it out. How long will they bring meals? When do the ladies come out? Holly and Lola arrived last night, but you're here at lunch."

"Technically, I'm working at the moment. I'm also a physical therapy assistant, remember? My next patient isn't until this afternoon."

"Oh! Will you be the one at the appointment tomorrow?" His eager expression melted her heart. Did he want to see her?

"No, the physical therapist will do the initial assessment, and someone will be assigned to your file. I thought the initial was last Wednesday?"

He nodded his head slowly as he chewed. "Yeah, I might have called and delayed it. You know, because of the kidney stones."

She snorted. "The initial assessment isn't going to be very taxing. You were putting it off, weren't you?"

He grinned. "Ahh! You caught me!"

I want to catch you between my legs. Holy crap, she needed to chill out. She took a sip of water.

"So, you work at the hospital on weekends and as a PTA during the week?"

The Soldier Gets His Girl

She swallowed a bite to reply, "Yep, I put myself through nursing school by working as a PTA. When I was hired at the hospital, the weekend was the only shift available. I'm hoping to switch to day shift soon."

"But you like it? Working both jobs?"

She nodded as she chewed, then said, "Yeah, mostly. Day shift is better for family life. But like I said, I enjoy helping people. Why? Thinking of becoming a nurse too?"

He shook his head and frowned "No, I've been thinking about the future, even before you mentioned it at the hospital about finding something I love to do. This leg thing kinda messed up my life plans, so now I need to reevaluate."

She nodded in sympathy. "I can understand that. What was your original plan?"

He took another bite. "Twenty or years in the Army. Then move back here, I guess. Never really thought about getting out."

"So, twenty or thirty years at a job you didn't love? I can't imagine. But you know there are tons of ways to find jobs you actually like. When I was in high school, they gave us a lot of aptitude and personality tests. You could take some of those. Or make a list of your hobbies, your likes, your dislikes, things like that," she said, spearing another bite of her food with her fork.

He laughed.

"What?" She looked up at him.

"You can't help it, can you? You have to help people. Your grandma. Your job. Doing meal trains for the church on your lunch break. Now you're trying to help me figure out life." He chuckled and shook his head as he took a drink of water.

She smiled and shrugged. "I guess so. You picked up on all that? You're pretty sharp."

He grinned. "Not bad for only knowing you three days."

Had it only been three days? He was so easy to talk to. It was like they'd known each other much longer. After cleaning up her plate and fork, she put the leftovers in the fridge.

"Any chance you can be my PTA when those sessions start up?" His half-smile made her stomach twist in knots.

She shook her head. "It's frowned upon to request a patient. But good news? I checked Holly's California rolls. They're definitely chicken." Their eyes met as they smiled at each other.

When he brought his plate to the sink, she walked around the island, trying to get some distance from him.

Being in the house and not the hospital with him standing upright was seriously messing with her body. He was so tall! She sighed at the way his body moved at the sink as he rinsed his plate. Tall, dark, and handsome was her kryptonite.

Her cheeks heated as she picked up her now empty food warming bag and folded it. She didn't have time to be mooning over him like this. When he wiped his hands on the dish towel and turned back to the island, she smiled as she met his gaze.

"I didn't answer you earlier but the meal train is at least two weeks, Monday through Friday. Some ladies might come together. Times aren't really set but it's usually in the evening."

He grimaced, and she knew he hated relying on others but wouldn't turn down the kind gesture of the church ladies. Only three days together, and she already knew that much about him. "I appreciate the heads up."

She patted his arm sympathetically. "No problem, just trying to make things a little easier for you."

"Sure thing. I have to go to my next appointment now. Thanks for letting me eat lunch with you. " She grabbed her food warming bag and headed to the door. His steps behind her echoed on the hardwood floor. Before she could reach the door, the heat of his body seeped into her back. His big arm reached around her to grab the doorknob.

They both froze, and time seemed to stop. They were close enough to touch, simply hovering in each other's personal space, breathing in the other's scent.

If I turn my head, he might even be close enough to kiss.

She kept her facing forward as her heartbeat raced. Her chest was going to explode before he opened the door. The hot air hit her in the face and did nothing to cool the heat rushing through her body. She had to get out of here before she did something stupid.

She stepped quickly onto the porch and was halfway to her car before turning to wave.

"Thanks again." Her voice was breathless and higher pitched than normal.

He stepped onto the porch, the shade masking his face. "Wait! When will I see you again?"

She opened her door and shrugged, before saying loudly, "Who knows? I'll be around. It's a small town and bound to happen."

That was the whole point, right? This town was small, and she was here to stay. If something happened like what happened with her ex, she'd have to move again. Nope, she couldn't pursue whatever this was.

She jumped in the driver's seat and started the vehicle. He stood on the porch, one forearm propped on the porch post, his left knee bent to take pressure off the leg.

She breathed deeply as she drove slowly down the lane. When she'd made the fried chicken last night for dinner, she'd wondered if being out of the hospital would change her opinion of him.

She'd half convinced herself that he'd be gone and she wouldn't have to see him at delivery today.

She'd also half convinced herself that whatever it was about him that made her stomach flutter was all in her head.

But damn. It wasn't. When she'd seen him in all that shirtless glory... Well, Maryanne was right. It had been years since she'd been in touching distance of a half-naked man. Well, outside the hospital anyway.

She groaned, knowing she couldn't touch. She had her own reasons because of her ex, but Andy was dealing with not only his injury but an identity and lifestyle crisis. He didn't need the added pressure of her or all her baggage too. On that, Suzie was right.

No ma'am. She would *not* give in to these feelings. It must be because she was about to turn thirty.

She'd heard hormones changed around this age. She was simply getting a jump start on them by drooling over the first guy to cross her path in a while.

And what about Dr. Kendall? a voice whispered that sounded suspiciously like Maryanne.

She snorted, saying out loud, "He doesn't count. He's my boss, for crying out loud!"

And still a hunk. Just like this guy, he's tall, dark, and handsome.

"He's nothing like Andy. Andy's..." She couldn't finish the thought. She didn't have time for this. She had patients to see before picking up the boys and getting groceries.

Grabbing a pen and a receipt from the center console, she turned up the radio and made a grocery list.

Chapter Eight

Andy knocked and immediately walked through the front door of the house Landry shared with his brother, Parker.

"There you are!" Landry said, walking to the dining table with a plate of food. "I wondered if you'd join us tonight."

"Eh, I wanted out of the house. Nice place," Andy said as he set the case of beer down on the dining table.

Landry's grin widened, his eyes sparkling with pride. "Thanks! I poured my heart and soul into this place. Bought it last year, a rundown old farmhouse on the edge of a new neighborhood development, and fixed it up from top to bottom. Once I updated the kitchen and bathrooms, the rest was just cosmetic."

Andy chuckled in appreciation, taking in the country interior of the home. The natural varnished wood floors matched the side tables and dining table, the light color matching the couch and fabric pieces in varying shades of blue. The open concept living room, dining room, and kitchen flowed seamlessly together, giving off a cozy and welcoming vibe. "Yeah," Andy agreed with a nod. "A man's gotta eat, but it looks like you've made a home here too."

"Exactly!" Landry's booming laugh echoed through the spacious living room. He gestured for Andy to follow him, and they made their way around the kitchen to the hallway. "Let me give you a tour before the rest of the guys show up."

When they came back from the bedrooms, The mouth-watering smell of grilled meat wafted into the bedrooms as they toured them.

Landry walked across the hall and pushed open a door. "This is the guest bedroom, just like the other."

"What's that smell?" Andy asked.

"Parker's grilling brats out back. You hungry?" Landry asked, leading him back down the hallway to the front of the house.

"I could eat," Andy replied, his stomach growling in agreement as he entered the living room. "But how's it going living with your brother again?"

Landry let out a rueful chuckle. "Well, it's difficult sharing a space with someone after having your own place for years, but we make it work. And luckily, we have a split floor plan, so we each have our own space."

Andy laughed, following Landry into the kitchen. "Is Parker still the ladies' man?"

Landry rolled his eyes and opened the fridge to grab condiments. "Always."

"Hey, don't be telling tales!" a voice shouted from the living room. Parker came into the living room carrying an empty tray. He chin nodded to Andy.

"Welcome home, man. Good to see you again, but don't let my bro fool you. He sound proofed the bedrooms so he could sleep in, not because of my extracurricular activities.

Unlike the rest of the world, he doesn't have to wake up early."

Andy grinned, stepping out of the kitchen and to the dining table so he wouldn't be underfoot. "Parker! How have you been, man? You're looking good, for a city boy."

Parker's barking laugh filled the room, his chocolate-brown hair falling into his eyes. He had a trendy haircut, shorter on the sides and longer on top, perfectly styled to allow it to fall forward when he moved. In stark contrast, Landry's shaggy, thick, and wild locks sprung around his entire head every time he ran a hand through it.

All the Williams' boys looked alike with their hazel eyes and brown hair, but Parker's eyes sparkled with mischief while Landry's were happy-go-lucky, hiding a deeper and more contemplative side. Irish twins, they were not even a year apart in age.

"You're just jealous that I'm younger and better lookin' than you," Parker said as he put the empty tray on the kitchen island.

The front door opened and several men stomped into the room, laughing and talking. Andy smiled and shook hands with Nick, Kendall, and Gunner.

"How ya doing, man? Heard you had a few rough weekends in a row," Nick said as he headed towards the kitchen sink to wash up.

Gunner, another Williams' brother, wrapped him into a hug. "Andy! Man, I'm so glad you're back. It's been too long. Already causing trouble and not even home two weeks?"

Andy laughed as Gunner slapped him on the back and released him, "It wasn't all me, I swear! Got hit by a truck and had a kidney stone. Stuff happens."

Kendall snorted, "Yeah, Holly was freaking out for days over it. I can't believe she hit you!"

"Holly's his hot sister," Parker said, wiggling his eyebrows as he grabbed a clean tray and headed back outside.

Kendall said, "Hey, stay away from my sister! She's had it rough."

Andy's brows rose. He remembered Kendall's sister at their basic graduation and a few years later. He hadn't recognized her at all. Then again, they hadn't spent that much time together. He'd been so wrapped up in his own injuries the past year and a half that he had no idea what Holly's story was.

They all washed up and grabbed plates and beers, talking about how he and Kendall knew each other from their Army days. Their conversation continued as they all went out the back door to join Parker.

A spacious concrete patio stretched along the back of the house, its flat surface covered with a faded gray rug and lined with mismatched furniture. Parker, tongs in hand, leaned over the grill and expertly flipped burgers while the rest of the guys hovered nearby, eagerly awaiting their turn to pile their plates high. As they settled into their chairs, the orange and pink hues of the Texas sunset painted the sky, accompanied by a gentle breeze provided relief from the early fall heat. They chatted quietly, content in each other's company as they enjoyed the peacefulness of the moment.

They each picked a seat while Parker finished cleaning the grill.

Andy turned to Kendall, hands full of the brat as he said, "I had no idea that was Holly, though. She's grown up."

Kendall sighed, his shoulders slumping a little. "She has.

The Soldier Gets His Girl

She even got married and was expecting her first baby, when there was a car accident."

"Oh, I'm so sorry," Andy murmured, images of his cousin Sarah's car accident going through his head. Deployed when she'd died, he still didn't know the exact details of it. His mind was his own worst enemy.

"Thanks. When I got out of the Army, she moved here with me and opened the yoga studio. It's been tough for her, but she's doing better."

Parker turned with his own plate and sat in one of the rocking chairs. "See? Better means I can totally ask her out, right?" Parker winked.

Kendall growled and threw a wadded up napkin at him, but Parker just laughed and caught it. Landry handed Kendall another clean napkin and shook his head as Parker held both his hands up.

"Hey, man, I'm just kidding. Don't worry so much! We've all been watching out for her. Well, except Andy. But if he had known about her, he would've watched out for her too. Hey, maybe he could've avoided getting run over."

Everyone laughed as they ate. Gunner cleared his throat and asked, "So what's the plan now that you're home, Andy?"

Andy shrugged and took a drink before saying, "No clue. I was going to be a lifer. There wasn't a back-up plan."

"Do you even need one? Aren't you drawing retirement pay?" Nick asked.

Andy nodded as he chewed. After he swallowed, he said, "Yeah, retirement pay is good, especially since I'd bought the house with cash from Aunt Suzie and Uncle Mike a few years ago."

Nick started choking on his food. Gunner slapped him

on the back before Nick took a drink and finally choked out, "Suzie is your aunt?"

They all chuckled as Andy winced and shrugged. "Yeah, you know her?"

Nick nodded, blinking owlishly. "Man, she's terrifying! She rented a tiller for her garden the first year I set up the shop. It was a nightmare, between the complaining and going back and forth. Next thing I knew, I'd tilled half her garden for her. *Then* she found 'the perfect tiller for the job.' Whatever the fuck that means."

Andy snorted, looking over Nick's chest and arms. He exchanged an amused glance with Landry, who just grinned as Andy asked, "Did you till it shirtless?"

As a look of horror crossed Nick's angular face, the guys busted out laughing.

Landry wiped tears from his eyes. "Oh, that's classic Suzie!"

"She'll twist everything around to the way she thinks it should be," Gunner said shaking his head.

"I remember soccer practice in high school. She'd stop by to have a 'meeting' with some church ladies in the bleachers," Parker said, using air quotes.

Gunner grinned, "I think Ma was in that group too."

"Eww!" Parker said, scrunching up his nose.

"I asked her about it once in high school. She was embarrassing Jake and I over some guy she was clearly ogling. She said it wasn't a crime to look, just touch, and Uncle Mike liked her looking because it always made her sweeter in bed," Andy said with a grimace.

"Oh my god!" Nick said. "She said that to her nephew?"

As Landry wiped tears from his eyes he said, "And Jake

is her son." Nick's stunned expression just made them all laugh harder.

"Even I know all about Suzie. She came to our basic graduation," Kendall said with a chuckle.

"Holly says the girls at yoga were talking about how she has already taken back the reins at the church for the Ladies' Auxiliary Club."

"Ma mentioned something about that too," Gunner said as he finished his hot dog.

"Said there were lots of events between now and Christmas," Landry said with a groan.

"What?" Nick asked. "What's so bad about that? We all like parties, and you can't deny, the food is excellent."

"True," Parker said. "But with Suzie home, she'll have them all organized and bigger than anything you've seen yet. And that means Suzie will rope us into volunteering for all of them.

"Setting up, hauling things, building sets for floats and plays and who knows what else," Landry sighed.

"We can boycott Tuesdays. Those will be non-negotiable, right? Poker night is sacred," Landry said with a straight face. They all nodded and chuckled.

Andy smiled. This was what he'd been missing. Not the bar or the deployments or the firefights, but simply the comaraderie of guys in similar situations. He was definitely not going to miss any poker nights. It was better than even being at the gym on Main Street.

Andy turned to Parker. "Hey, Landry showed me the gym last week. It's a great set-up."

Parker finished his food and wiped his mouth with the napkin. "Thanks, it was a fun project. Now it's almost managing itself, so I need to find another project."

"Whatever you do next, just make sure it helps keep the teenagers occupied. The gym is definitely helping with that and keeps the jails free," Gunner said. Last time Andy checked, he was a deputy officer. "The kids who normally run around doing stupid shit are now working out to impress the girls at yoga."

"Holly's giving teen yoga classes after school too," Kendall told Andy.

"It's kind of funny, though. The boys watch the girls at yoga while hanging out on Main Street. Then the girls go watch the boys at the gym," Parker said with a laugh.

They talked about all the stupid shit they did as teenagers to get the attention of girls. By the time the sun was gone and the bugs came out, Parker and Landry stood up to move back inside.

"Time for some poker?" Gunner asked as the rest of them shuffled inside.

"Wash your hands. I don't want any relish on the chips this time," Gunner laughed, slapping Parker on the back. They dealt the cards while the conversation flowed.

"Nick, what made you open the equipment rental shop after the Marines?" Andy picked up his cards.

Nick shrugged, "I was part of logistics and transport while in. My goal after was to be outside. Had some landscaping jobs, saw the need for the equipment rentals, and opened the shop."

"That makes sense." Andy looked at his cards and sipped his beer. He had no idea what he wanted to do when he grew up. God, he felt so old to be starting over.

Nick finished his beer before asking, "What did you do in the Army?"

Kendall nodded towards Andy and said, "He was a COMSEC guy."

"Y'all kept in contact after basic graduation?" Nick asked.

Andy nodded, "Yeah, our first duty station was the same too. After that, social media was a thing so it was easier to stay in contact."

Kendall shuffled his cards in his hand. "Andy's the reason I even knew where Crimson Creek was on a map. He always talked about this place. Small town but still central to anything in the Dallas-Fort Worth area."

"And has it lived up to expectations?" Gunner asked, placing his bet.

"Oh yeah. I love this little place. It's quiet, and everyone knows each other. I can picture myself settling down here with a wife and kids someday."

Parker gagged, adding chips to the pile. "Raise. A wife? You're not even that old yet! Why are you thinking about a wife? Live the free life, dude!"

Kendall laughed and tapped his cards on the table. "Check. I'm almost thirty-five. I'm not that old! Besides, small towns can be rather lonely if you don't have anyone to share it with. If I'm married, then all the little old church ladies will stop trying to set me up with their granddaughters."

Andy tossed a chip into the center, and the turn moved on to the Nick, who stared at his cards intently.

"You have Holly, so you can't be that lonely," Gunner said, leaning back in his seat and watching Nick.

Kendall shrugged, his voice tinged with annoyance. "It's just different with a sister, you know?"

They all shook their heads as Nick checked, and the turn moved to Landry.

"Wait, none of y'all have sisters? Weird. Well, sisters turn everything upside down. Her friends all become my friends, which puts me firmly in the friend zone with almost all the eligible ladies around here."

"Check," Gunner said, glaring at Landry, whose foot was bouncing fast under the table.

"Wait, there are a ton of girls around your house all the time? Raise," Parker said as he laid some chips down on the table.

Gunner elbowed Landry, who just rolled his eyes and shifted in his seat.

Kendall rubbed his forehead and let out a deep sigh. "Yep, they're over there now working on a bake sale for the school. Raise."

Nick's brow furrowed with confusion. "But... you don't have kids. Why would she bake for the bake sale? I thought only parents had to volunteer."

Kendall shrugged nonchalantly. "Yeah, but Cindy has kids. Remember her from the hospital, Andy?"

Andy nodded as he stared at his cards. Oh, he definitely remembered her. He couldn't stop dreaming about her.

And the way she'd stared at his chest earlier when she'd stopped by... like she wanted to lick it clean. He shifted in his seat as his pants became a little too tight thinking about her. He tapped his cards against the table to check.

"Her oldest is on my soccer team. He's pretty decent," Parker said, sitting back to wait on Nick to make his choice.

"Yep, that's her. She's in charge of the bake sale, which is good because her sister is the owner of Half Baked on Main Street," Kendall said.

Gunner groaned and closed his eyes. "Oh, what I wouldn't give for one of her bear claws right about now."

Landry rolled his eyes at Gunner. "I thought you cops loved donuts, not bear claws."

Gunner tried to swipe his shoulder, but Landry just

ducked in his chair with a laugh. Nick tapped his cards against the table, and Landry tossed a chip onto the table.

Andy cleared his throat and shifted in his seat. "So Cindy and Holly are baking at your house right now?"

Kendall nodded and waited his turn. "Yeah, and Maryanne, Cindy's sister. And probably Lola, because wherever Holly goes, Lola goes." He shrugged. Gunner folded and Parker checked, both of them leaning back in their chairs as if mirror images. It must've been a brother thing, which just made Andy miss his cousin, Jake, all the more.

Gunner took a sip of his beer, his eyes narrowing on Kendall. "How long will they be there?"

Kendall shrugged and checked. "They rarely leave 'til I get home from poker night. Why?"

Landry grinned, elbowing Gunner in the ribs. "He's thinking of swinging by your place when he leaves to see if he can make an early donation for the bake sale. Grab some of those bear claws."

Andy checked and finished the last of his beer.

Nick shook his head and stared at his cards, murmuring, "They don't make bear claws at home. They make those in the shop."

Kendall ran his hands over the back of his neck. "Bear claws aren't bake sale food. They'll be making brownies, cookies, pies. That sort of thing."

Nick checked, then Landry called it. They finished the game with Nick taking the pot.

Nick's voice boomed with excitement, and his shit-eating grin lit up the room. "I'm taking this to your house, Kendall," he declared. "Gonna snag some of those bake sale cookies."

Kendall let out an exasperated sigh as Gunner cracked

open another beer. Parker shuffled the cards on the table, his eyes focused on the game ahead.

Gunner tipped his beer toward Andy. "I'm surprised you don't remember Maryanne and Cindy, Andy. They actually spent a lot of summers here growing up. Their grandmother lived here. Mrs. Espinoza?"

Andy tilted his head to the side. "The middle school lunch lady?"

"Yeah, she died a few years ago, but Cindy and Maryanne both moved back to take care of her. Or maybe Mrs. Espinoza helped take care of Cindy, I'm not real sure."

"Why would she need taken care of?" Andy asked, his stomach twisting at the idea of her being in trouble and needing someone.

Landry sat back in his chair and sighed. "Remember when she first moved here? She was always on edge, avoiding people and keeping to herself. Ma said her marriage was a nightmare. Probably why she only focused on work and church."

Gunner nodded knowingly. "I heard he's locked up in prison now."

But Parker shook his head and interjected, "No way, I heard he died in some accident." Landry dismissed their speculations with a wave of his hand, "It doesn't matter now. She's clearly moved on from him, since she's been out socializing more than even Maryanne. Of course, she still focuses on the church and her kids."

"She's so different from Maryanne," Parker said, causing Gunner to glare at him. "Of course, Maryanne has grown up a lot."

Landry ignore him and said, "Remember how wild Maryanne used to be? She's the life of every party during those summers back in high school."

Andy sat there with a furrowed brow, trying to recall any memories of those years. "I don't remember either of them."

Gunner grumbled, crossing his arms, "They're a few years younger than us. You might not have noticed them before you left." It was weird how they'd grown up together, but Landry was his best friend and always had been even though Landry was actually a few years younger than he and Gunner.

"Not too much younger," Parker said, dealing the cards. "I think Maryanne is my age, and she's the younger sister."

Andy did the math. Twenty-six? Twenty-seven? Nick was working on his third or fourth beer, but the rest of them had gotten their second between hands. Andy thought back to everything Cindy had told him.

As everyone organized their cards, a natural break in the conversation led Andy to ask, "Did Mrs. Espinoza have diabetes?"

Kendall nodded, "Yes. Cindy had just finished nursing school when they moved here because Mrs. Espinoza got worse. She blacked out while driving and wrecked a few times."

"That's bad, but not as bad as what happened to Holly," Landry said. They talked about various car wrecks before moving on to trading stories of dumb stuff they did when they were younger.

Even though his leg ached, Andy was having a good time. It was relaxing. He hadn't merely sat around, hung out, and laughed with a group of guys like this since... well, since the deployment. It had been a few nights before the convoy was attacked, and he lost his leg.

He smiled as Gunner won the second game.

"So, are we going to play a third game, or wrap it up?" Gunner asked.

Nick grinned and said, "Why don't you ask Kendall to text Holly and see if they're still baking? You and I can take our winnings and spend them wisely."

Landry crossed his arms and leaned back in the chair, grinning slyly. "Question is... is it the bear claws he wants to eat or something else?"

"More like someone else," Nick said with a chuckle. Gunner's cheeks turned red even as he avoided their eyes.

"Aww, Gunner! I didn't know you could blush!" Andy said peering at him closely.

"It better not be my sister," Kendall growled, causing quite a few of them to laugh.

Landry cleared the table of empty bottles and said, "I doubt it. He's goes to the bakery every morning at seven. I don't think the bear claws would make him *that* punctual."

"Hey, I've always been punctual! Way more than you. And how would you know? Don't you always sleep in?" Gunner said as he shoved Landry on the arm.

Parker laughed as he threw an arm around each of their shoulders. "Enough. You're stalling. Let's go see Gunner crash and burn with the bakery lady."

Andy frowned as he eyed Nick, who had stood up slowly on wobbly legs. "You want a ride, man?"

Nick grinned, "I'm not *that* drunk. I bet I can still out-flirt Gunner. But never fear! Gunner picked me up!"

"I'll take that bet!" Kendall said. They made their bets on whether Gunner or Nick would be the better flirt. Andy didn't know which he was more excited for: poker night and having a group of friends or seeing Cindy again.

Chapter Nine

The open-concept design filled Holly and Kendall's modern house with natural light. The spacious kitchen boasted a massive island, where Maryanne and Cindy were busy making cookies while Holly and Lola whipped up brownies on the opposite end.

"I'm so glad Mom has the boys tonight," Cindy said as they rolled chocolate chip cookie dough into balls and placed them on the pan. "If they'd been here, they'd have half of this eaten by now."

Maryanne laughed, setting her dangle earrings swinging. "That's the truth. What movie did Mom bring over?"

"*Finding Nemo*. You know how Owen loves anything animal related right now."

Maryanne grinned and plopped another ball onto the pan. "Honestly, Mom was probably as excited as he was."

Flour and sugar covered every surface, creating a chaotic yet delicious scene that reminded Cindy of a bakery explosion. She wrinkled her nose at the mess and quipped, "Good thing Kendall's not here to see this!"

Holly laughed as she carefully poured the brownie mix into a pan. The warm, inviting scents of chocolate and sugar wafted through the air, tempting them all.

"He's so uptight. Living here is like we're kids again. His side is all ninety-degree angles and not a speck of dust. Mine? I wouldn't be able to tell you which clothes in my room are clean and which are dirty."

They all laughed, and Cindy said, "I kind of want to look at your room. I mean, if it's worse than my boys, with all three sharing a room, we need to stage an intervention."

Holly shrugged sheepishly and wiped her brow. Her silver hair had come out of the messy bun, and she had a streak of flour on her forehead and under her collar bone. Flour and probably eggs covered her tank top, while fingerprints were all down the sides of her yoga pants. Honestly, the only clean part on Holly were her cute, manicured toenails.

Lola rolled her eyes as she finished whipping up another batch of brownies. "You do not want to do that. It's a nuclear hazard."

"Hey, you sound just like Kendall!" Holly said, hip checking her friend.

Lola grimaced. "Never say that! He's so irrational!"

Cindy and Holly busted up laughing.

"What are you talking about? Kendall is the most rational man in town!" Maryanne said, eyebrows raised in shock.

Lola shook her head and rolled her eyes. "No, he's definitely not. Last week, I got a flat tire on Highway 80 and who shows up to 'save' me? Kendall. And what does he do? He starts mansplaining how to change a tire. Can you believe it?"

Her look of outrage made the three of them laugh. Lola

narrowed her eyes into furious slits, and her cheeks flushed a deep red to rival her hair.

"Seriously, it's ridiculous. Just because I'm a woman and he's a man, he thinks I don't know how to change a tire?" Lola huffed as she angrily whipped the batter for the brownies.

Holly glanced in the bowl with a sly smile. "Are you sure you're not imagining that bowl of batter is my brother?"

Lola looked into the bowl, glanced at Holly, and frowned as she slammed the bowl onto the counter. "Whipping your brother wouldn't do a bit of good!" she said as she walked to the sink to wash her hands.

"Oh wow, you're totally crushing on Kendall," Maryanne said as she washed her hands too.

Cindy slid the cookie pan into the oven as Holly slid the brownies in beside it. Holly turned to pour Lola's batter into a pan. After setting the timer, Cindy joined Lola at the sink and both sisters peered at Lola intently.

Lola frowned even deeper. "What? I am not," she said before flicking her watery hands into their faces. They squealed, and Cindy jumped back behind Maryanne. But Maryanne grabbed the faucet, pulled down, and sprayed Lola in the face.

"Wha—" Lola screeched, her jaw dropping in surprise.

Maryanne giggled as she turned off the water and lowered the faucet. Holly slid the other brownie pan into the oven and grabbed a dishtowel to wipe her hands. Cindy stepped away from the sink toward Holly, laughing so hard at the look on Lola's face.

"Admit it," Maryanne demanded, holding the faucet at the ready.

With a face of fury and water dripping from her chin, Lola lunged for Maryanne with a roar. Maryanne sprayed more water on her angry friend. Cindy grabbed her side, leaning over the counter.

"Oh, you laugh, do you?" Lola roared as she lunged forward, snatching the faucet from Maryanne and flinging it towards them. Water splashed Holly, who shielded herself with a dish towel, but they all ended up soaked with icy water.

Cindy gasped at the shock of the water, then joined in on the screeching and lunging chaos as they tried to restrain Lola's arms. Maryanne laughed, doubling over as she pointed and watched the chaos unfold. As they struggled to hold on to Lola, the front door suddenly burst open and several more people entered the open living area.

The girls paused and turned to the newcomers, caught like deer in the headlights.

Kendall stood just inside the house, his jaw hanging open in amazement. Behind him crowded a bunch of tall hunks in jeans.

"Hey, man, let us in." They all stepped in as Kendall raced to the faucet, shutting it off.

"What the hell is going on here?" Kendall's face was red from anger. Lola shook off Cindy's hand and crossed her arms.

"What's it look like, Ken doll? We were just washing up," Lola said, tipping her chin up.

"That's not how you clean up!" he roared, waving his hands around at the mess. Water was dripping from the cabinets, the drawers, and even the oven behind them.

Cindy and Holly inched back, watching as they argued. Holly handed her a towel, tossed one to Maryanne, and wiped off the dripping water on her neck. The guys hovered over the dining room table, and Cindy glanced at each of them. She'd only lived here a few years, but she recognized them all. Her breath caught in her chest. *Andy* was here too.

The guys ignored Kendall and Lola arguing and poked at the baked goods. One guy she didn't know reached for a cookie, but Holly whipped the dish rag and snapped it on his arm.

"Ouch!" he said, rubbing at his bulging bicep.

"Who are you and why are you stealing cookies from little kids?" Holly demanded.

"Nick. You must be Holly? I've heard so much about you from your brother here at poker night," the man bowed —literally bowed—and grabbed her hand to kiss it.

Holly giggled, blushing as Parker elbowed him out of the way.

"Holly! Can we help clean up? Will work for cookies." Parker took the dish towel out of her other hand and kissed the back of it.

Holly laughed, "Well, two gentlemen kissing my hands and treating me like a queen? How could I say no? Of course you can have some cookies."

"Only if you donate to the bake sale," Cindy said, as she wiped off the counter. Maryanne walked to the pantry to put up the flour and ingredients. Gunner grabbed the baking soda and sugar and followed her.

Cindy turned to see Lola and Kendall almost nose to nose arguing over… she listened. The hair on the back of her neck stood up as Andy neared. When she turned, his face was close to hers.

She sucked in a breath, smelling that scent of leather and the outdoors. Their eyes met as he said, "I think they're arguing about… fish?"

She glanced at his lips. They were so close. She wanted

to lean in... his eyes widened as he caught her movement, glancing down at her own lips.

She cleared her throat nervously and pulled back. God, how embarrassing. She looked away to finish wiping off the counter. "I don't know why they're arguing about fish. But then again, they argue about everything."

Andy leaned around her and placed his hand on top of hers. "Here," he said softly, "Let me help."

It felt like lightning going up her arm. Her entire body tingled as his front pressed into her back. She sucked in an uneven breath as she slid to the side so he could finish wiping down the counter.

She cleared her throat and raised her voice. "Y'all can donate to the bake sale and help us clean up. More cookies and brownies will come out of the oven in ten minutes."

"Fresh, warm cookies? Count me in," Parker said, winking at Holly.

Landry came out of the garage with a step stool. Nick grabbed a rag as they started to wipe down the ceiling and the tops of the cabinets.

Cindy stepped around the island and stood awkwardly. She needed to do something; she couldn't let the guys do all the cleaning.

She turned towards the dining table and wrapped up the pies in saran wrap.

"The cookies in the oven will take a while to cool down and eat," Holly said as she helped Cindy at the table. The guys complimented the baked goods, flirting with Holly the entire time and arguing on the perfect temperature to eat cookies.

Gunner and Maryanne returned. Was her sister's lipstick not as bright as it'd been earlier? Landry finished the dishes as the timer dinged. Cindy walked around the island to take out the cookies, but Andy was already there with the oven mitts.

"Which things come out?"

"The cookies," she said. His biceps flexed when he placed the cookies on the island. Cindy reset the timer for the brownies and took a drink of water. His nearness made her parched.

Landry, Parker, and Andy hovered around the fresh cookies until Cindy shooed them away. "You can't eat these yet. They're too hot."

Parker looked at his watch. "I'm timing it. I'll give them two minutes to cool, then I'm taste testing them. I'm telling you, that's the perfect cool down yet still preserves the warm, fresh cookieness."

Holly waved a cookie from the table at them. "You want something to compare the fresh out of the oven ones to? These are ready and still slightly warm! Who's been a good boy and wants a treat?"

Parker's hand shot up in the air. "Me, me, me!"

"No, me," Nick said, elbowing him out of the way. Holly laughed and waved the cookie at the two men as they swaggered toward the table.

Cindy glanced behind her, but Kendall had pulled Lola down the hall, whispering furiously. His arms waved, and Lola's jaw clenched hard, her arms folded over each other.

"What do you think is going on there?" Andy whispered near her head. His breath tickled the hair around her ears, causing goose bumps.

She breathed in deeply, his scent overpowering the smell of sugar and spice in the kitchen. It was a heady combination, making her a little dizzy.

Cindy shrugged and tried to act unaffected. "Lola's still mad at him for patronizing her a few days ago."

"Ahh," he said, "He can be a bit of a know-it-all sometimes. But he's usually right, so—"

"Yeah, he's like that at work too. But he's never argumentative. Only with her." She cut him off, nerves making her jumpy and too talkative. She leaned against the counter to face Andy, placing her hands behind her.

"So what are y'all really doing here? Wasn't it poker night tonight?"

His intense gaze swept down her body, pausing for a moment on her chest before meeting her own eyes. He couldn't be looking at her breasts. She was just wearing an old t-shirt with leggings.

And yet, his rugged face wore a hint of a predatory smile that made her shiver in anticipation. Perhaps he was as drawn to her as she was to him. Then he blinked, as if waking from a trance.

"We heard about the baked goods. We brought the poker pots too, to make our donations."

She smiled, her heart racing at the look in his eyes. "Oh good! Will you be at the bake sale too?"

"Are you going to be there?" He shifted to stand directly in front of her. She tilted her head back and pressed her legs together. He was so tall and muscular. She wondered how his lips would feel trailing down her neck, his hands on her body.

The air around them seemed charged with electricity, the memory of her body pressed to his from his time in the hospital warming her from within.

Her cheeks flushed as she remembered the dreams she'd had about him the past few weeks too.

"Yes," she whispered, her voice a breathy, throaty sound that made her immediately think of sex, sweat, and *him*. She sucked in a shuddering breath, and his eyes dipped to her chest once more at the movement. Oh god, he *was* interested.

No, he was just a red-blooded male. It wasn't personal. She wasn't sure if she was trying to convince herself or trying not to get her hopes up.

"Then I'll try to swing by," he said. Was it just her or was his voice deeper than before?

Chapter Ten

As they stood beside the oven, she couldn't take her eyes off him. The spicy outdoors scent of him mixed with the sugar and cocoa powder, flooding her senses. He leaned his hip against the cabinet and crossed his ankle over his leg, and she recognized the gesture as him taking pressure off his prosthetic foot. She longed to tell him to sit down and keep his foot up, but she wasn't his mother. She wouldn't baby him.

"Hey, Andy, I think Lola should take Parker and I home. Is that alright with you?" Landry asked. Andy blinked again, breaking their locked gazes before looking behind her shoulder and nodding with a smile.

"Sure. No worries," he said.

Landry grabbed a cookie for each hand as he said, "We're on Lola's way home. I know you're in the opposite direction."

Parker nodded. "Yeah, and Cindy is going your way, so you can take her home, ok?"

Cindy tensed, glancing quickly at Andy. Would he want

to give her a ride home? The grin on his face made her shoulders relax.

"That sounds great! Is that alright with you?" he asked. She could only nod, her stomach fluttering.

Lola stomped down the hall. "Landry, your timing is impeccable as always. I'm done here. Grab your warm cookies, and let's go?"

Landry nodded, slapping a twenty on the table and loading his hands up with a stack of cookies.

Nick sat at the dining table and waved to the pile of cash on the table. "I put the poker wins on the table for the bake sale. Let me know if it's not enough."

Cindy smiled and thanked them both.

"See you guys later!" Parker said with a wave before shoving the last cookie into his mouth, his other hand full of a stack of cookies. At this rate, it would've been better to have brought her boys. These guys were taking way more than her boys would've. But at least these guys were paying for what they were eating.

Landry followed Lola and Parker out the door, his voice carrying in the open room as he shut the door. "Man, I was afraid you were going to lose it and throat punch Kendall. Remember that one track meet in high school? Man, that was a good punch."

Before Cindy could process his words, Kendall stomped back into the kitchen, his furious gaze landing on his sister.

"Why don't you go take a cold shower and cool off?" Nick said with a smirk.

Holly giggled again as she said, "Yeah, you look like you could blow a gasket."

Nick leaned his forearms on the table, drawing Holly's eye to his biceps. "There's always the sink faucet?"

They all laughed. All except Kendall, that is. He just

huffed and stormed down the hall to his room. Holly waved at the table.

"Y'all want to help decorate cupcakes or were you only here for the cookies?" Holly smiled, her eyes twinkling.

Cindy glanced around as she and Andy walked towards the table and sat down to decorate the cupcakes. "Where's Maryanne and Gunner?"

Andy chuckled, and the sound sent shivers up her spine. She shifted on the chair, her panties now damp.

"I think she took him home," Andy said as he slid into a chair. "Is that alright?" he asked. Holly handed out bags of icing and showed them how to pipe it onto each cupcake.

Cindy shrugged. "Why wouldn't it be? She's a bit of a player, kind of like Parker and Nick. But she's helping me out with the boys on the weekends. She needs to relax on weekdays." She didn't know Nick well, but she knew of him. Nothing escaped a small town gossip mill.

Her eyes locked on Andy's hands as they decorated the cupcakes, his muscles flexing under his shirt. The colors of the frosting and sprinkles were a beautiful contrast against his tanned skin.

Nick was concentrating on decorating his cupcake so hard that he didn't even glance up to say, "Hey, I may be a player, but I own that shit. I mean, none of the girls I've been with expect anything but what I give them."

"Oh yeah? How do you know they don't?" Holly asked as she daintily frosted another cupcake. Andy's leg brushed up against Cindy's, making her squirm in her seat.

"Because I tell them I'm not looking for a relationship. Before I even ask for a number or offer to take a girl home. I'm honest about what I want; one night or a weekend of fun."

Holly snorted. "And that works?"

He nodded as he finished the cupcake and set it on the tray. It looked terrible, icing lilting to one side. He reached for another one and started anew.

Holly frowned. "So no girlfriends, huh?"

"Hey, I've had girlfriends," Nick argued. "Why do you think I only do hook-ups now?"

"Ahh," Andy said as he finished his cupcake. It had swirls on the top. "Bad breakup, huh?"

Nick nodded and said, "Yeah, she ended up in bed with the rear detachment commanding officer while I was deployed."

Andy grimaced. "Damn. That sucks."

"That's when I decided to never get played but to be the player." Nick said, raising his cupcake in a mock cheer.

"I got you beat," Cindy said. Her heartbeat fast and her palms sweat. What was she doing? *Am I really going to talk about this?*

Yes, maybe it will help scare him away.

"Two stories, actually. The first guy was in high school. He knocked me up before ghosting me, transferring out of state to go live with his mom. Didn't even know he was leaving. His dad showed up to a military function and got in my dad's face. He told my dad that there was no way the baby was his son's. And I'd never get a dime out of him."

"What? That's insane!" Holly gasped. Nick winced. She refused to look at Andy to see how he'd reacted. She had to keep going, get it all out there. If she scared him away, she wouldn't have to deal with all these crazy emotions.

"That wasn't even the worst one," she whispered. His knee pressed against hers again, and she drew a deep breath, somehow comforted by his touch.

"Got pregnant again a few years later, only this guy wanted to get married. Fast forward six years, cops show up at my door with a warrant to search the place, notifying me that they had caught my son delivering drugs to the park down the street. He was seven."

The guys stopped decorating and stared at her. Cindy looked down at her cupcake and continued, "They picked up James from daycare and sent them both to CPS while they arrested *me*, while I was pregnant."

Holly gasped. "You?"

Cindy's hand trembled as she tried to frost the cupcake. "I couldn't believe it when they found drugs hidden in between the wall joints in the garage. They were all prescription drugs that my husband had stolen from the nursing school I was attending. I didn't know they were there, my prints weren't on any of the drugs or in those shelves of his supply."

"Jesus," Nick said harshly.

Cindy ignored him, picking up the cupcake to put it with the others. Still avoiding eye contact, she said, "Cody told the cops his dad made him do it, which matched the security cameras at school that showed my husband giving my son the backpack of drugs. The day after they released me from jail, I filed for divorce."

The silence stretched. Andy slid his arm around the back of her chair and squeezed her shoulders. "Yeah, I think that's the winner of the worst break up story ever," he said.

She chuckled hoarsely as she rubbed her forehead with her hand.

"Oh, hun. Why didn't you tell me before now?" Holly asked.

"Where is he now? I have a machete in my truck. We can cut off his balls," Nick said, his tone serious.

She glanced at him in surprise. His expression didn't

change. He was just ready to jump in and have her back. She glanced at Holly who was nodding agreement, and warmth spread through her chest at their support.

She smiled and shook her head, "Prison."

"I know a guy in prison," Andy said, perking up. "Which one is he in? We can arrange someone to shiv him."

They all laughed as she replied, "Nah. No need. As long as I never have to see him again, and the boys are safe, it's all good. Leave the past in the past."

As she picked up another cupcake to decorate, Andy leaned back, lowering his arm from her shoulder to her hip. She could feel the heat from his body seeping into her skin as he stretched out his legs under the table. She instinctively clenched her legs together, trying to hide the growing wetness between them caused by his fingers gently tracing up and down her hip.

"Tell me about your boys," Andy said to her. She glanced around and saw Nick staring intently at Holly and her tongue as she licked icing off her fingers, flirting and whispering.

Cindy turned, so she was semi-facing Andy as she kept decorating cupcakes.

"Cody is twelve. He's really into soccer. James is eight. He's the quiet one, an artist and reader. Owen is four. He's pretty hyper and tries to be an artist like James but loves animals."

"Where are they tonight?" he asked, tracing circles on her hip with his fingers. Even through her shirt, she could feel every caress. Her breathing grew shallower and faster. The warmth of his body next to hers was like a magnet, pulling her in and igniting every nerve. His touch on her hip was electric, sending shivers down her spine and making her heart race.

"My mom is watching them at home," she breathed, reaching forward with a shaky hand to place the cupcake on the tray.

"Where's your dad?"

She swallowed hard. "Heart attack a few years ago. He was carrying a box inside the house and then dropped. I think the boys were too young to remember, but it was a rough few years. It was about eighteen months before losing my grandma, right before all the drama happened with my ex."

He squeezed her hip, and she met his eyes. He didn't say anything, and she was grateful. The empty words after the funeral didn't help.

She sucked in a breath and her shoulders relaxed as a wave of comfort enveloped her. His blue eyes stared into hers, and she wondered if he could see her soul. He glanced down as she licked her lips.

The timer on her phone beeped, and she jumped. She dismissed the timer and stood up quickly. When his hand fell away from her, she suddenly ached at the emptiness.

"Hey, Holly, I gotta get going. Mom will need to head out." She reached for the bake sale goods.

Holly waved a hand at the table. "Don't worry about all this. It can keep here just fine. I'll bring it to the bake sale this weekend. Y'all better head out too. Kendall won't be up for entertaining." She laughed as she nudged Nick's shoulder.

Nick rolled his eyes and glanced around. "Umm, Andy? Can I get a ride?"

Andy slapped his forehead and groaned. Cindy giggled as he said, "I guess I'll take you both home."

Holly shrugged, "I would offer, but I've not had the best of luck trying to drive in the dark lately."

Andy smirked, rubbing his hip as he stood and pushed in his chair. "Yeah, we figured that out."

They all laughed as Holly winced, offering him an apology cookie. He laughed and waved it off. His smile made him look so carefree. She couldn't take her eyes off him.

Her phone dinged, and she glanced at it. "Boys are all in bed. Mom said to take my time."

"Perfect."

She grabbed her big purse from beside the door and hugged Holly good night.

"Shotgun!" she said, as Nick grabbed Holly's hand and kissed it goodbye.

Nick grumbled, "Damn it," making her laugh as she went out the door behind Andy.

Chapter Eleven

As they walked to the truck, the excitement in the pit of his stomach skyrocketed. He could drop Nick off first. If he saved Cindy for last, he could sneak a kiss... wait, what was he thinking? He'd only known her for two weeks!

It's just a kiss, man. Lighten up.

Yeah, but she's a mom, he argued with himself. He glanced at her as she buckled up beside him. Would she even want a kiss? Or would she have expectations of something more? Did he even want something more? Nick climbed into the back seat of his crew cab truck.

Andy shook himself out of his reverie and smiled as he backed out of the driveway. When he came to the stop sign, Nick directed him to a neighborhood on the other side of town. Cindy said, "Oh, I live near there too!"

Andy nodded, "Okay, I'll take Nick home first then." An old George Strait song came on the radio, and Cindy started humming along.

"You like country music?" he asked.

He saw her shrug out of the corner of his eye as she

said, "I like all music. I mostly listen to pop from the early 2000s. The old country songs were my grandma's favorite, so I grew up on that too."

He nodded as they talked about artists and songs. Cindy turned to talk to Nick when the song changed. "What do you do, Nick? I don't remember you here from when I was a kid, but I've seen you around sometimes."

"I own the equipment rental place at the end of 6th Street. Construction, gardening, any heavier outdoor equipment, really," he said with pride.

"Oh, nice. You sound like you like it," she said. Was that a twinge of envy in her voice? Andy glanced over. Her smile wasn't the natural one, but definitely forced and fake.

"I love my job!" Nick said, "I get to fix and tinker with stuff when it needs it. I'm also a silent partner in a local transportation and logistics company, which is similar to what I did in the Marines."

He felt her gaze on him as he drove. "What did you do in the Army?" she asked.

Andy tapped his thumbs on the steering wheel in time to the music as he answered. "I was a communications security guy, but it was mostly electrical fix-it stuff. I'd rewire the radios, transmitters, even some cyber security things. They'd mostly bring me broken ones, and I'd fix them, but the last deployment... I rotated going to different bases to oversee other COMSEC guys, sometimes coming in to fix things the younger guys couldn't fix."

"Is that how you lost the leg?" she asked quietly.

He nodded, even though she probably couldn't see him in the darkness. "Yeah, the convoy on the way to the next base was attacked," he said, clearing his throat.

Nick said softly from the backseat, "Shit, man. I'm sorry."

"Yep," he replied. There was a pause in the conversation as he turned into the neighborhood. Almost immediately, Nick tapped on the window.

"This is me, second house on the left. Thanks for the ride, man!"

"It was nice meeting you," Cindy said as he jumped out. They waved at each other as Nick shut the back door and walked away.

He tapped on the steering wheel, missing the beat to the music from the nerves of being alone with her. "Which way for you?" he asked.

She directed him three streets over. He couldn't think of a thing to say, so he just listened as she crooned a Shania Twain song.

"This one," she said, pointing to a small apartment complex on the outskirts of the old neighborhood.

"Is this new?" he asked, putting the truck in park in front of the middle three story building. He didn't remember this place growing up.

She shrugged as she stared at it. "Newer. I lived with my grandma for almost two years, then this place became available. It's only a two bedroom. But the bedrooms are both masters, so the boys all fit in one room. For now, anyway." She laughed, the sound drew him like a moth to a flame.

He smiled softly as he reached out a finger and ran it down the side of her face. She froze, then turned her face to look at him. "I love your laugh," he whispered lamely. How could he tell her he dreamed of her smile, her luscious lips and twinkling brown eyes? Words would never do her beauty justice.

In the dim light of the parking lot, her eyes glimmered like pools of liquid honey. He continued to trace the contour of her jaw with his finger, feeling her leaning closer towards him. When he reached her chin, he tilted it up, never breaking eye contact as he waited for her reaction.

The sound of their breaths mingling filled the space between them, a symphony of anticipation and longing. The thumping of his heartbeat seemed to grow louder as he closed the distance between them. Her eyes fluttered shut and he hesitated, wondering why she was allowing this intimacy. She could do so much better than a busted up old soldier.

But she didn't pull away. With closed eyes, he leaned in and pressed his lips against hers. Her lips were like velvet, soft and smooth and fitting perfectly against his own. She gasped, and he swept his tongue inside, deepening the kiss and savoring the taste of her.

Their tongues tentatively meshed. He angled his head, searching for why this woman, of all the women he'd met in the past few years, drew him closer and made him want more. When she moaned, he cupped the back of her head.

She was still too far away. He wanted to be—no, *needed* to be closer. He pulled her sideways onto his lap, her ass pressing against his erection and making him groan as her feet rested on the bench seat. The scent of her skin mixed with sugar and spices, and he breathed her in, filling his soul with a peace he'd not known before.

The sound seemed to surprise her because she jerked back. He barely caught her before she laid on the horn of the steering wheel, twisting her back to the driver's side window.

He held her in his arms as they both chuckled softly. Damn, holding her felt right. It was like his arms had been empty his entire life.

But now, there was fire, energy, and life heating him up.

He'd never felt like this before. It was like ambrosia, like he was drunk on her kisses.

He stared into her eyes, so expressive. He had a window to her soul, and he couldn't fault her for being surprised by the kiss, confused by the intensity of these emotions, and overwhelmed by the desire that flowed between them. Her arms around his neck played with the short hair on his head, making his arms break out in goosebumps. He rubbed circles on her back with his hands, causing her to shiver and gasp.

"I—I—What is this, Andy?" she stammered, her back arching under his hands. He groaned as her breasts pushed against his chest.

He kissed her chin before raining kisses down her neck as he replied softly, "I don't know, Cindy. There's something about you that's invaded my dreams. I've been wondering about your lips for weeks. It's so much better than I imagined."

His finger traced the curve of her jaw to the fullness of her lips. In that moment, time seemed to slow down and the world faded away, leaving only the intensity of their connection. He couldn't find the words to express the depth of emotion he felt, but hoped his touch and kiss spoke volumes. His heart swelled with the beauty of this moment and the woman before him.

She gasped as his scratchy chin found the soft spot between her neck and shoulder. He kissed her there, sucking gently and making her squirm on his lap.

"I—I can't," she gasped. "I'm not... I don't..."

Disappointment speared him, but on some level, he'd known all along that she'd reject him. Any sane woman would, with all the baggage he brought to the table.

He swallowed hard and kissed the side of her neck. "Please, just let me kiss you. A final goodbye kiss?" Slowly, he trailed kisses back up to her chin, then the corner of her mouth.

She whimpered softly against his mouth, and he felt her body relax against him. *She'd feel so good if she just straddled him naked*, he thought. God, that was a bad idea. If he'd spent the past two weeks wondering about her lips, he'd spend another two wondering about every inch of her body.

She tilted her mouth and set it fully on his. He groaned as passion exploded. What was soft and teasing before suddenly became a wild and deep frenzy.

He ground up onto her, his hand fisted into her dark, curly hair pulled back in a low ponytail. Their mouths continued to devour each other's as their tongues danced in a desperate battle for more.

The heat between them was palpable as they continued kissing, his hands roaming over her body eagerly. Desire pulsed through him, urging him to take things further.

The slamming of a car door startled them both back to reality. He released her lips gently as she looked around, disoriented. Then determination took over as she seemed to shake herself out of the trance they had been in.

Jerking back across the seat, she scrambled to throw open the passenger door. The truck interior light caused him to blink but at least he could see her clearly now as she stepped to the ground on shaky legs.

Swollen pink lips. Her curls disheveled. Her dark eyes wide and blinking quickly, she murmured a quick, "Bye." Then she slammed the door and walked away.

He started to open his door, but he spied Maryanne walking to the stairs. He watched as Cindy followed her up, swaying hips making him groan and adjust himself in his pants. How long would it take to forget her kiss, the feel of her body?

He put the truck in reverse and drove home. There was just something about her that differed from other women he'd dated. It'd been so long since he'd been with a woman. He thought back and did the math.

Had it really been over three years? Damn, that was longer than he thought. The deployment and rehab had consumed him. All he'd focused on after being injured was getting back to normal.

And now... this was his new normal. He worked out every day. Now he had poker night once a week. Thinking about the crowd at the bar, he knew he didn't want to go back there.

But he didn't want to stay home alone either. After so many months of the rehab facility and living with people a room away, the house was too quiet, not that he'd ever tell Aunt Suzie that.

There *would* be some church events, though. Would he be able to handle them or Aunt Suzie pushing him? He knew it was only a matter of time before she manipulated him into helping with something or other. He didn't begrudge her and didn't mind helping. But when it was constant, it drew on his nerves.

He sighed, feeling at a loss on what to do. He wanted more than just killing time until the next time his Aunt Suzie needed him to do something. His thoughts turned back to Cindy.

Having all this time wouldn't be so bad if he could spend it kissing her. Hmm... she'd said she couldn't request patients for physical therapy, but could he request her?

Suddenly, he was looking forward to his intake appointment tomorrow with the physical therapist. He smiled. If he played his cards right, he could tell Cindy at the bake sale that he'd be her new patient.

Chapter Twelve

The next day, a knock sounded on the front door. Andy turned off the kitchen sink and wiped his hands on the hanging dish towel. He took a deep breath and opened it.

Smiling, he thrust out a hand for the short, little old lady in baggy blue scrubs. "Hello, you must be with the physical therapy company. I'm Andy."

She shook his hand with a wide grin, eyeing him up and down over her black, pointy glasses. "Nice to meet you, Andy. I'm the physical therapist at our office, Maggie. How are you doing today, hun?"

"I'm good. Thanks for asking. Where would you like to sit?" he asked, opening the door wide and gesturing around the house.

She nodded to the living room. "That recliner looks mighty comfy."

"That works for me," he said. "Would you like something to drink first?"

"I'm fine, dear. I have a bottle of water in this big ole

bag," she chuckled as she sank into the recliner and brought her bag onto her lap. She pulled out a clipboard and a pen and handed it to him.

"Can you fill out this first page? Then we'll talk, and I'll ask some more questions before taking your blood pressure and doing some muscle and movement assessments."

He took the clipboard and sat on the couch, quickly filling in his basic information. She popped the foot rest on the recliner like this was going to take a while. He didn't care if it did. It's not like he had anything else to do.

After finishing the paperwork, she led him through a series of questions about his health history, the incident and his recovery, and even his lifestyle habits. Then she lowered the recliner's footrest and got the blood pressure cuff out of her bag.

"How do you feel about being home?" she asked, putting the cuff on his bicep.

He decided raw honesty was the best policy. "I'm bored. I want to work. I'm not used to having so much free time."

She nodded as she pushed the blood pressure machine on and then wrote on the clipboard. "What kind of work do you want?"

He shrugged, the machine tightening on his arm. "Not really sure. I fixed radios in the Army but if I got a job in that, it'd be driving into Dallas or Fort Worth. And yeah, I can drive fine because the truck's an automatic, not a manual. It doesn't require pressure on my left leg, but I don't like traffic."

She chuckled and the machine beeped, the pressure easing off his arm. She checked the screen and wrote on her clipboard as she talked. "No one does, dear. That's okay. What have you been doing in your free time?"

She pulled the cuff off his arm as he replied. "I've been working out at the gym in town and running around the property here, making a trail along the fence line."

"How's your leg done with the terrain?" she asked, tapping the pen against her lips.

"It's fine. I mean, it's definitely been an adjustment from the treadmills in D.C., but I ran in the public parks there too, so not too different."

"What are you hoping to get out of your physical therapy sessions?" she asked.

He shrugged, "Nothing much. I mean, what's next after Level 4? I don't think I need more physical therapy, honestly. But I made a deal with my aunt, so here I am."

"Hmm, okay," she drawled. "Let's talk quality of life. What haven't you been able to do yet with the prosthesis?"

He sat back and thought about it. He hadn't tried to push himself too hard, not since a few months into his recovery when he'd literally made himself sick.

"Or perhaps a different question? Before your injury, where did you see your life going? What did you see yourself doing when you turn forty or fifty?" She sat back in the recliner but didn't prop the footrest up.

He smiled as he said, "I would have retired from the Army by fifty. Maybe have a wife and some kids. We'd end up moving here. It's why I bought this place originally."

"And what would you be doing here?"

He looked around the room, picturing a life that'd never happen. His stomach knotted as he sighed. "I'd be tinkering with something or other, sitting on the couch for family movie night, going to ball games and warning guys away from my teenage daughter. The kids would grow up, move off. The wife and I would sit on the back porch and sip coffee, watching the sun come up."

The Soldier Gets His Girl

"That sounds lovely!" she said with a smile. "I don't have a lot of patients your age. But I have a few grandsons who have probably never even thought of getting married or settling down."

He chuckled and crossed his arms. Before his injury, he hadn't thought of settling down either. An image of Cindy flashed through his mind as the therapist kept talking.

"There's good news about all this transition in your life. You can look for that wife now. You can still make that dream a reality. And the tinkering? I'm sure there's some local fix-it jobs you can find. I'll keep my ear open. You're going to be fine."

He smiled, thinking of the inside joke with Cindy. But he was so tired of people telling him it's going to be alright. No one knew that! Why would they say it if they didn't know?

"Alright, let's see how you move. Can you walk for me around the couch?" He did, then she directed him stand and sit, bend and squat to pick things up. It reminded him of Mandy.

"Oh yeah, this part was frustrating. So my niece was here a few weeks ago—she's three or four—and I couldn't just pick her up. Is that something we can work on?" he asked, his brows wrinkling.

She nodded, "Most definitely! When you get married and have babies, you'll want to pick them up."

Jerking back, he stared at her. He'd not even thought about babies. In his mental vision of the future, he'd just skipped that phase for his kids. He didn't just want a woman who could handle his brokenness, but his kids would need to put up with that baggage too. What would a baby think of his peg leg?

"Alright, let's see how you run. You'll want to play with

those kids of yours too," she said, standing and slinging her bag over her arm. "Shall we go outside?"

He followed her to the door, asking, "You want me to run in this leg or the running one?"

She paused and turned with big, wide eyes, the glasses making them appear bigger. "You have multiple attachments? Oh wow! Most people around here don't. You'll need to repeat these movements with each attachment."

An hour flew by before he realized it. He was sweaty from being outside, doing different exercises while Maggie watched and directed him from the front porch. She'd finished her bottle of water up as they headed back inside, so he grabbed a fresh one for each of them.

"Alright, that's it for me. I'll assign your case worker—who will be a certified Physical Therapy Assistant—and she'll contact you to figure out the best schedule. I'm only going to assign once a week for now, but if something changes, you need to tell your PTA."

He cleared his throat as he chugged the water. Swallowing, he said, "Actually, can Cindy be my PTA?"

Maggie nodded in surprise, "I can look at her case load. She might be full. But you have to listen to her and do what she says. Even if you don't want to be there or do it."

"Yes, ma'am. When I was in the hospital for the kidney stone and then the car accident, she was great. I didn't mind her telling me what to do, and she doesn't treat me feel like an invalid either. If her schedule allows, I would probably cancel less appointments if she was the PTA." He chuckled as she smiled and shook her head, making a note on her clipboard.

"I'll see what I can do. But why didn't you say something about the hospital when we were going over your medical history? Haven't you only been here a few weeks?" She tapped the pen against her chin again.

He chuckled and ran a hand over the back of his head. "Honestly, I try to forget about all hospital visits." They chuckled, and he continued. "But about three weeks ago, I got a kidney stone, then a truck hit me in a dark parking lot two weeks ago. Got a nasty bruise on my hip, but I'm fine now."

Her brows shot up in surprise. "Oh dear, are you sure you're alright? Did any of the physical assessments outside agitate your kidneys or your hip?"

"I'm fine," he said, thinking of Cindy and their joke as he held up his hands, palms up. "See why I don't really think I need the PT anymore?"

She laughed as she walked out. Waving goodbye, he shut the door, unable to contain his grin any longer.

He'd get to see Cindy at least once a week now. Would he be able to kiss her again? God, he couldn't stop thinking about how soft and inviting her lips were, like the most perfect puffy pillow made just for him.

He frowned as he walked towards the bathroom to wash off the sweat. Would she even want him? She had seemed to when they were kissing, but then she'd raced out of the truck.

Maybe he'd pushed too much. Maybe she just didn't think he was... well, man enough, with his bum leg.

He turned on the shower to warm up, then sat down on the chair outside the shower. He took off the prosthesis and hopped in on one foot, the gripper mat keeping him from sliding on the tile.

He wouldn't know anything until he saw her again. Hopefully, the bake sale would give them more time together without being too busy and overwhelming. Steady traffic, he could handle. A swarming hoard, he could not.

He'd know by her reaction to him. There was nothing he could do but wait and see.

The worry eased from his shoulders as he sat down on the shower bench under the spray of water. He hoped she'd smile that smile of hers, the one that said she had a secret. It made him want to unwrap her until he found out what it was.

And he so wanted to unwrap her. She'd been wearing leggings and a t-shirt yesterday, but the way the water from the faucet had clung to her curves, plastering the pale green shirt to her chest... He'd found himself hypnotized like some horny teenager.

He groaned and glanced down, his dick bobbing up and demanding attention. It'd been so long since he'd had any attention, from himself or a female. He closed his eyes, wrapping a hand around himself.

He could see the outline of her bra through that shirt. It had been lace, based on the pattern on the wet shirt.

And not padded, because her nipples stood at attention from the cold water. She never even noticed. She never noticed how she affected him either.

And when he'd kissed her... her gasps, her moans. The hint of icing on her tongue had been the literal icing on the kiss cake. That kiss was better than any cake he'd ever had in his life. It was soft and hard, teasing and demanding.

He imagined her kneeling in the shower, the t-shirt stuck to her curves, that secretive smile of hers as she looked up at him. Then she'd wrap her mouth around the tip of his cock.

God, that was all it took. He jerked, releasing into the shower with a groan. That was all it took last night too. Just one swipe of her pretend tongue, and he was a goner.

What was he going to do? She *had* to like him. The desperate need for her clawed at his chest. Having her around kept the loneliness at bay and was quickly becoming a need he didn't want to live without.

He used to be a pretty good flirt, if a cautious and slow one. It'd been years, but surely he could make her smile. He stood up on one shaky leg and washed off.

Chapter Thirteen

"What do you mean, she's not here?" Andy asked with a frown. Maryanne was behind the table in front of him at the bake sale, but Cindy was no where in sight. People were milling around the concession stands and the bake sale table at the soccer game. He was tense, but the open air and space made the crowd tolerable.

"She works at the hospital on the weekends, dude. Isn't that how you met?"

He was going crazy from not seeing her. It had been days, and he wanted to see her. He needed to see her.

"I was, yeah, but she works every weekend?" He rubbed his forehead.

Maryanne tilted her head to the side, eyeing him critically. "She has three boys, Andy. She has to work two jobs to keep them all clothed, fed, happy, and healthy. One job during the week and one on the weekends."

She smiled as another mom approached the table. Andy stepped to the side, letting Maryanne chat with the mom and her kid. The kid grabbed a cupcake and shoved it in his mouth, half of it crumbling down his shirt. The mom rolled her eyes and handed Maryanne some cash.

He'd known about her kids, since they'd talked about them several times. But until now, they hadn't been real people in his mind. He rubbed a hand over the back of his head, frowning at what a selfish bastard he was.

"You could help," Maryanne suggested after the woman walked away.

He took a step back toward the table. "What do you need? I'm not great at sales, even delicious ones like these."

She rolled her eyes and shook her head. "No, Andy. You could help with Cindy's son. You have a phone that takes pictures and videos, right? Go watch the soccer game and take some of number twenty-one. That's her oldest, Cody. Normally, I have the other two boys at games. We take pictures and video and cheer. But since I'm manning the bake sale booth and my mom took the two younger boys today…"

"Ahh," Andy smiled, his shoulders relaxing at such a simple task. "I can definitely do that. Number twenty-one? Red jerseys?" She beamed at him and nodded, turning to the next person to walk up to the bake sale table.

He grabbed a cookie and a bottle of water, left more than the suggested donation, and headed to the stands with a wave. She grinned at him and waved, turning back to the customer.

The cookie—warmed from the sun—melted in his mouth, the chocolate gooey and soft just like he liked it.

He walked to the stands, but Parker stopped him at the sidelines. "Hey, man! What are you doing here?"

"I—Well, I'm supposed to take pictures of Cody for Maryanne?" Andy said. The question hung in the air, and Parker grinned slyly.

"For Maryanne, or for Cindy?" he said, slugging Andy in the arm over the chain link fence. Andy shrugged him off, which only made Parker laugh out loud.

"Relax, man, and just enjoy the game. You can sit with my mom, if you'd like." Parker waved at a woman in the stands, and Andy glanced over to see Mrs. Williams wave back. He nodded gratefully at Parker and then walked towards her, feeling less out of place in the crowd.

"Andy! Welcome home! I didn't expect to see you here. I'm bringing you a casserole on Monday," she said, standing and wrapping him in a hug.

His shoulders relaxed a bit as he hugged her, careful not to crush remaining half of his cookie.

"Hey, Mrs. Will, you haven't aged a bit. I think Hunter looks older than you do now. Saw him at the grocery store the other day." Andy grinned as he sat beside her. The brothers got their laugh from her, but they otherwise favored their dad in looks. She was a tough, take no shit horsewoman who didn't let her sons get away with so much as looking at each other wrong.

"Oh, you're so sweet," she laughed, pushing a stray hair out of her eyes and tucking it back into her long braid. "I've told him to wear sunscreen, but he's never listened."

Andy bit into his cookie and nodded as she talked about their ranch. He practically grew up on it too, running between Aunt Suzie's and their place.

"I didn't even ask why you're here. Who are you taking pictures of?" she asked suddenly.

He grimaced and lowered his phone. Aunt Suzie would hear about this before the end of the game, but he couldn't really give any excuse so the truth it was.

"Number twenty-one? Cody? Maryanne at the bake sale

table can't take pictures of him for her sister so she asked me to do it."

"Ahh," she said with a wide smile, her ball cap shading her eyes and making her look mysterious. "They always say the way to a man's heart is through his stomach. Looks like they're right!" she laughed. Her brown haired braid shook down her back.

He frowned, "Wha—"

"Oh, Suzie is going to go nuts. Maryanne can stand up for herself, though. Never fear!" She jumped up and stepped down the stands.

He blinked at her sudden departure. Why did everyone immediately go call his aunt in this town? "Where are you going" he asked, his voice slightly higher than normal with borderline panic.

"Going to the bathroom! Be right back!" she smirked. He ground his teeth. Aunt Suzie was going to think he liked Maryanne after this, he just knew it. Ugh, sometimes small town life sucked. When he was in D.C. for a year and a half, no one knew who he was, and it'd been nice, if lonely.

He took videos as he thought. They were down by two when Mrs. Williams came back. She talked about the holiday events in town, but then Cody got the ball. Andy swiped quickly on his phone and hit the record button.

The other parents were whooping and hollering, and Mrs. Williams even got so excited she stopped mid-sentence and stood up to scream. He stood up with everyone else, yelling for him to go, go, go. The phone got a little wobbly when Cody scored and everyone went nuts, including him.

"That was amazing! That boy is going all the way. Further than even Parker," Mrs. Williams said, her face beaming.

"Do you come to all the games?" he asked, stopping the recording as they sat back down.

She shrugged, "Now that Parker's home, yeah. Turns out I missed it. With him coaching, it gives me an excuse to be here."

He looked around. "I can see why you like it. The energy is good here." It wasn't overwhelming, even with the crowds.

He stayed in the stands through half-time. Mrs. Williams left for a lunch date with her husband before everyone surged towards the concession stands and bathrooms.

Parker came to the chain-link fence that separated the small stands and kissed his mom's cheek before she left. Then he waved at Andy, and he made his way down the stairs to the fence.

"Hey, man! What do you think?" Parker asked, bouncing from foot to foot with excitement.

"You're doing an outstanding job with them," Andy said. It was completely true too. Parker made a brilliant coach, somehow reminding Andy of Parker's stern mom but with Parker's fun-loving personality still shining through.

Parker beamed at him, hands gripping the top of the fence. "Right? They're a pretty talented group of kids. You catch Cody's goal?"

Andy nodded and patted his back pocket. "Yep, got it all on camera!"

"Good. Cindy will like that," Parker winked. One of the other coaches whistled for a huddle, so he jogged away. Andy went to the bathroom, then made his way back to the stands. He nodded at a few people but otherwise kept to himself as he took videos and pictures of Cody, finding himself engrossed in the game.

At the end of the third quarter, Maryanne came up and

sat beside him. "How'd the bake sale go?" he asked, putting down his phone.

"Awesome! Totally sold out, so I can take over picture duty now. Did you get any good ones?" She grabbed his phone and scrolled through the pictures.

"Oh my God, you've got like a hundred on here! I thought you'd only take maybe a dozen!"

He grinned sheepishly, shrugging his shoulders. "I wasn't sure how many. Look at this video when he scored!"

"Oh, wow, you got his face in a couple of them too. Look how happy he is! Oh, and look at that swagger. So confident for such a little man." She handed him the phone back as the whistle for the fourth quarter sounded.

"I can tell how much he loves this game. And he's got skills too."

"He's worked hard for it. When they first moved here, he'd never played before. But soccer really got him out of a dark place. Both Cindy and I—we'll drive him to any practice, any game, any camp… anything that keeps him happy."

Now that he wasn't locked behind the phone, Andy soaked in the game, never taking his eyes off Cody. Based on what Cindy had said at Kendall's the other night, Cody had had a really messed up father.

"Cindy told us about her ex at Kendall's the other night. It affected the kids pretty bad?"

He saw her nod out of the corner of his eye. "Yeah, it was really hard to get the kids out of CPS. They were there for two weeks before I got temporary, emergency custody. Mom was up here, but I was in culinary school in Houston and closest."

"How long before she got the kids back?"

"A month. They wouldn't let her go back to their place

for over a week. So she crashed at my house. But when I got custody, she had to go home and could only do supervised visits until they finished the investigation. It was brutal for all of us. She'd never been away from the kids, and the boys were so small and scared."

He tried to do the math on the ages. "Cindy said Cody was seven?"

"Yeah," she said, "James was three. He's pretty reserved now. The chaos and uncertainty subdued him."

They cheered for Cody when he got the ball again, who passed it to his teammate to score. They were one point ahead, but Cody appeared to be slowing down in this quarter.

"You realize I'm only telling you all this because I saw you in the parking lot, right?" Maryanne asked, turning to him and pulling her sunglasses down to stare him directly in the eyes. He froze, blinking but not looking away.

"You... saw what?" The hair on the back of his neck stood up. Had she seen them kiss or had she seen Cindy run away from his truck? He held his breath, waiting to see what she had to say.

She snorted, raising one eyebrow as she put her sunglasses back on normally. "That tonsil tennis. I'm all for it, by the way."

He sucked in a breath in relief. Even though the game continued in front of them, Andy was hyper aware of Maryanne next to him on the bleachers. She popped a bubble and turned back to the game, ignoring Andy staring at her as she continued talking.

"That being said, she's been hurt deeply, Andy. Not once, but twice. As her sister, I'm telling you to treat her right or I will make that leg injury the least of your physical problems. As a woman, I'm telling you to take it slow and

The Soldier Gets His Girl

sweet if you want to make something that lasts. If you're wanting some fling, go back to the bar."

She jumped to her feet and cheered for Cody, who passed the ball to another teammate. When she sat back down, Andy cleared his throat, saying gruffly, "I'm not going to hurt her. I'm not that kind of guy."

She shrugged, flipping her dark ponytail over her shoulder. "I didn't take you for that kind of guy. I'm just saying, she's not some piece of ass. If that's what you're after, go somewhere else."

She kept her eyes on the game, so he turned back to watch too. Not seeing, he took a drink of his water. He hadn't ever been the fling type. Ever since the therapist had left the house Wednesday, he'd been thinking long and hard about what he wanted from life.

"I'm not just after a fling," he finally admitted. When he laid down at night, he imagined the house full of kids and a good woman in his arms. It might not be Cindy, but it could be. There was only one way to find out.

He saw her nod beside him, and she changed the topic to the bake sale goods. When the game was over, he waited for everyone to leave. She stood up and frowned down at him as he stretched his legs out in front of him. "You're not leaving?"

He shook his head, "Nah, I don't do crowds. I'll wait for them to clear out, then I'll head home. Thanks for asking me to take pictures and stick around. It was actually pretty fun."

She smiled, tilting her head to the side. "You know… why don't you come grab some ice cream with us? It's tradition when they win for the team to go get ice cream."

He shook his head, rubbing his shin where his leg ached. "No thanks. The entire team? That's a lot of people in one little restaurant." There were only two restaurants in town, and neither was large.

She waved to Cody as he jogged over to the break in the fence. "It's outside, dipshit. Sonic has outdoor tables."

"Oh, you didn't say *Sonic* ice cream," Andy laughed as the stands emptied of people. The team huddled on the sidelines until the bleachers only held a handful of people. Maryanne kept up a steady stream of conversation about how to pair ice cream with different bakery treats that she offered at her shop.

When the huddle broke up, Andy followed Maryanne down the stairs. Several of the boys headed for the break in the fence while others went towards the locker rooms. Cody reached the fence in front of them.

"Did you see any of the game?" the kid asked Maryanne as she stepped off the last of the stairs from the bleachers.

She nodded, reaching across the fence to ruffle his sweaty hair. He grinned, pride shining in his eyes.

"Yeah, I caught the last quarter. Your team work was amazing! Great job!"

"Thanks!" he said. "I got winded that quarter, but by then, their defenders were gunning for me, so it left some good opportunities for the rest of the team to score."

Big brown eyes turned to him, and Andy reached out a hand to shake.

"Hi, I'm Andy. Great game! I took videos while she was at the bake sale."

Cody's dark brown eyes twinkled in the light as he brightened. "Thanks! Can you go grab ice cream with us so I can see them? Coach says we need to watch our plays to see how to get better."

They walked to the emptying parking lot. Andy nodded

The Soldier Gets His Girl

as Maryanne grinned wide and said, "See? I told you it'd be best for you to get ice cream with us. It's always better when people just do what I say."

Andy laughed. "Oh no, I'm not admitting that. But as a soldier, I know when to pick my battles."

The dark haired boy between them reached Maryanne's shoulder, and he glanced up with bushy brows raised. "You're a soldier? That's cool. My grandpa was in the Army, but I don't remember him much."

Andy nodded, his stomach twisting, afraid he would say the wrong thing. "I was until I retired a few weeks ago and moved back here."

Maryanne stopped next to a little red sports car as Cody said, "Hey, Auntie M, can I ride with Andy to Sonic?"

Andy stumbled, putting a hand on the car. Maryanne looked surprised, her eyebrows raised high on her forehead.

Andy pointed to his truck across the parking lot. "That's me. I'm fine with me, if it's fine with you. And if you think Cindy would be fine with it." His lips twitched at the overuse of the word fine.

She nodded and smiled a sneaky smile that Andy didn't entirely trust. "I'll follow you. As long as I don't let you out of my sight, she'll probably be alright with it."

Cody threw his soccer bag into the backseat of her car, then turned and walked beside Andy to his truck.

"So the Army, huh? I want to play soccer, but I don't expect to make it professionally. I mean, yeah, that'd be awesome, but let's be realistic, right?" Cody said, talking fast as they got in the truck and buckled up.

"Does the Army have a soccer team?" Cody asked.

Andy frowned, as he started the truck and backed up. "I don't know about the Army specifically, but I'm pretty sure there's an Armed Forces soccer team. That's cool that you're looking long term like that."

Cody patted his dirty hands on his grass stained shorts in time to the music. "Yeah, I don't like surprises. Like, if I go the professional route, there's a lot of pressure and you can get traded, right? But the Army would be steadier. Consistent, I guess? Plus doesn't the Army have insurance?"

Andy nodded as they drove the few minutes to Sonic. "Yeah, definitely, and the insurance is good. I loved having a steady paycheck, but I also loved knowing exactly what I was going to do every day. I knew what I had to do, how to do it, and did it well. It was absolutely consistent."

He saw Cody nod out of the side of his eye. "That's what I'll aim for then." The beat of silence didn't stretch long before he went to the next topic.

"So... you like my aunt? Like, like her, like her?" he asked curiously.

Andy sucked in a breath and let it out slowly as they pulled into the Sonic parking lot. He'd been up front with the therapist, and he wanted to continue that. He didn't hide things and was an open book with everyone, since it usually meant less drama to deal with. He parked, unbuckled, and turned slightly to look at Cody.

He looked so much like Cindy, sitting in the passenger seat of his truck. Was it just a few days ago he'd taken her home and had that amazing kiss? It seemed like forever ago.

He shook his head slowly. "Actually, no. I don't like her, like her. I actually like someone else."

Cody frowned, his face falling. "Oh. Well, alright then."

He reached for the handle to open the truck as Andy blurted, "Has anyone ever dated your mom?"

Cody's hand froze mid-air. He turned and stared at

Andy. Andy swallowed hard. Maybe he shouldn't have pushed it. Maybe he shouldn't have said anything.

Damn, maybe I should have made sure Cindy actually liked me back before having this conversation. What the hell am I doing?

Cody leaned back against the seat and crossed his arms in silence, not looking away.

Andy took a deep breath and waited, not breaking eye contact. It was eerily similar to how Maryanne had stared him down earlier, but he held his ground and waited the boy out.

Finally, Cody pursed his lips and said, "No, no one has dated mom since Dad went to prison. Is it *her* you like?"

Andy slowly nodded his head.

"Does she like you?" the boy asked, narrowing his eyes.

"I—I'm not sure." What else could he say? They sat in silence, and Cody finally looked away to stare out the window. His teammates were already in front of the Sonic outdoor tables, chatting and laughing. But Cody just looked back at Andy, frowned and nodded, then opened the door. "

"I guess we'll just wait and see then, won't we?" Cody asked, shutting the door behind him.

Andy sighed in relief and got out to join Parker, Maryanne, the team, and the other parents as they ordered their ice creams. If Cindy did like him back, he'd need to win over each one of her three boys, and that wasn't even considering her mom and sister's approval.

The memory of the kiss left him hot and bothered, so he took an overly large bite of his ice cream to cool down. He had his work cut out for him, but that kiss haunted him, promising the effort would be worth it.

Chapter Fourteen

"Thursday's are my favorite night of the week!" Maryanne sighed, as they finished their child's pose.

Cindy flopped onto her stomach and breathed deeply. "Me too," she said softly, "It's almost as relaxing as a massage."

"Speaking of... Holly, are you available next week? My shoulder's been hurting," Lola said as she sat up and stretched her hands above her head.

"Sure thing, I'm pretty open during the day."

"How's business going?" Cindy asked as she stretched.

"It's slow, but I knew it would be when I moved here. Doing the teen yoga class after school has helped a ton, though." Holly moved to a one legged tree pose.

"What about more specialty classes?" Maryanne asked, following Holly's directions.

Cindy climbed to her feet and balanced on one foot, breathing deeply. She could feel the tension seep out of her shoulders from the rough weekend at the hospital, followed by an even harder week at her PTA appointments. She ignored the lingering tension from her first kiss in years. It'd been over a week. She had to let it go.

"What do you mean?" Holly asked, her lilting voice ringing throughout the bright room. The yoga studio was on the middle of Main Street, next door to Parker's gym. Maryanne's bakery was a few doors down.

Way back in the 1950's, someone split one long brick building into different businesses with varying facades. It was charming, quaint, and a bit run-down. Across the street were the pawn shop, theater, and pharmacy.

Holly had installed windows along the front to let in more light. She'd brought the old place up to date by refinishing the hardwoods, remodeling the bathroom, and adding a small locker room and floor to ceiling mirrors along one wall.

"I mean, the teenagers need a hangout spot. But don't we all? So have a yoga class for different groups. Like the little old ladies at church. Oh, and one for parents, like a Mommy and Me class or—"

"No, not a Mommy and Me class," Holly said sharply, causing the others in the rows behind them to glance up. Holly's voice wavered, and everyone stopped, frozen as they all realized what had been said.

"Holly... I didn't mean—" Maryanne said softly. She stopped talking as Holly smiled at her sadly and shook her head and led them into warrior pose.

"It's alright. A senior citizen class would be fun. Oh! And what about a singles night? We could all pair up with a new partner every five minutes!" Holly said, shaking off the memories and her face lighting up in excitement. Cindy's chest ached to comfort her friend, but she knew now wasn't the time or the place.

"Oh, I like that idea!" Maryanne said. "It could be like

speed dating, where you do a yoga pose and talk to a partner before changing partners and poses!"

Lola snorted. "And who exactly would come? Manly men won't come to yoga. It would end up being an old maid and senior citizen singles night!"

Cindy laughed, thinking of all the older patients she had. "Just don't let them get hurt. My case load for physical therapy is already pretty big."

Maryanne's sneaky smile shone through, causing Cindy's heart to race. That look never led to anything good.

"And what about your new patient? Don't you start with Andy tomorrow?"

Cindy gasped and stumbled out of her warrior pose. "How'd you find out about that?"

"Maggie came in to the bakery today and told me," Maryanne said.

Cindy rolled her eyes. "That woman does not understand HIPPA laws or privacy!"

Maryanne laughed as Holly squealed, "Oh my God, that's not the point!"

Cindy shrugged as she resumed warrior one pose. "So what's the point?"

Holly scolded, "There was serious chemistry between you two when we were baking! What happened when he took you home?"

Cindy stumbled again as her face flushed. Her lips tingled and her underwear became uncomfortable as she remembered his soft lips.

Dear Lord, what is wrong with me? I've never gone from zero to sixty by fantasizing about a guy before!

She shook her head furiously. "Nothing!" she cried.

Maryanne shook her finger. "Oh no you don't, missy.

You dish it. I *saw* you in the parking lot. You spill it or I will!"

Cindy gasped, "What? But you didn't say anything! We've talked every day for over a week!"

The whine in her voice was obvious, but she didn't care. Her sister had ratted her out! She thought she'd gotten away with ignoring what happened and how it made her feel.

Maryanne shrugged as they followed Holly into some seated yoga positions. "Girl's night was canceled last Thursday, and I wanted to wait to talk about it here."

Cindy groaned as she got into child's pose and hid her face on the floor. The studio was big enough that groups naturally formed. The three of them were the closest to Holly, and there were three other groups of women spread out around the open space. After several deep breaths, she raised up and sighed, keeping her voice low so the others wouldn't hear. "Alright, fine. He took me home, then we kissed in the parking lot."

Lola gasped, following Holly into the next pose. "Are you crazy? You've only known him for what? Two weeks?"

Cindy wiped her forehead with her shirt. "I know! It's completely ridiculous. I can't believe I kissed him. I mean, we've only hung out three or four times in the past month!"

Holly sighed, her face dreamy as she stared across the room. "I think it's romantic. I mean, you definitely had chemistry the other night. He couldn't keep his eyes off of you."

"I'm surprised you noticed, with all that flirting you were doing," Cindy said sarcastically.

Holly laughed, the sound like music filling the large room. "They're just silly boys. We were only messing around. It's child's play compared to what you and Andy had. I mean, I could practically see the heat sizzling from your side of the table!"

"Well," Lola said matter-of-factly, "Let's hear it. How was the kiss?"

Cindy couldn't stop the dreamy sigh. Her lips tingled again. Goose bumps rolled across her arms and the hair on the back of her neck stood up.

"Oh man," Lola said quietly. "That sigh says it all."

Cindy shrugged and followed Holly into the next pose. "It was the best kiss of my life, to be honest."

Holly giggled and said, "See? It's the real deal, guys. Just you wait. This is going to be epic."

Cindy groaned, brushing her hair out of her face. "No, it's not. It's not going *anywhere*. You guys know my track record. I don't pick the best guys. I don't even pick halfway decent guys. It won't work out with Andy."

Lola nodded, "I agree. I think you should stop it right there. And he's going to be one of your PTA patients?"

Cindy groaned and placed her head in her hands to mumble, "Starting tomorrow."

"Well, just explain you can't fraternize with patients. It's probably against company policy or something, right?" Lola asked.

Cindy nodded, her anxiety twisting her stomach. Oh shit, Lola was right. It was so against company policy.

Lola continued, "Exactly. So let it go, and move on. You don't need him anyway."

Maryanne shook her head. "I don't know, I think she should go for it. Y'all didn't see what I did. She was sitting on his lap! I've never seen her lose her cool like that before. Even with the previous two losers. And that's another thing! She's only been with the two! This is a prime opportunity to get experience and have fun for a change."

"That's true," Holly said. "You work all the time. Girl's night is the *only* thing you do for yourself. Live a little! Have fun and see where it goes."

"And if he causes problems at either of her jobs?" Lola asked with a frown.

Holly shrugged and Maryanne said, "Then we beat his ass." They all busted up laughing. The laughter lifted her heart. She could always count on her friends.

"I'll keep it professional tomorrow. And every PTA appointment after that. If not, I'll ask to transfer him to a different PTA. We're training a new one anyway."

Maryanne smirked, that sneaky smile back on her face as she leaned forward. "Want to hear something else?" Holly nodded quickly, leaning in closer.

"He came to the bake sale to see her last weekend. He was clearly bummed that she wasn't there. Then he sat and watched Cody the entire game, taking all kinds of videos and pictures!"

Holly and Lola gasped.

"Seriously?" Lola asked, her brow wrinkled in confusion. "Guys who are only after sex rarely spend a lot of time with their target's kids."

Maryanne rolled her eyes. "Exactly. Not only that, but *Cody* asked to ride with him to Sonic."

Cindy jerked back in surprise and gasped. "But Cody doesn't trust men! And you're just now telling me this? Oh my God! What'd they say? What happened?"

They'd all completely given up on yoga and were now sitting in a tight circle on their yoga mats, the other groups doing various independent stretches.

Maryanne patted her arm. "I knew you'd over-react like this. It's alright! They were talking about the Army and Cody had questions. Although…"

"Although what?" Cindy screeched. Holly put her hand on her arm and mimed deep breathing.

Cindy breathed in slowly and deeply with her before Maryanne replied, "Cody didn't want to sit with the team for long. When they'd almost all left, he put the heat on Andy. He asked a lot of questions about when you and Andy had met. Cody didn't seem as open and friendly after they arrived at Sonic."

Cindy frowned and thought aloud. "What changed his attitude like that?"

Holly giggled and rolled her eyes. "They probably talked about you, silly."

Lola nodded, leaning back on her hands. "Yeah. That makes sense. If they left talking about the Army and acting like buddies, then came back with Cody being a moody teenager and asking questions involving *you*..."

Maryanne nodded, laying on her back with a sigh. "That's exactly what I think."

Cindy frowned and rubbed the sweat off her forehead with the bottom of her shirt. "But what does that mean? What did he *say*? Oh my God, what if he told Cody about the kiss? Oh my God—"

Maryanne slapped her lightly on the leg. "Chill out, chica! This is why I didn't tell you. Because if we would've talked about it before, you would've obsessed all week over it. Now you don't have time to think and worry yourself sick before you see him tomorrow."

Lola bobbed her head side to side. "There's no way he told Cody about that kiss. I mean, good guys don't kiss and tell. Douchebags kiss and tell. But not good guys. Andy is definitely one of the good ones. When we were growing up, he was always lending a hand, and I never heard of him

The Soldier Gets His Girl

treating a girl wrong. And didn't y'all just stick up for him as *not* being one of those jackass players?"

Cindy glanced between them as they all nodded and stared at her. She breathed deeply, fighting the panic. "So… facts? One, we kissed, and it was out of this world amazing."

"Like can't stop thinking about it in the shower kind of amazing?" Maryanne asked. Holly giggled as Lola rolled her eyes. Cindy couldn't stop the blush and nodded quickly. They burst into laughter in triumph.

"Two," she said loudly, clearing her throat and ticking off a second finger on her hand. "He spent time with Cody —and Maryanne—so he might not be just after sex. Those are positive facts. But, and this is the biggest but of all time," they all snickered before she continued.

"I have to work with him tomorrow. I can't do anything with patients. I literally can't see this going anywhere but horribly. In a romantic sense, it's best to not even go there. I should only see him on our PTA appointments. If I can stay away from him and him from me… it'll all be fine."

Cindy's smile was bittersweet at the word fine. The idea of only seeing Andy for PT made her chest ache, but she was afraid to spend more time with him too.

"Counter arguments," Lola said, continuing the game they'd played since they were kids. "You don't really know what he wants, sex or something more. You have no idea who he is, what his likes and dislikes are, anything. You've freaking met him four times for crying out loud! I think the negatives outweigh the positives here, girl."

"Closing positive arguments," Maryanne said. "You can quickly find out what exactly he wants, a hook-up or something more, by simply asking him tomorrow. You will see him once a week for the next few months. Get to know him!"

"As long as you guys aren't having sex or making out while you're on the clock for PTA stuff, I think you'll be fine," Holly said with a hopeful look on her face. Even with all she'd gone through, she still believed in love and happily ever afters.

Cindy sighed and rubbed her temple. "Final decision? I will be professional tomorrow and get to know him. If he tries to kiss me or something, I will ask him what he wants and try to see if we're on the same page. Like, I'm a mom. I can't just do casual hook-ups."

Maryanne shrugged and wiggled her brows. "I think it'd be the best thing for you. You're so tense and stressed all the time!"

Holly and Cindy giggled as they all rolled up their mats. Half of the class had already left by the time Cindy walked to the stairs on one wall and called, "Boys! Are you ready to go?"

When thumps and footsteps sounded above, she turned and walked into the locker room to gather her things. She listened with half an ear as Holly talked more about the events she could host for the yoga studio.

Washing her face at the sink, she breathed heavily through her nose. She could be professional. Surely she could look him in the face and do her job without thinking of repeating that kiss. She sighed as she wiped the water off and shoved her dirty workout towel into her gym bag.

Problem was, she hadn't stopped thinking and dreaming of that kiss. She looked in the mirror and frowned. The lack of sleep had given her dark circles. When she left the locker room, the boys were coming down the stairs as Kendall walked through the door.

The Soldier Gets His Girl

"Holly," Cindy said into the locker room through the open door behind her. "Kendall's here!"

"Coming!" she shouted from inside.

Cindy smiled as she walked towards the front door ahead of the boys.

"Hey there! How's your week going?" she asked Kendall. His blond-brown hair fell into his eyes, Elvis style. He was tall and handsome, but he didn't make her heart skip a beat, even when he smiled and a dimple showed on his left cheek like it did now.

"Going good! We have shift together this weekend?" he asked.

"Yep, are you ready for the craziness?" He frowned, his brows wrinkling as she laughed and continued. "Full moon this weekend."

He slapped his forehead and groaned, rotating his shoulders. "That's this weekend? Ugh, maybe I can switch with Dr. Jensen for next weekend."

She laughed and slung her bag over her shoulder as the boys approached. "Probably not. It's Halloween next weekend."

"Fuck my life," he groaned.

Owen gasped and yelled, "Bad word! Bad word!"

Kendall spun on his heel, his eyes wide and mouth gaping in shock. Cindy doubled over with laughter and held onto her stomach. Cody grinned ear to ear, and James ignored them as he read a book.

Maryanne grinned as she followed the boys toward the front of the studio. "That's a dollar into the swear jar, Doc."

Kendall rolled his eyes and fished out a dollar. Instead of handing it to Cindy though, he handed it to Owen, whose jaw dropped as he took it.

Kendall said, "Sorry, little man. I'll do better."

Owen smiled and said, "Want to see my loose tooth? Look!" Kendall inspected the tooth like he would with patients.

Maryanne and Cindy grinned as he gave Owen his professional diagnosis—that all the Halloween candy next week would make it fall out faster than normal.

"All right, guys. Let's go home before it gets too dark," Cindy grabbed the snack tray she'd brought, now empty. They filed through the door, Maryanne behind her.

As they were loading into the SUV, Maryanne whispered, "No sparks at all between you and Kendall. But Andy? My lanta!"

Cindy shushed her as she buckled Owen into his seat, then got into the driver's side with a wave to her sister. As they headed home, she glanced over at Cody sitting in the front seat.

"Hey Cody," she mumbled, not wanting to catch the other boys' attention. "Umm, your Auntie M says you rode with a new guy in town to Sonic last week. You know that was incredibly dangerous, right?"

Cody rolled his eyes and crossed his arms. "Yeah, Mom, but Auntie M followed us in her fast little car. She was riding his tail the entire way to Sonic. Plus, I thought he was there *with* Auntie M. As a boyfriend. They were chatting it up in the stands after the game."

Pain speared her chest at the idea of Andy and her sister. She frowned as he continued.

"But they aren't in like. He's in like with you, apparently." The background song changed as they pulled into the parking lot of the apartment complex.

She parked and looked Cody in the eye. "And how did you feel about that?"

Cody stared at her, his face motionless. Owen squirmed

in the backseat and unbuckled. James looked up, saw they were home, unbuckled, and opened his door. Their chatter rolled over the two of them in the front seat.

Cody shrugged and reached for his buckle. "He seems like a decent guy. I mean, Grandpa was in the Army and so was he. And they don't just take anyone into the Army. No criminals or anything like that. Good guys only, right?"

She smiled slightly and nodded. Oh, the simplicity of childhood, when it was all cops and robbers, good and bad!

He opened his door and grabbed his stuff as he said, "Then we'll see what happens."

She got out and trudged up the stairs behind them, locking her SUV behind her. Huh.

She wasn't exactly expecting him to be so aware of adults, or that he'd be so calm about it. She expected him to throw a fit or something.

But wait... she opened the apartment door, and Owen ran to their room. James threw himself down on the couch with his book, and Cody walked to the kitchen for a snack.

"You have twenty minutes until bath time," she said to James before she followed Cody into the cramped kitchen.

She went to the sink and turned on the water. "We're not dating or anything, Cody. He's actually going to be one of my patient's starting tomorrow. So we won't start dating either."

Cody chewed a bite of banana and swallowed. She started washing the dishes as he threw away the banana peel.

Suddenly he was hugging her from behind. She turned and wrapped him in a hug.

He squeezed and said softly, "It's alright if you want to date though, Mom. If you're happy, we're going to be happy. And maybe he could make you smile more and worry less."

With that, he walked out of her arms and the kitchen, leaving her stunned. She turned to shut off the water.

Was he right? Could she find happiness? Was Andy the key? Or would this be her third strike and she's out kind of thing?

She was hesitant to take the risk and find out. But it didn't matter anyway. He was a patient.

Chapter Fifteen

She sighed as she pulled up to his house in the woods. The knot in her stomach hadn't left since her talk with Cody the night before. She couldn't even tell if it was worry or excitement.

Shutting off the engine, she grabbed her therapy bag and stepped up to the front door. She'd barely knocked once before the door opened.

The light from the mid-morning sun fell over his tanned face, bringing out the brightness of his icy blue eyes. His black hair was still wet from a shower and his green t-shirt clung to his broad shoulders.

Black basketball shorts fell at his knee, revealing his prosthetic foot. His right leg was lean and muscular. Glancing at his bare foot, she noted that even his toes were sexy.

Good Lord, get a grip! She swung her gaze back to his intense gaze, a thrill at seeing him shooting down her spine.

He smiled and held the door wide, stepping back.

"Good morning! I'm so glad you're here! Would you like to come inside?"

She swallowed nervously and stepped around him. Her body tried to brush up against his, but she jerked herself away and into the living room.

"Hey, Andy, how are you today?" she asked, trying to sound casual over her beating heart. She sat on the couch and pulled out her binder.

She flipped to a blank page and glanced at him as he brought two bottles of water from the kitchen and handed her one. She assessed his walk with a nurse's eye, but it was the woman side of her that glanced at his crotch as she reached up to take the water bottle.

She squirmed in her seat and felt her cheeks heat. The brush of his fingers on hers sent an ache straight to her core. She smiled tightly, glancing down at her binder. "Thank you."

She cleared her throat as she took a drink. He was so close. The butterflies in her stomach danced in time to her beating heart. He leaned back on the other end of the couch. The awkwardness stretched, the words on the page in her lap blurring. All she could think of was that kiss and how she wanted a repeat performance. Curiosity niggled at her. It could've been a fluke occurrence. Surely it wasn't as good as she remembered.

He leaned forward, putting his elbows on his knees. "I need to be totally honest, Cindy. I requested you to be my PTA."

Her eyes widened in surprise as she looked back up at him, half turning on the couch to face him. "I told you we couldn't request patients!"

He held his hands up in surrender, leaning back against

The Soldier Gets His Girl

the couch. "I know, I know. But you didn't request me. I requested you, so I figured it'd be alright."

She shook her head slowly. "Andy... in the spirit of honesty, I don't think this is going to work. I mean, after that kiss, I don't think I can work with you."

He reached over and grabbed her hands, bringing them away from her binder. His touch was gentle but electric, lightning shooting up her arm.

"It's not about the chemistry or the kiss, although there's no denying either. Cindy... on a purely medical level, I don't need a PTA. I'm at a Level 4. I'm good."

She frowned and opened her mouth to argue, but he squeezed her hand and continued.

"Yeah, there are goals to work on. But the truth is... if anyone else was my PTA... well, I'm not the friendliest guy with nurses and therapists. I went through a lot of them back in D.C. With you?"

He stared into her eyes, his chiseled features softened in a smile, his thumb gently gliding over the back of her hand.

"Well, I'm comfortable with you. I complied in the hospital without even realizing it. I think PT sessions with you would be similar. I'd be making improvements and working towards my goals without even realizing I'm putting in the work, you know? And at this point, I need that."

She frowned and tilted her head to the side. "So on a purely professional level—"

"On a purely professional level, I need *you*," he squeezed her hand. Tingles raced up her arms and hit her heart. Had anyone ever really *needed* her? Other than her kids, she didn't think so.

She breathed deeply. Damn it, he still smelled like

leather and sunshine. She didn't even realize that sunshine had a smell!

She sighed. "Fine, I'll do the sessions, but we're keeping it purely professional," she shot him a glare as she dragged her hand from his.

His grin was so full of joy, she felt a piece of the wall around her heart melt.

"Fine," he said.

She giggled at their joke as she opened up the binder and asked follow-up questions from Maggie's notes.

"Alright, so I see some of your goals are squatting, picking things up, running sprints, and moving and stopping quickly. Is that right?"

He stared at her intently, then nodded. She reached for his water bottle sitting on the coffee table and knocked it to the floor. It rolled away from the couch, towards the fireplace.

She glanced at him with an innocent stare. "Oops. I seem to have dropped the water. Could you grab that for me?"

He looked at her with a raised brow. Then she winked. He burst out laughing and stood up. "See? You're totally going to get me to practice, and I'm going to have fun doing it. This will be great, Cindy, you'll see."

She shrugged, unable to stop the smile that spread on her face as she watched his fine ass squat to pick it up. "It's just a water bottle, Andy. Don't make a big deal about it."

When he held it up in triumph, she grinned. He had such a magnificent smile, she couldn't help but want to smile with him.

"Now what?" he asked.

She glanced around and nodded to the shoes beside the front door behind her. "The shoes by the door. Can you squat and straighten those up? Make a row against the wall?"

He saluted her with a grin, then walked over and did as she asked. For the next hour, he squatted and picked things up around the house.

At one point, they laughed as he re-arranged the cleaning supplies under the kitchen sink, squatting and getting up repeatedly.

They talked about music and movies while they floated between the living room and the kitchen. They both loved action films like classic Jackie Chan and all the *Lethal Weapon* movies.

When the hour was over, a light sheen of sweat shone on his forehead and neither of them had stopped grinning. Her cheeks actually hurt from smiling so much! She finished the bottle of water and wrote out some notes.

He flopped onto the couch beside her, closer than before. "Will you stay for lunch?"

She glanced at the clock on the wall. It was nearly eleven-thirty. "I suppose, but it wouldn't be the professional thing to do."

He sat up, his face full of eager expectation. "Yeah, but your hour is up, right? So you're off the clock and can do whatever. Ya gotta eat, right? Might as well be with me. We can be friends, right? If I were Lola or Holly, you'd eat lunch with them, right?"

She frowned. His argument was solid, but it was a slippery slope. He looked so hopeful, sitting there. How could she turn him down? She finally nodded and smiled. He grinned, grabbing her hand and squeezing it before pushing off the couch.

"All right! Let's get you some food." He sauntered into the kitchen. His limp was more pronounced after the PT session, and she made a note of it in the binder, finished up her written reports, and put it away in her bag.

"Are you still getting deliveries from the church ladies?" she asked, joining him in the kitchen.

He nodded as he pulled a third casserole out of the fridge and added it to the kitchen island.

"We have Mexican cornbread casserole, chicken and pasta, or breakfast casserole. What would you like?" he grinned, waving to the spread of food.

She looked them over and chose chicken and pasta. He grabbed two plates and placed one in the microwave while she grabbed another bottle of water from the fridge.

"Do you only drink water?" she asked, grabbing two and following him to the dining table.

He shrugged as he placed the napkins and forks on the table. She noticed him place one on the end and one right next to it, so they'd be close but could see each other's faces as they talked. She liked how he listened to her when she spoke.

"I always got ripped during deployments because there wasn't anything else to do. In rehab, I realized I wouldn't be able to work off the calories like before. So I switched to mostly water, maybe a soda or tea at lunch. How about you?"

She smiled as she switched the plates out of the microwave and handed him the warm one.

"We always have a pitcher of lemonade and a pitcher of sweet tea in our fridge. The boys have lemonade at dinner but the tea has caffeine. So I drink that in the mornings for a pick me up."

"You don't drink coffee? Coffee is in a category by itself. It doesn't count. I always have coffee in the morning," he said, making her laugh.

He pulled her chair back at the table, and she sat with a smile of thanks.

"I don't do coffee," she said, placing the napkin in her lap.

"So uncivilized," he teased. She chuckled as he placed his hand palm up next to her. She hesitated, then remembered when she'd eaten lunch with him before and placed her hand in his.

"God, thank you for this food and the women who made it. Please tell Cindy to let me kiss her today, Amen."

She gasped and jerked her head up to catch his eyes. He was grinning, then winked at her. She laughed as he said, "What? A guy like me needs all the help he can get!"

She snorted as she stabbed her food with her fork. "Yeah, right. A guy like you? All the girls at church are desperate to date the newest eligible bachelor in town. You don't need any help in that department!"

He laughed quietly, spinning the pasta over and over on his fork slowly. But he didn't eat it. Eventually he placed an elbow on the table, his chin in his hand.

"Remember when we talked about what I could do with my life? I think I'm getting an idea of what I want."

He stared at her intently as she swallowed her bite and took a drink of water. His comment made her stomach twist into knots but she didn't know why.

"Oh yeah? What kind of job are you thinking about?"

He blinked several times before smiling softly and picking up his fork to eat. Before he took a bite, he said, "I'll probably look online this weekend for radio repair jobs down in DFW."

"You'd commute?" she asked. She took another bite as he swallowed his.

"Yeah, but that's alright. It would give me something to do. I mean, this isn't a big town. It's incredibly boring."

She laughed, almost snorting out her water. "It's not boring. You simply don't have a lot of purpose yet. Be patient. When you find it, it'll be the perfect fit!"

"But how do you know?" he asked, his brow wrinkling with a frown.

She shrugged. "You don't. You just have to step out on faith and give it your best. What else can we do but that?"

He nodded, taking another bite. "I suppose," he said. "So how's Cody this week?"

She smiled, pleased he'd remembered his name. Most guys didn't even bother once they learned she was a mom of three.

"He's good. Struggling with pre-algebra but that's normal for him. The soccer season is going really well, which makes him happy and easier to live with," she chuckled.

"Oh hey, I have pictures for you!" he said. "I didn't have your number and forgot to ask Cody or Maryanne so I could send them to you."

"I'll give you my number before I leave. Just text them to me. I appreciate it!"

"Are you sure text is fine? There's a lot of them," he said, one eyebrow raised.

She rolled her eyes and nodded, scooping another bite onto her fork. "Yeah, it's fine. And thanks for taking them."

He smiled, and took another bite, eventually saying, "It was my pleasure. And I'm not just saying that. I enjoyed watching his game. Does he have another one tomorrow?"

"Yeah. Every Saturday for a while."

"Can I have a copy of his schedule? Can I watch? Like I

said. I'm pretty bored around here," he laughed, looking unsure of himself.

She shrugged, her chest growing warm at the idea of him watching Cody play. "You're free to do whatever you want. If you want to spend a Saturday watching some middle school soccer, be my guest. I'll text you the schedule."

His grin lit up his face, and her heart skipped a beat. She was happy she'd made him smile, but he probably didn't realize how much it meant to have a male watching her son's soccer game.

He placed his hand on her knee as he said, "Thank you."

His touch sent sparks up her leg and straight to her clit. She cleared her throat with another drink of water.

"Will you be there? Do you work every weekend at the hospital?" He finished the last of his pasta.

She pushed back her empty plate. "I work this weekend, yes. But I only work half of next weekend as it's the last weekend of the month. That means I'll get to take the boys trick-or-treating."

"Oh cool! Are you guys dressing up?" he asked, gathering their plates and taking them to the sink. She wiped down the table and threw away the napkins.

"The boys are, yes. Owen is going as Spider-man, James as a ninja, and Cody as a soldier."

"You don't dress up?" he teased, leaning against the kitchen sink. She stood at the end of the island, not wanting to leave yet.

"Oh no, definitely not. Sometimes I'll wear my scrubs from work." She waved a hand at the green scrubs that she was wearing now.

They were the ones that made the green flecks in her

eyes pop. Not that she'd worn this pair because she knew she'd be seeing him today. Nope, absolutely not.

He stepped closer and slid a hand along the counter top where he ran a finger along her knuckle.

"I could see you dressing up as a sexy nurse. One of those little short skirts? Not gonna lie. I've dreamed of it a time or two."

She snorted but couldn't move away from his fingers traced lazy patterns along the back of her hand. "Must've been the drugs from the kidney stone," she whispered.

His fingers traced up her wrist as he stepped closer, his grin spreading. "Nah, the drugs are long gone, but the image of you in a little nurse's outfit won't leave me alone."

She breathed shallowly and rapidly, her breath almost as fast as the beating of her heart. She couldn't reply. Her mind was drawing a blank. *What do I say to that?*

"Well, that's fair, since you without a shirt has caused some problems with my sleep cycles." She huffed, her cheeks heating like a furnace.

Dear God, had she really admitted that? And what was with that voice? That wasn't the way she normally talked.

He smiled wider and his eyes lit up. "That makes me feel so much better," he said, leaning in. She could feel his breath on her lips, and she tilted her chin up, waiting. Her lips tingled in anticipation.

"I'm glad I'm not the only one suffering from this want," he mumbled.

He dipped his head forward slowly, giving her time to move away. But she couldn't. She didn't want to. She forgot why she should.

In this moment, in this place, she was exactly where she needed to be. There weren't any of the outside worries crowding her head. She was fully in the moment.

His lips brushed hers softly. Once. Twice. The third time, she licked her lips just as his mouth touched hers. He groaned and crushed his mouth to hers, his tongue sweeping in to dance.

She gasped, giving him greater access. The hand that had teased hers slid behind her shoulders, drawing her flush against him. Her entire body shivered at the contact of her breasts against his broad chest.

His other hand wrapped around her waist. Her groin slammed into his, and he spun her, pressing her against the counter. Wrapping her hands around his neck, she pulled him down closer.

Goose bumps broke out on every inch of her flesh. The hairs on her head stood on end. He lifted her onto the kitchen counter and stepped between her legs. She gasped as his hard cock pressed against the thin fabric of her scrubs.

When he ground against her, she jerked, so close to bursting already. She couldn't breathe. It was too much, too fast. She broke the kiss and leaned back.

His hooded eyes met hers, glazed in lust. His hands gripped her hips hard, his cock still pressed against her, causing a pulsing down there that she'd never experienced before. She blinked, trying to remember why she'd stopped.

"Andy," she whispered. He groaned at the sound of his name and pulled her in for another kiss. He tasted like sunshine and happiness.

She couldn't remember why she'd stopped before, so she met his lips eagerly. He growled his approval, grinding against her clit again.

Their kiss mimicked the movement of his hips until she was gasping. She was so close. She whimpered, begging him for release as her hips bucked. He growled into her mouth, pulling her hips almost off the counter top to grind into her harder. He held her legs captive, and she lost it.

Everything fractured as she cried out into his mouth. He kissed her as she came, holding her legs as they shook. His lips softened as the spasms slowed down, holding himself still against her.

When she turned liquid in his arms, he broke the kiss and pressed his nose into her neck. He held her until their breathing slowed.

Eventually she wiggled on the counter, and he let go of her legs. She jumped down, and her legs nearly gave out. He pulled her flush against him, catching her.

She gasped at the contact. They were touching from knee to chest, and it still wasn't enough. She wanted to push him to the floor and ride the hard cock that was pressed against her.

She jerked out of his arms with a gasp. "Andy! We can't do that!" She glanced at him as she rounded the dining room table, using a chair to help hold herself up.

Swollen lips from their kisses, hard jaw and clenched his teeth, and yet his eyes still shone with lust.

"Why not?" he demanded gruffly. "We're both consenting adults. Do you not like me?"

He said it as a challenge, as an accusation. But she could see the vulnerability that lay beneath that false bravado. She shook her head. She couldn't lie to him.

"It's not that! I—I told you! You're a patient. We can't do this." She waved a hand between the two of them. "If we're going to end up kissing, then there will be no lunches, nothing but our PT sessions, alright? This *has* to stay professional."

He raked a hand through his hair, frustration clear in his body language. He rubbed his temples, not looking at her for several long seconds as his nostrils flared with deep breaths. She pulled herself together, adjusting her clothing a bit.

Finally he dropped his hands and nodded, his blue eyes piercing her soul and looking lost.

"Fine," he said, a wry smile twisting his lips at the joke. She smiled softly back to him, then turned to get her bag from the living room.

"I have to head out now. I'll see you next Friday then? Purely for PT?" she asked, hoisting her bag onto her shoulder and standing there. The idea of him rejecting her PT session caused her heart to skip a beat.

He nodded, opening the door for her. As she passed, his fingers grazed her arm as he said, "See you next week, then."

Chapter Sixteen

Holy shit. That was the most beautiful thing he'd seen in his entire life. The way her face lit up when she came, the feel of her in his arms. It was so damn perfect, he nearly bent the door frame under his grip as he watched her drive away.

He shut the door softly and turned. Surveying the living room, dining room, and kitchen, he pictured her there on the couch before the fireplace, reading a book and sipping hot chocolate on a cold winter's night. He pictured her in the kitchen, baking more things for a bake sale.

Walking down the hall to the master bedroom, he pictured her sitting up in the bed, a baby girl in her arms. She'd glance up at him with that soft smile of hers.

He wanted that. He wanted the family. And not just any family. The more time he spent with her the more sure he was that he wanted a family *with her*.

How crazy was that, considering he'd only hung out with her five times in the past month?

Maybe he should formally ask her out. No, she'd simply turn him down because of those stupid professional rules.

Maybe he should ask for a different PTA. The fear of asking her out and switching to someone else for therapy lingered within him.

And honestly, why would she date him? He was a bum with a bum leg. He didn't even have a job. Although the house was probably a perk over her apartment, he had nothing else to offer her.

He needed to make himself worthy of her, worthy of the risk she'd take on him. And that started with getting a job. He'd shower first, then he'd run to Denton and buy a laptop so he could search for jobs. He turned on the water and sat down in the chair outside it as he pulled off his prosthetic.

Did he even have the internet here? He had a lot to do. And he couldn't forget the soccer game! He pulled out his phone to text Parker as he waited for the water to heat the shower.

Hey man, what time is the middle school soccer game tomorrow?

He sat the phone down on the counter and hopped into the shower, carefully holding on to the handle. He sat down on the bench and noticed his cock standing tall and erect, waving at him. Groaning, he leaned forward and washed his hair.

But damn, the taste of her on his lips still lingered. His hands tingled from the feel of her, and he could almost smell her scent even over the smell of his shampoo. His breathing deepened as he imagined her sitting on the kitchen counter, her legs spread, a sexy nurse costume barely covering her pussy.

He pictured himself kneeling, sucking, tasting, lapping. In his head, he could practically hear her moan, could almost feel her grinding on his mouth. She'd taste so good. Sweet but tart.

He wrapped a hand around himself and in moments, he was groaning into the spray of the water as he came.

A few moments later, he leaned back against the wall with a sigh. He hoped she'd come around to the idea of them being together because he honestly couldn't picture living here without her anymore. Standing on shaky legs, he turned off the water.

Scratch that. He couldn't picture living without her, period. In theory, he knew he could. These same thoughts had consumed him when they'd amputated his leg. He couldn't imagine life without a foot.

Logically, he knew he could live without her, but he didn't want to. He needed to play the long game to win her. First step? Get a laptop and find a job.

He dried off, put on his leg, and got dressed. Looking at his phone, he saw Parker had texted him. He read it as he stepped out of his room and walked down the hall with his socks.

10am, bright and early!
But it's down in Ponder.
You coming?

Yeah, I'll be there.
It was a good game last week.

You don't happen to have videos of Cody, do you?

Actually, yes.
But I don't have Cindy or Maryanne's numbers to give them to him.
Send them to me?

I can get them to him, but obi can't give you his #.

You got it....
There are 17 of them tho. You want all of them?

Holy shit!
Did you video the entire game?
WTF man!
🤦 😊 But yes, I want all of them.
Thanks.

Sending now.
It may take a while to go through.

He set the videos to send and leaned down to put on his socks. A knock sounded at the door, and he glanced at the clock. It was barely after noon. Before he could open the door, Aunt Suzie pushed her way in.

"Hey, Aunt Suzie. You do realize that you don't own this place anymore, right? You can't just barge in."

She laughed, waving her hand daintily as she said, "I saw you sitting there through the window, dear. It's not like there's anyone else here or anything."

Cindy could've been here. He definitely wanted her here long term. Thinking of Cindy, he breathed deeply, hoping to catch a hint of her scent still in the air.

"I heard your physical therapy appointment was today. How did it go?" she asked. She plopped down onto the couch and her poodle skirt floated down around her. Pushing her ballet flats off, she curled her feet under her. Her bright pink t-shirt had a picture of Elvis on it today.

He shook his head, checking his watch. It'd only been an hour since Cindy had left. "How'd you hear about that?"

She shrugged with a smile. "Well, I ran into Maggie at the grocery store."

"Ahh," he said, nodding. "Well, it was good. I was sweating by the end of it, so I guess I have things to work on."

She flipped her hair. "Of course you do. You can always grow, improve, and get better. Level 4 was not the finish line, right? Isn't that what the doctors have all been saying?"

He rolled his eyes. His doctor and nurses back in D.C. had on him that the pace he took to reach Level 4 was not sustainable. They kept harping on slow and steady wins the race.

"I know, I know," he sighed. "It's not a race to the finish line. It's more of a cross-country hike, with no end date in site. The key is to keep moving, not necessarily how fast I get somewhere." He grimaced as he nearly quoted the doctor.

Aunt Suzie looked pleased that he'd remembered though.

"Did you just stop by to check on me?" he asked with a lift of his eyebrow.

She nodded, blinking owlishly at him, "Of course. I'm about to grab Mandy from school so I wanted to stop by and see how it went first. This is her first week there. And I think she's doing great with it! She loves her teacher. She's in Owen's class, so she's absolutely having a blast."

He frowned at the familiar name. "Owen?"

She squinted suspiciously at him, tapping her chin. "Yeah, Maryanne's youngest nephew. You were at the soccer game with her, right?"

"Not really. Just wanted to get out of the house and heard there were cookies. I'm glad Mandy found a friend though. Cindy is my therapist."

She nodded slowly and picked at her nails. "I thought she may have been. She's the best, according to Maggie, and I told her you needed the best."

He grinned and stretched his feet out in front of him. "Cindy has been pretty great. She was amazing in the hospital and today's session was pretty good too." He bent over to lace up his shoes.

Aunt Suzie cleared her throat as she said, "You know who else I ran into at the grocery store? Mrs. Williams. She said you sat with her at the soccer game. That was sweet of you."

"Nothing sweet about it. It was a good game. I'm going to the one tomorrow too."

She tilted her head to the side, gazing at him. He straightened and waited. There was no telling what she was thinking, and he'd learned long ago not to prompt her about it.

"Why didn't you tell me you wanted cookies? I would've made you some," she finally mumbled.

He shrugged and smiled. "Poker night was that week, and we had stolen some cookies from Kendall's house while his sister and the other ladies were making them. I wanted some more. Didn't occur to me to bother you, Aunt Suz." Was she feeling left out?

She nodded and waved her hand. "Ahh, okay. Well, tomorrow I'm going to be prepping the garden for winter. It's been in terrible shape since we did nothing with it this year while we were gone. If you're going to the soccer game, can you take Mandy too? The weather should be fine."

He frowned, thinking about the day tomorrow. "Does Ponder still have that playground next to the fields? That's where the game is tomorrow."

"Perfect! That playground will wear her out." Aunt Suzie beamed at him and stood, pacing to the kitchen island and straightening his mail. "You know," she said slowly, "This will be the first time you've taken her out by yourself."

He frowned again and shook his head, thinking back to the past year. "Surely not. We did a ton of stuff in D.C. with her."

"Yeah, but it's always been with me or your Uncle Mike there too. This time, you'll be alone," she smiled sadly, a frown line remaining between her brows.

"Huh, I guess you're right," he rubbed his jaw. "Well, it'll be fun. We'll play all day."

She sighed and gripped her hands. "Don't get carried away. You'll probably bring her back after lunch. You know how hard it is at naptime."

They both laughed as they thought back to all the times in the past year they'd needed to schedule around Mandy's nap time. He stood and went to the island to grab his keys, wallet, and phone.

"Where are you going?" she asked, walking to his refrigerator and inspecting the contents.

"Oh, I'm going into Denton to get a laptop. I'm going to look for a radio repair job."

She closed the door and turned to face him. "Are you sure you're ready for a job? I mean, you've been here less than a month. You need time to heal."

He rounded the island and took her hands. Squeezing them gently, he looked down into her concerned blue eyes.

"I can't just sit around and do nothing, Aunt Suz. I need a job. It's the first step in my new life plan, okay? I won't overdo it or take on something I can't handle. It's fine, alright?"

With a chuckle, he realized he really did say fine way too often. He'd never really noticed that about himself before.

She sighed and pulled him into a hug. "Alright, just don't rush into major life changes. Moving is hard enough to handle without adding other baggage to it."

He patted her back and replied, "I won't, don't worry. Now, I need to go if I want to get back before traffic starts."

He let her go and stepped around to the front door, grabbing a light zip up sweater hanging on a peg. They walked out together and after one more hug, he jumped in the truck and followed her down the driveway.

Chapter Seventeen

"All right, we're here!" he said early the next morning.

Mandy bounced in her booster in the back seat, clapping her hands and pointing to the playground. "Yay! Slides *and* swings!"

He smiled as he parked the truck and turned it off. He opened the back door and grabbed the small backpack Aunt Suzie had packed for her for the day. She tried to bounce out of her seat as he leaned over and unbuckled her.

She hopped down and held out her arms, so he picked her up. Placing her on his right hip, he swung the backpack onto his left shoulder and closed the door. People were parking and unloading all around him.

"There's the playground!" Mandy squealed, pointing to the right of the soccer field.

"How about we go play first? Later, we'll watch the soccer game and eat a snack, come back to the playground if you're good, then go to Sonic for an ice cream. Does that sound like a good plan?"

"Yay! Ice cream!" she shouted as he walked through the parking lot. She wasn't heavy but after weaving between cars, he was already feeling the pressure on his left leg. He set her down on the side walk and held her hand.

She chatted the entire way, bouncing from what flavor of ice cream she wanted, to the butterflies they saw, and finally the colors of the flowers.

His heart was light, and the sun was shining. It was already a great day, based on how much he'd smiled already just from Mandy's antics. He'd been smiling more in general since he'd moved back and was definitely less tense and fearful.

"Yo, Andy!"

He looked around as they arrived at the playground. Mandy climbed the equipment.

"Parker! How's it going? Ready for the game?" Andy said as Parker and the team walked past. Cody stopped next to them as the rest of the team and coaches kept walking towards the field to warm up.

"Hey, Mr. Andy. Thanks for sending those videos. I watched them over and over. Coach helped me work on this technique that should be killer today," Cody said with a grin.

Andy smiled back and shoved his hands in his pockets. "Just call me Andy. And you're welcome! I'll take more videos today, if you'd like? Although, I doubt I'll be able to get 17 of them, since I have Mandy today." He nodded to the playground beside him where he could see her little legs running back to climb the stairs to the slide.

Cody shrugged, bouncing on his feet as he stared anxiously after his team. "That's alright. Auntie M is coming today, so she'll probably video some."

"Go warm up now," Parker said gently, nodding to the

field. Cody waved with a smile and jogged off to join his teammates.

Parker smirked, "So... you here for Maryanne or what?"

Andy's brows raised in surprise. "What? Definitely not," he said, shaking his head.

Parker held up his hands, palms out. "I'm just fishing for info because Mom said y'all were pretty cozy when she left last weekend."

Andy watched Mandy on the playground. "Yeah, we're friends. Nothing more."

Parker shoulder checked him. "Yeah right, I've heard that one before. You're probably playing both sisters, aren't you? We'd all made that bet on whether I could out flirt Nick a few weeks ago, but damn!"

"Man, you're crazy. I'm bored out of my mind, staying at home. Soccer is a great excuse to get out and get some sunshine. That's all."

"Uh-huh. Then why aren't you going to the football games on Friday nights too?"

Andy shrugged, digging his hands deeper into his pockets. "They're too crowded and by the time night falls, my leg hurts. I'm easing my way back into things, and I don't want to go out on a Friday night with a crowd of people and overdo it."

"Yeah, I guess that's fair. I mean, you went to the Electric Cowboy one time and *bam*! Look at what happened! I'd probably avoid Friday night fun too, if I were you." They both laughed, and Parker turned towards the field as a whistle blew. "Well, I better head over. That's the 5 minute warning. See you later?"

Andy nodded. He turned to call Mandy. Her little pink

tutu skirt was sticking out of the slide tube, her legs kicking back and forth in the air as she laid on her stomach.

"Mandy! Let's go find our seats for the game!" he said.

"Unca Andy, come look at this bug! It's so squishy!"

"Don't touch it, Mandy. Let me see first. It could hurt you."

Andy looked at the stairs that led up to the round tubes. He could probably climb in, although he had no idea how he'd get back out again.

He slipped the backpack to the ground and climbed inside. It was a tight fit and bear crawling through the long tube gave him slight flash backs to the Army.

But this was more fun and cleaner than bear crawling through the mud under barbed wire for training. He reached the opposite side of the tube and climbed up a few more stairs to Mandy.

"Isn't it so squishy?" she asked, as she poked the green, fat caterpillar. "See? It doesn't hurt."

He sighed and pointed. "You still have to be careful. It may not hurt you, but you can hurt it."

"Oh," she said, pulling her finger back. "But look at those little spots."

Andy took a picture of it and Mandy with his phone. "What colors does it have?"

"Green, black, and white," she said, grinning proudly.

"Good job! Now, why don't we take this little guy over to that tree? We don't want him to get stepped on."

She nodded with a frown. "You carry it without hurting?"

He chuckled, as he grabbed a nearby leaf and scooped up the caterpillar. Mandy took the stairs up to the slide.

"Slide with me like a train!" she sat at the top of the

slide. They'd never done this before, but he'd seen other kids doing this at the parks in D.C. when they'd visit.

He awkwardly held the caterpillar on the leaf in his palm and sat down, his legs sliding around hers. Pushing off with one hand, they slid forward down the long slide.

She squealed the entire way as he wrapped his free arm around her stomach. It's a good thing he did, because their combined momentum pushed them off the edge of the slide. He stumbled as he juggled Mandy and the caterpillar and stepped slightly wrong on his left leg. Pain shot down his leg, and he winced.

Hobbling forward, he set her down. She jumped up and down, clapping.

"Now the bug!" she squealed, racing over to the tree beside the playground. He limped carefully after her. It didn't hurt too much, just a twinge, but he didn't want to overdo it.

He sat the caterpillar next to the tree on the ground, near some big oak leaves.

"What does he eat?" she asked. She grabbed his hand, and they watched the caterpillar for a minute.

"All he needs are leaves. He eats all green foods." A whistle blew on the field, and they walked hand in hand to the stands, grabbing the backpack on the way.

"Is that why he's green?" she asked. He nodded as she continued talking about some girl who ate all pink things and turned all pink. He spied Maryanne in the stands and made his way to her.

When Mandy saw a little boy about her age sitting there, she stopped mid-sentence and yelled, "Owen!"

The boy's head jerked up from his tablet, and he smiled so big it took up nearly his entire face. Mandy let go of his hand and climbed up the stands to give her friend a hug.

He nodded at Maryanne and grinned. "Mind if we sit by you?"

She looked surprised but said, "That's good with me. I didn't expect to see you here today."

Andy sat beside her, Mandy and Owen in front of them. He took off the backpack and set it by his feet. Another little boy sat on the other side of Maryanne, reading a book.

"You must be Owen. I'm Mandy's Uncle Andy," he said, the boy turning when he heard his name. He smiled shyly and nodded. He was slightly bigger than Mandy, with chubby cheeks and freckles on his tanned face. He had the same brown hair as the boy next to Maryanne, and they were clearly brothers.

"Say, it's nice to meet you," Maryanne prodded Owen.

"It's nice to meet you," he said, then held out his hand.

Andy chuckled and shook his hand. "It's nice to meet you too. And who's this?"

Maryanne nudged the boy beside her, and he looked up, blinking quickly. He waved and said, "Hi, I'm James."

"Nice to meet you James. What are you reading?" Andy asked.

He turned the book so he could see the cover. "*Hatchet*. It's pretty good. This boy is stranded in Canada and has to survive for months."

"I remember that book. I spent the entire summer camping with my cousin, Jake, pretending like we were stranded and had to survive in the woods," he chuckled.

James perked up and lowered his book further. "You did? Where did you camp? I've never been camping and want to so bad!"

He nodded as the players on the field took their positions. "I have a cabin just outside of Crimson Creek that's on ten acres, all wooded. That's where I learned to camp.

You're welcome to come camp anytime. I'll even show you how."

"That would be so cool," he said in awe, his eyes shining as he turned to Maryanne. "Do you think Mom would let me go camping?"

"Probably not without her and your brothers. She's very protective." Maryanne's grin spread wider, and he saw her wink through the sunglasses.

Andy grinned and stretched out his foot. "They are, of course, invited to camp too."

"Whoohoo!" James yelled, throwing a fist in the air. "Alright, I'm going to finish this book. I'll do some research at school next week about camping. This is going to be so awesome!"

He wiggled as he leaned back and pulled up his book with a grin, tucking his head in intently as he read.

Andy chuckled as he leaned towards Maryanne to whisper. "Cool kids. Cindy's?"

She nodded and leaned closer to whisper back. "Yep, now you've met all three. What do you think?"

"What do I think of what? Cindy? The boys?"

"Yes." Her deep, throaty laugh rang out. "Let's start with the boys."

Maryanne took out her phone as the whistle blew, and he asked, "You want to rotate filming? You get first and third and I'll take second and fourth quarters?"

She nodded and pressed icons on her phone. "Sure, but don't leave me hanging here."

He kept his eyes on the game and Mandy and Owen in front of them. "The boys are great. I've been around Mandy a lot the past year and a half. She's adorable, but you know how kids are. They get bored, cranky, and fussy. Kids are kids, no matter how old they are. There are pros and cons to most kids, but there's not really any telling until you get to know them. Maybe Mandy just makes all kids look easy, and I wouldn't know the difference."

The comment made Maryanne chuckle, and he checked that none of the kids were listening to him. Mandy and Owen were both watching something on his tablet. Cody got the ball and both he and Maryanne cheered him on.

When the ball was stolen, Maryanne put her phone down. "Yeah, I guess I could say the same for my nephews. They're good kids, but maybe I'm partial because of how close we are. There are drawbacks though. I mean, Cody is hitting the age where hormones are starting, and he's getting a bit of an attitude sometimes. Cindy's not always sure how to handle that. It makes me worry for when they all grow up."

"What do you mean?"

She shrugged, still leaning close and talking low so as not to be overheard. "What all did Cindy tell you about her exes?"

He relayed the gist of what she'd said at Kendall's house while they were decorating cupcakes. By the end, Maryanne was staring at him instead of the game.

"What?"

"I just… I can't believe she said all that. She *never* talks about her past. Like, ever. It took so long for Mom and I to get her to open up. For her to come out and say all that? Not just to you but to others too? That's a huge thing for her. She must really like you."

He grinned, thinking back to yesterday on the kitchen counter. "Maybe, but I'm not so sure. She's turned me down twice now."

She gave him the side-eye before pulling her phone back up to take more pictures of Cody. They yelled for him as he got the ball, spun around two opponents, and passed it to a teammate who kicked it in for a goal. They clapped and cheered with the crowd.

"What exactly did she turn down?" Maryanne asked, pushing her glasses up her nose.

He tried to think of her exact words. "Umm... she said no more kisses because we needed to keep it professional? I mean, I straight up asked her if she liked me and she said... well, now that I think about it, I don't think she actually answered that question. She just kept talking about being a professional and not dating patients."

Maryanne sighed and rolled her eyes. "Dude, you gotta spell it out clearly with her. She may have told you a little about the previous two guys, but you need to ask her about how it all started with them both. Learn where they messed up. Then don't do that."

"Well, I won't steal prescription pads or do crazy illegal stuff, so that's not a worry," he chuckled.

She laughed softly as she explained, "No, but they both treated her alright... until they got what they wanted. Then the story changed."

"How so?" A timeout was called on the field, and Cody waved at them as he jogged to the huddle. Maryanne and Andy both waved back.

Maryanne sighed and looked behind them. No one was around. The early morning games combined with being visitors meant less of a crowd on that side of the stands.

Once satisfied that there was no one nearby, she continued. "When she married the jerk, she became withdrawn and sullen. She didn't talk to me or Mom as much as she did before the wedding. She completely stopped talking to Dad, and that was hard on her, especially when he died so suddenly."

Andy wanted to offer condolences but he had no words. His family situation was different than most, and he hadn't been close to either of his parents.

Maryanne kept talking, not waiting on him. "I don't know exactly what the jerk did to her, but she hasn't dated anyone since. Five years is a long time to be alone. She's afraid of starting up with someone who seems great but is secretly a jerk."

He nodded as she snapped some more pictures.

"I don't intend to be a jerk," he mumbled.

"Well, what *do* you intend? Date her? Casual hook-ups? Because that last one isn't something she's going to go for. She has kids and work to think about."

He nodded, crossing his arms and leaning back slightly. "Yeah. She's a long-term kinda girl, and I like that about her. I definitely want to date her. I'd like to see where it goes, give it a real chance."

"How do you feel about marriage?" she asked. Her blunt gaze missed nothing. He met her eyes and refused to look away.

Perhaps he should give it more thought, but the more time he spent with her, the more he wanted to make it last.

"I'm not opposed to it, but it's not something to jump into. Both of us have to be 100% committed and in love, and quite frankly, we're not there yet. I've had a few short-term relationships before. When I realized it wasn't leading to marriage, I broke it off."

She nodded, turning back to the game as the crowd cheered. She whipped up her phone as she took a video. The other team scored and their side cheered.

"If it's not going that direction with Cindy, clearly communicate that to her. Then back off. Request a different therapist or something."

"I'll do that, but it's hard to figure out if it'll lead to marriage and love if she won't spend time with me outside of the Friday therapy sessions."

The buzzer called to end the first quarter. Mandy had to use the bathroom, so Maryanne offered to take both her and Owen. Then she offered to take them to the park for a few minutes, since it was Andy's turn to take pictures of the game.

After she left, he thought about what she'd said. He could picture the boys at the house too. James would read on the couch, and Cody'd play soccer with him out front in the driveway.

He frowned. Could he play soccer, with his leg? He'd dreaded his limitations. But now he wanted to see if he could push them and maybe play soccer, be a real dad. He glanced around at the crowd. It wasn't too overwhelming like the bar had been.

Had a few weeks really changed him that much?

He was more comfortable in his own skin now. He hoped this thing with Cindy would turn into something real, something lasting. Despite the fear of it not working out, he wanted to try anyway. Now he just had to convince her.

Chapter Eighteen

Cindy stumbled through the front door of her apartment Sunday night.

"How was your weekend at work?" Maryanne asked.

Cindy groaned, kicking her shoes off. "So. Long."

She threw her stuff down in the entryway and fell onto the couch. Maryanne handed her a glass of wine, so she took a long sip as she propped her aching feet onto the coffee table.

"Was it the full moon?" her sister asked, looking impeccable as always with her spooky themed leggings and pumpkin shirt.

"Yeah, it wasn't anything too terrible, just constantly one thing after another. There wasn't a spare minute. Even the hours I needed to sleep in the break room kept getting interrupted. I don't think I've gotten more than three or four hours of sleep at a time since Thursday."

Maryanne jumped up. "Let me go run you a bath." Cindy took another sip of her wine as the water turned on.

Soft footsteps padded back down the hallway, and she opened her eyes. She didn't even realize she'd closed them.

"Come on, sis. Let's get you in there." Cindy groaned as she sat up and grabbed Maryanne's outstretched hand.

"Why are you sticking around? Don't you have to be up at three to make donuts?" she whined as Maryanne pulled her gently down the hall.

"Yep, and I'm going to leave. But not until I get you settled into bed."

"Aww, you're my favorite sister." Cindy sighed as she got into the bathroom.

Maryanne laughed and went into the closet. "I'm your only sister."

Cindy quickly undressed and slid into the bath, the bubbles covering her body. She leaned her head back and sipped her wine. The warm water soaked through, and she called through the open door of the closet. "It's a good thing you said bed and not bath, because if you left while I was in the bath, I might fall asleep and drown."

Maryanne laughed and came out of the closet, pulling up Owen's little step stool to sit on and staring at her nails. She could feel her sister's need to talk. Maryanne wouldn't have stuck around if there wasn't something on her mind.

Cindy grumbled without opening her eyes, "What is it?"

"So... Andy came to the soccer game yesterday," she said. Cindy's eyes shot open and heat spread across her cheeks.

Maryanne grinned. "You blushing or just turning pink from the hot water?"

Cindy scowled and turned off the water, the bubbles to her chin now as Maryanne pressed for more information. "How did his therapy session go?"

Cindy took a sip of her wine. God, she'd tried not to

think about him all weekend, but he'd never been far away in her mind.

She finally sighed and leaned her head back. "The session itself was fine. We laughed a lot, but he did excellent work. Then he invited me to stay for lunch which ended with…"

Maryanne leaned forward, clasping her hands together on her knees. "With? Girl, do *not* leave me hanging."

Cindy gulped the rest of her wine before handing Maryanne the empty glass. She shrugged a bubble covered shoulder. "We kissed and stuff."

Maryanne's brows rose. "What kind of stuff?"

"Like, I ended up sitting on the counter with him between my legs and…" She put her face in her hands, getting suds all over. She scooped up some water and splashed her face, angling away from her sister.

Maryanne leaned in, her voice raised in hope. "And you totally got naked and had sex on the counter?"

Cindy's head popped up, and she jerked in the tub, sloshing bubbles over the side.

"What? No! We both kept our clothes on the entire time! But… well, I did have an orgasm." She whispered the last word, as she wiped bubbles from her chin.

Maryanne screeched quietly and bounced her feet on the tile. "Oh my god, *yes*! Finally, you're getting some action!"

Cindy looked at her and frowned. "What? No! This is not good, M! He's a *patient*!"

"Yeah, I heard you the first thousand times you said it." She rolled her eyes. "But he's not looking for a casual hook up."

"How do you know?" She leaned her head back and

closed her eyes again. She refused to give in to the hopeful flutter in her chest.

"He told me," she said. Cindy popped her head up and stared at her sister.

"What?" Maryanne asked with a shrug. "I asked, and he answered. It's as simple as that."

Cindy groaned. None of this was simple. "Go find my pajamas. I'm getting out. This is *not* helping me relax."

While Maryanne was gone, she got out, dried off, and wrapped the towel around her body. Her mind and body wouldn't stop thinking about the kitchen incident with Andy. Her face heated, but she wanted to look at it objectively.

When she'd gotten pregnant with Cody, she hadn't even realized they had sex. It wasn't a topic she was very knowledgeable on, and she'd never once orgasmed.

With her ex-husband, she thought she'd orgasmed. It was nice and relaxing, that first year while they were dating and pregnant with James.

But from a physical standpoint, what she'd experienced with Andy was so much more than anything before. She'd lost all ability to think and was purely in the moment. The orgasm had been undeniable too.

After Owen had been born, Maryanne had gotten her a dildo for Christmas. She hadn't used it very often, but she knew what a real orgasm was. She now knew that her ex had never given her one or made her feel as… well, as taken care of as Andy had Friday.

If she pursued something with him, would he always make her feel like that? Or would he eventually turn back into a pumpkin jerk too?

A pajama shirt hit her in the face, and she caught it.

The Soldier Gets His Girl

Maryanne, who had changed into one of her large t-shirts, walked through the closet to the bathroom door.

"You staying over?" Cindy asked, brows raised.

Maryanne turned, one hand on the door frame. "Yep, we're not done talking about this. This is a major development in your life."

Cindy sighed as Maryanne went out of the room. She was so tired, and the wine had made her even more sleepy. Quickly, she finished dressing, braided her hair, and brushed her teeth before crossing the hall to check on the boys. By the time she turned the light off and walked to her own bed, Maryanne was already curled up under the covers on her side, eyes closed.

"Hm, I'm awake. Talk to me," Maryanne mumbled.

"I guess it is major," she said, climbing into bed and facing her sister like when they were kids and shared a room.

Maryanne snorted, not bothering to open her eyes. "Yeah, because you've literally not gone out with anyone since the jerk screwed you over. The fact that you've kissed or done anything at all with Andy means something, Cindy. Pursue it and see where it goes. You owe it to yourself."

"But what if he changes after the first year? What if he turns into a jerk? What if he loses interest or if we have sex and he's disappointed or disgusted? What if—"

"Don't *what if* this all night, Cin. You always look at the negative possibilities and see none of the positive ones. You don't dare to dream because you're so stuck in the past. In fact, you're barely living now because you're letting it drag you down!" Maryanne whispered, ending on a yawn.

Cindy sucked in a breath and closed her eyes. "I am not. I work my butt off—"

"Exactly. You work, Cindy. You aren't living. Think

about how tense and stressed you were tonight. When was the last time you partied? And don't say a kid's birthday party! When was the last time you did anything for yourself? Even when we're at girl's night, you still take care of others, bringing snacks and helping clean up."

"What is living except helping people? I—"

Maryanne cut her off as she grabbed Cindy's hand. "Everything you do is an obligation. Is there anything you actually look forward to doing in your week?"

Cindy thought about it and rolled onto her back, dislodging their hands. "I look forward to eating dinners with the boys. This school year, they each take a night to cook with me. It's led to some pretty cool conversations."

"And it gives them that one-on-one time with their mom that they crave. I mean, I'm an amazing aunt, but I'm not you. They need you, Cindy. Have you heard from the job applications?"

She sighed. "No, just an email on one saying they'd gone another route."

"Maybe you're looking at this from the wrong angle. Have you considered other nursing jobs not at the hospital? They're out there, right? What about telehealth? Then you could be home when the boys are home."

"Hmm, I hadn't considered that. I'll look into it on Tuesday."

"You're getting burnt out, Cindy. You're running ragged. In the past year, you've been getting random colds and sicknesses because you're not taking care of yourself. I'm going to give you your Christmas present early. How about a massage with Holly once a week until Christmas? If I do that, will you go?"

"Yeah. It will be good business for Holly. But are you sure you can afford it?"

"There you are, trying to take care of everyone else again. Don't worry about the money. Now, about this Andy thing…"

Cindy groaned and pulled the covers over her head. "Maryanne, let it go. I'm tired, and you have to be up early."

"No, I'm not letting it go. Look, this weekend is Halloween, right? And you only work at the hospital Friday to Saturday. Why don't we take the boys trick or treating, then you and Andy go on a late date? Give it a real chance. What's the worst that could happen?"

Cindy didn't have to think long about it. "I could lose my PTA job."

Maryanne reached out and found her hand in the dark again. "Yeah, and you're already working to find a new job so what's it matter if you did?"

Huh, she'd not thought of it like that. If she got a better paying job at the hospital, then she wouldn't be his PTA anymore. The thought of not seeing him every week put pressure on her heart.

If she got a new job that was weekdays only, she could see him more. Or at least on weekends when she wouldn't be working. But finding a new job was taking a while. What if he moved on in the meantime? It was likely, especially if she kept putting him off.

The idea of him with someone else made her heart skip a beat. Maryanne's hand went slack in hers and a soft snore echoed through the room.

She lifted her head and made sure Maryanne's phone was plugged into the bedside outlet. Then she turned onto her side and closed her eyes.

The last image she saw before sleep claimed her was

Andy running down the driveway toward her without a shirt, his chest glistening in the sun.

Chapter Nineteen

Cindy pushed open the door to the yoga studio and called out, "Holly? Are you here?" It was mid-morning on Wednesday and Cindy had already finished her one PT patient for the day.

"Up here!" a faint voice rang out. Cindy walked up the stairs in the back. An old, tall window let light in at the landing to the second floor, revealing a wide hallway and three doors on the left. A new wall separated the hallway and doors with a new living area in the front half of the second floor.

Holly stood in the open double wide doorway that led to the living area, a bright smile on her face. "There you are. Come see what we've done so far."

Cindy walked through the doorway, following Holly into a completely empty room. Light poured in from the floor to ceiling windows in the front of the building, and the floors shined with new varnish, but it was an empty shell of a room.

"Wow, I didn't think you were renovating this floor until next year. It looks so fresh and new," Cindy said in surprise.

"Yeah, I couldn't wait any longer. Kendall is driving me crazy, and I need a place of my own, like yesterday. So this is where I'll put the kitchen."

To the left, painter's tape marked the floor with an L shape, and Holly pointed to it. "This is the kitchen. The plumbing will be easier with the bathroom behind this wall. This will be the kitchen table, a couch here, and this entire wall will be a storage space."

"What about a bed? Is this a studio or one bedroom?" Cindy asked spinning around slowly to take everything in.

Holly shrugged. "A loft bedroom above the kitchen, probably. I mean, these tall ceilings make the room feel a lot bigger."

"What is it, twenty feet tall?" Cindy asked, looking up at the patched ceiling.

"Twenty-five."

Cindy frowned, trying to picture the space. "Did you have someone inspect the roof? Is it leak proof?"

Holly laughed. "Yeah, the roof company inspected it before I even opened up the yoga studio. It's fine. I might even put in a roof top terrace."

"Wow, going fancy, huh?" Cindy teased.

Holly grinned and shrugged, rocking on her feet back and forth as she looked around. "Not fancy. But this place feels like home, and I've been missing that."

Cindy leaned over and hugged her. "What about the bathroom?"

Holly's face lit up as she said, "Oh, you have to see it. It's so cute!"

They walked out of the living area to the hallway with the three doors, and Holly opened the closest one. It had a jetted tub shower combination in front of the door. To the left was the one sink but with extra-long counter space on either side. Behind the door was the toilet.

"Oh my God, Holly, this is so cute! It's the cutest little bathroom I've ever seen! Did you do all this tile work?"

Cindy ran her hand on the counter. She looked at herself in the large oval mirror and winced. The dark circles under her eyes were getting noticeable.

Holly laughed. "Mostly. Landry made sure to evenly space and straighten all the tiles. He's a fantastic handyman. There's no way I could've done any of this without him. Are you ready to see my massage room?"

They walked to the next door in the hallway. A tall stained-glass window across from the door let in natural light while preserving privacy. Against one wall stood a plush armchair and a sleek counter with bottles of essential oils neatly arranged on top. In the center of the room was a massage table, draped in crisp white linens. A diffuser hummed quietly in the corner, filling the air with calming scents of lavender and eucalyptus, while gentle ocean waves played from a small speaker nearby.

Cindy breathed in deeply and the tension in her shoulders eased.

Holly smirked, "That lavender works wonders, huh? Get undressed and lay on the table, face in the hole. Sheet's right here."

Cindy set her purse on the chair as the door clicked shut behind her. When she was ready, she called out to Holly.

Holly knocked and opened the door and said, "Ready?"

Cindy hmm'd into the opening where her face rested as Holly moved around near the counter behind her.

"I'm glad Maryanne made these appointments for you.

You've been looking pretty tired. Have you not been sleeping well?" Holly folded the sheet off her back.

"Not really, but it's the season, really. With school, soccer, and all the stuff that goes along with the boys and two jobs," she mumbled, before groaning as Holly began her massage.

"It's good, right? You are so tense. Is this normal tension for you?" Holly's lyrical voice soothed Cindy's nerves.

"Well, I'm trying to find a better-paying job, so I can only work one and be home more. I'll be able to relax, enjoy the boys, and hopefully sleep better."

Holly hummed as she rubbed warm circles up and down her spine. She used a combination of essential oils and massage oil to work the knots out from between her shoulder blades, and Cindy groaned.

"I heard you started giving PT to the new guy in town, the one who came by the house when we were baking?" Holly asked softly. Cindy jerked slightly on the table.

"Whoa! That was a powerful reaction at the mention of one guy. Or was it the mention of your work? We don't have to talk about that. We don't have to talk about anything if you don't want to." Holly asked as her hands soothed Cindy's shoulders back down.

Cindy swallowed hard and kept her eyes closed as the knots in her shoulders slowly dissipated. "A little of both. Work being work, but Andy is—well, things happened at his PT session, things I can't talk about."

"Oo, like medical things and patient confidentiality? Or sexual things? Because the way you two were acting at my house the other day was hotter than hell."

Cindy sighed, "Sexual things, I guess."

"Well, as your friend, I'm happy to listen and cheer for you to find a happily ever after. But I won't pry if you don't want to talk about it, like I said. Lord knows y'all have been patient enough with me the past few years." Holly said with a tinkling laugh.

After a few minutes, Cindy sighed into the table. "Holly... can I ask something that you might not want to answer?"

Holly's hands moved to her arms, kneading the muscles there. "Sure."

Cindy cleared her throat. She didn't want to hurt her friend, but she didn't really have anyone else to ask.

"My parents' marriage was... good but tense. Dad had some serious PTSD. And while they loved each other, I don't think that they were *in* love with each other. Does that make sense?"

"Yes, there's definitely a difference," Holly said softly as she moved to the other arm.

"I thought I loved my husband, but that backfired. What does being *in* love look like?" She waited, knowing this was a tough question for Holly.

Holly sighed, and said, "I'm going to hold up the sheet so you can turn over. Let me know when you're done."

Cindy groaned as she turned over on the table, then Holly slid the pillow under her knees as she talked. "I don't have a good way to describe what it looks like, per se. But I can tell you how it feels."

Holly paused and moved to massage her feet. Her soft voice mixed with the ocean sounds and filled Cindy with hope. "Being in love is the best feeling in the world, Cindy. It's like being wrapped up in a hug all the time. Like you're safe in that hug and nothing can hurt you."

Cindy's throat choked up in sympathy for her friend, knowing how the loss of that love affected her. She'd never met Holly's husband, but she'd heard nothing but good things about him.

Holly continued. "He's there to pick you up, dust you off, and set you on your feet again. Love is when he listens to you and supports your crazy ideas even if he doesn't agree with them or think they're going to work."

She laughed softly. "Especially when he doesn't think they're going to work. Being in love is when you're the most important person to someone else. Light takes up your entire body, and there's no darkness hiding anywhere because when it creeps up, your best friend is right there beside you, ready to talk about it."

The silence settled as Cindy thought about her words. Longing filled her soul, but it had been there all along. She'd been searching for love her whole life, it seemed like.

"I've never had that, but I think I want it. The pain from my ex… it wasn't worth it. Is the… possibility of pain worth the risk? If it's actual love involved?" Cindy asked.

"I think you're the only one who can answer that, Cin. For me… yeah, it was worth it. I wouldn't trade those years with him for anything."

The silence stretched as Holly added more oil to her hands and worked the knots on the top of her shoulders and neck. The last of Cindy's tension gave way as she thought.

She wasn't in love with Andy. She didn't know him enough for that, surely. but she couldn't deny the way he made her heart beat faster. The way his kisses made her melt, the way they made her relax and forget about all her worries.

"All done," Holly whispered. "Take your time getting up. I'll be downstairs cleaning out the locker room. You can even take a nap. Just relax." She closed the door, and Cindy let her mind drift.

What would happen if she went out with Andy? What if they started dating? She didn't ask Maryanne about him meeting Owen and James, but James had been talking nonstop about some camping trip.

Owen had told her about seeing Mandy at the game with her big uncle. If Andy had Mandy by himself, did that mean he was father material?

She put on the brakes on her thoughts. *Let's not get ahead of ourselves,* she thought. First, she needed to figure out if she wanted a relationship. Then she could think about him and the boys and them as one big happy family.

Unbidden, she pictured them in front of his cabin. All four boys would play soccer while she set the food on a picnic table. She drifted off to sleep as the image played out in her head.

Chapter Twenty

When she left Holly's, she was the most relaxed she'd ever been. She walked down the street to meet Maryanne and her mom for lunch at the Texan Cafe. Spying them, she walked to a booth on the right in front of an enormous window.

Their mom, Margarita, was still a beautiful woman, with her dark hair streaked with solid chunks of white like the woman on the Munster's. She was barely five feet two and dressed in a khaki pants suit, red silk blouse, red pumps, and pearls.

"Hey Mom! Hey M!" Cindy said as she slid into the booth. The two glanced up with a jerk. Cindy narrowed her eyes as her Mom looked at her guiltily.

"What's going on?" Cindy asked as she tilted her head. She glanced at Maryanne who grinned.

"I've told Mom about Andy," Maryanne said. Cindy shot her the evil eye, which made Maryanne laugh loudly. The waitress Dot came over and took their orders.

"Oh, hun, this is fantastic! You've been alone for so

long!" Margarita gushed, reaching across the table and squeezing Cindy's hand.

Cindy raised her eyebrows pointedly. "Yeah, and so have you. When are *you* going to start dating, Mom?"

Margarita just rolled her eyes and waved her hand. "Who knows? Whenever I feel like it, I suppose. Maybe I'll meet someone on the cruise in February." Their mom was going with some of the other ladies from church on an over fifty cruise. Mr. and Mrs. Williams had volunteered to be the old single ladies' chaperones, which Maryanne found funny.

When their food arrived, Margarita demanded details. "So tell me about this Andy."

Cindy chewed her burger and swallowed with a sigh. "He's Suzie's nephew, the one with the prosthetic foot. He's a retired Army guy, did the radios and such, and seems to get along well with his niece who is in Owen's class."

"So, what's the problem?"

"He's my physical therapy patient. It's a breach of policy, so nothing can happen with him."

Her mom waved a fry at her and said, "Being a patient doesn't matter when true love is on the line. Love is no respecter of persons after all."

Cindy shook her head as she took a drink, then said, "Who said anything about love? And I thought God was no respecter of persons."

"Him too," her mom said cheekily. "I know you were hurt pretty badly the last few relationships. I understand your need to protect yourself. But for me to figure out whether Maryanne is right and you should go for it, or if you are right and you shouldn't even have anything to do with him… well, we've invited him to join us for lunch."

Her mom said with a sneaky grin that made her look exactly like Maryanne.

Lifting her hand in a wave, her mom glanced over Cindy's shoulder as the doorbell dinged and someone came inside.

Cindy turned to see Andy standing in the doorway, backlit by the soft light. Her breath caught in her throat at the polite smile on his face as he greeted Dot by the door, who promptly disappeared into the kitchen. When he turned and met her gaze, his smile widened and lit up his face.

His sneakers squeaked against the hardwood floor as he stepped forward, his well-worn jeans hugging his muscular thighs. He wore a light blue long-sleeved shirt, the sleeves rolled up to reveal toned forearms that made Cindy's heart flutter.

He raked a hand through his hair, looking nervous and unsure as he approached, glancing from her to Maryanne and then to their mom.

"Hey," Cindy said softly.

He looked back at her, and it felt like the butterflies inside her were going to fly out of her throat.

"Hey," he said before sliding into the booth next to her and extending his foot slightly to stretch it out. He glanced across the table, eyes twinkling. "Thank you for inviting me to lunch, Maryanne. I didn't know y'all had another sister."

He reached a hand over the table to shake their mom's hand.

She laughed as he grinned. "You can call me Margarita. I'm their mother, and it's so nice to meet you, Andy. I haven't signed up to bring you a meal from the church yet, but everyone's so happy you're back in town."

"I'm happy to be here. Especially now," he said,

The Soldier Gets His Girl

glancing at Cindy with a smile. Her cheeks flushed as she broke eye contact and looked down at her food. She took a big bite of her burger as he continued.

Dot approached the table carrying another plate of food. "This must be your burger?"

"Yes, thank you. Can I have a sweet tea with it?" he asked. Dot just blushed as she set the plate down, then went to get him his drink order. He picked up a fry and said, "I called ahead to place my order. Didn't want you lovely ladies waiting on me."

"I don't know," Maryanne said, her lips twisting in a mischievous smile. "I hear you might be worth the wait."

Cindy glared and kicked her sister under the table, making Maryanne jump and laugh at the same time.

"Girls, enough of that. We don't want Andy to get the wrong impression."

He grinned and swallowed his bite, nodding at Dot as she set down his drink and walked away. After he drank, he said, "Don't worry about me, ma'am. I'm just blessed to be here. I mean, if you would've told me I'd be eating lunch with three beautiful women this time last year, I would've called you a liar." He laughed, using his French fry to point at the three of them.

Her heart skipped a beat at the sound. His laugh made her shoulders relax almost to the post-massage level.

"So, Andy, I've heard you've met my grandsons," her mom said as she wiped her mouth with her napkin.

He nodded his head yes as he swallowed a bite of his fries. "Oh yes. Cody's a beast at soccer. I love watching him play."

Maryanne nodded as she finished eating. "That reminds me. Give me your phone while you eat. I'll text the pictures from Saturday to Cindy."

Andy unlocked his screen and handed it over. "You might want to text the videos directly to Cody. I had to send all the ones from two weeks ago to Parker to give him."

Maryanne raised her eyebrow at Cindy in question. Cindy huffed out a breath and nodded. She was very picky about who got Cody's number, always making him get permission before giving it to friends at school.

"Did you have Mandy on Saturday or did Suzie go with you to the game?" Cindy asked, thinking of what Owen had said about it. He wasn't that clear, and details were hit or miss with her baby.

"Oh, Aunt Suz had some gardening to do, so I took her for the day. It was actually my first time to have her all to myself, but we did pretty good, considering." He laughed as he wiped his mouth. "By pretty good, I mean she only cried for about twenty minutes at naptime on the way home."

"Wow, twenty minutes isn't bad for a three-year-old. I still struggle with Owen when they stay with me. What'd you do?" Margarita asked.

"When we got back to my place, I rocked her in the recliner and then bribed her with a movie if she'd take a nap first." He laughed as he leaned back, placing his arm behind Cindy's shoulders on the back of the booth.

The hairs on the back of her neck stood up at his nearness. Maryanne glanced down at his nearly empty plate. "Man, you eat really fast."

He laughed again, and the knot in the pit of her stomach loosened. "Habit from the Army. In boot camp, if you didn't eat fast, you didn't eat."

Her mom nodded as she finished her fries and said, "I can understand that. We used to invite the platoons over for barbeques when their father was still in the Army. When we said the food was ready, it was like a hungry pack of lions descended and picked it all clean in five seconds flat. It was so funny to watch. Do you girls remember those barbeques?"

They both nodded and smiled at each other. "Of course, Mama," Cindy said.

Maryanne snorted, "I remember when Daddy stopped having those barbeques too. It was that one pool party, remember?"

Cindy rolled her eyes as Margarita laughed and told the story to Andy. She finished her burger as her ears burned in embarrassment. He laughed when he heard how her swimsuit straps unraveled in the pool.

"Marty kicked all the guys out and never invited them back," her mom laughed.

Cindy shook her head and whined, "It wasn't my fault! I told you the swimsuit was too small!"

Her mom nodded her head as she wiped the tears from her eyes. "I know, dear, but your father didn't want to admit you had grown up on him. That last deployment was the hardest, not because of the work over there, but because when he came back, both of you had turned into women."

Maryanne rolled her eyes and crossed her arms, leaning back in her seat. "Yeah, and Cindy always ruined it right when things got interesting. Those BBQs were some good eye candy."

"It wasn't me who shut them down, but Dad," Cindy pointed across the table. Andy's hand rubbed up and down her bicep, the warmth of his arm cocooning her and keeping her calm. She breathed deeply and relaxed back into the seat and his hand.

Margarita cut in. "Now, girls, none of that. I swear, these two fought like cats and dogs growing up. Some of that comes back every once in a while. They're not normally like this."

"That's alright," Andy said. "It's good to be passionate, and it sounds like your husband was a good man who was just doing the best he could. Cindy told me about him and Mrs. Espinoza passing, and I was sorry to hear it."

Margarita paused, her eyes tearing up. "Thank you," she said softly.

Andy looked uncomfortable and took a sip of his drink. "I can understand where he was coming from about the last deployment being the worst too."

"Oh, that's right. How are you recovering?"

"I'm doing well, especially now that I have the best physical therapy assistant in North Texas working with me." He winked, and she blushed and glanced down at her food. When had she finished it all?

She put her hands in her lap as her mom said, "Oh, she definitely is. When she was working with my mother when she first lost her leg, it was like an angel had descended from heaven. I didn't think anyone could get her to work and recover!"

"Was Mrs. Espinoza your mom or your mother-in-law?" Andy asked.

Margarita perked up. "That would be my mother. Did you know her?"

Andy nodded, and Cindy looked at him in surprise.

"You knew my grandmother?" she asked. When had they met? He hadn't grown up here. She would have heard about it from Lola or someone.

"Oh, yes, she was my middle school lunch lady. Always gave me extra mashed potatoes. Said it'd help the meat stick to my bones."

The light from the window reflected off his teeth as he

grinned. His clear blue eyes called to her soul, drawing her closer to him.

She leaned back as Maryanne said, "That must have meant you were a scrawny kid. She said the same thing when Cindy was pregnant."

"I was pretty scrawny. When I was in elementary school, I lived in downtown Dallas. My mom wasn't... in the right frame of mind to raise me and—well, food wasn't always a priority. So, when I moved in with Aunt Suzie and Uncle Mike, it seemed like I never could eat enough."

"You went to school here? Why didn't we ever run into each other when we were in town?" Cindy asked with a frown.

He shrugged, his hand drawing closer around her. "I hung out with the Williams' a lot. Landry was the third of the Musketeers with my cousin Jake and me. But most summers I had to spend with my mom."

Cindy looked at him closely. His mouth was tight at the corners and there was a tenseness to his shoulders that wasn't there earlier. She put her hand on his thigh, causing him to twitch before relaxing under her palm.

Maryanne sucked the last of her drink through her straw, then set her cup down. "We were only here in the summers and holidays, so that makes sense on why y'all haven't run into each other before now. You about ready, Mom?"

Cindy tore her eyes from Andy's face and glanced at her mom. "Where are y'all going?"

"Oh, we're going to pick up Owen from school, then go get some supplies for the bakery. We'll pick up James and Cody and take them to soccer practice later too," her mom said as she took a drink of her soda.

Cindy's eyebrow arched in surprise. "Oh, you are, are you? And what am I supposed to do?" She sipped her coke.

Maryanne grinned slyly, "Andy."

Cindy choked on her drink. Andy slapped her on the back, and she squeezed his leg as she took another drink to ease the coughing fit.

Her mom snorted and slid out of the booth. "Not literally, dear. Although I'm fine with it, in case anyone was wondering. But anyway, the Williams' are having their Halloween bash and you don't have a costume. If you have a costume, you won't have an excuse not to go. I bet Andy doesn't have one either, him being new and all. So, you two go on down to the costume store in Denton and pick something out."

Maryanne slid out of their booth and followed Margarita to the door. Andy stood and offered Cindy a hand. She took it without thinking.

As he helped her up, he asked, "So sounds like we have a date in Denton. That is, if you *want* to go costume shopping with me?"

Cindy blushed as he kept hold of her hand and tossed her purse over her shoulder with her other. "I—I guess it'd be fun. I know the boys would love for me to actually dress up this year."

He grinned and kept hold her hand as they walked to the cashier's stand. "Wonderful." Maryanne opened the front door, and Andy squeezed her hand before letting it go.

"I got it, Margarita," he said, stepping forward and reaching for his wallet. Cindy opened her mouth to argue, but Maryanne tugged Cindy out the door, leaving their mom to fuss at Andy for paying.

Maryanne let her go when they reached their mom's

The Soldier Gets His Girl

car. They each leaned against the hood, and Cindy tilted her head up to the sun to breathe deeply.

Chapter Twenty-One

"You going to be alright? You don't have to go costume shopping with him, you know, but it would do you some good." Maryanne's voice was soft but no-nonsense. This was going to be a lot of alone time with Andy, but they'd be in public. They could learn a little about each other, see if they could become friends at least.

"I... think so. You and Mom both think he's a good guy, though?" she asked. With her track record, she really didn't trust herself to make this decision. Maryanne reached over and squeezed her hand, her sunglasses hiding her eyes.

"We really do. We've both talked to some of the church ladies who've dropped food off for him, and he's not made one flirty remark or pass at any of them, not even Lizzie or Katie. They both whined about it," Maryanne said with a throaty chuckle.

Cindy smiled even though the knot in her stomach returned. At the sound of their mom's voice, she opened her eyes. Andy swaggered towards them, his dark hair shining in the sunlight.

Even though the swagger was deliberate, to cover up his limp, she found it as sexy as she did last Friday when he was barefoot and in basketball shorts.

His blue eyes caught hers, and the knot in her stomach dissolved. She wondered how his smile made her feel better like that.

She hugged her mom and sister and said goodbye, then she and Andy walked along the sidewalk.

"Want me to drive or do you want to?" he asked, pointing to his truck. "I'm fine either way."

She was surprised. "You'd let me drive?"

He looked at her in confusion. "Why not? You have to be an excellent driver to handle three kids in the car, right?"

She laughed and nodded. "Oh, I am. I just—I guess I didn't expect it to be an option. All the men I've been around... well, man's gotta drive and prove his manliness."

He laughed and shook his head as they walked. "There's a difference between a real man and a boy being macho. I don't necessarily care about who drives, but I can get pretty antsy in traffic. I've been told it's part of my PTSD."

"Are you more likely to have a PTSD traffic moment if you're driving or if you're a passenger?" They stopped at her SUV, and she waited as he looked down, rubbing the back of his head as if embarrassed by this small thing.

"Less likely if I'm driving. I wasn't driving when the IED took out the humvee." She studied his face, lined with time and burdened by memories. His eyes were distant, lost in a reverie of days gone by. It was clear that he was still haunted by his past.

She placed a hand on his forearm and stepped closer. "Then you drive. I don't like driving on the interstate in Denton anyway, so it works out."

They turned back to his truck two parking spots away.

"Are you sure you're alright going shopping? I don't want you to feel pressured into going if you don't want to." He waited expectantly, his hand holding the handle of the passenger side.

"This is fine," she said softly. "Wednesdays are the closest thing I have to a day off, and I wouldn't mind spending it with you."

He beamed at her and held the door open. She climbed into his truck, the leather seats worn but comfortable, and she took a deep breath as he opened his own door and joined her inside. After buckling, he revved the engine and pulled out of the parking spot. It had been so long since she'd felt that flutter of excitement in her stomach and even longer since she'd gone to the city on an afternoon adventure.

The smell of him made the tension in her shoulders ease, and she sighed as she glanced past the blurring trees.

"You ok?" he asked, as he stopped at the one stoplight and plugged in the directions on his phone.

"Yeah, why?" she asked as they turned toward Denton.

"I don't know. You sighed kinda funny." Country music played softly in the background, but she couldn't tell what the song was.

She blinked in surprise. He'd noticed such a little thing like sighing. Jerry had never noticed or said anything like that. Maybe Andy really was different from her exes.

"I'm fine. I was just wondering about shoulder tension. Holly gave me a massage earlier. It was great and all, but the tension is creeping back up, and I'm not sure why."

"Hmm, is it chronic?" he asked.

"What do you mean?"

"Well, if you've been a single mom for—what is it, five years now?"

"Yeah."

"Well, that would make anyone tense. And if you haven't taken regular breaks to recharge, you might have chronic stress or something going on. I'm just guessing, based on what you said earlier about not having any time off. Did you work today?" he asked.

Cindy fiddled with her purse on the seat beside her. "Yeah, but it was only one PT patient this morning."

"Yeah, but it's not like you're getting a full weekend to recharge. And how long have you been working like this?" He turned onto the main highway and sped up.

She shrugged and leaned into the window away from him. "Four or five years I suppose. Ever since I got hired at the hospital right after 'Buela died."

"'Buela?"

"Oh, my grandmother. Mrs. Espinoza? We called her Abuela but shortened it as kids." He nodded, both hands loose but still at ten and four on the steering wheel.

"So you didn't get to grieve her either, did you?" he asked softly.

She turned and looked at him. "Where is all this coming from? You're tuning in to a lot of emotions here, and I'm not used to that from anyone, much less a guy."

He laughed, making her smile. "I had to do a lot of therapy while I was in recovery. Every weekday for fifteen months is a long time to figure out how to process things like grief and trauma."

He met her eyes quickly, dark and mysterious as he said, "Like recognizes like." Then he looked back at the road. "So did you ever grieve for her?"

She frowned and looked out her window, thinking through that whirlwind of two years. First her dad had died, then she'd been arrested and her kids taken away, then the divorce and moving in with her grandma, only to then have her grandma die.

She shook her head, her chest tight. "Mom was the priority. She'd already lost Dad by then and 'Buela's death hit her as hard if not harder. I guess I had focused so much on finalizing the funeral, taking care of Mom and the boys, and cleaning and doing all that normal stuff that I still haven't really thought about it."

He nodded, and the silence stretched in the cab. It was a comfortable silence, and soon she hummed to a George Strait song. He turned up the music, and they both started singing *Check Yes or No*.

When the song was over, he turned the radio down as the ads started playing. "Do you want to be my friend?" he asked softly.

She smiled and tugged at the seam on her shirt. "Definitely." The silence stretched, like a warm hug wrapping around her.

"Do you want to be more than my friend?"

He had a slight wrinkle between his eyebrows, like he worried about the answer. He didn't make eye contact, but she could tell by the way he was holding himself tense in his seat that the answer meant a lot to him.

"Yes," she whispered. "But I'm scared."

He glanced at her and reached over to squeeze her hand. "I know. But how can I make you not scared? I'm not even sure what you're scared of."

"Well, it's against policy to date patients at—"

"Don't, Cindy. We both know that's not the real reason. That's just the convenient excuse." He squeezed her hand again before placing his back on the steering wheel.

As they pulled onto the interstate, she squirmed in her seat and twisted her t-shirt. With a sigh, she shrugged, "I guess I'm afraid of being hurt again. The boys' dads... well, they weren't good guys, even though I thought they were."

She huffed out a sigh and crossed her arms.

"Are you afraid to trust that I'm a good guy?" he asked. His voice was curious, not judgmental like most people, so she nodded.

When he didn't respond, she picked at her nail polish. "I think you're a good man, Andy, I do, but I can't trust my instincts with dating and men. Both times before, I didn't make good decisions, and I can't handle a third strike. Or the boys! Now that they're older, they're more aware. They could be hurt too."

"I would *never* hurt them. Or you," he growled. She'd never heard him talk like that, gruff and so certain. It made her heart race in excitement and hope.

"I'm not looking for a forever thing, Cindy, but I won't turn it away if it finds me. I just want the opportunity to get to know you and the boys and see where this goes." He exited and pulled into a parking lot.

He turned and faced her, his face a mixture of determination and vulnerability. His eyes bore into hers, pleading for a chance. "I can't promise a perfect future, but I'm willing to give us a shot. Will you try with me?"

He flipped his hand up, like he'd done that first day at his house when they'd prayed over the food.

She met his gaze, searching for any sign of doubt or hesitation. But all she saw was hope and an eagerness to make things work. She placed her hand in his, and he squeezed it gently before bringing it to his lips for a soft kiss. The simple gesture sent shivers down her spine and ignited a spark deep within her.

With a sharp inhale, she watched as he released his seatbelt. She mirrored his actions, unbuckling her own and scooting closer to him. As he leaned in closer, she could feel his lips pressing gently against each of her knuckles. Slowly, they moved towards each other until their hips were aligned and their knees touched under the steering wheel. The tension between them was palpable and electric.

And when his mouth bent and took hers, she sighed. It was better than her massage earlier, better than their previous kisses because it was slow and thorough.

She moaned and leaned into him, but he pulled back, breaking the kiss softly. He touched her forehead with his as their breathing slowed.

"Don't want to start something I can't finish yet," he said apologetically, as he cupped the side of her face in his hand.

He dipped his mouth and gave her a light peck on the lips before pulling back. "Ready to go in? I want to see if they have any sexy nurse costumes," he said waggling his eyebrows. She laughed and grabbed her purse.

"I don't think that's going to be fit for the Williams' Halloween party," she said as they rounded the front of the truck and walked toward the store.

"Have you ever been to one of their parties?" He grabbed her hand and linked his fingers through hers. Tingles shot up her arm at his touch. She felt safe as he looked both ways before crossing the parking lot.

"No, I always take the boys trick or treating in our apartment complex. Then we head home, divide the candy, and watch a Halloween movie together."

"Well, you can still do that. The Halloween party doesn't start until ten-ish anyway. Is your mom going to stay with the boys so you can go to the party?"

"She's offered to do just that every year, so maybe, if I actually go to the party."

He stopped inside the doorway and grabbed a basket with his free hand. He pulled her to a stop and looked her in the eyes. "Can I go trick-or-treating with you and the boys?"

He'd met the boys. This would give her a chance to see how they acted together, but it was too fast. The boys would know that something was going on because she'd never brought a man around them before. Despite her reservations, the hopeful look in his eyes had her nodding.

"Sure, we normally have a potluck around seven at the park in our complex, all the residents. Then we go door to door to whoever is home. Some years we go to the nursing home to trick or treat."

"What are they going to dress up as for Halloween again? Spider-man, a soldier, and what?"

"A ninja," she walked past the scary costumes for zombies, clowns, and monsters. "I think we're in the wrong aisle. I don't like the scary costumes."

He chuckled, taking her hand in his. "How do you feel about scary movies?"

"Nope, not a fan. Rule Number 1: No scary movies in the house." She grinned as they turned to go down another aisle, her fingers tingling as they walked.

"Ahh, now we're talking. These are much better than the scary costumes anyway."

She laughed, her head tilting back as he released her hand and reached for a costume. "You're a guy. Of course you'd say that."

"Hey, if you don't want to be a sexy nurse, maybe you could be a sexy cheerleader?" he looked so hopeful as he held up the bag with the costume.

She laughed and shook her head. "No way. Look how short that skirt is!"

"Exactly!" he said, reaching for the next costume.

"What about Cleopatra?"

She looked at it and placed her chin in her hand. "Hmm, that could work. Do you think they have a matching Roman soldier outfit for you?"

He looked from the costume to her and grinned. She couldn't help but smile in return. His joy was infectious. He grabbed her hand and took off around the corner.

She laughed, feeling more carefree than she had in years. "Where are we going?"

"To find that Roman gladiator costume, of course," he said, as they walked down the aisle for men's costumes. They slowed, finding a few options.

"Ah-ha!" he exclaimed, his arm shooting up in a triumphant gesture. She turned and giggled at the sight of him holding a bright red costume bag. She walked back to him, and his eyes glanced up and down her body. She smirked, her eyes scanning the bag's picture of its contents.

She circled around him, taking in his bulky frame and military style haircut, until she tapped a finger to her chin. "I don't think that's going to work."

"Why not? It's perfect!" he said, his jaw dropping along with his hand holding the bag.

"Nope, you're too big and burly."

He grinned, the twinkle in his eye catching the overhead lights, making him look like a little boy on Christmas morning. "You think I'm hot."

She blushed at the heat in his eyes. She hadn't felt this desired or pretty in a long time. "I didn't say *that* exactly."

His grin widened as he stepped closer, making her heart race. "If you think I'm too big for the costume, I guess I'll have to try it on and find out if you're right. Come on, I bet there's a changing room back here somewhere."

They rounded the aisle and saw the sign for the changing rooms. As they walked all along the back of the store, she only saw one other person, and that was the teenager on his phone behind the counter.

This was one reason she loved having Wednesday's free; no crowds anywhere.

Chapter Twenty-Two

As they neared the changing rooms, he realized there were only two of them. He handed Cindy her costume bag to try on and stepped into his changing room. This was going to be tricky. There wasn't a chair in the room.

"Umm, Cindy?" Hopefully she could hear him through the wall.

"Yeah?" she called.

"Do you have a chair in there?"

"Yeah, do you not?"

"No, and I kind of need it to get my pants around my foot."

"Alright, we can switch." She kept talking as he opened the door and stepped around to her door. She propped it open, and he sucked in a breath. The white toga dress clung to her generous curves like a second skin. As his gaze raked her from head to foot, he noticed her nipples perked up hard against the fabric.

Just looking at her made his cock stiffen, especially when he realized she wasn't wearing a bra with the costume. He stepped into the small space and shut the door behind him. She gasped softly and her pupils dilated as they stared up at him.

"I should be able to take my pants off standing up, since I'm a Level 4 and all, but it's not something that I've really tried to accomplish yet. Think that could be something you help me work on in PT?" He sat in the chair in the corner, trying to act nonchalant.

She stood there as he pulled his sneakers off. He found it telling that she didn't turn around and leave. His gaze landed on her breasts, right in front of his face.

He couldn't touch her yet. Not in public. Not like this. It might scare her off, and he'd *just* gotten her to agree to date him. He had to let her watch him change. But maybe he could turn her on as much as he was.

He stood back up and pulled his shirt over his head. Her jaw dropped as her gaze landed on *his* chest this time.

Running a hand down his stomach to the button on his jeans, her eyes followed him like a hungry tiger. He flicked open the button, and she licked her lips. His heart raced as his smile grew.

He groaned silently as he slid the zipper down and pushed his pants down his thighs. As they caught on his prosthetic foot, he sat down in his boxer briefs and pulled his pants off.

When he was free, he grabbed the costume bag from where it'd fallen at his feet and opened it. He glanced up at Cindy, who was still rooted to the spot. But now she had both her hands pressing her lips in surprise.

It covered up the nipples of her costume but he could see the bright pink panty outline through the white fabric. He glanced down and held up what could only be called a glorified leather skirt.

He stood as he pulled it up over his boxer briefs to his waist. Standing in only two items of clothing was a challenge to his patience, when she was so close. But he turned slightly and looked at the long mirror. He stepped back to stand beside her and took in both of their reflections.

Her long, dark curly hair hung down past her shoulders, nearly grazing her nipples. She barely reached his shoulder, she was so short, but it was the perfect height for him. They were only inches apart, but he sucked in a deep breath when he heard her raspy, shallow breathing.

He caught her gaze in the mirror and just stared into her eyes. Would she give in to the temptation that proximity had given them? She licked her lips, and he turned to face her.

She turned too. He could feel her breath on his chest, slightly stirring the dark patch of hair that ran down his chest. She looked up at him, her eyes glazed and blank with lust.

"Cindy," he whispered, "I want so much with you, but I'm afraid if I touch you right now, I won't be able to stop. And I don't want our first time together to be in a store changing room."

She licked her lips and a slow smile spread across her face. His heart skipped a beat at that smile. "Well, I don't want it to be either. But last Friday… that was all for me. This time can be for you."

She placed a hand on his chest, and it was like fire straight to his cock. She pushed him slowly until the back of his legs hit the chair. He sat hard as she kneeled in front of him and reached under the gladiator skirt to grasp him.

It was his turn to gasp as her fingers wrapped around him through his boxer briefs. She found the slit and pulled him free as she leaned forward and kissed him on the mouth. Thus far, he had started and led all their kisses.

But this one, she was clearly in charge of. He groaned into her mouth as she stroked his tongue with hers slowly. His hands came up to grip her head softly, tangling in her curls. Her hand mimicked her mouth, and she twisted her wrist slightly when she reached the tip. Then she moved back down slowly. He shifted to the edge of the chair.

She broke the kiss and gasped as he reached out to flick her nipples through the dress. It made her jerk and squeeze extra tight, making him gasp in pleasure.

His hands tweaked her nipples before she pulled back with a groan.

"No," she whispered, sinking to her knees. "Just for you."

She flipped up some of the long, leather pieces of the skirt to reveal his cock. He saw her eyes grow wide as she licked her lips, leaned forward, and wrapped her mouth around the head.

He gasped, wrapping his hands in her hair so he could see her face and mouth.

It was the hottest thing he'd ever seen in his life, and that was including his wild teenage years and twenties. She swiped her tongue around the entire head before lowering her mouth slowly. She made it halfway before she pulled back up and repeated the process.

Shit, he wouldn't last long like this. It'd been too long, and she was too good. She stopped swirling her tongue and started going up and down faster, her hands holding the leather back on his thighs. Her hands squeezed his legs, and he imagined them wrapped around his cock.

He gasped as he pulled her head onto him. He kept his

hips locked on the seat, but her wet, little mouth was all he needed. She slid down farther and farther.

When he hit the back of her throat, he wasn't even three-fourths of the way in, but it was exactly what he needed. He gasped and held her still on his cock as he released.

She took a deep breath through her nose, swallowing with a "mmm" that he interpreted as good. He hadn't even thought to ask her if she wanted to swallow or not, but it looked like she didn't mind too much.

He sighed as she pulled back slowly. When she got to the tip, she sucked hard, making him jerk.

When she sat back on her haunches, she smiled the satisfied smile of a woman proud of her work. He blinked at her, still panting. "Hot damn, I was not expecting that."

"Was it alright?" she asked, the vulnerability in her eyes and the worried wrinkle on her forehead enough to crack his heart.

He tucked himself back into his boxers and reached for her, pulling her onto his lap. Her legs dangled over the side of his thigh, and he pulled her head into the crook of his neck.

"Cindy, it was perfect. It was the hottest thing I've ever seen. In my head, with that dress, you're my very own sex goddess," he whispered as he kissed her forehead. He smiled as she hummed and relaxed in his arms.

He hugged her and just sat there. It was the most at peace he'd felt in... well, ever. Had he seriously never felt this before? How had he survived before now, without this, without her?

Footsteps sounded outside the door. Someone entered the changing room next to them. She sat up slowly, her eyes big as she seemed to realize where they were and what they'd done.

He grinned and placed his forefinger over his lips to say silently, "Shh."

She smiled and stood up, glancing around. He held up a hand and mouthed, "Wait."

Silently, he took off the gladiator costume, then handed it to her with the bag. She folded it and put it in the bag while he put on his pants and his sneakers. Finally, he pulled on his shirt and sat back.

"Now you can change," he mouthed silently with a lascivious grin as he waved for her to change. She smiled shyly, her cheeks turning dark pink, before pulling her hair over one shoulder. She pulled down the exposed wide strap of her dress and exposed a breast.

His breath caught, and he sat up in the chair. His hands twitched, wanting to touch her. He shoved them under his thighs with an exaggerated pained expression.

She chuckled softly, making her breast bounce slightly. His jaw dropped as she pulled down the strap of the other shoulder. Both breasts hung free, high and full and perky. Their caramel color made his mouth water for a taste.

She slid the dress down her waist. It fell to her feet, and she turned her back to him slightly and bent over to pick up her pants. He groaned out loud. It was a damn pink lacy thing that cupped her ass exactly the way he wanted his hands to do. He wanted to trace the outline of her panties.

As she shoved a leg into her pants, he couldn't stop himself. His hand shot out from under his own leg where he'd trapped it. He couldn't seem to control it.

He watched as his finger traced the edge of the silk, gliding from her hip down under the curve of her ass where it disappeared.

She froze, one foot in her pants, one foot out. She glanced over her shoulder at him and met his eyes with an arched eyebrow. He jerked back and shoved his hand back under his thigh with a sheepish grin.

She smirked as she finished pulling her pants up. She bent forward and grabbed her bra, but turned and faced him. He licked his lips. She was so close; he could practically taste her. She leaned forward, whether by accident because she was trying to put on her bra or on purpose he didn't care. He leaned forward to meet her and sucked a hard nipple into his mouth.

Her gasp rang out in the silence, and she stumbled. His arms came up to catch her, and he pulled her between his legs. One hand came up and fondled the other breast before he switched. She threw her head back with a silent gasp, and he reached around and grabbed her ass through her pants. He squeezed. She squirmed. He wanted to shove his now hardening cock inside that tight pussy.

He let her go and licked each nipple with the flat of his tongue. She whimpered with each lick. He went to the other, but she stepped back on shaky legs before he could latch on. She panted as she finished putting on her matching pink lacy bra. He leaned forward and grabbed her t-shirt, handing it to her. She grabbed it quickly and shoved it on as she slipped her feet into her slip-on ballet flats.

When they were both dressed, she stood on the opposite wall from where he sat as they stared at each other. They both panted. Judging from the look in her eyes, she wanted to finish this as much as he did.

The other changing room door opened and closed. He stood, opened the door of their changing room and looked around as he stepped out.

Chapter Twenty-Three

Waving her through, they walked along the back wall of the store once more. Breathing deeply, he said, "So."

She sighed dreamily. "So. What now?"

"Um, not sure. My brain isn't working yet. You tell me. Do we need anything else? Wait, where are the costumes?" he said looking around and behind them towards the changing rooms.

She chuckled again and raised her hand. She held the basket with their costumes in the bags. He sighed in relief. "Why don't you go find gladiator shoes or a helmet? It'll be in the accessories over by the changing rooms. I want to look for another Spider-man costume for Owen because I think his might be too small."

He nodded as he turned around. "Meet you at the checkout counter in a few?"

Before she could take a step away from him, he leaned in for a quick, deep kiss. He tasted himself on her lips but instead of disgusting him, it just made him want her all the more. He groaned and pulled back with a grin.

Her cheeks flushed as she smiled and walked off. He watched her hips sway before he turned to find the gladiator shoes.

After checking out, they walked hand in hand back to the truck. He placed their bags in the back seat and opened her door. Before he could close it, she grabbed his t-shirt and pulled him in for a kiss.

He groaned as he fisted her hair and pulled slightly. He nipped at her bottom lip with his teeth, then soothed it by sucking gently. Her moan drove him wild again.

Pulling back to cup her face, he kissed her softly, trying to break the spell they were under. Finally, he shut her door and adjusted himself as he walked around the truck.

He couldn't believe he was hard again, but had he really been soft after he'd come in that tight mouth? He didn't think so. She just made him want more and more.

Starting up the truck, he glanced at the time. "Well, it's only two-thirty. Do you want to do any more shopping? Do you need anything else?"

She stared at him intently before she whispered, "I—I think I just want to go back to your place."

He blinked, his heart racing as he ran a hand over the back of his head. "Are you sure? What about... protection? I don't think I have any condoms, so we'll have to stop somewhere."

"I'm on the pill, and I'm clean. Are you?"

He nodded his head and started the truck. "Yeah, I got checked right before my last deployment and there's not been anyone since so I'm good."

She nodded shyly, her cheeks flushing. "Well then, alright. Don't get a ticket getting home." He grinned as he pulled up the GPS and backed out.

They sang to the radio the entire way to his house. They

both might have been too wound up to hold a conversation. If anyone asked what they sang, he wouldn't be able to tell because he didn't remember. His entire body was strung tight in anticipation.

When they pulled up to his house, he shut off the engine and turned to her. "You still good? You sure you still want this? Because when we go inside, I'm not sure I'll be able to stop." He gripped the steering wheel hard.

She looked into his eyes, the want shining brightly in the afternoon sun. She nodded, biting her bottom lip as she unbuckled and grabbed her purse. He unbuckled, grabbed the keys, and they both got out. Racing her to the front door, he unlocked it.

As he closed the door with a resounding click, he grabbed her by the waist and spun her against it.

He spun her around, his rough hands gripping her waist, pulling her closer until their bodies were flush against each other. They both let out a low moan as their lips collided, igniting a fire deep within him. Their tongues danced in a frenzy, exploring and claiming every inch of each other's mouths. Her hands snaked under his shirt, sending shivers down his spine as they both moaned in pleasure.

He thought that was a brilliant idea and slid his hands under her shirt, lifting it up and over her head. She unhooked her bra as he stepped back, pulling his own shirt over his head. She'd barely gotten it off when he scooped her into his arms and carried her back towards the bedroom.

"Your leg!" she protested. "I'm too heavy."

"Never. I bench press more than you, darlin'. We're good."

He stepped into the bedroom and swung her so she

could kick the door shut. The light from the window slanted over the bed as he placed her gently on it.

He stepped back as he reached for his pants. She grabbed her own, and they took them off at the same time. But the light falling on her breasts and torso called to him. He couldn't stop staring at her, even as he tugged off his shoes. She lay spread on his bed like a buffet, and he knew —as soon as he touched her—he'd be a goner. The idea didn't scare him though, and he scanned her body, taking in every curve, every freckle.

When they were both naked, he walked around the other side of the bed and laid beside her.

Leaning on one arm, he traced the outside of her breast with his other hand, fingers light. She sucked in a breath as one finger circled first one nipple, then the other. Slowly he made his way down her stomach. He circled her belly button before dipping to her hip and the crease of her leg.

She quivered next to him when he neared her pussy. Her eyes widened as he brushed a finger down to her clit. It was like a furnace as she bent her knee and spread her leg out, tilting herself towards him. He'd gladly be consumed by this fire.

He circled her clit once, twice. The third time, he pressed into it gently, applying more pressure with each passing second until she bucked against him with a gasp. She jerked, so he repeated it. Once. Twice. Gently, but with steadily increasing pressure. She jerked again.

He did it again and again until she was gasping and writhing. Then he traced down her slit and slowly pushed a finger inside her dripping pussy. She gasped and bucked against his hand. He curved his finger, and she grabbed his bicep and pulled him on top of her. His finger slid out, and he used it to line himself up with her.

The Soldier Gets His Girl

He wanted to wait a little longer, had to make this so good for her that she would never walk away. He leaned down and sucked on a nipple. She twisted under him, her moans getting louder and her hips bucking, trying to get him closer. Her nails bit into his biceps until he raised up and kissed her. When their mouths met, he tilted his hips and traced her entrance with the tip of his cock.

She squirmed, and he slid the tip in. He swept his tongue into her mouth, pulled out, and slid in again. He repeated the move, going deeper each time until he was fully sheathed inside her.

Damn, it was perfect. She was tight and wet and when he pulled out and slid all the way in one thrust, she moaned into his mouth and arched her back. So he did it again, harder and harder until she was bucking up against him. Her arms wound around his shoulders, gripping his biceps. Her nails dug into his shoulders, and he loved every minute of it.

He thrust harder, deeper, hitting a wall. She broke the kiss and screamed as she came. She spasmed around him twice before he groaned into her neck and lost himself inside her.

Breathing deeply, soaking up the scent of her shampoo, he tried to keep most of his weight on his arms, but she was still twitching around him, and he didn't want to pull out yet.

He leaned back, keeping them together as he glanced down. His stare must have roused her because she opened her eyes.

He brushed the dark hair back from her face gently. The light fell on her face now, and her open, trusting smile was so full of happiness that it made his heart flip over.

"You're—that was—incredible." He couldn't even think

of what he wanted to say. Perfect? The best he'd ever had? He couldn't imagine going the rest of his life without her and that kind of sex ever again.

She wrinkled her brow with worry. "Was it alright? It's been a while, and never like that."

He grinned, pride filling him at her blush. "Took the words right out of my mouth. Hell, that was amazing. *You're amazing!*" He kissed the blush on each of her cheeks gently, making her smile widen.

He rolled to the side, finally slipping from her tight sheath, and sat on the edge of the bed. Grabbing a tissue from the box by his bed, he handed her one and cleaned himself off. Then he laid back down. When she tossed her napkin into the trash, he pulled her back down into his arms.

Her head on his chest felt like home. He wrapped his arms around her. She breathed a contented sigh as she slid a leg in between his. He drifted off to sleep, content and happy for the first time in years.

Chapter Twenty-Four

Cindy slowly opened her eyes to sounds coming from down the hallway. She stretched, thinking the boys must be getting ready for school. But the room was shadowed. She frowned, realizing it wasn't her room.

She sat up with a jerk, the sheet falling down to her hips. Glancing around, she remembered where she was. Her cheeks heated in embarrassment. She was naked in Andy's bed.

When footsteps and ringing sounded down the hall, she pulled the sheet up to cover herself. Andy stepped in, wearing nothing but his black basketball shorts.

With a smile, he handed over her purse. "Your phone is ringing. Dinner's almost ready, if you're hungry." He leaned forward and kissed her swiftly on the lips, causing her inner muscles to clench. Then he strode out of the room and back down the hall.

The ring of the phone broke her trance; his ass was really amazing in those shorts. She dug it out of her purse and answered it without looking.

"Hello?" she asked breathily. He still took her breath away.

"Yes, is this Cindy?" a male voice said from the other end.

"Yes, may I ask who's calling?" she said, clearing her throat.

"My name is Alan. I'm the HR director at Wise Health Center in Decatur. We received your application for the emergency room nurse position?"

"Oh, hello!" she said, her spine straightening as her heart skipped a beat.

"Hello!" the man chuckled. "We were wondering if you could come in for an interview next week."

"Absolutely." Her heart raced again with excitement.

"What day works best for you?"

"Wednesdays are best. Any time." She prayed as she gripped the sheet tightly. She set the time for just before lunch and hung up. Andy appeared in the doorway and looked at her with a wrinkled brow.

"Everything alright?" He walked towards her.

She couldn't stop grinning. She jumped off the bed and launched herself into his arms as she squealed. "I got the interview! I got the interview!"

She could feel his deep laugh down in her stomach. He lifted her up off the ground and spun her around, making her laugh. Then he sat down with her straddling him on the edge of the bed.

"What interview is that?" He placed small kisses along her jaw line.

She shivered, her nipples puckering at his closeness. "The one at the hospital in Decatur."

"Why do you want to work there?" he asked as he nibbled on her ear.

She moaned, closing her eyes. "So I don't have to work two jobs and can be home when the boys are home. The ER pays better."

Suddenly realizing that she was fully naked, she ground down on his cock, rubbing her clit through his shorts. The friction from the material caused goose bumps to run along her arms.

"That would be good." He kissed his way along her jaw and to her mouth. When their lips met, she whimpered as his hands pulled her hips harder onto his cock.

"Wrap your legs around and lock them," he demanded softly, breaking the kiss.

She did, and he stood up. His hands left her hips to pull down his shorts and underwear. Then he sat back down on the bed and impaled her with his thick cock at the same time.

His gaze caught her nipples, and his head dipped, taking one into his mouth. He grabbed her hips and set a fast rhythm, lifting her up and slamming her down. He was basically jerking off with her body, and she loved every minute of it.

Every time he slid deep she quivered. Every time he pulled out, she clenched as she tried to keep him inside. Her breast popped out of his mouth, and he buried his head in the crook of her neck.

She gasped as he nipped softly on her shoulder. There were star bursts behind her eyes as she orgasmed. She moaned as he kept slamming her down, moving through her orgasm and making it build higher and higher until he stilled beneath her.

Wrapping her arms around his back, she held him tight as he pumped inside her, her own muscles twitching in response.

As their breathing slowed, he kissed up the side of her neck. She giggled when his five o'clock shadow scratched a sensitive spot. He leaned back with a grin, catching her eyes. His were glazed and happy.

She took a certain amount of pride in putting that look on his face.

He blinked several times, as if wakening from a dream. "Congratulations on your interview. I can't wait to see how we celebrate you getting the job." He smirked and kneaded her ass.

She giggled and slapped him on the bicep. She started to pull up off him, but he held her secure.

"Want to take a shower?" he asked, wagging his eyebrows.

She laughed and pushed off him. He let her go this time, his hands staying on her hips as she found her legs shaky.

"I'd love to take a shower. Did you say you made dinner? What time is it?"

He shrugged and looked around her to the clock on the wall. "Almost five-thirty. What time do you need to be home?"

Walking towards the open door of the bathroom, she shrugged. She could feel his eyes on her ass, and it made her warm inside. He followed her as she started the water for the shower.

"Not quite sure. Cody will get out of soccer practice at six. Then I guess Mom will take the boys to church at seven." She tested the temperature of the water.

"Do you normally go to church on Wednesday nights?" He pulled his shorts and boxer briefs down and tossed them into the hamper.

It blew her mind that they were standing here having a

random conversation while naked when a month ago she didn't even know he existed. She was just so… at home with him, although that didn't quite describe it fully. It was more than that.

She felt the water's temperature again and stepped inside. He sat in the chair outside the door and rolled down his sleeve for his leg, pulling it off. He stood and hopped inside, using the arm rail as he made his way to the built-in bench.

She stood in the spray as he sat, his hands sliding up and down her thighs as she ran her hands through her hair to wash it.

"I expected this to be awkward." He said after a few moments of silence. She opened her eyes and met his blue smiling gaze. She smiled and cupped his face with her hands.

"I did too, but it's like we've been doing this for years." She kissed him lightly on the lips.

He reached up and grabbed her palms with his hands, turning and kissing the center of first one, then the other. "This feels right, Cindy. With you… I don't feel broken. I'm complete. Whole. Home."

Her heart skipped a beat. She had thought the same thing about him feeling like home, but it was too soon. They couldn't rush into this. She simply nodded and leaned forward to kiss him more deeply.

His hands ran along her back and down to her ass. She gasped as he squeezed, and she pulled back with a laugh.

"No more, Andy. Not today. We need to slow down." She lathered up her hair.

He grinned and shrugged as he reached for the shampoo. They talked about her work schedule for the week and finalized their Halloween weekend plans. Stepping out before her, he dried off and put his leg back on with a snap.

When he walked naked out to his bathroom to grab clean clothes and check on dinner, she sighed. Showering with him and talking was an eye opener. There was no shame or self-consciousness between them. And she loved that while they talked naked, there were no secrets between them either. No secrets, no barriers.

She could see herself falling for him, and if she were totally honest with herself, she was already halfway there.

But was it the flash in the pan kind or the last forever kind? She rinsed her body as she thought back to her previous encounters with the exes.

Cody's dad, well, they'd still been kids. Raging hormones played more of a factor than any feelings of love. He'd been sexy in a gothic, depressed, drummer boy kind of way. They'd fooled around, but when she found out she was pregnant, he'd ghosted her.

Both times it had hurt. She hadn't climaxed at all. With Jerry… she frowned. She couldn't help but compare Andy to him, but it was like comparing watermelons to blueberries. With the watermelon, she couldn't wait to sink her teeth into Andy. The more she ate, the more she wanted it.

With the blueberries, they'd been bitter. Like they'd been under-ripe or picked too soon. And they were so easily bruised. Jerry had gotten his feelings hurt a lot. When that happened, it hadn't been pretty. She frowned, thinking of how Jerry had made her feel.

The woman he'd made her into… she wasn't that woman anymore. Her spine straightened. She wasn't insignificant or useless. Now, she was independent, even though it took her two jobs to take care of her family.

She smiled, thinking of her interview. If she got the job,

she could quit both her current ones. It'd replace her income and even give her a bit more.

She hoped the hours were during the day. As she turned off the water, she saw Andy had set a clean towel on the chair. She smiled at the thoughtful gesture. He was really kind, making her dinner, taking her shopping, getting her a clean towel. It was the little things Jerry had never done.

She wrapped the towel around herself and walked to the bedroom to find her clothes. But after searching, she realized her shirt and bra were still in the living room by the door.

Spying the master closet, she walked towards it and found the stack of neatly folded t-shirts. Slipping on a dark green one, she heard voices down the hall.

Shifting on her feet, she worried on what to do. She didn't want to just waltz out. There wasn't exactly shame over her hook-up with Andy, but she didn't really want to advertise what she'd been doing here. Heaven forbid, it could be one of the church ladies out there. She could be fired from the PTA position.

She took a deep breath to calm her nerves and walked to the bathroom to towel off her hair and brush it. She threw the dirty towels into the hamper and tidied up before going to listen at the door. There were still multiple voices outside.

Sitting on the edge of the bed, she pulled out her phone to text Maryanne and her mom in the group text.

How are the boys?
How was soccer?
Are y'all going to church?

Soccer was good.

*We're on our way to church now. We ate leftover fried chicken that
Mom made yesterday.
It was so good.*

*Dang it!
I love that fried chicken!
Did you save me any?*

*Nope. The boys were extra hungry tonight.
I'll make you some next week, hun.
Did you get a bostume?*

Cindy smiled at the typo. Her mom was not the best at texting but she was still better than most of her generation.

I did. A Cleopatra one.

*Oh! I can't wait to see it!
We moved your car back to the apartment btw.
You coming to church tonight or just want us to bring the boys home later?
Stay out with Andy longer. Is it going well?*

*Not sure about church.
He cooked dinner and we're about to eat.*

😊
Yay!

She sighed with a smile. The fact that both her mom and sister approved of Andy meant more than anything. They'd not liked either of the exes, which just showed that she needed to trust their judgement over her own.

So far, she was glad she'd trusted them about this today. How could she regret the best sex of her life? Standing up, she walked to the door again.

She listened. No voices now. As she walked out, Andy walked in through the front door and locked it behind him.

Meeting him in the kitchen, he grabbed a large spoon. "Aunt Suzie stopped by. I wasn't sure what to do, so I just got rid of her as quick as I could."

"What'd she say?" She slid into her chair at the table. He scooped a casserole onto two plates and added a slice of French toast before bringing it to her.

"She wanted me to take Mandy trick or treating. I told her I was going to the Williams' party, but she said to just bring Mandy home to her first." He went back into the kitchen and grabbed some waters.

"Oh, Owen will love trick or treating with her! I've heard nothing but her name for weeks now. He's thrilled to have her in his daycare class." She picked up a fork, the chicken and cheesy rice scent making her mouth water. He held his hand up on the table, and she placed hers in his with a smile and bowed her head.

"Thank you, God, for teaching me how to cook and for Cindy taking a chance on me. Amen." His prayer was simple, but she blushed as she let go of his hand. Even after the sex, his touch still sent a thrill through her body.

"You cooked this? It's fantastic."

"Thanks," he replied after he swallowed. "I got a little tired of reheating all the meal train food, and I enjoy cooking. One of my first jobs was as a chef in a little restaurant in Dallas."

"Oh cool! My first job was as a waitress," she said, taking another bite. They talked about growing up and their teenage years as they ate. Occasionally his knee would nudge hers under the table, and she'd feel a pull toward him, like the physical touch just pulled the emotional connection tighter.

When they'd finished eating, they took their plates to the kitchen sink where he rinsed them off and placed them in the dishwasher as she wiped down the table. "How long did you live with Suzie growing up?" She asked.

He led her to the living room where they sat on the couch side by side. He reached out and wrapped his arm along the back of the couch, drawing her closer to his side. The hand on her shoulder drew lazy circles on her shirt as his other hand reached across his body and held hers.

"From fourth grade to tenth grade. Every summer I had to go to Dallas and stay with my mom. That summer was the worst, and I got into some trouble. They sent me to military school after that, and I only came home for two weeks at Christmas and two weeks at the 4th of July." His voice grew softer as he looked away.

She leaned her head on his chest and yawned. "What kind of trouble?"

He sighed as he wrapped a curl around his finger. "My mom was a drug addict. Her dealer came around, and she didn't have the money. I walked in on her... paying him on her back, but he had her pinned down. So I beat him up and tossed him out. The cops showed up and took both of us to jail. I was a week from turning fifteen, and I think Uncle Mike knew someone who knew someone because they offered me a choice. It was juvie or military school." He blurted, his words running together.

"That's terrible! I can't imagine how scary that must have been for you. You were still a kid!" she mumbled. He nuzzled the top of her head, and she rubbed her cheek on his chest. "What happened to your mom?"

"No clue. I haven't seen or heard from her since. Aunt Suzie says she's dead, but no one has produced a body or an obituary report or anything," he said frankly.

"How do you feel about the not knowing?" She asked, burrowing deeper onto his chest and offering what comfort she could. He shrugged slightly, making her head move.

"Relieved that I don't have to see her every summer. I always dreaded summer breaks while all the other kids looked forward to it."

She nodded, and they sat in comfortable silence for a while.

Later, she opened her eyes and blinked. A soft light glowed from the kitchen, illuminating Andy. She was sprawled on the couch almost on top of him, his arms wrapped around her. She glanced at the clock on the tv and winced. It was nearly ten o'clock!

She tried to ease up but his arms wrapped around hers once more. He was frowning in his sleep, his eyes closed and a wrinkle on his forehead.

She leaned down and kissed his rough cheek, the dark stubble making him appear to have sharper edges in the near darkness.

His eyes fluttered open, and his sleepy gaze met hers. She saw the awareness come into them as he recognized her, and he whispered, "Cindy."

He pulled her down and their lips met. She sighed and relaxed. She wasn't going home anytime soon.

Chapter Twenty-Five

"I'm sorry, Maggie. But I need to switch Andy with a different PTA," Cindy said the next day. She was on the phone watching Owen at the playground but this had been nagging at the back of her brain since she'd woken up.

"I'm sorry, dear. But the new PTA already has a full case load. We can't switch it less than 24 hours out. Are you alright? Are the boys sick?" She was so sweet to ask. It almost made Cindy feel guilty about needing to quit and find a better job.

Cindy sighed, rubbing her forehead. "We're alright. It's just—Andy asked me out, and I want to say yes."

"Oh. Oh my, alright. Well, you can't do that while he's your patient. Oh, of course! That's why you're trying to switch him to someone else. Alright, well, tell him to wait a week. You need to do his therapy tomorrow. I'll find someone else before next Friday, alright?"

Cindy breathed a sigh of relief as she replied and hung up. She chewed her lip and glanced at her watch. "Only about fifteen minutes left, Owen!"

Hands wrapped around her eyes from behind as a soft voice said, "Guess who?" The scent of cinnamon and sugar filled her nose, making her stomach growl.

"My favorite sister in the entire world," she laughed. Maryanne came around the bench. Today her black jeans were ripped, and she wore heeled lace up black boots with a tight purple t-shirt that read *"I eat dudes like you for breakfast"* and had a picture of a cartoonish zombie girl. Her hair was piled into a messy bun, and she grinned as she plopped down next to Cindy.

"Whatcha doin'?" She turned and crossed a leg over her knee, bopping it up and down.

Cindy smiled and shrugged, turning to the playground. "Watching Owen play before going to get the boys from school. What are you up to today?"

"Finding you so you can dish on the date yesterday." Maryanne grinned, and Cindy's cheeks heated. Her sister squealed and pushed her softly on the arm. "Oh, tell me it had a happy ending! Please, oh please!"

Cindy laughed, hands going to her cheeks as she shook her head. "You're crazy!"

Maryanne smirked and leaned toward her, brown eyes meeting hazel ones. "But I'm right, right?"

Cindy's mouth tipped up in a secretive smile as she glanced down and away. Maryanne squealed again and grabbed her hand to squeeze.

"Tell me everything! No, wait. Wait for girl's night tonight. Then tell all of us." She practically bounced up and down on the bench.

Cindy leaned forward and grabbed her sister's hand. "Absolutely not, M. I'll tell *you* but you can't tell anyone, not even the girls at girl's night. I had to tell Maggie that he's asked me out. If she finds out we started fooling around while he's still my patient, I'll be fired. Tell me you won't talk to *anyone* about this."

Maryanne huffed and sat back, crossing her arms. "Fine," she said, making Cindy smile as she thought about the night she'd met Andy when everything was 'fine.'

"You'd better tell me now, because the boys have to be picked up soon." Maryanne arched to her eyebrow, her foot still bobbing.

Cindy rolled her eyes and sat back to watch Owen some more. "We went to the Halloween store and—well, I gave him a blow job in the changing room."

"You did *what?*" Maryanne yelled loudly, catching Owen's attention. He waved at his aunt, but she didn't see him. Her eyes were bugging out, wider than Cindy had ever seen them.

She laughed, one hand on her cheek as she said, "Oh my God, you should see your face right now!"

Maryanne blinked as she lowered her voice and leaned in closer. "So you didn't give him a blow job in the store?"

Cindy smirked and whispered, "Oh, I so did."

Maryanne sat back on the bench, stunned into silence. Cindy enjoyed it. She didn't shock her sister often. Usually it was the other way around. After a few moments, Maryanne asked, "Wow. How did that happen? What happened after that? You didn't come home until nearly midnight last night."

"We went back to his place and had sex." She shrugged, trying to be nonchalant but feeling her cheeks burn in embarrassment.

Maryanne grabbed her face and turned Cindy so she could look in her eyes. Cindy rolled her eyes but her sister wouldn't let her go. She refused to release her cheeks and held her still as she asked, "And how was it?"

Cindy blinked, her gaze going hazy as she thought back to the three bouts of sex yesterday. She grinned, her mouth pushing against Maryanne's hands. Maryanne gasped and leaned back, letting go of her face. "That good?"

"It was the best I've ever had," Cindy said dreamily as she pictured that last time. Slow paced but gentle, he built her up to the hardest orgasm of the night.

Maryanne snorted. "Best out of three isn't saying much."

Cindy frowned and slapped her sister's arm. "Don't be a hater. It was... well, imagine the best chocolate cake you've ever tasted. But every time you taste it, it tastes better than the last until you can't imagine eating any other cake in your entire life... it's like that."

Maryanne blinked at her in shock, and Cindy shrugged. Her sister's language was food, being an excellent baker. She understood the metaphor.

"Is it love?" she asked softly.

Cindy frowned as she thought about it. "I might not know what love is, exactly. I mean the exes weren't much to measure up to, but Andy blows them out of the water."

They sat in silence, watching Owen play. He waved from the top of the jungle gym at someone across the playground. She spied Mandy running toward Owen, and Cindy's heart beat faster as she hoped it was Andy.

She sighed in disappointment as Suzie circled the playground towards them.

"This should be interesting," Maryanne mumbled.

"Don't say anything, do you hear me?" Cindy whispered furiously, a false smile on her face as the woman neared. She was wearing a bright orange pencil skirt today with a black t-shirt. It had a skeleton playing guitar on it.

Maryanne nodded to her shirt. "Hi Suzie! Love the shirt!"

"Thanks, dear! I love yours too! Where did you get it?" She nodded to each of the girls before sliding onto the bench beside Maryanne. They talked about their favorite online retailers while Cindy watched Owen and Mandy play.

"What are your plans for trick-or-treating with the boys?" Suzie asked. Cindy glanced over as Maryanne leaned back and looked at her expectantly.

"We're going to have a potluck at my apartment complex about six-thirty. Then we'll go door to door," she smiled. "What about you and Mandy?" she asked, knowing perfectly well what Andy had said last night about it.

Suzie waved a hand that sparkled from all the rings. "Oh, Andy's going to take Mandy around to the nursing home, I think. Maybe she and Owen can meet up. She's excited to show off her costume at school tomorrow."

Cindy laughed as she said, "Owen too. I just hope he keeps it clean. Last year I had to do a fast wash so he could wear it for trick-or-treating. At least this year, I'll be able to wash it overnight instead of same day."

Suzie nodded, sitting primly with hands on her lap. "Last year, we were in D.C. and there was an enormous trunk or treat at the church we went to. She fell asleep in her costume! Sticky mess and all!" She laughed.

"Where was Andy?" Maryanne asked. Cindy was glad she'd asked because she was curious too.

Suzie frowned as she replied, "He couldn't handle the crowds at that point. He had just been released from the hospital to the in-patient rehabilitation center. We visited him for trick-or-treating before going to the church. He was so withdrawn and sullen... but these past few weeks, he's really come out of his shell. Much more than I would have thought."

Cindy glanced at Maryanne, who winked, before looking at Suzie. Suzie kept her eyes on the kids on the playground so Cindy faced forward and said nothing. Maybe she had a suspicion, but the less they talked about it, the better at this point. The alarm on her phone went off.

"Owen, time to go get your brothers!" she called out.

His little head popped out of the tube and he whined, "Awwww. Do we have to? Mandy just got here!"

Maryanne said softly, "I can stay with him a while."

Cindy reached out and squeezed her sister's hand. "Thanks, sis. I appreciate it. Can you have him home by five? That way we can eat before going to yoga?" Maryanne nodded and Cindy stood, slinging her purse over her should. "Alright, Owen, Auntie M is going to stay with you, but be good."

"Yay!" he whooped from inside the tube.

"It was nice seeing you, Suzie, as always," Cindy said. Suzie nodded and smiled. She didn't feel any of the attitude from that night in the hospital. Maybe Suzie had forgotten about it. She let it go as she walked to get the boys.

A few hours later, they all sat down at the kitchen table to eat. James had finished a book report and won an award for the most read books that month.

Owen's tooth was even more loose, and Cody had gotten in trouble at lunch for accidentally dropping his tray and sending it spraying onto a teacher. Maryanne told of a new dessert she'd come up with. The boys ate quickly, knowing that Auntie M brought samples of the new sweet.

Sure enough, the little cream puffed pastries came out of the fridge and into their little mouths. They practically melted on the tongue.

She wanted to save a few for Andy so she placed some in a baggie and put them in the fridge. When they were ready, they all headed out for girl's night at the yoga studio.

The next day, she knocked on the door, but no one answered. She turned and looked around behind her. He wasn't jogging up the driveway like he had a few weeks ago. She listened but didn't hear any sounds from inside. She spun slowly back around and tried the handle of the door.

It opened, and she stepped inside. "Andy?" she called softly. All the lights were off in the house. Frowning, she wondered where he could be. She shut the door softly and set her bag down by the couch.

She tiptoed down the hall, peering into the other bedroom doors that were opened. All three of them were empty. His bedroom door was cracked, so she pushed it open slowly.

The blinds were closed, and the lights were off. The faint light let in from the hallway shone on the bed, where his rumpled form was twisted up in the blankets. She closed the door behind her and walked across the room towards him. Even in the faint light, she could tell his shoulders were drenched in sweat.

Frowning, she reached out a hand to smooth down the dark, matted hair on the back of his head and said softly, "Andy? Are you alright?"

He moaned and turned his head toward her. His hand came out from under the covers as he groaned, "Cindy? What time is it?"

"It's ten-thirty. It's time for your PT session. What's wrong?" She stroked his head.

He groaned some more and pushed up onto his forearms, his biceps bulging. He flopped back down on his stomach with a moan. "Nightmares. Migraine. Couldn't sleep."

"Oh, alright. Let me text my boss and tell her you didn't answer the door. I'll let you get back to sleep."

"No, stay." He reached over and grabbed her hand like a drowning man after a life raft. "Will you just—stay?"

She nodded, as she kicked off her shoes and got her phone out of her pocket to text Maggie. She set the timer on it for an hour and set it on the bedside table as she crawled into bed with him.

He wrapped his arms around her, spooning her, and sighed. She stroked his arm and linked their fingers together.

She didn't think she'd be able to take a nap, but she must have. Her eyes popped wide open as her alarm sounded, and she reached for it quickly and silenced it.

He was still spooning her but his breathing was deep and even. She slid out of the bed and grabbed her phone and shoes. Tiptoeing out, she shut the door softly and went to the kitchen. She checked the fridge and noted that he still had some of the casserole from last night.

She grabbed the puff pastries from her bag and slipped them into the fridge. Finding a notepad with a grocery list on the side of it, she ripped the page under it out and found a pen from her bag. She wrote him a note and left, shutting the front door behind her.

Chapter Twenty-Six

Cindy went to work at the hospital early that afternoon and barely got a break for the next twenty-four hours. She stumbled home around noon on Saturday to find the boys already hyped up on candy, and Maryanne baking in the kitchen. Her stress skyrocketed at the noise.

Maryanne glanced over her shoulder as she kicked off her shoes by the front door. "Hey, you're home! Let me pop this in the oven, then I'll take the boys to go run off some of that energy in about half an hour."

"Perfect. I'm going to go take a shower," she yawned.

Maryanne nodded, "I'll tell you when I head out with the boys. You take a nap until about five, alright? Then we'll get ready and head down for the potluck."

"Sounds good." Cindy walked to her bathroom. When she got out of the hot shower, the house was quiet and Maryanne's text said they'd headed out. She threw on the green t-shirt that she still had from Andy's house from Wednesday and fell into bed.

She breathed deep, loving that the shirt still smelled like

him. She imagined him spooning her like yesterday and fell into a dreamless sleep.

When she woke, Owen and Mandy's faces stared at her from less than two feet away. She groaned and rolled over, making them both giggle as Andy came into the room and whispered loudly, "You guys get out of here! You're not supposed to wake up Sleeping Beauty like that!"

Mandy and Owen danced around the bed singing, "Kiss the princess. Kill the princess."

Andy rounded the bed and tilted her onto her back. He leaned in before he kissed her softly on the lips. Cindy's eyes flew open, and Mandy and Owen whooped, "Hooray! Sleeping Beauty's awake!"

Andy pulled back, staring down at her with his bright blue eyes so full of promise. The kids' little feet carried them out of the room, and the sound faded.

Andy lowered his head and swept his tongue into her mouth. She groaned and melted, lazily sliding her tongue along his before he broke the kiss. She opened her eyes and saw his smiling face close to hers.

"I think they're wrong. You're not Sleeping Beauty. You're Sleepy from Snow White," he teased. She snorted, sitting up and rubbing her eyes.

"What are you doing here? What time is it?" She caught him staring with hunger at her nipples, hard and perky against the t-shirt.

"Is that my t-shirt? I've been looking for that one. It looks even better on you." He grinned, tucking a stray curl behind her ear even as his eyes turned predatory.

She blushed and swung her legs out of the bed. He ran a hand up her thigh, groaning when he found her pantiless. She gasped as he slid a finger along her clit before he jerked himself back and walked toward the door stiffly.

She stood next to the bed and stared at him blankly. He leaned against the door jamb to her bedroom and glanced behind him in the hall before looking back at her.

"It's about five-thirty, and we're ready to go downstairs for the potluck. We thought we'd meet over here early and head down with you."

"How'd you find my apartment? I thought I told you seven?" She grabbed her costume bag from on top of her dresser and walked to her bathroom.

"I texted Maryanne and asked," he said. He followed her to the bathroom and shut the door. Leaning against it, he glanced around at her shower/tub combo and a single sink with a long counter.

She shivered at the predatory look in his eyes as he locked the bathroom door behind him. She licked her lips and whispered, "But the kids—"

"Are with Maryanne. And we'll be quick," he said, grabbing her hand and pulling her gently to the bathroom sink. He grabbed her around the waist and lifted her up easily.

She gasped as the cold counter hit her ass, making her grab his biceps. Then he gently stroked her clit. She squirmed on the counter and leaned back slightly, her head and shoulders on the wall behind her.

He dipped a finger inside and moaned. "God, you're so wet." He flicked the button on his jeans and ripped the zipper down.

Pulling his hand away, she whined until she saw he was pulling his pants down. He grabbed his cock and pumped once, lining up with her before easing himself home.

It seemed like it'd been a hundred years since they'd last had sex. She gasped as he filled her up slowly, letting her adjust to his size. When he was all the way inside, she met his gaze, his eyes hazy with lust. He gripped her hips and shifted his hips. "Ready?"

She bit her lip and nodded. He pulled out and slammed back into her, making her gasp. His hands on her hips held her still as she wrapped her legs around his waist and held on. He couldn't pull out like he wanted though, so he slid his arms under her knees and held them out, pumping wildly back and forth.

She clenched, gasping and arching her back. It was too much. Too hard, too fast, too everything. She felt it in every cell of her body. Way too quickly, she was crying out as her orgasm swept over her. She was still spasming when he gasped and swelled within her, spilling inside.

He leaned forward and kissed her slowly. The tenderness he showed her was like none she'd ever had before. It made her feel loved and cherished. Is that what this was? Her heart skipped a beat in excitement but her head denied it. No, she couldn't be *in love*. Not yet, it was too soon.

He slid out and set her legs down gently, helping her stand. He turned on the bathroom sink and washed himself off before pulling his pants up.

She stood there watching him. Her heart still raced as he kissed her and buttoned his jeans.

"I'll be right back with my costume. Then we'll get changed, alright?"

She nodded as he left the bathroom. Had she really had sex with her kids in the apartment? Did that make her a terrible mom?

She really had no basis to judge that on though. Did other single moms do this kind of thing? She had no one to ask. All her friends were single and kid-less. No wonder she felt like a workaholic outcast in their group sometimes.

She cleaned up, then slipped off the t-shirt. Pulling the

Cleopatra costume out, she slipped it over her head. The bathroom door opened. She pulled her head through the neck in time to see Andy's head bend down and his mouth latch onto a nipple.

It was like an electric wire ran from her nipple to her pussy at his touch.

"Andy!"

He chuckled as he released it, then kissed the other one with a quick nip.

"I like how you say my name," he winked. Giggling, she pulled the dress down and adjusted it.

For her makeup, she did Egyptian eye liner. Then she fixed her hair, so it didn't look so much like bed head.

She kept catching glimpses of him in the mirror as she worked. He made her feel so desired and wanted, whether she was in a big t-shirt or dolled up like this.

He pulled his shirt over his head and his muscles bulged. She admired the view before he pulled on the red cape and snapped it in place.

Sitting on the closed toilet seat, he pulled the jeans off his prosthetic foot.

She frowned as she finished her makeup. "I didn't even think about your leg with that costume. Are you alright showing it off in public?"

"Hmm? Oh, yeah it's fine. I got used to it in D.C. when I'd go running in the summer. Although, it didn't get much of a second glance there. I am uneasy about it, but this is my hometown. If I can't be myself here, then where can I be?"

She nodded and smiled. Turning around, she leaned against the counter and watched him strap on the gladiator sandals, wrapping the straps all the way up his calves.

"Did you try those on? Are you able to walk in them?" she asked.

He rolled his eyes as he stood up. "Yes, Cindy. Since I slept through our PT session yesterday, I put them on and actually walked to the mailbox and back in them. I'll be fine."

She pursed her lips and crossed her arms. "Fine, but if they get too uncomfortable or something, let me know. We can work with it, or we'll leave early or something."

"Yes, ma'am," he pulled her arms down and wrapped her in a hug. "I like that you worry about me. It means you care."

"I do care," she said into his bare chest. She breathed deeply, smelling that sweat and leather that she loved.

"I know you do. You care about everyone and their dog," he chuckled. Was she really that obvious? "But it makes me feel like you care about me as something more, as someone special."

She pulled back and looked into his eyes. They were vulnerable, his teasing smile hiding the worry she saw. She smiled and rubbed her hand on his cheek, feeling that five o'clock shadow scratch her hand in the best way.

He kissed it as she said, "You're special, Andy, and I care about you, not just as a patient, but as *you*."

"Like, you care about me as boyfriend/girlfriend type of caring?" He kissed her hand again.

She nodded and put her hand on his chest. "Yes, but we can't call it that until you're no longer my PT patient, alright?"

He sighed but nodded. He grabbed her hand, and they walked out of the bathroom.

Chapter Twenty-Seven

They passed Owen and Mandy playing in the boys' room. In the living room, James and Cody were playing a video game, so they headed into the kitchen.

"There you two are. And don't you look adorable, all matchy matchy." Maryanne was dressed as a sexy witch, her black dress sleek and form fitting. The slit on the side of her dress went to the crease of her hip and her black high-heeled boots came up to above her knees.

"Separately, you both slay, but together? Hot damn, you're a smoking hot couple." Maryanne winked, making Andy chuckle.

Cindy looked into the living room and held her hands out. "Sh, the kids might hear you."

Andy looked at her, the confusion clear on his face. "Mandy and Owen saw us kiss, and Cody knows I'm in like with you. I think they get it."

Cindy bit her lip and sighed. "Maybe so. Between wanting to do right by them and needing to keep my jobs, it's a little stressful start for me."

Andy took her hand and kissed the back of it. "But it'll be worth it."

She sighed, some of her tension floating away at his touch. When she was with him, the things that normally stressed her out seemed alright. "I hope so, but for now, if anyone asks, we're just friends, alright? At least until I get you moved to another PTA."

Andy's lips pursed, but he didn't try to argue.

"Don't mind me. I'll just take this food downstairs after slaving away on it all day." Sarcasm dripped from her sister's voice, but the look on her face just made Cindy laugh. She stepped over and hugged her.

"Thank you for getting all the food done and for watching the boys while I took a nap. I don't know how I would've made it this far without you. Not only are you the best sister, but tonight, you're the sexiest witch in town. Let's get this party started, shall we?"

"That's the spirit!" Maryanne said. "I'll go ahead and take this down, if y'all will get the rest?"

In a burst of energy, Mandy bounced into the hall, the extra tutu under her Batgirl costume making it extra poofy. Owen followed on her heels, his new Spider-man costume slightly hanging on his tiny frame, but not so much that he was going to trip in it.

"Mama, Mama, next year, I wanna be Batman, okay? And Mandy's going to be Batgirl so we can match." He barely paused for breath before continuing to outline their costume plans. Cindy helped him get his shoes on while Andy helped Mandy. James saved their video game, and Cody put his controller up. After they all slipped on their shoes, Cindy and Andy grabbed the spider cupcakes with Twizzler legs and the tray of white chocolate ghost strawberries to take downstairs for the potluck.

The apartment buildings had just four units each, two on top and two on bottom. In between two of the buildings, fold out tables were decorated in plastic orange and purple table cloths, food covering every spare inch already. Mandy and Owen immediately ran to the two metal swing sets while some kids played basketball on the single hoop court. Maryanne was already talking with the other adults mingling around the food.

Cindy introduced Andy to their neighbors, and he shook hands. One was an old retired teacher who had been in the Navy during the Vietnam War. She left them to talk military as she helped with the food.

"He seems nice," Mrs. Willowby said as she set a meat and cheese tray next on the table and nodded to Andy. "How long have y'all been dating?"

"Oh, we're not dating. We're just friends. He's new in town, so I'm showing him around." Her cheeks heated, and she turned away to rearrange the food so everything would fit.

Mrs. Willowby chuckled. "Uh-huh. Sure."

Kate slid up next to her, one hand propped on her hip. "Darlin' if you're not dating that hunk of meat, I'm gonna go after him. Women like us don't get a chance at prime Kobe beef like that every day."

This year, Kate wore a low cut princess dress, too short for someone of her fifty years. She ran the biggest hair salon in town, but her niece, Katie, owned the bar. Kate could usually be found there on the weekends, hunting for a younger man who could keep up with her.

Cindy clenched her jaw at the thought of Kate setting her sights on Andy, but she tried to play it cool as she shrugged. "You'll have to ask him. Like I said, we're just friends."

She averted her gaze as Kate sauntered over to the two men lounging at the picnic table. Every fiber of her being wanted to intervene, to assert her claim on Andy, but she was bound by her own words for another week. Her stomach churned with anxiety that she might lose him to the alluring charms of Kate. She took a deep breath and popped a strawberry into her mouth. If he was so easily turned by a pretty face, no matter how old, then she didn't want him anyway.

The familiar knot of worry annoyed her, and she pushed it aside as Maryanne whistled and called everyone over. After they said grace, the elders got their food and the rest of the neighbors lined up on both sides of the tables. Many had already set up camping chairs in semi-circles around the picnic tables. Most of the kids took their plates to the basketball court and sat down in groups.

As Cindy made Owen a plate, Andy came up behind her and ran a hand up her forearm. "There you are. Your neighbors are pretty good people. One question though. What do I make for Mandy's plate?"

He stared at the table with a bewildered look, eyebrows raised, and the knot in her stomach dissipated as she chuckled.

"Just give her all the same things that I've got here for Owen. Those two are peas in a pod, so they'll probably only want the same things and refuse to eat the same things."

They took the plates over to the basketball court and placed them next to James and Cody, who sat with a group of other kids. Cindy called the two youngest off the swings, and they jumped off and raced over. Andy came back with two juices, the straws already popped into them and ready to drink.

Andy's fingers grazed hers as they walked back to the

tables to fix their own plates. Cindy linked their pinkies together, wishing she could hold his hand openly like they'd done at the store in Denton this week. Thoughts of Kate were gone. Somehow, when she was with Andy, he made her feel like the only woman in the world. She smiled as they sat on the picnic bench and made small talk with the adults nearest them.

The rest of the evening was loud but mostly due to laughing as they went door to door at the apartment complex then down the street. Eventually they all piled into Cindy's SUV and went to the nursing home and visited them too. Cindy was really proud of the way the kids were patient and respectful to the residents there.

"Okay, where to next?" She asked, sliding into the driver's seat. Cody and James buckled in the back row while Maryanne helped Mandy and Owen with theirs in the middle.

Andy glanced back at Mandy from the passenger seat and saw her yawn. "Looks like Batgirl's ready to go home. Let's go to Suzie and Mike's house next."

"Then we can head to Mom's with the boys. They're going to stay over with her, since she'll take them to church in the morning anyway," Cindy said, starting the SUV and pulling onto the road. She turned the music all the way down as the kids' chatter flowed all around. James and Cody were bickering about who got the most candy while Owen and Mandy were singing the Wheels on the Bus and making up lyrics. It was loud, chaotic, and filled her heart with so much joy, she just smiled and soaked it all up.

Andy gave her directions to a large ranch house a few minutes outside of town. As they parked, the knot of anxiety returned, and she took a deep breath. What would Suzie say about all of them here? Logically, Cindy knew she knew they were together, but the woman didn't know they were *together*.

"We're here," Mandy called, clapping as Maryanne unbuckled her. "Gamma's house, Gamma's house."

Andy opened his door then the back door, helping Mandy and then Owen out of the SUV. "Let's make this the best trick or treat yet," he said, offering a hand to Maryanne as well. Cindy smiled, probably a goofy smile, at how much of a gentleman he was.

They all tromped up the front steps to knock on the door. It swung open to reveal Suzie dressed in a regular Wonder Woman costume. Thank God it was a more conservative version than the sexy ones they'd seen at the costume store.

As the group of children shouted, "Trick or treat," Suzie's eyes scanned over their costumes, a smile on her face and hands on her hips.

"Well, who do we have here? A soldier! Thank you for your service, sir."

She saluted Cody and reached for a large bowl of candy on a nearby table. Carefully, she dropped three pieces into his bag. Cody's grin widened as he saluted back and thanked her before retreating back into the night with his loot.

"Spider-Man! I'm surprised to see your feet on the ground, Spider-Man. You be sure to not go jumping off of buildings tonight, alright? It's more dangerous at night," she said, dropping a handful of candy into Owen's bag as he giggled. He made the *pew pew* Spidey hands and did a hop back down the sidewalk to where Cody waited.

"Batgirl! Well, you certainly look familiar. Didn't I see you saving some kids over at the playground the other day?" She dropped a handful into Mandy's bag.

Mandy giggled and pulled off her mask. "Gamma! It's me! Mandy!"

Suzie placed a hand on her heart as she cried, "Mandy! My goodness! I didn't realize that was you! Well, give Owen a hug goodbye then go show Papa your costume. I bet you fool him too!"

Mandy skipped down and hugged Owen before turning and slipping in behind her, swinging her bag of candy and calling for her Papa. A tug on Cindy's chest made her sigh, since her boys didn't have a Papa to talk to anymore.

Suzie glanced around, frowning as she said, "I could have sworn there was another trick or treater here who wanted candy, but I can't seem to find him..."

James laughed as he popped out from behind Cindy and made a 'hee-yah' karate chopping move to present his bag of candy. Suzie laughed as she dropped the last of her candy into his bag. "Oh there you are! A karate master, are you?"

He shook his head and hunched his shoulders, his shyness peeking through again. "No, ma'am, I'm a ninja!" Then he did a roundhouse kick as he went down the sidewalk back toward the SUV.

Maryanne, Andy, and Cindy stood on the doorstep with Suzie, who narrowed her eyes at their costumes. Andy stepped forward and kissed his aunt's cheek. "Mandy was really great tonight. She ate good at the potluck and didn't whine at all, even when we told her it was time to go home."

Suzie sniffed, her eyes misting, but all she said was, "She's usually pretty good around Owen. He brings out the best in her."

"She brings out the best in him too," Cindy said with a smile. "Thanks for letting her trick-or-treat with us tonight."

Suzie glanced at the SUV as James and Cody helped Owen pile in. "Y'all off to the Williams' shindig?"

"Yeah, we're going to stop by Mama's first," Maryanne said.

Suzie patted her sister on the arm. "What a sweet daughter you are. Say hi to your mama for me!" She waved as they turned and walked back toward the SUV, Cindy's lips pursed as she replayed Suzie's words over and over.

Maryanne climbed into the back seat and helped Owen buckle again. At the image of her kids in the rearview mirror, Cindy decided to let it go.

Cindy breathed a sigh of relief. "That went well. I don't think Suzie suspects, despite our matching outfits." Once everyone was buckled, she backed out of the driveway.

"I don't think you have to worry about that," Maryanne said from the backseat.

"Oh? Why's that?" Cindy turned onto another highway, trying to hear over the arguing in the very back as Cody and James compared bags of candy.

"Suzie thinks I'm the one seeing Andy," Maryanne said casually. Andy looked over and caught her eye, blinking in confusion.

Then he turned and looked at Maryanne and said, "What do you mean, she thinks you're the one dating me?"

Maryanne sighed and shrugged. "Well, we were at the park Thursday after Cindy went to pick up the boys, and she was asking some rather personal questions about my previous dating history. I think she talked to Mrs. Williams after that soccer game and bake sale."

"Ohhh," he said, "And I've been going to all the soccer games, including the one from this morning, and sitting by you."

"Yep," she said. "It probably threw her off a bit to see

you two matching, but it'll be ok." Cindy had none of the same jealousy with her sister as she'd had earlier with Kate. They'd become closer as adults, and she was literally her best friend.

She didn't like the idea of anyone with Andy, much less her sister, but she knew Maryanne would never do anything to hurt her. It could actually work in her benefit if Suzie and Mrs. Williams thought Maryanne was the one dating him, at least for the next week.

She parked in front of their mom's house. Formerly 'Buela's, it was Margarita's childhood home. They'd de-cluttered a lot in the past few years, but the bathrooms and floors all needed redone. It was looking pretty worn down, and Dad's retirement pay only went so far.

Everyone climbed out and the boys raced up the steps to knock on the door. Margarita answered, hand on her chest. "Oh my stars! Look at all these handsome young men!"

"Trick or treat!" The boys yelled and held up their bags.

Margarita grinned and held the door wide, stepping back. "Well, look at all these heroes, Spider-Man, a ninja, a soldier, and a gladiator! Oh my! Do these strapping young men want to come inside for a cookie or two? I'm already out of candy, but I bet you'll love these cookies. They just came out of the oven!"

The boys scrambled past her and through to the kitchen, various shouts of yes and whoops for cookies following them. Margarita turned to follow them, laughing as she asked over her shoulder. "How'd it go tonight?"

Maryanne chatted about the night, her heels clicking against the hardwood floors as Andy closed the front door. The living room was filled with cozy, overstuffed furniture and a large fireplace in the corner. They made their way through the sunken room to the kitchen, Andy's hand on her lower back sending a tingle up her spine.

The scent of freshly baked cookies wafted through the air, and the boys sat at a worn, linoleum-covered table, eagerly digging into their candy bags.

"Wait, boys, you know the rules."

"But Mom—" Cody whined, making Andy chuckle. Cindy shook her head and reached for a cookie. "No buts. Pick out five pieces for tonight, then we're putting the candy up. If I were you, I'd space them out and eat throughout the movie."

"Movie?" Owen asked, perking up and swinging his head toward Margarita. "What movie?"

Her mom held up *Finding Dory*, and he jumped up, screaming, "Yes, I was hoping for this my whole life."

They laughed as he hugged Margarita around the knees and then bounced up and down. "Can we start it now?"

"Did you pick out your five pieces?" Margarita countered. Owen spun around and started to count out loud as Cindy bit into the cookie.

She moaned, the gooey warmth filling her mouth. "Mom, these are perfect!"

"Where do you think I get my recipe from," Maryanne said as she bit into her own cookie. Andy reached for two and bit into one. He nodded, eyes widening, and quickly scarfed down both. The boys dumped out their candy bags and finished counting them out.

"Andy, was this your first trick-or-treating with kids?" Her mom took up the candy bags and rolled them up, placing them on top of the fridge.

"Yeah, but I think it went well. I had Mandy, but we just dropped her off with my aunt and uncle." He looked at Cindy, and she nodded, reassuring him.

Margarita poured the boys glasses of water. "She's a precious thing. I was so sorry to hear about Sarah." She placed her hand on Andy's back, patting lightly.

Andy's eyes flashed with pain and his smile turned sad and haunted. "Thanks, I was too. Aunt Suzie took it the hardest."

"Nanarita, can we watch our movie now?" James asked. Owen looked like he was about to fall asleep in the chair.

"Oh, right away, dear! To the den we go!" she said, grabbing the movie from the counter.

Cindy scooped up Owen and turned to carry him back to the den/living room. Andy followed them out with Maryanne on his heels. She placed Owen on the couch with James, and Maryanne handed her a wet washcloth. Cody sat on the love seat and curled up with Margarita, popping the recliner on his side, as Cindy wiped the chocolate from Owen's face. He groaned, his lashes fluttering and waking slightly.

"Movie?"

She smiled and kissed his forehead. "Sh, yes, the movie is starting. Love you."

He grunted, his head lolling so he could see the television turn on.

"You kids have fun! Don't drink and drive, and I'll see you sometime tomorrow? No rush." Margarita said, pointing the remote. Cindy then Maryanne kissed her on the cheek, and Cindy kissed James and Cody too. They filed out the front door and climbed into the SUV.

"Freedom! Now for the real party to start," Maryanne said, tugging her dress down to show more cleavage and adjusting her bra.

Cindy laughed at her in the rear-view mirror as she

started the vehicle. "It's only nine-fifteen. Doesn't it start at ten?"

Andy nodded, his shoulders hunched almost up to his ears. "Yeah, but Landry said we could come early. And, honestly, I'm not sure how big the crowd will be or how I'll handle it. I've only been in one crowded place since I've been here, and it didn't end well."

"Oh? Where was that?" Cindy backed out of the driveway.

"The Electric Cowboy. The second night we met, when Holly ran me over." He chuckled, running a hand over the back of his neck.

Cindy giggled, "Yeah, I guess that counts as not ending well."

"Oh, I don't know," Maryanne said from the backseat. "It gave you two more time together, so I count that as a win. Especially since he wasn't really hurt."

Andy reached over and laid his warm hand on her thigh, making her breath stutter in her chest. "Hmm, I guess you're right. Anything that lets me spend time with Cindy is a win in my book too." His thumb stroked the outside of her thigh, and her body tingled at his touch.

Cindy sighed, her voice breathy. "So to the Williams' ranch?"

He nodded, squeezing her leg before releasing her. "Yeah, we can help Mrs. Williams set up or have pre-party drinks with the band."

"There's going to be a band?" Cindy asked.

Maryanne laughed from the backseat. "Girl, you don't even know what you've been missing! Just wait. I look forward to this party every single year."

Chapter Twenty-Eight

They pulled onto the dirt road that led to the Williams' ranch. Some of Andy's fondest memories were here, since he'd practically grown up with the Williams' boys. He loved the wide-open spaces and the gently rolling hills. It was one of the biggest spreads in the county.

"This the barn?" Cindy slowed near the big barn on their right. It already had a few cars parked around it.

"Yep, they have other barns closer to the house, but this one has almost direct access to the highway. They use it for big events like cattle auctions," he said as they pulled to a stop. His leg was already pulsing with a dull ache, but he wanted to see Cindy relax and have fun. She'd been smiling all night, but he'd occasionally see her frowning, obviously worrying about something. He unbuckled, and they made their way to the open cattle door on the end of the big red barn.

The floor was concrete for easy cleaning, but someone had decorated the walls and rafters in faux spider webs. A fog machine was already going in the opposite corner, spreading a haze over the dimly lit room. Orange Christmas lights wrapped around rafters above, and they'd strung big Edison bulbs along one wall where the food and drinks were located.

"Andy! You made it!" Landry said as he caught sight of them. He stepped off a raised platform where the rest of his brothers were setting up and shook his hand. Landry's grin widened as he looked Maryanne up and down.

She cocked out a hip and said, "Like what ya' see, handsome?"

He laughed. "Damn right, I do! Too bad Gunner called dibs."

Maryanne snorted and rolled her eyes. "Yeah right, as if he'd ever call dibs on anything but bear claws. Where is he, anyway?"

Landry shrugged, turning back to the stage to check on Parker and Hunter's progress with the equipment. "No idea. He told me he'd help, but here I am. All alone. Like always," he pouted, making Maryanne laugh as she walked away.

Landry smiled at Cindy. "How's it going, Cindy You're looking lovely as always." She blushed and chatted with Landry. Andy spied Mrs. Williams walking in a side door carrying an enormous cauldron. He walked over to her and grabbed it before it slipped out of her fingers.

"Oh thank you, Andy! I'm surprised to see you tonight, but I'm so glad you came! Just put it on this table." She pointed to an empty spot on the drinks table.

"I'm happy to be here. At least until the crowd moves in." He tried to ignore the knot in his stomach. A panic attack at the party might embarrass Cindy, and he didn't want that.

"Well, come help me set this machine up. It's supposed

to make a fountain in the cauldron of punch. Oh and taste it. Tell me what you think." She ladled up a cup for him.

He took a sip and coughed. "Man, that's strong!"

She laughed and waved her hand. "That's the point, deary. This is our night to cut loose before the stress of the holidays."

He shook his head as she talked about the holiday events that would happen this year. Before he knew it, people were trickling in, and he'd lost sight of Cindy.

He went back to the band area where Landry, Parker, Hunter, and Gunner were all warming up their various instruments and doing sound checks. The party would officially kick off at ten and end with a countdown like they did for New Year's at midnight.

"Have you seen Cindy?"

Landry shook his head no. Circling the perimeter of the party, he finally found her standing outside the bathrooms along the far wall. The tightness in his chest released at the sight of her. He took a step toward her before he registered the events unfolding before him.

His icy blue eyes narrowed and his normally friendly expression hardened into a stern glare. His footsteps were silent but purposeful as he made his way towards Cindy and the man, his fingers curling into fists, ready to defend and protect Cindy at any moment.

He wrapped an arm around Cindy's waist, offering comfort and sanctuary. She leaned into him with a smile, her shoulders relaxing at the rescue as his fingers pressed into her side, anchoring her to him. He pressed a kiss to her cheek, effectively staking his claim on her in front of the man.

"Hey, sorry I lost you. Had to help Mrs. Williams set up. Oh, hello, I'm Andy," he said, holding out a hand to shake.

The man frowned and reluctantly shook Andy's hand. "Patrick. Nice to meet you."

"You been here before, Patrick?" Andy asked.

He shrugged, looking around like he wanted to escape. "I'm from Decatur but heard about this party from one of my friends who lives here."

"Well, welcome to Crimson Creek." Andy stared at him, letting the silence stretch awkwardly as he caressed Cindy's hip.

"Oh, there's my friend now! I'll see you guys later." Patrick turned and walked off.

Andy squeezed her hip and looked down. "I hope you don't mind me stepping in like that."

Cindy's brown eyes crinkling at the corners as she arched a brow. "The kiss was a bit much, but thank you for getting rid of him. He already smelled like beer and reeked of cigarettes." The band started the party with announcements and their first song.

"Want to dance or get a drink?"

"Dance." She grinned and tugged him to the dance floor. They played four fast songs that had him sweating by the end of them. His leg throbbed after the long day, but dancing with Cindy and seeing her laugh at his lack of moves was too good to miss.

They sat on bar stools, sipping the bubbling cauldron punch and watching the other party-goers. Cindy couldn't get enough of the sweet, fruity flavor and hummed with delight after each sip. That hum did something to his chest, and he gave her his glass and ordered a beer from the bartender. They continued to chat and laugh, occasionally pointing out funny moments on the dance floor or observing the wallflowers huddled in small groups along the edges of the room.

Maryanne bumped into them and ordered a drink. "Hey, I forgot to tell y'all, don't wait for me. I'll find my own way home or to someone else's," she winked as she swayed to the music, waiting on the bartender.

Cindy rolled her eyes with a laugh and finished her second drink. He downed the last of his beer as she pulled him back onto the dance floor. As the band transitioned into a series of slow songs, he wrapped his arms around her and pulled her close. He buried his nose in her hair, the smell of her shampoo grounding him. With her so close, the growing crowd didn't bother him.

The fabric of her Cleopatra dress created a thin barrier between their skin, driving him wild with desire. He was grateful for the black boxer briefs he wore, as they helped contain the raging erection that formed from having her pressed against him.

Without hesitation, he reached down and squeezed her ass, grinding her hips against his. She looked up at him with a mischievous grin as the song came to an end. He leaned in for a kiss, but she playfully spun out of his grasp as the music picked up again. Groaning in frustration, he followed her lead on the dance floor once more.

After an hour, he was glistening with sweat, his leg making him limp as they went for another round of drinks.

"You feeling okay with the crowd?" The roar of the music nearly drowned her words. He grabbed a water, and she grabbed two of the punch. He motioned her to go out the side door.

Brightly colored bean bags flew through the air as people play corn hole, while others took turns rolling plastic lawn bowls towards giant pins. A group gathered around the giant Jenga, focusing intently as they carefully remove blocks. The flickering flames from the fire pit cast a warm glow over the scene, and the sweet scent of toasted marshmallows mingled with the fresh cut grass and wood smoke.

The laughs and murmured voices blended with the crackling of the fire, but it was significantly quieter, even with the occasional cheers and groans as players took their turns.

"Oh, a fire pit! I want to make s'mores!" Cindy said, holding her arm and hunching her shoulders as she shivered.

He wrapped an arm around her. "We could go back to my place. I have a fire pit in the back yard."

She looked at him in surprise. "You do?"

"Yep, I also have a hot tub that I've been dying to get you in," he growled, kissing her jaw.

She giggled again and finished one of her drinks. Her skin was warm under his touch as he leaned against the cool, rough wood of the barn. As he pulled her against him, he felt the curve of her spine and the softness of her hips against his body.

The shadowy corners of the barn gave them a semblance of privacy as they watched the Jenga game play out in front of them. He nuzzled his lips against her bare neck, making her shiver. She leaned forward to finish her second drink, pressing her ass against his cock. He groaned, holding her hips tightly as he tried to control the urge to thrust. They were in public and anyone could see.

She finished her drink and stepped to the right, dropping both cups in the trash can beside the door. Her cheeks were flushed from dancing and the dim light of the fire pit highlighted the desire in her eye.

Her mouth found his in a ravenous kiss. She rocked

against his cock, nearly climbing him to get the friction between her clit. He broke the kiss and looked around. "Ready to get out of here?"

She swayed into him and kissed his jaw, humming her agreement. He slid his arm around her shoulders and led her to the SUV. He opened the passenger door for her, but she smirked and walked to the trunk. "I have a naughty idea."

She opened it with a giggle and pushed some buttons. The seats folded flat, and she hopped inside. When she turned to look at him, she arched a brow in invitation and patted the spot beside her. "What do you say?"

He grinned and climbed in beside her as she pushed the button to close the trunk. "How can I refuse? You're not Cleopatra. You're Aphrodite."

She giggled as the trunk finally closed. It was a tight fit for someone his size, but he made it work. At least, until she pushed him back and threw a leg over him. Her dress slid up, exposing her thighs, and he ran his hands up and under it.

He groaned, his fingers digging into her flesh. "Damn, if I'd known you were going commando, we wouldn't have stayed at the party this late."

She giggled as she found the slit in his boxer briefs, slid the leather of the gladiator skirt up, and then sank down on him with a groan. "I've wanted to ride you since the Halloween store," she panted.

She started a rhythm, and he pulled her dress straps off her shoulders, exposing her breasts. The SUV rocked and, on some level, he worried someone would walk by and see her in all her glory. But the thought was fleeting as she took him deep, deeper than before.

He moaned as she placed her hands on his chest, pushing her breasts together and making them bounce. He reached one hand under her skirt and rubbed a circle around her clit, making her buck harder. Then he reached up with the other hand and pinched her nipple slightly.

She jerked again, going down harder with a moan as she came on his cock. He reached for her hips and set a fast rhythm, fucking her through her orgasm until she was coming again and again and again, moaning incoherently.

When he finally burst inside her, she gasped and fell onto his chest. He wrapped his hands around her and held on tight as they both spasmed.

When their breathing slowed down, she began to snore softly and went limp on top of him. He shifted her onto her side, and she hummed softly, but didn't wake up. He settled her dress over her thighs and sorted her straps, covering her magnificent breasts. Then he fished out her keys and hit the open trunk button.

He went around to the driver's side door, opened it, and turned it on to start the heater. The temperature had dropped in the dark.

Walking back to Cindy, his heart melted as he looked at her. She curled up like a little kid, one hand tucked under her face. He didn't want to disturb her, but they couldn't stay here all night.

"Cindy, darlin', are you going to wake up so we can go home?" He reached up and massaged her calf. She moaned but didn't move. He sighed and went to the passenger door, opened it, and laid the seat back.

Then he gently pulled her towards the edge of the trunk, slipped an arm under her shoulders and butt, and picked her up before settling her on the passenger seat. She kept sleeping which made him grin. He closed the door then shut the trunk, jumped in the driver's side, buckled them up, and drove home.

He smiled as he realized his little cabin really was home. When she was in it, anyway.

Chapter Twenty-Nine

The first rays of sunlight peeked through the curtains, casting a warm glow on Andy's face. He stretched his arms above his head, more contented than he'd felt in a long time. He looked over at the woman sleeping next to him and smiled. Her dark hair was splayed across the pillow, and her face was relaxed in peaceful slumber. He couldn't wake her, especially knowing how tired she'd been yesterday after working the grueling overnight shift at the hospital, so he quietly got out of bed and tip-toed to the kitchen.

As he cracked eggs into a pan and flipped slices of bacon on the stove, he thought about how lucky he was to have her here with him. He quickly whipped up a hearty breakfast and headed back to their room, eager to wake her up and start their day together.

When he saw how peaceful she looked, he decided to let her rest and went for a solo run through the woods around his property. As the crisp fall air cooled his cheeks, he thought about the past few weeks. A month ago, he'd still been in D.C. Sure, he had Aunt Suzie, Uncle Mike, and Mandy, but he'd still been alone and useless.

But now... he had hope for a life that was full of laughter. Last night had been so much fun, both with the kids and then with Cindy at the party. He'd not even been stressed about the crowd that much.

He couldn't believe he'd known her for such a short time and already his life trajectory was completely different. It'd only been a week since he'd made out with her on the kitchen counter, but already he couldn't imagine life without her.

He wanted her and the boys to move in with him, but what could he offer her? He wanted to give her the world, but with a bum leg he needed more than just his house and himself.

As he completed the circle and jogged down the driveway, he saw Aunt Suzie's vehicle in the drive and frowned. What was she doing out this early?

He walked up the steps and opened the front door. This wasn't good, he thought as he saw Aunt Suzie dressed for church, hands on her hips and her face pinched in righteous indignation.

Cindy stood frozen in between the kitchen sink and the island in another one of his t-shirts, a bottle of water halfway raised, as if she was about to take a drink. Her hair was curling every which way and falling down her back in tangles.

He caught the tail end of what Aunt Suzie was saying as the door shut behind him.

"You're a hussy. We all knew it when you moved back to town and had three kids with two different men. I told you to leave Andy alone, but you didn't listen." Aunt Suzie's finger wagged at Cindy across the kitchen island.

The Soldier Gets His Girl

His nostrils flared as he breathed heavily, trying to calm the storm of emotion within him. The loud thumping of his heart echoed in his ears, like a war drum beating out a dangerous rhythm. With each step he took, it grew louder and faster, fueling his fury. His fists clenched at his sides, the muscles in his arms tensing with the urge to lash out at Aunt Suzie.

Anger on her behalf raged within him, but he had to protect Cindy. Aunt Suzie jerked out of the corner of his eye when she realized he was there, but he kept his gaze on Cindy, determined to reach her side and offer his protection. She looked sad, like she'd known what they'd said about her. He rounded the island as she set the bottle of water on the counter and took a deep breath, her bottom lip wobbling.

"Look at me. You're alright," he reassured, tipping her chin up and meeting her eyes. He saw the last edges of sleep fade away as the pain set in. The look in her eyes was like a bullet to the heart. "You're nothing of the sort, so don't even let those words take root in you, you hear?"

She nodded, even as tears pooled in her eyes.

Wrapping her up in his arms and nestling her face against his sweaty t-shirt, he drew soothing circles on her back. His jaw was tight and he gritted his teeth, feeling the tension spread through his body like a wildfire, only Cindy's hands on his back keeping him from his aunt. Turning his head, he met Suzie's shocked face.

"What is wrong with you? Is this how you treat people? Is this how you treated my mom when she first got in trouble? It's no wonder she ended up the way she did. You can't talk like that. You don't know other people's stories, Suzie. You can't sit there and judge."

"I'm not—I haven't—" she stammered before taking a

deep breath and lowering her hands from her hips. "She's not what you need, Andy."

His brows rose. "And you know what I need? You're not me, Suzie. You're not my mom, and I'm not eight anymore. I may be broken, but it's not for you to fix me, alright?" He fumed, stroking her hair slowly even as he shot daggers at his aunt.

"I know I'm not your mom, but I practically raised you, and I thought I did better than this—"

He cut her off with a growl. "There is no one *better* than Cindy. And I mean *no one*. Go on to church or wherever you're going, but you'd best have an apology for Cindy the next time you see us. While I am grateful for all you've done for me over the years, I am severely disappointed in you today."

She opened her mouth and closed it repeatedly, before huffing a breath, spinning on her heel, and leaving. She slammed the door behind her. As the quiet settled around them, he kept stroking her hair and rubbing her back until the tension left her shoulders.

"You okay?" he murmured as he kissed the top of her head. She squeezed his shirt with her tiny hands. Her body shook from repressed emotions.

"Yeah," she sniffled. He wrapped her into a hug and just held her for what seemed like hours. He didn't have to wait long before she sobbed onto his shirt. Her pain tore his heart to shreds, and he just held her while she cried it out.

After her sobs turned to quiet sniffs, he leaned back to look into her red-rimmed eyes. "Why don't we eat some breakfast and put it behind us, hm? Are you hungry? I made breakfast."

She sighed and pulled away. Taking a drink of her water, she stared out the kitchen window into the trees.

He leaned a hip against the counter and crossed his arms. Waiting was the hardest part. He just wanted to fix it already! To take away her pain and make her smile and laugh. Instead he held his tongue.

"I knew they said stuff like that, but it still hurt to hear it out loud," she mumbled as she capped the water bottle. He nodded and listened, determined to be patient and exactly what she needed.

"I heard a lot of hurtful things in high school when I had Cody so young. Between having him and helping 'Buela in the summers and taking care of her, I knew I wanted to be a nurse. So I set out to prove to them I wasn't just some whore looking for a sugar daddy."

Her hazel eyes trapped the light from the window and a frown marred her lips as her spine straightened. "I can take care of myself. I don't need you—"

"Hey," he said, holding his hands up. "Ease up. I'm not the enemy here. You can take care of yourself. You're the strongest, most giving person I've ever met, Cindy. I'm not looking to swoop in and rescue you. You don't need me to because you're perfectly capable of handling yourself. You've been raising those boys and doing a fine job of it without needing anyone else."

He took a deep breath and grabbed both her hands. "I'm the one who needs you though, and I'll take you however I can get you. I'll get Suzie straightened out. Then we can get on with seeing where this relationship is going to go, alright?"

He held her hands and waited, never taking his eyes off hers. She sighed again and nodded with a yawn. "Okay, I'm going to go take a shower then. My stomach is still queasy from all the punch last night. I don't want to eat yet."

He smiled and kissed her on the cheek. As he wrapped

an arm around her waist, they walked down the hallway together. He glanced into one of the open bedroom doors and stopped.

Memories slammed into him. "Go on. I'll be right behind you. I think I have some of Sarah's clothes still in that dresser. Something should fit, so you don't have to wear the dress when you go home later."

She smiled and drank her water, walking down the hall as he stepped into the bedroom. It was bright and airy, not too musty. The dresser beside the window held a picture of him, Jake, and Sarah when they were kids. She'd always stayed here when she'd come home from college.

He snorted as he rifled through the drawers. She'd always claimed that Aunt Suzie was too smothering, but he'd never seen it until he'd gotten injured. Now he totally knew where she was coming from. Finding a few pairs of yoga pants, he pulled them out and walked through his bedroom to his bathroom.

The steam from the shower already had the mirrors foggy. He sat the pants on the counter, then sat on the chair to take off his foot. She was already washing her hair when he slid in, hopping around her and sitting on the bench.

"Do you have any prosthetics that can get wet?" she asked. He nodded, leaning forward, and putting his head against her stomach. She reached her hands around to the back of his skull and started massaging it.

He groaned, her fingers working miracles on his head. "Yeah, but I use it sparingly. If I want to go running in the rain or something like that."

A few minutes of silence passed before she asked, "How are you? You still mad at Suzie?"

He smiled at her need to take care of everyone, even though she was the one who'd been hurt. He leaned back, grabbing the shampoo and lathering up. "Yes, but it's not that. I just didn't realize Sarah's stuff was still in there."

"You miss her," she stated matter-of-factly.

"Yep." He rinsed off his hair and body, then leaned back against the shower wall.

"Tell me about her." Her smooth voice coaxed him to remember. He closed his eyes and sighed again.

"She was in a car accident with her roommate from college. I'd actually dated her roommate, not many people knew that. We'd only gone on a few dates before I deployed. When I came back, they were just... gone."

"Did you love the roommate? What was her name?"

"Stella. No, we weren't in love. It was more of a casual hook-up situation. She was a free-spirited college girl, living it up, and I was a tied to the Army. It never would've worked, and we both knew that."

She stood in the spray, water flowing down her body and distracting him. "It was hard on Aunt Suzie. Sarah had Mandy and didn't even tell Aunt Suzie until the car accident."

"What?" she asked, a wrinkle on her brow.

"I know, right? So weird. Stella died on impact, but Sarah lingered for almost a week, in and out of consciousness. She told Aunt Suzie about the baby and made her the guardian. The day after she signed the papers, she slipped into a coma. She died a few days after that."

"Oh, Andy. That must have been terrible for her and Mike both."

He nodded, his chest tight. "Yeah, I think Mandy is what kept them from losing it completely. Gave them something to focus on. Jake stayed with them as he'd just finished his four years in the Army for months."

"The mechanic in town? He's still in the military though, I thought."

He nodded, lathering the loofah and soaping his body. "Yeah, he re-upped into the Reserves and deployed. I think that's how he handled losing Sarah, by going back into it all. I was deployed when Sarah died, based out of Hood at the time. I came home a month or so after, but ended up only being home a few months. They shuffled me to another unit that deployed, so back I went for the last time. Ended up with this over halfway through." He waved at his stump, the skin twisted below his knee.

She knelt and reached for it, but he flinched away. She raised a brow. "Does it hurt? You do realize I'm a nurse, right, and have seen way worse?"

He wanted to open up to her. Some part of him needed her approval, her acceptance. He sucked in a breath and moved his leg back toward her.

But she didn't flinch or look disgusted. Instead she rubbed her hands over the end of it. He couldn't feel it, not until she reached closer to his knee. Then she massaged his thigh, which was huge in comparison with her little hands.

When she massaged up and down his thigh, his cock twitched. The smirk on her face drove him insane with want. Moving a hand to his other leg, she massaged slowly on the outside, up, then down on the inside.

She repeated the move but wrapped her mouth around the tip of his hard cock as she moved forward. He leaned his head back and gasped.

Her mouth was like heaven. He thought he was tense before but with every swipe of her tongue, he started bowing up way too quickly.

He leaned down and pulled her up by the shoulders.

Falling into his lap, she straddled him and slid down his throbbing cock so slowly he groaned.

This was a different angle than last night in the SUV. Sitting up, her breasts pressed to his chest, he leaned forward and captured her mouth.

She placed her hands on his shoulders as she rode him, his hips guiding her down harder, faster. Their pace quickly descended into a frantic, uneven mess. He couldn't think to slow down or touch her. She clenched around him as she broke the kiss and pulled back to grind onto his pelvis harder.

Her gasp turned into a moan as he exploded inside her, causing her to jerk with her own orgasm. She slumped onto his chest with a murmur of nonsensical sounds.

Kissing the top of her shoulder, he worked his way to her neck. He loved hearing her sounds almost as much as he loved her.

Squeezing his arms around her in surprise, he sucked in a deep breath. Releasing it slowly, he pursed his lips. His heart raced and his mind whirled fast as lightning.

Yes, he definitely loved her. He didn't know when or how. Maybe it was when he'd first seen her, when he was consumed with pain, and she'd been the haven in the storm.

He should have known when he couldn't stop thinking of her, when she made him feel useful and supported, when she didn't treat him like an invalid but like a bit of a hero when she looked at him with that awe on her face. She made him feel needed even though she swore she didn't need him.

She stirred in his arms. He kissed the side of her head as it rolled onto his shoulder. He caught her sleepy gaze and smiled, "Want to go back to bed, sleepy head?"

She giggled softly and sat up, then lifted a leg off and sat next to him on the bench. He reached over and linked their fingers together. They sat in comfortable silence until the water started to turn cold.

He reached up to adjust it again. She stood and rinsed off again, so he did hopped to the chair outside the shower and dried off. When he heard the water shut off behind him, he handed her a clean towel with a kiss on the cheek before he walked into the bedroom to get some clean clothes.

They spent the rest of the day in his room. He brought her breakfast in bed after their shower, then fell back to sleep for a few hours, waking up only to make love again. Margarita had texted that she'd keep the boys entertained for the day, so he had her all to himself until dusk.

They finally got around and headed out to Cindy's apartment. They sang together as they drove. He was content, happy for the first time in so long.

A knot had settled in his stomach at the realization that he loved her. It had grown bigger throughout the day. If he didn't tell her soon, he was going to burst.

He knew she wasn't ready. They weren't even 'dating' yet, not until she was officially no longer his PTA. Before they climbed out of her SUV, he leaned over and cupped her cheeks.

Looking into her eyes he smiled. He hesitated then said, "Outside of Aunt Suzie, today was the best day I've ever had, Cindy. Thank you." He kissed the blush on her cheeks, then hopped out of her vehicle.

He handed her the keys back, then walked around to where he'd left his truck yesterday when Mandy and he had come to the potluck.

"Tell the boys I said hi!" He waved and jumped into his truck to head home.

Chapter Thirty

Cindy sipped her tea as she sat at the playground on the bench. She saw Maryanne arrive this time, her orange sequined top falling elegantly off one shoulder. Her brown pants and leather boots were spotless; whereas Cindy's scrubs had a stain on the knee and a new rip on her shirt pocket.

She sighed as her sister sat down.

"What's with that face? Normal Monday or did something happen?" She turned on the bench and pulled one leg up so she could face Cindy.

She rubbed her forehead as the pressure increased on her chest. "Well, Suzie found out about Andy, and she was *not* pleased."

Maryanne gasped, "What? No! How?"

Cindy shrugged and tucked a stray strand of hair behind her ear, her braid already too loose. "I stayed at his place after the party Saturday. He went for a run Sunday morning, and I got up to get a bottle of water. Then in walked Suzie, ready for church. She read me the riot act about being a hussy trying to trap Andy with another baby and child support."

"That bitch! How dare she!" Maryanne whispered furiously, her cheeks blooming red from anger.

"Right? But honestly, I don't blame her. She's just trying to watch out for him. That being said, I'm not going to the ladies' meeting tonight at church. I don't want to stir up any drama or have her make a scene."

"You think she would?" Maryanne sat back and placed both feet on the ground. They watched Owen as Cindy nodded.

"I know so. It could be really bad. Just tell Mom I'll call her tomorrow, okay? I'm going to take the boys home after soccer practice, make dinner, and go to bed early."

"Fine. If that's what you want to do. But if it were me, I'd march up to that woman and give her a piece of my mind."

Cindy laughed, reaching over to squeeze her sister's hand. "I know, and that's why I love you… oh! I didn't tell you! I have an interview!"

"What? When? How?" Maryanne squealed, nearly bouncing on the bench in excitement.

"Wednesday morning at the hospital in Decatur. I'll be back in time for our lunch with Mom."

"That's fantastic news! Oh Cindy, I know you'll get it."

She laughed, nerves twisting her stomach. "I sure hope so. It'll be a bit of a drive, but not too much. The pay will hopefully be equal to what I'm making now between the two jobs, but with better hours."

They talked about the bakery and Maryanne's newest flavor for November that she was going to spotlight. Soon, soccer practice was releasing, and Cody jogged over to them.

"James! Owen! Time to go!" she called. "Hey, how was practice?"

Cody's brown hair flopped into his eyes as he grinned. "It was awesome. Coach says I've improved a lot the past few weeks. I think it's the videos Andy has been filming. It lets me see more of what I'm doing."

Cindy nodded with a smile and called James and Owen over again. It had been eye-opening to see Andy interacting with the kids on Saturday. When the boys finally made it over, she said, "I had a rough day at work, so we're just going to go home, alright? No ladies' meeting tonight. What do y'all want for dinner?"

Owen said, "Aww, no Nanarita?" James shrugged, and Cody narrowed his eyes at her.

"What?" she asked.

He shook his head slowly. "Nothing." Owen took her hand as they walked towards the SUV and told Maryanne goodbye.

As they all buckled up, Cody said, "It's cool to go home early. Can I help you cook tonight?"

She smiled as she drove home. "Sure, I'd love the help. What are you thinking we should make?"

"Chicken Alfredo," he said. She grinned. He always chose pasta when it was his night to help with dinner. She looked forward to a nice normal night with her boys.

The bell rang above the diner's door as Cindy walked in. She wore her best suit and had come straight from the interview. Spying her mom and sister in their usual booth, she hurried across the floor.

They both glanced up at her expectantly. Grinning, she slid into the booth across from them.

"The interview went amazing! We even talked about pay and hours. It would be a slight increase and—drum roll please."

She paused as Maryanne used her fingers to make a drum roll.

"It's daytime hours!" she squealed. Maryanne whooped, and her mom clapped.

Cindy laughed as they congratulated her. "I'm so excited! I'd be working four days a week from seven am to seven pm."

"Maryanne can handle soccer practice and school pick-up, and I'll take over for dinner and bedtime. When will you know for sure?" Margarita asked as she sipped her tea.

"They said they'd call next week."

After Dot took their orders, her mom set her chin in her hand. "Now tell me *all* that happened this weekend with Andy."

Cindy blushed but told her mom the highlights. She'd talked to her briefly when she'd come home Sunday and gotten the boys from her house, but they had been loud and wanted to get home quickly.

"It sounds like you had a wonderful time. I knew he was a good man, but I am partial to military men, so there's that." They all laughed, and the conversation turned to other things.

"You missed little from the ladies' meeting the other night," Maryanne eventually said.

"We're going to work on the floats this weekend, since

the Veteran's Day parade and the Fall Festival and Homecoming will all be next weekend."

Cindy groaned, as Dot delivered their drinks. "It's going to be such a busy weekend! Are you guys going to be able to handle it all?"

Maryanne nodded, "Absolutely. We'll be working throughout the next two weeks baking for the Festival, so I'll be working longer days for a while, but it'll be fine."

"Got room for me today?" Andy said suddenly from behind her. Cindy jumped and swung her head around with a big grin on her face.

"Hey, what are you doing here?" She slid over as he sat beside her. He kissed her on the cheek, and she blushed.

He grinned and slid his arm along the back of the booth. "I wanted to see how the interview went. I figured you'd be here, it being Wednesday and all."

She gushed about the interview, turning in the booth to face him. She caught Mom and Maryanne whispering to each other furiously before Dot came and took his order. When his order came, the conversation quieted as they ate.

"Oh, girls, I forgot to tell you. I'll be going out of town for about a week. There's a reunion down in Houston that I want to go to," their mom said.

Cindy frowned, her shoulders tensing at even the mention of Houston. "A reunion?"

"Yeah, a bunch of us from the military widows group are going down there. We're going to have a blast. Hotel, pool, spa—"

"Damn, can I come too?" Maryanne asked, making Cindy giggle.

Margarita shook her head with a grin. "Nope, you're not part of the club. Sorry."

Cindy smiled and wiped her lips with her napkin. "You're going to have so much fun, Mom! Get a massage for me, ok?"

Maryanne pointed a fry at her. "You didn't get the massage from Holly today, did you?"

Cindy shook her head. "I had the interview, remember? I'll just go next week."

"If you need to relax, there's a hot tub on my back porch that you're welcome to. It's not as good as a massage, but it's the next best thing," Andy said. Dot came and refilled their drinks.

"Cody has soccer practice until six tonight. Maybe we could all come over for dinner? Or did you want to hit up the hot tub now?" she blushed, picturing all they could do with a spare hour or two.

He smirked and winked at her. "We can hot tub it up now. Then grab the boys and bring them by for dinner tonight. Are they picky eaters?"

"Heavens, no. James doesn't like spicy food and Owen prefers chicken, but they'll eat just about anything," Margarita said. Cindy nodded as she swallowed a bite of her food.

They talked about their favorite foods and restaurants from all the different places they'd been stationed. They laughed when they found a few that all of them loved and even one that they all hated.

When lunch was over, Andy once again paid by pretending to go to the restroom. Cindy grinned at the look on her mom's face when she realized it and pretended to get indignant with him. He teased Margarita as they all walked out the door, but Cindy stopped short on the sidewalk. Suzie and Mandy walked hand in hand toward them.

"Hey, if it isn't my favorite girl!" Andy exclaimed as he

leaned over and picked up Mandy. She squealed and laughed as he tossed her into the air.

Cindy's heart flipped an extra beat. He was great with her. They said kids and animals could tell if a person was trustworthy or not. If it was true, then Andy was a keeper.

"We wondered where you were. We just came from your house." Suzie's voice was more reserved than normal, and she stared at Andy, ignoring Cindy completely.

Cindy frowned, her mind racing to why Mandy was here. "Was today an early release day for the daycare?"

Suzie arched a brow, giving her the stink eye as she finally looked at her. "Yes, didn't you realize? Oh, poor Owen. If we'd known, we would have brought him to you."

Cindy and Maryanne exchanged a glance then both of them swiped on their phones to check the school calendar. With a groan Maryanne said, "Yep. It's right here. Why the notification didn't go off?"

Cindy shook her head. "Mine didn't go off either. It's fine though. I'll just go grab him." She put her phone away and walked around Suzie toward her SUV.

Andy placed a hand on her arm before she'd taken more than two steps away. "Can you bring Owen over to play? I bet Mandy would love to see him some more this afternoon."

Cindy glanced over her shoulder and caught Suzie's furious gaze. She pursed her lips.

"Looks like you should ask Suzie about that first. Text me. I'll see you later, M. Love you, Mom." She turned and walked to her SUV before she mouthed off and said something she shouldn't.

Suzie'd said just the right thing to make her feel like the worst mom in the world. How could she not know that it was an early release day? Owen must have been sitting there for half an hour already. She pulled into daycare and rushed inside.

When she finally got back into her SUV, she glanced at her phone. Andy had texted, so she replied.

I have Mandy and she'd love to play.
I can also make dinner?

We normally pick up James at four and go to the playground by the soccer field during practice.
Do you want to go to the park?

Yeah, that works. I was hoping to see you before then. I've missed you.

I saw you at lunch.

Not for long enough. It's been three days since I've seen you.

lol I've missed you too.
Do you have a crockpot I can use? I can bring Owen by your house now and set dinner to cook while we go to the park, if you want to carpool.

No, I don't have one. I can get one though.

Nah, it's alright. I'll bring mine.

Sounds good! I'll be home by 2.
Helping Aunt Suzie pick up some stuff from the feed store first.

She sent the thumbs up emoji, then backed up and

drove to the grocery store. It was easier to shop with just one extra kid, and she'd make sure she had extras for two more mouths to feed tonight. The entire time she gathered ingredients, Owen talked a mile a minute. She only listened with half an ear, smiling at the thought that Andy had missed her.

Chapter Thirty-One

"Mandy!" Owen squealed as she opened the SUV door. He ran up the porch and squeezed his friend in a hug. They giggled and ran through the house. She closed his door and walked to the back to get the dinner supplies.

"Need a hand?" Andy asked. She grinned at him but before she could answer, he grabbed her around the waist and pulled her quickly flush with him. She gasped, and his mouth descended on hers, his tongue plunging in.

It was hard, fast, and intense. When he released her and pulled his head back, she swore she swooned, but he kept his hands locked behind her back. She blinked and caught his gaze with a smile.

"What was that for?"

"I wanted to do that earlier but couldn't bring myself to do it in front of your mom," he chuckled, giving her a quick peck on the lips before letting go and turning to grab the crock pot.

She snorted, "Mom's fine with it. It's Suzie you gotta

worry about." She grabbed the three grocery bags and pushed the button to close the trunk.

He sighed as they walked towards the front door. "Right, she avoided talking about it today. She went on and on about nothing in particular, never shutting up long enough for me to push her to apologize or talk or anything."

He shrugged open the door with his shoulder, and Cindy stepped through, closing it behind her. "It's fine, Andy. She's just a mama bear protecting her cub. Even though he's a grown ass man now."

He chuckled as they stepped into the kitchen. "What are we making tonight?"

"Crack Chicken," she said, laying out the ingredients on the island. "We need a cutting board, knife, and a pan to cook the bacon now. Do you know how to cook bacon?"

"Yeah, I cook it on a flat griddle though. That work?"

"Can I use a pan instead? I'll cook the bacon, and you can put all the ingredients into the crock pot. Just dice the chicken and the cream cheese and the packet of ranch dressing mix."

"You just throw it in?" He looked skeptical which made her giggle.

"Yep, once the bacon is done, we'll put it in the fridge and pull it out to add with the shredded cheese when we get back from the park. I have green onions too. Is Mandy fine with them?"

He shrugged, pulling out the pan. "No clue. Normally, she either eats it or she doesn't."

Cindy laughed, opening the packages of chicken in the sink and rinsing it. "That's alright. She's going to love this. All the kids do. We'll throw the green onions in with the chicken too."

He set two cutting boards and two knives on the counter, then took one and cut up the green onions. Cindy took the other and cut the bacon into small chunks.

"I've never seen anyone cut their bacon up like that."

She kept chopping. "I don't like to crumble bacon by hand. It's too messy, and you always get big chunks. Kids don't do well with that, so I started cutting up the bacon before cooking it when Cody was old enough to eat it."

"And now all the pieces are nice and uniform. I like that," he teased.

She grinned, feeling her cheeks heat. "Yeah, I like things tidy. With three kids, I don't always get that so I appreciate when I can make it happen. It's the little things, you know?"

He shook his head sadly. "Not really. I'd love to someday, though."

"What do you mean?"

"I mean, I'd love to have a bunch of kids like you someday. I think... I think it'd keep the darkness away."

She frowned at him and waited. She slid the bacon into the pan on the stove and stirred it around as it sizzled. He tossed the onions into the crock pot, then started to cut up the chicken breasts. She washed her hands, but when he didn't say anything else, she finally asked, "What do you mean by darkness?"

"The nightmares. The PTSD. The loneliness and... stuff like that. It was hard in the hospital and rehab because of the loneliness. Then Suzie and Mike brought Mandy. She was barely a year and a half, and she came barreling into my room, straight to the bed. She grabbed my fingers and kept trying to climb onto the bed."

He laughed as he slid the chicken into the pot and then washed his hands and the cutting boards and knives.

"Aunt Suzie stressed me out with all her fluttering

around, but she was amazing with the doctors. She got shit done. And while she was reading them the riot act, Mike would grab Mandy and place her on the bed with me. We'd play, and it just brightened my day, every time. I think it'd be nice to have that... that light around every day. Does that make any sense?"

She nodded, a small smile playing around her lips. "It does, actually. When my dad died, then 'Buela... the kids helped me get through it. Yeah, I was probably a terrible mom, always crying and yelling at them, but they were sweet. Still are. I like taking them to the park and watching them play. The things they say and do are so funny sometimes."

He smiled, drying off his hands. She turned to stir the bacon, and he wrapped his arms around her from behind.

"You do it too," he whispered into her ear as he kissed up her neck. She shivered.

"Do what?"

"Bring in the light. Banish the darkness."

She set down the wooden spoon and turned in his arms, wrapping her hands around his neck. She sighed as their lips met, molding together.

A pair of giggles made them pull apart. In unison, they both turned their heads and caught Mandy's skirt flying around the doorway and back down the hall.

He grinned, the light in his eyes making her heart smile. "See? Isn't that one of the most beautiful sounds in the world?"

"You'd better go see what they're getting into. Your house is probably not kid proofed yet," she chuckled as she turned back to finish the bacon. He laughed as he agreed and walked out.

Yet. Did that mean she *wanted* to kid proof it? Because

they would be over here more often? She frowned. She couldn't deny that she wanted to spend time with him. He was so different from any man she'd ever known before. He had helped with dinner—and washed the dirty dishes immediately! Without being asked or whining or anything! Perhaps she could spend more time with him.

"Mom, can we go to the park yet?" Owen called from down the hall. She turned off the stove as she drained the bacon grease and yelled, "Yeah, give me five minutes, and we'll be ready to go!"

It actually took her a little longer to turn on the crock pot, wash the counters, and put everything away. Giggling came from one of the spare bedrooms.

She pushed open the door and saw a computer desk set up on the right with a laptop and printer on it. The full bed was in the middle of the room with a sheet stretched from two of the bed posts to the wall, where Andy stood stapling it. She giggled.

"What are you doing?"

"Building a fort," he said it so matter-of-factly, like it was the most ordinary thing he'd ever done. It made her laugh out loud. Owen and Mandy giggled from underneath.

"No, it's a tent!" Mandy bossed.

"Come on in, Mama!"

"We're camping!" Mandy squealed. She rolled her eyes at Andy as he finished stapling the sheet to the wall. She crawled in, and Andy soon joined them.

They sat on one side with Mandy and Owen on the other. Owen handed her a piece of printer paper.

"You need to add wood to the fire, Mama, or we'll get cold and freeze."

She grinned as he showed her how to rip up the paper and add it to the growing pile in the middle of their fort tent. Andy kept his prosthetic foot stretched out of the tent.

"We have to go fishing," Mandy said as she patted her hands over the paper 'fire' pit.

"Is that what we eat while camping?" Andy asked. She glanced from Andy to Mandy and noted that they both had such beautiful blue eyes. She wondered if he'd give her a little blue-eyed girl.

Sucking in a breath, she glanced down at her paper quickly. Good grief, the man was sex on a stick but she did *not* want any more babies, even though Owen was starting to grow up and would start real pre-k next year. Then Suzie would really be pissed, thinking Cindy was just after a baby daddy.

Cindy cleared her throat and tapped her chin. "You know, if we go to the park now, we'll have enough time to swing by the gas station and grab some goldfish crackers. We could then eat fish while camping when we come back home."

Andy's gaze swung to her at the mention of the word home, but he didn't say anything. His smile widened though, which made her blush. She avoided his eyes, smiling as Mandy and Owen both whooped, then high-fived, their chubby little hands almost missing each other.

They scrambled out, Andy and she following much more slowly. He stood up first, then offered a hand to help her up.

"What a gentleman," she murmured. He grinned and leaned down and kissed her swiftly. "I like you calling this place home," he whispered, pecking her lips and then turning on his heel to follow the kids.

Her lips tingled, and she practically floated to the door to put on her shoes. She tried to remind herself that this was just playing grown up, pretending to be a family. They weren't though, and she had to remember that.

They took his truck to pick up James and Cody from school. Andy's shoulders tensed up the longer they sat in the pickup line.

"What's wrong?" She frowned, putting her hand on his thigh.

He breathed deeply, then released it slowly. "Traffic. I don't like it."

"Because of the deployment?"

"Yeah. Sitting still like this, barely crawling along... if we got in a situation like this in a village... well, it never ended well. I guess my body's just trained to tense up like this now."

"You can control it, to a certain degree. The rest will just take time."

"I know. The longer I get from my active duty days, the better it will be," he mimicked in an annoyingly snooty voice. She blinked as he leaned one elbow on the door's arm rest and leaned back in the seat a bit.

"Sorry, I just heard it over and over in D.C."

"From the doctors?"

"Yeah, I wasn't lying when I said that I wasn't a fan of doctors or nurses anymore. You're the only one I've liked in years," he glanced at her and winked. She smiled and tried to distract him with conversation.

They finally made it to where the boys were, and she had to roll down her window and wave at them as they didn't recognize the truck.

The two booster seats barely allowed the other two boys to crawl into the back seat. They crowded in, talking one over the other.

"Andy! What are you doing here?" Cody asked.

James said, "Mom! I made a 100 on my pre-spelling test so now I get to read tomorrow and Friday during spelling!"

She turned in her seat and grinned. "Congratulations, honey! That's awesome!"

"Hey, Cody. Hey, James. Mandy wanted to play with Owen at the park, so we decided to all ride together. Then there's dinner at my house. How does that sound?" Andy pulled out of the parking lot.

"Sounds good to me," James said.

"Sure. If you want to video some of my practice tonight, that'd be cool too," Cody said, trying to play it off as no big deal. But Cindy saw his eyes shining as she glanced over her shoulder. She wasn't sure if it was good or not that Cody was so hopeful for Andy's attention.

Andy pulled into the parking lot. "Sure, I can do that, if your mom is alright with watching Mandy on the playground."

She smiled, relieved that he didn't mind. "It's fine with me. There's a bench at the playground that has double seats. So you can watch the soccer field and I can watch the playground."

"Perfect!" Andy said as they all jumped out. He helped Mandy and Owen unbuckle, then swung them each to the ground. Cody grabbed his bag and jogged over to the field.

James grabbed his book and walked beside Andy, talking about a paper that he'd written in school about camping. Andy held Mandy and Owen's hands as they crossed the parking lot. She hung back to grab the little backpack and watched them. He listened to James and asked questions.

Her ex had never done that with either of the boys. She couldn't remember him ever even holding their hands or helping them get out of a vehicle. As she stared at him walking with the three kids, she stopped.

Her hands started clamming up as her heart tried to beat out of her chest. She loved him. Oh god, she *loved* him. It terrified her because she loved him more than she'd ever loved her ex.

She'd been curious with the first, infatuated even. And her ex-husband… she'd thought she'd been in love, but he'd lied to her, manipulated her, and verbally abused her until she didn't even want to escape.

Andy would never do that. She started walking again, slowly. Her head knew it, but her heart was still terrified. She grabbed a bottle of water from the backpack, her mouth cottony.

She saw the three kids run to the playground, James running to his favorite spot that was out of the wind but still gave him some sunshine so he could read. Andy stood waiting at the benches.

"Is this the one?" he asked, and she nodded. They sat, their seats sharing a back. They didn't sit back to back, but more as if they were sitting side by side so they could still talk to each other.

"You didn't have to agree to video him," she said to break the silence. She had to talk about anything else; otherwise, she'd admit her feelings and ruin it all.

"Eh, it's okay. I like watching him play. Reminds me a lot of Parker at that age."

"You're good with them, the kids. I can see why you'd want a bunch of them. You'll make a great father someday."

"Thanks," he said. The silence stretched between them, turning awkward. He asked about the interview again and the job details, then they talked about nothing really of consequence until a truck pulled up across the playground.

The blond haired bearded guy from Holly and

Kendall's jumped out and sauntered over. "Your friend is here," she said.

Andy turned and waved as he stood up. "Hey, man! How's it going? You remember Cindy?" He rounded the bench and shook the man's hand.

Nick grinned, his teeth brilliant white in the sun. "Sure! How could I forget such a beautiful woman?" He winked, making her laugh.

"Nick, wasn't it?" They shook hands, and he lingered, holding hers a beat too long.

Andy frowned and stepped beside her, wrapping his arm around her waist. She dropped his hand. Andy's body language gave an obvious message but his voice was still friendly and warm. "What are you doing here?"

Nick's eyes shifted from her to Andy, and he gave a dramatic shiver with a pitiful, hang dog look. "I ran into your Aunt Suzie today."

Andy burst out laughing as Nick nodded. "Yep, I tried to send one of the minions to help her, but they all scattered like elephants in front of a mouse. It was funny until I realized that only left me."

"What did she want this time?"

"She wanted to rent a pole digger. Now that the garden is winterized, they're apparently updating fences. She talked about *everything* but she reminded me of something. You were COMSEC, right? Do you know how to repair radios on big rigs?"

Andy shrugged, shoving his hands in his pockets. "I can. They're about the same as those in Humvees."

"Awesome. Remember how I was partnering with a guy to rent out semis for local deliveries and such? We have some repairs to make to the starting inventory—got some sweet deals down in Dallas at some police auctions—so I wanted to ask if you'd be willing to give 'em a shot. We'll pay, of course."

Andy nodded, his shoulders lowering as he smiled. "I'd love to. Do you know how bored I've been sitting around by myself?" He laughed.

He was bored? Had he just been killing time with her? Her heart raced, and she glanced at the kids on the playground.

Nick slapped him on the back with a grin. "Well, come by the office tomorrow, and we'll work out the details. Gotta go now. Bye, Cindy! It was good seeing you again!"

"You too!" she called out with a wobbly smile. Andy watched him walk away for a minute before turning and sitting beside her. He slung an arm around the back of the bench and pulled her in for a side hug.

"Oh my God, this is amazing! I'd submitted some applications in Fort Worth the other day, but none of them really appealed to me. And you know how I feel about traffic. Nick's is just down the road!"

"What about the pay? What if he doesn't pay enough?"

"Eh, I don't really need it. I mean, the Army has me at 100% disability, which is more than enough to live in this little town. If I wanted to move somewhere like Fort Worth where the cost of living is more, then I'd be pushing the budget. But here? Working for Nick would just be for fun. Won't turn down a paycheck, but it doesn't matter if all he offers is minimum wage. It'd still be worth it."

"I'm so happy for you, Andy. You've been searching for a purpose, and here it is! Falling right in your lap!"

He grinned and kissed her. His joy was infectious but there was still a heaviness in her heart. He pulled back and stood up, going back around the bench to take more videos of Cody.

Maybe this job would take up all his time. Maybe he wouldn't want to see where their relationship could go. Maybe he was just bored and killing time with her. Her heart hurt at the thought of not seeing him all the time, but the idea that maybe he didn't really want her was ten times worse.

He was too good-looking, too successful to want someone like her. She struggled to fight off the creeping invasive thoughts of not being enough. She knew she needed to sort out her feelings—and fast—before it consumed her.

Chapter Thirty-Two

The next day, Andy stepped into the shower after lunch to clean up. Wednesday night when Cindy had gone home with the boys, his heart had ached. He hadn't had time to think about it though because Mandy had stayed the night.

That had been fun but stressful. He'd never given a child a bath before but thanks to FaceTime with Cindy, he'd managed. She'd only cried once when the soap got in her eyes.

They'd both fallen asleep in the fort tent, an old lantern working as the night light. Eventually he'd gone to his own bed, but he'd been stiff and out of sorts since waking up.

He'd taken Mandy home so Aunt Suzie could get her ready for school—and so they could have a brief chat—but she wasn't home. He got her changed for school and repacked her little unicorn backpack with fresh clothes. After dropping Mandy off at school, he went to Nick's and took a tour of the business.

Of course, he'd started tinkering around with some of

the tractor radios, which had been fun. There were a few he'd brought home to work on, but he needed a shower from being outside at Nick's.

As he stepped out of the shower, he imagined Cindy and the kids at the table last night. They'd eaten dinner like an actual family. He'd laughed so hard at the crazy things the kids had said. It was loud, but fun and peaceful in the chaos.

His phone rang, and he answered it without looking.

"Hello?"

"Andy? This is Cody. Can you come pick me up from school?"

"What? Why? Where's your mom?"

"Mom's at work. I was going home with a friend from school, but his mom told him at lunch that she's sick, so I can't come over anymore. James is going to someone else's house, and Auntie M has Owen somewhere and isn't answering."

"What time does school let out?"

"I have one class left, so in an hour?"

"Sure, I'll be there. The middle school, right?" He'd been at the elementary school with James yesterday, but the two schools were practically side by side.

"Yeah, pull around to the gym parking lot. I need to drop something off with Coach."

They hung up, and Andy grinned. He cleaned up the house, thinking about how he could get them all back over for dinner and a movie. Or they could play card games. Mandy might be too young to learn Uno, but they could try.

An hour later, he waved at Cody in the parking lot. Kids milled around as the busses left.

"Hey," Cody said as he jumped into the passenger seat. "Thanks for getting me. I really didn't want to stay at the school until seven."

"What's happening at seven?"

"That's when Mom is picking up James from his friend's house. Auntie M is bringing Owen home, and my friend's mom was going to take me home then too."

"Sounds good. Do you have a key to your apartment?" When Cody nodded, Andy drove across town and pulled up to the complex. When Cody opened the door, and they stepped in, Andy glanced around.

How had he only been there once? He loved her. He should know what her space looks like. Walking around the living room and kitchen, he frowned as Cody came out of his bedroom.

"Do you know if she was going to cook dinner or were you all eating separately and just meeting up here later?"

"She was bringing food home, I think."

"Let's see if we can surprise her with something warm and fresh then." They walked into the kitchen, and Cody showed him where the pantry cabinets were. It was tiny and packed with food, way too small for a family of four.

"There are always pasta makings. I cook that with Mom once a week," Cody said, waving a box of noodles at him. Andy smiled as he grabbed a jar of spaghetti sauce. They started the meat for the spaghetti and talked about the school day and Andy's new job.

When the meat was done, he showed Cody how to strain it.

"Mom never lets me strain the meat," Cody said with a frown.

"She's probably worried you'll splash the hot grease on yourself. That stuff burns."

The Soldier Gets His Girl

"Do you want to start the sauce now?"

Andy thought about it, then turned the burners off on the stove. "Nah, we'll wait an hour at least. It's only four-thirty. Why don't we clean up the apartment a bit, then we can hang out?"

"We have video games and a soccer ball, if you want," Cody asked, looking down and hunching his shoulders.

Andy looked under the kitchen sink for cleaning supplies. "I love both, but first, let's take half an hour to clean, alright? What's your favorite video game? We played a lot during deployments."

He handed Cody a rag and the cleaning spray. They worked room by room until it sparkled and shined. Cody put up the toys while Andy swept and mopped. Cody found the vacuum for the bedrooms while Andy did the laundry.

When Maryanne came in with Owen at a quarter til seven, the place was spotless and the smell of spaghetti was making both he and Cody hungry. They'd each eaten a piece of the cheesy French toast he'd made, but it wasn't going to last very long.

"Wow, I'm not sure that I've ever seen the place this clean. What are you doing here, Andy? Did you just stop by to clean and cook? Can you do that for my place next?" Maryanne chuckled.

Andy grinned as Cody said, "No, I couldn't go to my friend's after all. And you and Mom weren't answering, so I called Andy."

Andy shrugged, putting down the controller. "I wasn't busy, so here I am."

James opened the door and threw his bag down by the door, catching sight of Andy and saying, "Andy!"

Cindy stepped through the door and saw him, her face lighting up. But then she glanced around, taking in the clean apartment and the food on the table with a frown. He ached to greet her with a kiss, wrap her in his arms. He wanted to see the stressed look on her face melt away.

The kids were crowding her though. Cody told her all about why Andy was there and how they'd cooked, cleaned, and played video games. She ran her hand over Cody's head, his brown hair falling forward again, then she smiled over his head at Andy. That smile made the effort worth it.

Andy stood and went to the kitchen. This was home because it was where she was. His house was empty without her there.

"Ya'll hungry? Everyone like spaghetti and cheesy bread?" They all talked over each other as they made their plates. The table barely fit the six of them, but they made it work.

There was no pressure to go or to be someone else. They all just talked and said what they thought. He loved that. Growing up with his mom and then the Army, he'd needed to watch every word out of his mouth.

He glanced at Cindy. Her hair shone in the light, her thick braid coming undone slightly after a long day of PT. He wanted to run his fingers through it and kiss her perfectly pink lips. Her groans and moans drove him to distraction, and it'd been too long without her in his arms.

Shifting in the chair, he tore his eyes from her. Tuning back into the conversation, he tried to think of ways he could convince her to let him stay the night.

Andy woke up on Friday on the wrong side of the bed. Literally. He tried to get out of bed on the opposite side as normal, forgot he was missing a leg, and almost fell on the floor.

Thankfully, he swung himself so he landed mostly on the bed, but it still pissed him off. When he finally made it into the kitchen, he found that the coffee was all gone and that made him even madder.

He decided to go for a run and clear his head. If he thought about it, the 'off' feeling had started last night when Cindy had gently waved him out the door so she could get the kids in bed. Texting last night wasn't enough.

He wanted to see her every day. He wanted to wake up with her in his arms. He wanted them to move in.

But how could he convince her? They'd only known each other a little over a month!

He was not the most patient man, but he knew that's what she needed—patience and time to see that he would not turn into an asshole.

As he jogged down the lane, he saw an unfamiliar little car in the driveway. Looking at his watch, he saw it was just nine and slowed to a walk.

A tall blond stepped out wearing Scooby Doo scrubs, her hair pulled into a ponytail. She pushed up the glasses on her wide nose and smiled nervously.

"Hello, I'm Monica. I'm the new PTA?"

He nodded slowly and smiled politely. "Yes, ma'am. I'd heard about that. But the appointment wasn't supposed to be until ten?"

She pulled out her phone and swiped with a frown. "It is ten."

He chuckled as he showed her his watch. "Time change isn't until Sunday, so I'm not sure what's going on. It's definitely nine, but since you're here, come on in and we'll figure it out."

She frowned as she grabbed her bag and shut her car door, still scrolling on her phone. She was probably older than him, based on how awkward she seemed with the phone. "This darn phone... I had to get a new fancy one when they hired me here, and it doesn't work the same as my old one."

He opened the door and held it for her. After he closed it, he grabbed his shirt off the back of the couch and a water bottle from the fridge.

He waved to the couch. "Would you like to sit for a minute or jump right into it? Do you need to ask me questions or anything?"

She pulled out her binder and looked around. "Can we sit at the kitchen table? I like to write as we go."

He nodded, and they sat.

"I don't have many questions. Cindy's notes were very thorough on the exercises you were doing and the goals. I noticed you were running. Will a session be too much on your leg or do you run every day?"

He answered a few questions before she directed him to do some very scripted and very boring exercises from his chair. Next he did some sitting to standing exercises, all very basic. He sighed with relief when their time was up.

After she drove off, he closed the door and took a shower. He was feeling dirty from the run and the PT. He scrubbed twice then hopped out, wondering if Cindy would want to swing by for lunch. He dried off and snapped on his prosthetic, threw the towel in the laundry, and walked into his bedroom toward his closet.

Hearing sounds in the kitchen, he threw on shorts and a t-shirt and walked down the hallway. The feeling of dread in his chest eased when he saw it was Cindy and not Aunt Suzie.

"Hey, I was about to text to see if you wanted lunch." He smiled as she looked up at him, her face open and relaxed just the way he liked it.

All the unease from being without her eased as he pulled her into his arms. He breathed deeply as his tongue dueled with hers, catching her moan and squeezing her to him tighter until she pushed away slightly with a laugh.

The sound of it shot straight to his cock, making him even harder. He looked into her eyes and smiled as she pushed against his chest softly.

"I missed you, so I thought I'd eat lunch with you. I should've texted, but I also wanted to see how the session was."

He stepped back as they raided the refrigerator. "No need to text. My house is always open to you. Are BLT's okay?" He almost asked her to move in, but the timing wasn't right.

"Did you buy bacon hoping I'd cook it for you?" she teased as he got out the ingredients and handed them to her to put on the island.

He laughed, "No, I was going to just throw it on the flat griddle. You're a wonderful cook though. That crock pot leftovers are already all gone. You should've taken that home because I gorged myself on it."

She laughed, and the sound filled his soul with joy. "At least I've got good cook going for me. And they say the way to a man's heart is through his stomach."

"You're on the right track," he said, not admitting that she already had his whole heart.

She rolled her eyes, her cheeks turning that pretty pink he loved so much. "Doubtful. I'm too much of a challenge with too much baggage."

"I wouldn't call you a challenge. I'd call you spicy," he

winked. They teased each other as they worked. The flirting was light-hearted as he made the bacon, and she built the sandwiches.

He asked about the PT appointment time, and she explained about the calendar mix-up. Monica had called after she'd left, and Cindy had helped her figure out what had happened.

She asked about the radios that were sitting on the side table in the living room, and he told her about the work at Nick's yesterday.

"Can't you stay a little longer? I think I need a little massage on my leg from the PT session today," he pleaded, pulling her into his arms after they'd cleaned up the dirty dishes together.

She giggled as she kissed his scruffy chin. Rubbing her hands up and down his biceps, she said, "I wish I could. I came early for lunch because I have a patient soon, and it's a farther drive than normal. Then I'm working the hospital tonight."

He rested his forehead on hers, whishing she didn't have to work both jobs. "Maryanne has the boys this weekend?"

"Yeah, like normal. She's too good of a sister." She leaned up and kissed him like a starving lion. It was a promise of passion, and he intended to hold her to it when she finally had time for him. He growled as their tongues twisted and lapped at each other.

Grinding his hips into hers, she pulled back and twisted out of his arms. She touched her bruised lips, that small secretive smile hovering on them as she backed up to the door. "I'll text you this weekend?" He nodded, stalking after her, wanting to wrap her up in his arms.

Leaning his head on the door jamb, he gripped it hard as she hopped into her SUV and drove away. She had to move in with him. He loved her and wanted to take care of her so she wouldn't work so hard.

Surely she was falling for him too? He glanced down at his legs as he shut the door. Then again, maybe she was fooling around with him, not wanting to get serious with half a man. She had baggage, but he had challenges too.

Chapter Thirty-Three

He sat in the living room and worked on one of the radios. He'd barely gotten started when a phone rang. He didn't recognize the ringtone, but he followed the sound to the kitchen. Cindy's phone was under a random paper towel on the kitchen island, so he answered it.

"Hello?"

"Andy? Oh my God, is Cindy there?" Maryanne gasped. He heard crying in the background and frowned.

"No, she left about ten minutes ago for a PT session somewhere. She forgot her phone. What's going on?"

"It's Owen. I picked him up from school and took him to the park. Somehow he climbed onto the outside of the playground tube thing and fell off! I think he's hurt and I— I—" she sobbed and the phone cut in and out.

"Maryanne, calm down. It's going to be fine. Stay there, alright? I'm on my way, and we'll figure it out. Is he awake?" he kept her on the phone answering questions as he jogged down the hall to grab his phone, keys, and socks. Putting on socks and sneakers in the living room, he raced out the door, making sure to keep his tone of voice even.

The Army had taught him it wouldn't help if she heard the panic that was pushing ice through his veins. He made the ten minute drive to town in six and slowed only when he reached Main Street.

Shoving it in park, he jumped out and hung up the phone as he ran over to where Maryanne and Owen both lay crying on the playground. No one else was around, but he knelt down beside them and gave a small, totally fake, smile.

"Okay, let's see what's going on, big guy. What'd you land on?"

He sniffed as Maryanne pointed. "His left side. I don't think he hit his head though."

"Is it your arm?" He gently touched it. Owen curled into Maryanne's arms, his bottom lip quivering.

"I have an idea. Let me go get something from my truck. Then we're going to put your arm on it to keep it still. That will help it not hurt while we drive to the hospital, got it?"

"The hospital? Is Mama there?" he mumbled into Maryanne's shoulder.

Andy shook his head as he stood up slowly. "No, she's not there yet, but she will be later. I'm going to call her, alright, buddy? Hang tight."

Jogging back to his truck, he saw the other box of radios that he'd meant to bring in yesterday. Now he was glad he'd forgotten it. He tore off two of the cardboard flaps on the top and grabbed some 550 cord from his center console.

Opening his phone, he called the office for the physical therapy place.

"Hi, can I speak with Maggie please? Yes... Alright,

then can I leave a message? Tell her that Cindy doesn't have her phone, but she needs to call Andy immediately. It's an emergency."

He thanked the receptionist and hung up as he knelt down beside Owen. He laid the bottom piece of cardboard on the ground, explaining every step in the process. Owen slid off Maryanne's lap slowly and laid down on the ground.

Andy praised him as he tied the five-fifty cord around the cardboard and helped him sit up. Maryanne twisted her hands, tears still streaming down her cheeks.

"There! Now you're ready to hop in the truck, right? Maryanne, do you have his booster? You can ride in the back with him and make sure he doesn't move it or bang it on anything, but the cardboard is extra special and will protect it." She jumped up and raced to her little red car to grab it.

Owen nodded but started crying more as he stood up.

"What is it, big guy?"

"I don't want to walk," he sobbed. Andy nodded and scooped him up gently in his arms.

"That's fine. Probably a good idea not to. Not until the doc checks you out. Will this work? Put your cardboard arm on your stomach, and I'll take you to the truck." He walked slowly, taking extra care to even out his limp so it wouldn't jar the boy.

Maryanne opened the door, and he slid Owen inside. He closed the door as he and Maryanne rounded the truck and each got inside, her in the back with Owen.

He started the engine and backed out. Owen started crying again, the noise filling the cab and giving Andy a headache. They pulled into the hospital parking lot minutes later. He carried Owen inside as Maryanne checked them in with the paper work.

Owen wailed, clinging to his neck. "Don't leave me, Andy! Don't leave me!"

"I won't, big guy. I'm right here."

"I don't want a shot!"

"They probably won't give you a shot."

"I don't want them to cut off my arm like they did your leg!"

He chuckled as he adjusted Owen on his lap in the small waiting room. He ran his hand over Owen's little head, cupping his face and hugging him tightly. "Don't worry, big guy. They won't do that. I won't let them, okay? Do you want me to tell the story of what happened with my leg?"

His heart pounded. He'd been careful to wear jeans around the boys. He hadn't thought about it when he'd raced out of the house in his basketball shorts. They'd seen his leg on Halloween, but none of them had said anything until now.

When Owen nodded, he said, "I was in a line of trucks called a convoy. We were going to a town in the desert where the radios had stopped working. The people needed those radios to call for supplies like food, water, and things like that. We were almost to the town when the truck in front of mine was hit with a missile and blew up."

"Did people die?" Owen whispered, his crying silent now as he listened.

"Yes, several of my friends."

"Does it make you sad? When Mama's 'Buela died, she was sad."

"Yes, I'm still sad about it, but we can't change the past. We can only make better choices in the future. Like today. We can't change that you fell and got hurt, but I bet you won't climb on the outside of the playground again, right? You'll make a better choice in the future."

Owen nodded against his chest as the nurse called them to go back into a room. Owen made him sit on the hospital bed and hold him, Maryanne fluttering next to the bed the entire time talking too fast about calling Margarita who was out of town.

He eventually sat in a wheelchair with Owen on his lap, carried him onto the x-ray table and held his hand, then held him in the wheelchair back to the room. Kendall walked in a short while later and blinked. "Andy? What are you doing here? Good to see you're not the patient today."

Andy chuckled and put his phone away, pausing Owen's video. "Yeah, I'm sort of seeing Cindy, so when Maryanne couldn't reach her, I came running."

"Is he going to be okay?" Maryanne twisted her hands anxiously.

"Do I need a shot?" Owen murmured, tensing up in Andy's arms.

Kendall smiled at Maryanne before sitting on a rolling stool. "Yes, he's going to be fine. And no, you do not need a shot. At least, not yet. You've broken your elbow though. Your bones are tiny, and you'll need surgery to fix it. I can call the ambulance to transfer him to Children's Hospital in Dallas, or you guys can drive him?"

Maryanne gasped, "Surgery!"

Andy rubbed soothing circles on Owen's back as he tensed. "That's going to be an adventure, huh, big guy? You might even get a cool scar out of it and get to pick out the color of your cast!"

There was a commotion in the hallway, and Cindy swept in, her curly hair coming out of her ponytail. Her eyes flashed as she walked straight to Owen who cried, "Mama!" He almost fell off the hospital bed as he reached for her.

Andy slid off the bed quickly as she gathered him up, careful of his arm that was now wrapped in soft gauze wrap.

"I'm going to guess you won't be in to work tonight, Cindy?"

She glanced at Kendall anxiously. "What's the verdict?"

"Surgery at Children's for the broken elbow. Do you want the ambulance?"

She nodded slowly as she checked Owen over for other injuries. "Yeah, that's fine. It'll be quicker that way."

Kendall nodded and left to order the transfer. Maryanne talked without taking a breath, telling her every single detail that had happened. When she finally stopped to take a breath, Cindy smiled tightly at her. Reaching out a hand, Cindy reassured her it was going to be fine.

Andy leaned against the counter in the room, taking the pressure off his leg. Carrying Owen around, plus the PT earlier, plus the run this morning was wearing it out. It throbbed actually, now that he had time to register it in his head.

The EMS team came in and wheeled Owen out of the room. They hooked him up to an IV which made him cry, but when he saw the ambulance, he stopped to ask lots of questions about all the parts.

Maryanne hugged Cindy as they stood outside the ambulance and waited. "I'm so sorry, sis. I don't know how it happened. I'll pick up the boys and take care of everything, okay? I'm so, so sorry!"

Cindy chuckled shakily as she hugged her back. "It's going to be fine, M. Boys get hurt all the time. Remember two years ago when Cody had to get stitches on his leg?"

Maryanne laughed as more tears streamed down her face. "But this one was my fault!"

"It's no one's fault. These things just happen. Kids are kids."

"I—I'm going to go to the bathroom."

"Here. Take my keys to the SUV. You can pick us up when we're released after the surgery?" Cindy handed over her keys and Maryanne nodded, walking back inside. Owen was still chattering with the paramedics, the pain medicine in the IV making him talkative.

Cindy turned to Andy and narrowed her eyes. He blinked at the fierce look on her face.

"What?"

"You swept in and solved all the problems, didn't you? Just like that? I saw you in there. I heard what M said. You're not his dad. You've not been here his whole life. *I* have. He's *my* baby. While I appreciate the help in getting him here, Maryanne should have been the one holding him. She's his aunt for crying out loud. You're nothing."

"Nothing," he said flatly, clenching his fists at his side. Where was all this coming from? That wasn't enough fodder for this kind of anger. Something else must've happened.

"Nothing but trouble. Do you have my phone?"

He pulled it out of his pocket and handed it over. She glanced at it and slid it into her purse, then crossed her arms. "I got back to the office and had a meeting with Maggie. She'd run into *Suzie* earlier this morning, who gave her an ear full."

His stomach churned and twisted, the heavy weight of dread causing his muscles to tense and knot. Her hands waved as she continued.

"Then when she got to the office and saw that there was a message from you saying for me to call you, she figured that everything Suzie said was true. So she fired me. I'll probably lose my physical therapy assistant certification."

Jaw set in a hard line and fists clenched tight, he trembled with the force of his rage. "She can't do that. You followed the rules and asked for a transfer. We're not patient-therapist anymore. We're apparently nothing," he said stonily. His jaw cracked, and he breathed deeply to let go of the tension. It was like a weight was pressing on his chest.

She snorted, "Doesn't matter. We had sex less than a week after your last therapy session with me. Luckily, the last therapy session that we were scheduled for was canceled when you were a no-show. I'll have a review in 60 days to see if I keep my certification. Of course, that's after Christmas, which now might not even happen because I'll have to pay for this ambulance ride and surgery… with only one income. So yeah. I'm pretty pissed because none of this would be happening right now if it weren't for *you*."

He could feel the heat of his anger radiating off his body, making his skin flush and tingle. His body seemed to pulse with pain from his head to his foot.

He growled, "Good God, Cindy. I'm not the one who fell off a playground so don't go blaming that on me. And it takes two to tango. I might have pursued you but you *always* wanted it."

Shit. As soon as the words left his mouth, he knew they were the wrong ones.

"Well, not anymore, buddy. This is over," she snorted, pointing from herself to him and back again. "Over before it even officially got started. Thanks for the help with Owen, but leave my boys alone, alright? We'll be fine. We always have and we always will."

He crossed his arms and glared at her. "Fine is over-rated, and you know it. You're the one who told me that."

A paramedic hopped down from the back of the ambulance and rounded the side where they stood facing off against each other.

He imagined they looked quite the pair, both with legs spread wide and arms crossed, glaring daggers at each other.

"We're ready to go, Cindy."

"Sure thing," she said, not breaking eye contact as she pursed her lips. "Bye, Andy. I'll be seeing you never."

She spun on her heel, stormed over to the back, and hopped up. The paramedic shut the doors behind her and walked around to get into the driver's side. He stood frozen as the ambulance drove away.

Kendall came out and saw him still standing there as it passed out of sight. "You can go down there with them. It's only in Dallas."

Andy slowly shook his head and breathed deeply, trying to shake away the anger and confusion and pain. "I think she just broke up with me."

"Damn. Sorry, man. That little boy is going to be upset about that."

Andy nodded as he thought about the boys. All three of them would be. Cody only had two more Saturday games before the season would be over, the last being the out-of-town tournament. His phone vibrated in his pocket with a text from Landry.

Decorating the float tonight at the old football field. BYOB!

Kendall glanced up from his own phone and Andy noted it was a group text thread. "This will be perfect, man!

They'll help take your mind off Cindy tonight. Sound good?"

Andy smiled wryly. "Sure. This is more my kind of Friday night. Building crap and drinking with friends."

Kendall laughed, and they said their goodbyes. Andy walked through the parking lot to his truck. He'd swing by the grocery store and grab some drinks. Then go soak in the hot tub for a while before going to meet up with Landry.

Chapter Thirty-Four

Andy was getting out of the hot tub when he heard a vehicle pull up in front of the house. He closed the back door and walked with the towel wrapped around his swimming trunks to the front door. As it opened, he saw Suzie, Mike, and Mandy tromp inside.

He pasted on a fake smile for Mandy's sake. "Hey, guys! Give me a second to change out of these wet clothes."

He thought of all the things he wanted to say to Suzie as he pulled on clean jeans and a thin long-sleeved shirt. Padding barefoot down the hall, he saw Mandy's feet poking out from under the sheet tent.

Grabbing a bottle of water from the fridge, he sat at the dining room table. Mike had a folder in front of him, and Suzie was fiddling with a coffee cup, her eyes downcast and refusing to meet his.

"I have several things to say but it seems like you do too. I don't want you here, Aunt Suzie. I don't appreciate what you've done and until you fix it or I'm no longer mad, I don't want to see you. That being said, it seems like you came to talk about something else. Otherwise, you wouldn't have brought Uncle Mike."

Uncle Mike looked back and forth from Suzie to Andy. "I don't know what's going on between you two, but this conversation is long overdue. We're going to lay all our cards out on the table, son." He rubbed a hand on the back of his neck and stretched it.

Andy crossed his arms and leaned back in the chair. "I'd appreciate that. I'm tired of the manipulation and drama."

Suzie sucked in a breath, her bottom lip wobbling as her eyes pleaded with him. He frowned and narrowed his eyes. He wasn't going to be taken in by that innocent expression. He'd seen it too many times on Sarah's face growing up to be fooled.

Uncle Mike slid the folder over to him. "These are official and legally binding."

Andy flipped open the folder and saw a birth certificate. The more he read, the more his hands trembled and his stomach twisted. The letters seemed to swirl and dance before eventually forming into recognizable words. Each line and number etched into his mind, burning into his memory.

"This is Mandy's birth certificate," he paused, not believing what he was seeing. He took in every detail of the document, from the font to the signatures at the bottom. There in black ink as clear as day was something he never expected. "That's my name."

A high-pitched ringing echoed in his head, similar to an explosion or the aftermath of a loud clap of thunder. The shock felt like lightning stabbing his chest, constricting his breathing. His muscles tensed and his heart raced.

Uncle Mike nodded. "It wasn't Sarah that was pregnant and had Mandy. It was Stella."

Stella's name at the top confirmed his words. He was filled with a mixture of shock, apprehension, and excitement as he read the name on the birth certificate—his daughter's name—Stella's, and his own. He kept glancing from one to the other, hoping he was mistaken.

His heart raced, and he flipped through the next few pages of legal paperwork, searching for answers. How, why, they all flew together in his mind. The last document had Sarah's signature, awarding Mike and Suzie guardianship. The timeline slowly started to come together.

Uncle Mike cleared his throat. "Not sure if you remember, but Stella was a pre-law student. She made sure that all legal paperwork for Mandy was signed three days after she gave birth. Sarah was to be the guardian if anything ever happened to her."

Stella hadn't had any family of her own. She'd been a foster kid, which was why she was going to work in family law and why Sarah had sort of adopted her as the sister she'd never had. His eyes widened in disbelief as he struggled to process the unexpected news. Everything seemed to slow down and blur together, making him dizzy and disoriented. He felt like he was floating outside of himself, watching the scene play out in slow motion.

He shook his head, his headache starting to return. "I don't understand. Why didn't she tell me?"

Mike shrugged. "You were deployed. From what Sarah said before she slipped into the coma, Stella was going to wait til you returned."

"But then they died," Andy said, his voice hollow and wooden to his ears.

Suzie started crying silently, tears rolling down her cheeks. "When we lost Sarah, it was the hardest thing I'd ever had to go through. And then there was this little blue-eyed baby girl who reminded me so much of what we'd lost that I—I couldn't bring myself to tell you when you returned."

She picked up her mug, holding it in both hands to keep it from shaking and spilling onto the table. Andy looked at Mike. Their gazes met, both filled with pain and regret.

"Mandy was the one ray of hope we had during that first year. Then, before we could even catch our breath, Jake left and you deployed again. We understood then why Stella didn't want to tell you while you were gone. We were afraid it would distract you from the mission and get you killed."

"It could have given me hope, a reason to come home," he said harshly, his eyes wide with disbelief, a flicker of betrayal and confusion leaving him rooted to the chair.

Mike nodded, a calming, steady presence. "I know that now, but back then, when we were grieving? Well, things that made sense then don't really make sense now."

"Why didn't you tell me when I came home?"

Suzie sighed, placing her forehead in her hand and rubbing. "You'd lost your leg, Andy. We knew that was going to take all your focus, and it did. We saw you struggle, what you went through, and couldn't put learning to be a dad on your shoulders along with learning how to walk and do all the things you used to do."

He leaned back in the chair and drank his bottle of water. "All this time, I've been lonely and wanting a family of my own... and I had one." Disbelief made his voice softer than normal, and the pounding in his head increased.

"Oh, Andy, you have a family. We're your family," Suzie said, reaching over and squeezing his hand. He jerked his hand back and glared daggers at her. She pulled back slowly, blinking more tears to drip down her face.

"Now, don't be like that, son. Whatever's going on, we

can work this out." Mike was solemn, the lines on his face deepening.

His jaw set in a hard line, eyes narrowed into slits as he glared at Aunt Suzie. "Family means love, and love doesn't lie. Love doesn't deliberately hide life-altering secrets like this."

"I know, we shouldn't have kept it from you for so long. You're healthy now, and settled back home, so here we are." Mike leaned back in his chair and crossed his arms.

Andy shook his head and grabbed his water, drinking as he gathered his thoughts. His voice was low and dangerous as he spoke to his uncle, a deep growl underlying his words. "Whether we work this out or not is entirely up to Aunt Suzie. Give me a few days to come to terms with this, and I'll adjust to being a dad. But what she's been doing with Cindy is inexcusable."

Mike looked perplexed, his head tilting to the side. "She's been doing what with who?"

Andy sat his water down and rubbed his temples. "I wanted to date Cindy, a nurse from the hospital who became my physical therapist, and she sabotaged it. Aunt Suzie not only verbally abused her in my own home last week, but she also got her fired today."

"Suzie!" Mike reprimanded.

Flinging up her hands, Suzie glared at Mike. "What? She's a hussy with three kids and two baby daddies. All she wants is another kid and child support. She's playing him!"

"She is not!" Andy roared, jumping to his feet and waving his arms. "Cody's dad refused to acknowledge him and ran off when they were in high school. The other ex is in *prison* because he stole prescriptions from her work, then used Cody to deliver them. There is no child support! From anywhere!"

He threw himself away from the table, the chair clattering to the floor as he paced. He could feel his muscles tensing, his jaw clenching, his fists tightening. All because of his aunt's actions, driven by her misguided sense of righteousness. He couldn't stand it, couldn't bear to see someone he loved be hurt like this. His anger burned like fire, ready to consume anyone who dared to stand in his way.

"She's a single mom doing a damn fine job raising three smart, talented, and kind boys. She's the *best* thing that's ever happened to me, outside of five minutes ago when I found out I'm a fucking dad!"

"You're a daddy? Where's the baby! I want to see the baby!" Mandy said from the hallway. He must have drawn her attention with his outburst. He spun around and picked his chair up, sinking into it as he stared at her. She came up to them at the table, her chubby little cheeks flushed from playing and her blue eyes wide and innocent.

He swallowed hard and leaned forward to balance his elbows on his knees. No more fucking secrets in this family. He was done with it.

He sighed and took a deep breath as she neared. "I don't have a baby. I—I have a Mandy. I'm *your* dad." He cringed. There was probably a better way to tell her this, but his mind was so overloaded he couldn't think of it.

Suzie half rose from her chair, but Mike reached across the table and grabbed her wrist. She froze and sat back down.

Mandy blinked owlishly, her jaw trembling. "I have a daddy?"

He nodded slowly, and her face lit up with a broad grin as she ran to him. He wrapped her up in a hug, pulling her onto his lap with a soft chuckle.

"I didn't know until right now, or I would've told you

sooner," he whispered as he breathed in her baby smell. She had Stella's blond hair, what he'd once thought was Sarah's blond hair. But his eyes and nose. Damn, even her name was from him! *How did I not see it?*

"Will you live with me here?" he asked her suddenly. She pulled out of his hug and glanced from Suzie to Mike and back to him, a frown on her face as she thought.

"Will it make Gamma sad?"

He glanced at Suzie, and she smiled a wobbly, wet smile, reaching out and stroking Mandy's hair out of her eyes. "I might be sad for a little while, but you're right down the road. I can come over all the time, and you can come stay with me and have sleepovers. This way I get to be Gamma, and your Daddy gets to be Daddy."

Mandy tilted her head to the side and hummed. "Okay, I'll move in after church." They laughed as she told them how it was going to be. He squeezed her tight and kissed the top of her head.

She wiggled off his lap. "I'm hungry, Daddy." His chest tightened at the new title, and his own eyes teared up. He coughed, choking back tears as he stood and walked to the pantry to grab a small, single package of gold fish that he'd picked up earlier.

"Will this work? I'll make something for dinner, if you'll all stay?" he asked, glancing at Mike and Suzie. They smiled. He opened the package, and she took off back to the tent to eat her fish over the 'fire.'

Mike stood up and stretched. "I'm going to see what this fire and tent situation is now that's all settled. Suzie, you settle this Cindy thing, you hear?" She sighed but nodded.

He gathered things for chicken and veggies out of the fridge and put it all on a tray. "I'm going to go fire up the grill and cook this. Will you open the door?"

She nodded, seeming unsure but resigned. She opened the back door for him. He walked to the opposite side of the back porch as the hot tub. He fired up the propane and set the tray down on the outdoor table. Suzie sat in a chair and stared into the woods.

"Tell me about Cindy," she mumbled, sounding miserable.

He prepped the food, unwrapping it. He was emotionally drained from the day and had entered a state of numbness that was probably for the best. "What do you want to know?"

She shrugged and rubbed her forehead again. "Start at the beginning, I guess. I've apparently made some pretty major assumptions about her. Tell me about her first baby daddy?"

He told her everything he knew, everything he could remember of what Cindy had told him. He might have over shared, which is not something he'd ever done before, but he wanted everything out in the open so all this confusion would stop.

He told her about the kidney stones and meeting her for the first time, how he'd felt even then with all the pain and medicine, and about the first PT session and how he'd pursued her but she'd always refused.

He told her about how her mom had tricked them into going shopping for costumes together and how she took care of him when he had a migraine.

She finally sighed. "Ahh, that makes sense then. I came over after your PT session, and there was a note on the counter. It didn't say who it was from, but I had assumed it was Maryanne at the time, judging from the pastries and the... tone of it. You were still asleep, so I didn't wake you."

He smiled, not telling her he'd saved the note. "The

crowd at the Halloween party at the Williams' was huge, Aunt Suzie. The place was loud with the band, people were crowded in... and I didn't panic."

"Honey, that's great! You're getting better!"

He turned from the grill and met her eyes, his own hard as he glared. "I'm better when I'm *with her*. She calms me, somehow. Not that it matters anymore. We weren't ever really dating, but she sort of broke up with me today after you got her fired."

"That's okay. You've got enough to worry about with moving Mandy in and all. It'll all work out in the end, whether that's with her or with someone else."

He gathered up the throw away trays the food had come in and breathed deeply through his nose. He wasn't numb enough for this conversation, as his anger at her cavalier attitude was climbing at an alarming rate.

He caught her gaze and held it a few moments so she'd know he meant business. "Suzie, there will be no one else but her. It's her or no one. I love her."

She frowned, blinking as she opened her mouth. "No," he said, his voice harsh. "You listened to everything I had to say, but you still don't get it. *You* don't get a say in this. *You* have done nothing but jeopardize her ability to feed three kids. You may not have wanted Cindy to take my money and for me to be her baby daddy, but I pray every fucking day that she does because *I love her*."

He picked up the tray and walked to the back door, kicking it open. It banged against the wall as he walked through the hallway. He saw it in her eyes. She didn't believe him. Even knowing Cindy's background, Suzie still disapproved.

Did anyone understand women? As he passed Mandy's room, he heard her giggling with Uncle Mike. He'd better learn quickly how to understand women because he was going to be raising one!

His heart beat a little faster as he threw away the trash, washed his hands from the raw chicken, and pulled out plates to set the table. He wanted nothing more than to cut Aunt Suzie from his life, but that wasn't fair to Mandy or to Uncle Mike. He would see how the rest of dinner went before he made a decision on that.

Chapter Thirty-Five

He pulled up to the old football field barely five minutes early. He was exhausted, both physically and emotionally. Physically from the PT session and run and carrying Owen. Emotionally from worrying about Owen, then Cindy, then Suzie and learning he's a dad… It had all really taken it out of him.

He got out slowly from the truck and grabbed the case of beer as he checked his texts. He'd asked Maryanne for an update on Owen; his surgery wasn't until tomorrow morning so they were spending the night in the hospital.

No messages yet though, so he started walking to the floats. The old track field had several trailers on it, each labeled with an era or war. He walked to the last one that said *Post 9/11* and found Landry and Nick.

"Hey, man! Glad you could make it," Landry said as he hopped off the back. Andy set the case of beer down.

"Are we the only one's working on this?" He glanced around. Looked like he was the last one there.

"Yeah, my brothers are playing at the Electric Cowboy

tonight, and Kendall's working this weekend. But three of the best can still put a good dent on it!" Landry replied.

"If I'd known there were only three, I wouldn't have bought the 24 pack," Andy chuckled.

Nick came around from the front with a smile and a beer already in his hand. "Eh, any leftovers, and I'll take care of them." Grinning, Nick slapped him on the back. Andy stumbled and Landry reached out to steady him.

"Sorry, man. Didn't think I slapped ya that hard," Nick said, taking the case of beer and putting it on the bed of the trailer.

"You didn't. I've just had a long-ass day, and my leg hurts. No worries. What do we need to do first, Lan?"

He directed them to the back of his truck, which he'd driven right up onto the old track. They took out some lumber and framed something out with the pieces. Landry had labeled the backs with some code that only he understood.

"What exactly is this?" Nick asked as Landry directed him to screw in two pieces.

"We're building a Humvee."

"What the fuck?" Andy asked, looking in surprise from the pieces to Landry, who just laughed and waved his hand.

"Not an actual Humvee, but a miniature version. If we get it framed out today, then we can finish the siding tomorrow, then paint it Sunday or next week. I needed something that could be done relatively quick and easy because I've got to help the other floats with their projects too."

"Whose idea was it to build a fucking Humvee?" Andy grumbled as he placed two pieces next to Nick.

Landry shrugged. "I think there was a committee or something. Not really sure. Lola gave me a list of people to work on each float and a main theme for each one."

"Ahh, Lola. Is she still hung up on Kendall?" Nick asked.

"Yep, and neither of them are acknowledging it. It's hilarious to watch."

"Did you ever get anywhere with Holly or did you move on to less defended territory?" Andy asked Nick, who laughed.

"Honestly, I haven't had a chance to do much of anything the past few weeks. The new partnership is taking up a lot of my time, which is why I'm so glad you're on board with the radio repairs. You're a life saver!"

Andy grunted as he pushed on the drill, the whirring not helping with his headache. "Don't mention it. I was bored anyway."

"You didn't look bored at the park with Cindy," Nick said slyly.

Landry stopped organizing the pieces and glanced over, but he ignored it and shrugged. "She sort of dumped me today, so that's that."

"That sucks. What happened?"

Andy gritted his teeth. "Well, we weren't really dating because she was my physical therapist and the whole can't date a patient thing. We were getting to know each other, just running into each other now and then, you know? And she had already requested her work to give me a different therapist. It was all going so well, until Aunt Suzie got her fired today. Now Cindy won't talk to me."

"Your Aunt Suzie, man. I swear," Nick said with a shake of his head.

Andy rubbed his temples as he paused and grabbed a beer, sitting down to drink. "Yeah, and with Owen in the hospital for elbow surgery, I'm worried out of my mind for the little guy. Thankfully Maryanne is keeping me updated."

Landry chuckled. "You've got some major dad energy going on with her kids, man."

Andy shook his head and barked a laugh. "You don't even know the half of it. Tonight, Aunt Suzie dropped a bigger bomb than anything we saw overseas."

"Oh? What'd she say?" Landry asked, taking the drill and picking up where Andy had left off.

Andy took another drink and stared across the football field "Mandy's my daughter."

They both paused and looked at him. He just stared, unseeing as he thought through all the things he'd missed in her life thus far. He'd been deployed during her first birthday, had only seen her two or three times before they'd shown up at the hospital in D.C.

Landry's voice broke through his thoughts. "You slept with Sarah? Your cousin?"

Andy choked on his beer, then gasped, "No! I slept with Sarah's college roommate before I deployed. Apparently she's Mandy's mom, not Sarah. Stella died in the same car crash that sent Sarah to the hospital for a week, before she died. In the hospital, Sarah gave Suzie and Mike guardianship and told them about me being the dad."

"Damn. And they've kept it from you for how long?" Nick asked.

"Just over two years," he said, finishing off his beer. He reached for another as they worked in silence. Andy just sat there, not really seeing them and trying not to think.

After a few minutes, Landry moved to the next piece of the float. "So what are you going to do now?"

Andy frowned, his thoughts shifting from the past and all he'd missed to planning for the future. "Mandy's moving in on Sunday. I should probably get a lawyer, but I'm listed on the birth certificate, so I might not need one."

"Is Suzie fighting you on her moving in?" Nick asked.

Andy shook his head. "No, she knows it's time to let her go. I think all the lies and the pressure of keeping it all inside was eating at her too much. Hell, that's probably why she took out so much anger on Cindy. Maybe she just needed someone to lash out at since she couldn't lash out at herself."

Nick whistled. "That's deep, man. You sound like a therapist."

Andy laughed. "Well, I had over a year of mandatory daily therapy. I learned a few things. You should try it."

Nick snorted as he finished up framing one side. "I know a lawyer if you need one."

Landry moved to the other side and talked Nick through attaching the two corners as Andy finished his beer.

Landry picked up the drill for the other end. "You need help moving stuff around the cabin? I can help you remodel a bedroom for Mandy."

Andy grinned and rubbed the tension out of the back of his neck. "Actually, she's already taken over one room. On Wednesday, I convinced Cindy to bring the boys over to play because I had Mandy. Mandy and Owen are thick as thieves, kinda like we were as kids."

Nick opened a beer and sipped. "Is that why you were at the park? Is Mandy the little girl that was there?"

Andy nodded. "Yeah, I think Aunt Suzie has been throwing Mandy and I together to see how well I do as a dad. Maybe she was testing me to see if I could handle it."

Landry shook his head and pointed. "Nick, grab that one and hold it up. I'll level it and drill it in place. And I don't think Suzie would test you like that. That's a dick move, if that's what she was doing."

Andy shrugged. "I don't know, honestly. I've never seen

this side of Suzie before. Sarah said she was overbearing, but neither Jake nor I saw it."

Nick's face darkened, his eyes dimming in the low light of the night. "Maybe it's how she's grieving. Like, the grief triggered her or something."

Andy nodded slowly and finished his beer. As he got up to help with the float, his mind wandered to how grief changed people. It was a possibility. Landry and Nick talked about their weekend plans.

"I can swing by to move furniture anytime tomorrow morning, if you'd like," Landry said as he tested the frame. When it held, he directed them to hold up the side panels so he could screw them in.

"That'd be cool. Before we went to the park this week, Mandy and Owen built a blanket fort in the spare rooms I'd just set up as my office. Mandy stayed the night and slept in the fort, so that's probably her room now."

Landry grinned ear to ear, and Andy scowled, "What?"

Landry's light brown hair fell in his eyes as he shook his head. "Man, you are *such* a dad! You were already doing dad stuff and didn't even know it!"

Nick agreed, grabbing another beer and opening it with one hand. "Let me guess. You slept in the tent with her for a while?"

Andy tried to ignore the burning sensation creeping up his cheeks, but he felt vulnerable and exposed in front of his friends. He forced a nonchalant shrug and flashed them a cocky grin, masking his discomfort., "Of course, how else was I to get her to fall asleep?"

Both of them laughed, so he rolled his eyes and opened another beer. "It's not that big a deal, guys."

"Isn't it? Let me see," Landry said as they moved to the other side of the float to hang up the side of the fake humvee. "You had Mandy and Owen at the park, but that's where soccer practice ends. Did you invite Cindy and the boys back to your house for dinner?"

He shifted uncomfortably, holding the wood as Landry tried to level it with one hand while he finished his beer with the other. "Yeah, so? Cindy and I threw this chicken crack stuff in the crockpot before we went to the park, so it wasn't a ton of prep. No big deal."

"You made dinner with Cindy? That's so domesticated of you," Nick teased.

Landry finished screwing in the board, and pointed out the smaller pieces that remained. "No big deal? Of course it is. Y'all were playing house like one big family. I bet ya'll sat down to eat together too, right?"

Andy opened another beer, his soul growing weary of the teasing. So what if he wanted a big happy family? It had been so loud and chaotic at dinner the other night, full of laughter. Sure, there'd been some squabbling, but it had reminded him of the military. It was a brotherhood, a family, and he'd missed that.

Andy moved out of their way and left them to finish the end of the float, saying over his shoulder, "Oh, shut up. You've been to my house. There's nowhere else to sit that has enough seats for all six of us."

The two of them laughed and poked fun at him as they framed out the back of the Humvee. He sat, legs dangling off the back of the trailer. The cicadas chirped and the ever-present Texas wind cooled the sweat on his neck from the manual labor. He sipped and checked his phone, but there weren't any more updates from Maryanne about Owen. After so many beers, his mind wandered with the pleasant dulled edges.

The Soldier Gets His Girl

When the others moved to the front of the humvee, he asked, "What else do we need to do?"

Landry waved a hand and stretched. "You don't need to do anything. You're drunk, and you're not touching my tools like that."

"That's what she said." Andy laughed, hiccuping at the end which made Nick laugh.

Landry threw a crushed beer can at him. "You've definitely had enough, but answer me this, Batman. If you're cooking dinner, hanging out with her kids, and going to all the soccer games, does that mean it's serious, even if y'all weren't officially dating?"

Andy shook his head slowly, feeling his head slosh from the alcohol. "Not anymore," he whined. "She said that I wasn't Owen's dad and never would be and was too much trouble. And that was all before I even knew about Mandy! She'll never want me now. Too much baggage." He guzzled down the beer and reached for another.

"Oh, no you don't. Nick can take these home." Landry grabbed the few remaining in the case and handed the cardboard box to Nick, who jumped down and took it to the back of Landry's truck. He nursed his last beer, holding it in two hands so Landry wouldn't take it too.

"Come on, Nick. Let's knock this out. Ten more minutes, and we'll be done. Then I'll take this love sick dog home."

"Hey, I'm not love sick. I'm drunk!"

Landry snorted and pulled out the next supplies. "Seems like you love Cindy to me. I don't recall you ever getting drunk over a woman before. Although, to be fair, there are several women involved here that would drive any man to drink alone, not to mention the combined power of Suzie, Mandy, and Cindy."

Andy nodded, his head bobbing and making him dizzy. "Yeah, I love Cindy. I love Mandy too. Aunt Suzie? I'm not sure I love her at the moment." He laughed, hiccuping again.

Nick laughed as he came back. "I don't know how your Uncle Mike can love her, honestly."

Andy shrugged, feeling a bit defensive of his uncle. "He picks his battles. When he knows she's out of line, he straightens her up. Problem is, he knew nothing about what all she'd done to Cindy until today. Hopefully he talks with her tonight, and Suzie comes around."

"Why doesn't she like Cindy anyway?" Landry asked.

Andy rolled his eyes and sipped. "Suzie thought she was drawing child support from the boys' dads. So she thought that Cindy just wanted me to knock her up so she could get another child support payment."

Landry's brows shot up in surprise. "That's nuts! Why didn't she go gossip with Cindy's mom? Or my mom, for crying out loud? They would have both been glad to set that straight."

Andy's shoulders sank. "I don't know. Who knows how women think, much less my Aunt Suzie. She's crazy."

"Got that right," Nick said. They finished the frame for the Humvee, and Landry laid out all the sides where they needed to go. Nick grabbed a tarp from the back of his truck, and together they covered the project.

When they finished, Andy shifted forward on the tailgate and swayed. Landry quickly grabbed him by the shirt and pulled him back. He guessed he was about to fall on his face, but he didn't feel like he swayed that badly.

"Whoa, there! Let's see how we can get you down without jarring that leg," Landry said.

"Much oblijjj—oblijj—ob. Lie. Jed," he said slowly. Nick and Landry laughed as they helped him off the trailer.

Landry put his arm around him and walked him towards the passenger side of his classic truck. They told Nick goodbye as he walked to his own truck.

When they were on the road, Landry said, "You know, Andy, if you love Cindy, you gotta find a way to fix it. Moping around like tonight isn't doing you any good. It'll make you feel like shit tomorrow."

Andy groaned and rubbed a hand down his face. "I already feel like shit. The hangover will be icing on the cake. Oh! Cake! Can we stop and get some cake?"

"No," Landry chuckled, "Nowhere is open." Andy nodded, pulling out his phone to text Maryanne.

Do u hv cake

Uh, no?
Why do you want cake?

Idk Cake is goood.
U da bake lady.
Why don u hv cake.

Are you drunk?

Yess

Why?

Cindy saaid too fuck offf.
Caake wld maake her lv meee.

"Hey, what are you doing? Give me that!" Landry said, taking Andy's phone out of his hands. *His hands? My hands. My hands are weird.* Andy stared at his hands as Landry stopped in front of his house.

Andy looked up and said, "Oh, we're here. But where's the cake? I thought Maryanne was getting us cake."

Landry snorted and got out of the truck. "Nope, but if you come inside and lay down, I'll bring you some cake for when you wake up."

"Score!" Andy opened the door and stumbled into Landry's arms. Then his vision faded to black.

Chapter Thirty-Six

Andy groaned the next morning. He'd slept in his clothes, which meant he'd slept in his prosthesis. He rolled over and sat up slowly on the edge of the bed, rubbing his knee as it throbbed.

"Well, good morning. Hope you like your coffee black. I'm assuming it hasn't changed in the past few years," Landry said as he waltzed into the room.

He placed the cup of coffee and a bottle of pain killers beside him on the side table. Then he pulled the curtains back on the window and let in the light from the mid-morning sun.

"No, turn it off," Andy grumbled, rubbing at his eyes.

Landry chuckled, "I can't turn off the sun, dumb ass. Are you still drunk?"

Andy started to shake his head but groaned instead. "What time is it?" He reached for the pain killers and swallowed some down with the coffee.

"Almost ten."

"Shit, I'm going to be late." He slid the empty coffee

cup onto the side table and stumbled into the bathroom, Landry following him to make sure that he didn't fall on the floor.

"I'm glad I crashed here last night. You can't go anywhere. Your truck is still at the field. I'll drive you over this morning to grab it."

"Thanks, I appreciate it. Don't know what happened last night, but you didn't have to stay over. I'm fine," he turned on the shower and sat down in the chair.

Landry leaned against the door jamb. "No worries, man. Parker had a date last night, and I didn't want to be home. So this was a win-win for me. Breakfast is almost ready. You probably don't want anything, but it'll help you kick that hang over."

Landry walked out as Andy pulled his shirt off.

An hour later, he was less grumpy and the pain was slowly fading. He'd put on a different prosthesis, one that allowed for the swelling from sleeping in the other one. Drinking a bottle of water at breakfast, Landry talked his ear off about the various building projects he had going on around town.

Soon, he was on his way to catch Cody's soccer game. Clenching his jaw, he realized Cindy may not want to see him anymore, but he would'nt let Cody down.

Maryanne hadn't replied to his text earlier about Owen, and he wondered how the surgery was going. He hated not knowing, not being there.

Pulling into the parking lot at the soccer game, he got out slowly and grabbed another bottle of water from under the back seat before limping to the stands. This was the last home game, surely Maryanne would be here?

His phone rang as he looked over the soccer field and

saw Cody. He sat on the bleachers as he answered it without looking.

"Hello? Andy? This is Maryanne. Sorry I didn't reply earlier; there's been an emergency at the bakery."

"Are you okay?"

"Yeah, I have James here with me, and we're working on it. But I won't be back in time to get Cody from the game. Is there any way you can bring him to me?"

"Yeah, I just got here. There's nine minutes left on the clock."

"Perfect, okay. I'll see you when you get here. Take him to Sonic if they go. This is going to take me a while, so I'll still be here. You know where the bakery is, right? At the end of Main?"

"Yeah, but wait! How's Owen? Are they still in surgery?"

"She hasn't called me yet, so I'm assuming so. When she checked in last night, she said they'd keep him at least twenty-four hours after surgery for observation."

"Is she there alone? She doesn't need to be alone. She'll worry herself sick," he growled.

Maryanne grunted, and he heard banging in the background. "No, Mom flew into Dallas around midnight last night. I gotta go. This damn thing is—"

The line went dead. He turned the phone back to video mode and watched the game.

When it ended, he waited for everyone else to file out of the bleachers. As he finished his water, he texted Cody to tell him the plan, then he waited.

Cody's frown took up his entire face as he jogged over. "How's Owen? Is he coming home? Did Auntie M go get them?"

Andy smiled tiredly, his leg throbbing. "No, he's still in

surgery. Maryanne had an emergency at the bakery. We're going to go help her out after Sonic. Think we should bring her and James some lunch?"

Cody nodded and talked about what they'd order, the game, Owen, and his mom. When they got into the truck and headed out, Cody said, "Thanks for being there when Owen got hurt. Auntie M told me all about it."

Andy shrugged, "It's all good. Hated to see him hurt like that though."

Cody told him of the stitches he'd gotten a few years before. At Sonic, Cody hopped out after Andy ordered the food and milkshakes. He hung out with the team as Andy leaned back on his headrest and closed his eyes.

An hour later, Cody directed him to drive behind the bakery and park next to Maryanne's little red car. They got out and carried the food inside.

James was mopping up the floor as Maryanne was moving goods out of the storeroom. A bulging hole was visible in the main work room and ran all the way across to the storeroom ceiling.

"What happened?" Cody gasped. Maryanne shook her head as tears rolled down her eyes.

"I don't know. I had a security alert this morning, so I ran over here after I dropped you off at the game, and the entire floor had flooded. Half the inventory is ruined!" she wailed.

"Did you shut off the water?" Andy asked, eyeing the still dripping ceiling. She burst into more tears, smearing flour across her face. Cody stepped up and hugged her. Andy fished out his phone and called Landry.

"Hey, man, you got a minute? I'm at Half Baked, and there's a leak upstairs. Do you know how to turn off the water to the building?" Landry directed him outside and under the outdoor stairs that went up to the second floor. There was a locked gate that Andy had to break with the crowbar from his truck. He finally found the water main and turned it off.

As he hung up, he walked back inside. Maryanne was now sitting in a small office beside the storeroom, trying to salvage paper files and move everything from the growing water spot on the ceiling. He sat down on the edge of the desk to take the pressure off his leg.

She looked up at him with eyes so similar to Cindy's it made his chest hurt from missing her. She looked so lost with tear streaks on her face, marring her normally perfect makeup.

"I don't know what to do now," she sighed as she looked around.

"Do you have insurance?" She nodded, so he continued, "You'll want to call them now. And your landlord so he knows about the upstairs problem. I asked Landry to come over and help. He's a general contractor and will know how to salvage stuff and what to do on the repairs, alright?"

She nodded again, wiping her eyes with a napkin. The phone rang. He stepped out of the office to help the boys clean up as she talked. Half an hour later, Landry arrived with Gunner and Parker.

Maryanne came out of the office when she heard the new voices, but burst into tears when she saw them. The guys all looked at each other, unsure what to do to help. Cody and James walked to her, squeezing her hand and giving her a hug.

Landry was already inspecting the ceiling, walking between the storeroom and the primary work space with a frown. Parker hung up from a phone call and said, "I called Mr. Pike on the City Council. He approved the request for the gym to open to the public, so I figured he'd know who the landlord is. Turns out he's the landlord. He's on his way over."

The back door opened, and Holly walked in. She frowned at the mess and the crowded space, "What in the world is going on here? Maryanne?"

"Back here!" Maryanne said, having retreated back to the office. Holly dodged around the lingering men and slammed the office door. Andy and Landry exchanged glances and shrugged. Women didn't make any sense sometimes.

They made a plan for Gunner and Andy to help the boys move items out of the storeroom and onto the various benches around the main room, while Landry and Parker walked upstairs to check on the damage and find a source.

Several hours later, Andy's leg was throbbing but most everyone else had left except for Gunner. Maryanne looked exhausted, pale, and shaky. Andy spied the Sonic bag and shuffled through it.

"Maryanne, you didn't eat. Here, this will help," he handed it over. As she ate, he asked, "Can I take the boys home? I think you've got enough to worry about here, and they're going to need dinner soon."

Maryanne swallowed her burger, which she'd eaten almost as fast as some of his Army buddies ate. She slurped a melted slushy and leaned back in her office chair, closing her eyes as she nodded.

"I forgot to tell you earlier, but Owen made it out of surgery fine. He's groggy and the meds are making him say funny things, but he's going to be fine."

Andy smiled in relief, shifting to take the weight off his leg. "What kind of funny things did he say?"

Maryanne snorted, "Cin said he now thinks he's part

robot, since they had to put in a metal funny bone to replace the shattered one."

Andy chuckled. "That kid. He's something else. Cody! James!" They poked their heads into the office, and Andy smiled. "Owen made it out of surgery but now thinks he's part robot." They howled with laughter, which made Maryanne perk up and smile.

"Boys, do y'all want to go with Andy? He can take you home or to his house. I need to stay here and deal with more of this, but I can pick you up later tonight."

Andy waved away the offer. "Don't worry about it. They can stay the night tonight, right?" They grinned and high-fived each other before rushing to hug their aunt and racing each other out the door. The back door banged open.

Maryanne gave him the rough time line for tomorrow, saying she'd go get Cindy, Owen, and Margarita tomorrow between noon and five. He said goodbye and limped out, nodding to Gunner who was doing a final mop from all the people who had made a mess.

The next morning, Andy felt much more himself. He'd soaked in the hot tub last night with the boys. James had made him laugh so hard with his swimming and diving antics. They'd taken over the biggest spare bedroom, which had two twin beds in it already. It was the room he and Jake had shared when they were kids when they'd come to the cabin for deer season.

His hangover was gone and his leg wasn't throbbing. It was going to be a good day, despite his reservations about seeing Cindy again. He slid into the shower and washed up, a knot forming in his stomach as he thought about Cindy coming home today.

She didn't want to see him, and she'd probably be mad that he'd kept the boys last night. She was so protective of them, such a mama bear. It was adorable when it wasn't directed at him.

Cody was already on the couch watching cartoons. Andy sat in the recliner to drink his coffee. Cody looked over and nodded at his leg. "You going running?"

Andy looked down and adjusted the running prosthesis as he nodded.

"Can I come with you?"

Andy blinked. "You want to go running?"

"Yeah, Coach says I need to increase my stamina with cardio. I can't really do that at the apartment. Plus, if I join the military, it'll be good to get used to morning runs, right?"

Andy grinned. "Yeah but will your brother be alright here by himself?"

"Let me go wake him up and check. He normally sleeps as late as he can." Cody threw off the small throw blanket and walked down the hall. A few minutes later, he came out with his sneakers and a smile.

"We're all good. He's already turned over and is back to sleep."

"We'll leave your phone here, and I'll take mine. So if anything happens, he has it. And we'll lock the doors, not that anyone comes out this way. Especially not this early on a Sunday morning."

As they walked out the door, they stretched and talked about what they normally did on Sundays. Cody explained about church with Maryanne and Margarita, followed by family lunch. After that, they did whatever they wanted until Cindy got off the hospital shift. As they jogged, Cody talked less and less until they ran in silence.

Andy matched his pace to Cody. Every so often he'd give him a tip such as running on his toes or how to regulate breathing. It took at least twice as long as normal, but when they returned to the house, Cody was gasping for breath even as he grinned.

"That... was awesome."

Andy chuckled as he unlocked the front door. "Longer distances are different from the sprints you run in soccer."

"No joke," Cody said. Andy tossed him a bottle of water from the fridge, and they guzzled each down.

"I'm going to go take a shower to help cool down," Cody said.

"Wake up your brother on the way. If we're going to go to church, he needs to get up. What do y'all like for breakfast?"

"Cereal is fine."

Andy turned and walked to the pantry. He grabbed all the breakfast things he had: one box of healthy cereal, a box of protein bars, and a box of pancake mix.

James rubbed his eyes as he rounded the kitchen door. Andy smiled. "What would you like for breakfast?"

James sat at the kitchen island and said, "Oh! Pancakes! Do you have chocolate chips? Mom makes them into the shape of a heart with chocolate chips. Sometimes she dyes them green and makes spotted dinosaurs too."

"Wow. And I thought Maryanne was the amazing baker in the family. Your mom is so talented."

James nodded as Andy got out the flat griddle and a bowl. "Can I help?"

"Sure, pour the mix into the bowl, then you can add water." Andy turned on the griddle and handed James the whisk to whip up the pancakes as they talked about school and books.

"Reading is pretty important. It's not just for education. A lot of people don't read enough, so it's pretty awesome that you read for fun," Andy said, flipping another pancake.

"I read fifty-two books last year. That's one book a week! I won an award at school for it," he said proudly as he bit into his pancake.

"That's fantastic. I read a lot while I was in the hospital and rehab. I need to keep track of how many in a year."

"Start now. I want to see if I can beat you in books read by the end of the school year. I've already read twelve since August 1st, which is when my teacher said I could start keeping count."

"It's a deal. We'll meet at the bakery the weekend after school lets out and compare. Deal?"

"Deal." They shook hands and finished eating.

"But why do we have to go to the bakery? You'll be around like now, right?" James asked, frowning down into his plate.

Andy shrugged as he took his plate to the sink and rinsed it off, placing it in the dishwasher.

"Technically, your mom and I were never dating. And she got really mad at me Friday. Not sure she's going to want me around. I know she's going to be upset with me that you and Cody were here last night."

Cody came into the kitchen, his face lighting up at the pancakes.

"Yes! Pancakes!" he sighed, going to the island where the plate and a cup of juice sat beside James.

"She was probably worried about Owen," James said.

A car door slammed outside, and Andy walked to the door to see who it was, saying to James as he went, "Go hop in the shower, so we can head to church."

Chapter Thirty-Seven

He swung the door open to see Suzie, Mike, and Mandy walking up the steps. His heart tripped a beat as he remembered; he was a dad!

When Mandy reached the top step of the front porch, she launched herself into his arms with a loud, "Dadddyyyyy!"

He swung her up in the air, making her squeal before pulling her in for a hug. "Hey, munchkin. What are y'all doing here this early?"

Mike smiled as they walked in. Suzie's steps faltered as she saw Cody sitting at the kitchen island. "Good morning," he said brightly with a smile as he hopped up and rinsed out his and James' plates.

Suzie sucked in a breath then smiled, "Morning! We've come to drag Andy off to church. We decided if he's going to stick around, he needs to get out and thank the ladies who brought all the food by for him in person."

Cody nodded, "Cool. We were just getting ready for church anyway." James yelled from the hall bath, and

Cody jogged down the hall to help him with the water faucet.

Mandy pulled Mike to her room, talking about painting the walls. Mike pulled out paint swatches from his front pocket and waved them at Andy as he passed by.

Andy laughed. "Knock yourself out. But I'm the boss here! I get veto power!" he yelled after them. He glanced at the clock in the living room and glanced at Aunt Suzie. "I need to go change for church, then I'll be ready."

"No rush, dear. We were going to make breakfast here and wake you up, but I see you beat us to it."

"If you haven't eaten yet, there's pancake mix still out. Help yourself." She nodded and moved to the kitchen as he walked to his room to clean up.

He came back out a few minutes later to find Mandy and Mike tucking into some pancakes at the table. He walked to the recliner and propped his leg up to wait on them all. Suzie flopped down onto the couch and put her chin in her hand.

"What's up?" he asked.

She shrugged, looking down before glancing at him worriedly. "Why are the boys here? Where's Owen and Cindy?"

Andy kneaded his leg. "Owen broke his elbow on Friday. He's been in Children's since then with Cindy. He had surgery for a metal elbow bone yesterday and will be home sometime today."

Suzie gasped, "Oh, no! The poor baby. What happened? Did Cindy not keep a close enough eye on him?"

He tried to ignore the flare of anger at her snide comment. "He climbed the outside of the playground equipment in the park after school," he said, glaring at her pointedly. "Cindy was at work. You know Maryanne watches him in the afternoons. You also know that if a boy takes it in his head to try something, there's not really anything you can do to stop it. Don't you remember Jake and me growing up?"

Her face softened as she laughed. "Oh, yes. You two gave me all my gray hairs!"

He smiled and shook his head. After a few minutes of peaceful silence, he said softly, "What will it take for you to see what a great mom Cindy is? What a great person?"

Suzie looked at him with a frown and shrugged, "Honestly, I don't know. I want to though. I want to believe in her, but I don't know how yet."

He nodded with a sigh. "Fair enough. I love you, Aunt Suzie, and I don't want to cut you out of my life. But if I need to, I will. I'm going to go check on the boys. Do you want to come over here for lunch after church?"

They made plans for lunch and less than half an hour later, they were all piling into their vehicles and on their way to church.

Uncle Mike and Suzie swung by their house and grabbed all the stuff they'd packed for Mandy. Cody and James helped them unload it as Andy pulled out all the toppings for the chili he had put in the crock pot before they'd left.

Once all the boxes had been moved into her room, they sat down for a rowdy lunch. The three kids bickered back and forth about little things, teasing and laughing. Suzie finally relaxed and laughed with them.

When it was time for Mandy's nap, Suzie laid down with her while the boys tumbled outside. James had asked about camping, and Mike swore there was an old tent in the shed out back. Sure enough, they found it and set it up in the tree line beside the house.

The boys giggled as both Mike and Andy grumbled over the complicated framing. When it was finally up, they raced back to the shed and found lanterns that still had working batteries and some sleeping bags that weren't too moth eaten.

They piled into the tent as Mike and he sat on the front porch in rocking chairs, beers in hand.

Suzie came out and shut the door quietly as Cody jogged up. "Andy, can you play soccer with me?"

Andy shrugged. "Probably. I haven't tried yet. You got a ball?"

Cody grinned as he nodded. "Never leave home without one!" Andy changed and met Cody in the front yard. Mike and Suzie rocked on the porch while Cody and he played. They laughed and tried to score on each other.

A truck pulled up as it began to rain.

"Finish the play! Finish the play! Next score wins!" Cody shouted. Andy barely registered Landry getting out, and James running to the house from the tent as he focused on the ball.

Andy was tired and ready to go inside, his leg throbbing, so he pointed behind Cody. "You're going down! Did you see who just pulled up?" When Cody glanced over his shoulder, Andy stole the ball and whooped a victory. Cody screeched and took off after him as Andy laughed. He stole the ball, but somehow Andy tripped and fell down on one side.

He gasped as he flopped onto his back, craning his neck to see Cody kick the ball and jump up and down in the rain as he screamed in victory. Andy laughed as Landry jogged over and offered a hand. When he was finally on his feet, Andy tested his weight and smiled, slapping Landry on the back.

"Hey, man! What are you doing around here?" he said through the rain, the water dripping into his eyes as they dashed up to the porch. Suzie was wringing her hands worriedly, so he held up his hands and said quickly, "I'm all right! I didn't land on anything vital."

She huffed a sigh and tilted her nose up as she stomped inside, the rest of them following behind her.

"Wanted to see if you'd heard anything from Maryanne about the insurance. Wasn't sure if they gave an estimated time for payout or if they'd gone to look at it today or what was going on."

Andy shut the door and took off his muddy shoes. "I haven't heard anything today about it. Let me go get cleaned up, and I'll check my phone."

"What happened?" Suzie asked.

"The second floor flooded out Maryanne's bakery yesterday," Landry said. Andy left them talking as he took a quick shower, washing and changing his prosthesis. He let the wet one dry and put on the spare.

He heard the hall bath water going as he passed and assumed Cody was washing up. James was lying on his bed reading, and Mandy was in her fort, introducing her toys to her new room.

He propped up his leg on the coffee table, as Mike had taken over the recliner. Aunt Suzie listened to Landry as he filled her in on the local gossip, so Andy checked his texts. He sucked in a shallow breath when he saw one from Cindy.

We're on the way home.

Maryanne has been talking for an hour about what happened at the bakery.
Thanks for taking the boys. I hope they've behaved.

He breathed a sigh of relief. She was talking with him! And she wasn't mad he'd watched the boys!

They've been great. They love the hot tub. lol
Went to church this morning, put up a real tent outside, and played soccer until the rain hit.
Be careful driving in it.

He saw the three dots and waited, holding his breath.

Maryanne is a nervous wreck, so Mama is driving.
She already owes $5 in the swear jar, but Owen is asleep beside me so it's okay. lol

Traffic sucks.
And in the rain?
She's a brave woman. Must be where you get it from.

I'm not brave. I'm scared shitless.
I need to apologize about the other day.
I said some things...
We need to talk.

I agree.
Why don't you pack a bag and come over here tonight?
I'm not gonna lie.
I think I'm getting an ulcer worrying over Owen. It'll make me feel better to see him.

And there are more bedrooms here, so if he needs more medicine in the middle of the night, he won't wake up the boys.

Sure.

He sighed in relief and glanced up, tuning back in to the surrounding conversation. Uncle Mike was asleep in the recliner. Landry was showing her photos on his phone. Suzie was frowning.

"See? Being a dad looks good on him. He's a natural at it," Landry said.

Andy frowned and reached for his water. "Who are you talking about?"

Landry snorted, "You. I saw you at Sonic a few weeks ago with Cody and Maryanne and snapped a picture. Then at the park the other day. You were there with Mandy, and Cindy was there with James and Owen. What were you doing facing away from the playground?"

"Soccer practice. Cody likes to watch videos of himself playing so he can see his mistakes and get better."

"Ahh, that makes sense." Landry turned and smiled smoothly. "So really, Suzie. You have nothing to worry about. Mandy's going to be fine. He's already a dad. He just didn't know it until now."

"But it's a rather sudden thing. If he'd known during the pregnancy, he'd have months to prepare and learn everything he could. But he's had just a few days! She shouldn't move in yet. It's too soon." Suzie twisted her hands, the frown line between her brows prominent.

Landry nodded and put his phone away. "Yeah, but he's been practicing for over a month now. And you can't deny that he's the strongest man we know. He's no stranger to hard things and major life changes."

They both glanced at his leg, and he frowned, crossing his arms. "I'm right here, you know. Don't talk about me like I'm not."

Landry grinned. "Don't worry, man. Cindy's going to take you back, and then you'll be one big, happy family."

Suzie pursed her lips in frustration.

"Don't you want him to be happy?" Landry asked.

She leaned back on the couch, sitting in between them. "Of course I do. But I don't want to see him hurt again." She crossed her arms like a pouting child.

Andy chuckled. "Life's full of hurt, Aunt Suz. You, of all people, know it. But let me ask you this. Knowing the pain of losing Sarah, would you rather she'd never been born at all? To save yourself from that heartache?"

She gasped and slapped him on the arm. "Never! She was the best daughter a mother could ask for!"

"Exactly," he smiled softly, grabbing her hand and squeezing. "I may get hurt, but it doesn't change the fact that I love her and those boys. That's all that matters at this point."

Mike grumbled awake as Mandy ran into the living room dragging a stuffed giraffe. "Daddy! When will Owen get here? Will he come see my new room?"

Andy pulled her onto his lap and held her close, his chest warming at her words. "They're on their way, munchkin. He's very sleepy from the surgery, so you'll have to be very gentle with him, okay?"

She nodded and introduced him to her giraffe. Then she pulled him up and drug him into her room to meet the rest of her toys. Landry said as he walked down the hall, "See? He's a great dad already!"

Chapter Thirty-Eight

Cindy woke up as Owen cried. They were about fifteen minutes from the apartment. Her mom looked back at them in the rear-view mirror and said, "Awwww, poor baby! Is your arm hurting?"

Owen nodded and wiped his eyes with his good arm, his wail getting louder with each passing minute. Cindy grabbed the bag from the floor and found his two day supply of pain killers and gave him two.

"No!" he screamed as she tried to get him to take the chewable tablets.

"It'll make you feel better," she cajoled, stroking his hair. He pulled away from her as tears leaked down his cheeks. "Come on, Owen. We're almost home. Then we can take a bath and curl up on the couch together, alright? Want to watch a movie?"

"No!" he screamed. "Mandy! Andy! Mandy! Andy!"

"Is he saying Mandy or Andy?" Maryanne asked from the passenger seat.

Margarita shrugged, turning into the neighborhood. "Does it matter?"

"Come on, sweetie. If you take this medicine, I'll ask Andy where Mandy is and if we can see them. But she won't want to see you if you're crying and hurting."

"Call him! Call him!"

"You're too loud. He won't be able to hear me. Are you going to take your medicine and stop crying?"

Owen grabbed his sippie cup and drank. She pulled out her phone and texted Andy, surprised when she saw a response just a few minutes after Owen had finally taken the pain killers.

When they pulled up to her apartment, he'd quieted down to just sniffles. She carefully pulled Owen out of his booster as Maryanne and her mom followed with her purse and the bag from the hospital.

"A nice warm bath will help you feel all better!" Her mom said cheerily as she unlocked the door. There were cereal bowls still on the kitchen table and the trash smelled. Cindy sighed, following her mom to the bathroom.

"What about Mandy?" Owen demanded as they carefully started the bath and took off his shirt over his new cast.

"We're going to get cleaned up and pack a bag. Then we're going to Andy's to see them both." Her mom glanced at her as she took his dirty clothes and the boys' dirty laundry to the washer.

She directed him to put his cast on the side of the tub and told him about not getting it wet. He played with his bath tub boats with one hand while she washed him, whining the entire time.

When he was out, dried, and changed, Maryanne took him to the kitchen to get some food. Cindy stepped into her own bathroom and showered quickly, changing and packing a bag. She rounded up school clothes for them all tomorrow and headed into the living room.

She flopped onto the couch as her mom came out of the boys' bathroom and said, "Alright, that's cleaned. Now what else do you need, dear?"

Cindy shook her head as she yawned, "Nothing, Mom. We're fine now. I'm going to go to Andy's tonight. There's a room just for Owen, so I can get up with him whenever he needs without worrying about waking the other boys."

Her mom sat on the arm rest of the couch and stroked her hair from her face. She groaned, some of the tension easing at having her mom take care of her. She was safe. Loved.

"I'm glad. Maryanne had told me yesterday that you'd broken up. Are you going to get back together?"

"We weren't even dating, Mom, so there wasn't any way to break up. But I think... I think I need him, and it makes me mad."

"You've been taking care of yourself for a long time, hun, but we both know that it's a lonely road. If you have the chance to walk that road with someone you love? Take it, dear."

Cindy groaned, rubbing her eyes and sitting up with a sigh. "I know. I'm tired of fighting it all."

"You need some sleep. You've hardly slept since Thursday night."

"I'll sleep tonight. I promise. But tomorrow, I have to see if I can pick up some over time at the hospital or talk to the HR lady about adding hours or getting a raise or something."

"I'm sorry about the PTA job."

Cindy shrugged as she got up and stretched. "It's a big misunderstanding, but it's not worth fighting about. I'm tired of all the fighting, not just with Andy but with Suzie and work and just all of it."

"I'm going to see if Holly can get you in for a massage tomorrow and Wednesday this week, alright?" Maryanne came out of the kitchen with Owen. He had chocolate sauce on his face but he looked much happier, his eyes less glazed in pain.

"That's a good idea. I'm going to grab my swimsuit too. Andy has a hot tub that I've been wanting to try out."

"I want to swim too!" Owen whined. Cindy smiled as she swung by their bedroom and grabbed trunks for all of them. She waved them at Owen, and he smiled.

Half an hour later, they pulled up in front of Andy's house. It was barely five, but the sun was already setting through the trees. Cody and James came running through the front door as she got out of the SUV. They hugged her before opening Owen's door.

They talked over each other asking questions as Owen showed off his cast. Cindy glanced at the house and saw Mandy walk down the steps with Andy right behind her. He was smiling, but it was a worried smile, the furrow between his brows standing out in the lengthening shadows.

Her heart ached to run to him and just let him hold her. He made her feel loved. Even if he hadn't said it, didn't his actions speak louder than his lack of words?

She helped Owen get out of the SUV—she didn't want him jumping down and jarring his arm yet—but as soon as his feet hit the ground, he led the kid parade into the house. Andy stood gripping the car door with white knuckles. He opened his mouth but closed it again after an awkward beat.

She sighed and grabbed the bag she'd packed in the back seat. "Are you sure it's fine for us to sleep over tonight? The kids can be rather loud sometimes."

He nodded, taking the bag. "I'm sure. I want you here. All of you. I wouldn't have offered if I didn't."

She nodded, grabbing her purse and keys and shutting the doors. She strolled beside him. Even though they weren't touching, his body heat seeped to her in the slightly chilled air. She breathed deeply of that leather smell that was all him.

When they opened the front door, they heard giggling coming from one of the rooms down the hall. Andy put the bag by the door.

"Are you hungry? We're about to eat, but it's just leftover chili from lunch today."

"Chili sounds good. Owen already ate, so I don't know that he'll eat again."

"You want to go tell them all to wash, and I'll bowl it up?"

She nodded and walked down the hall. She stepped into the spare bedroom where they'd set up the sheet fort and stopped. There were boxes stacked against one wall, and toys were all over the bed and floor in front of the tent. She saw feet kicking out of the tent and walked over toys to bend down and see inside.

She grinned, "What are y'all doing?"

"Playing camping doctor," Mandy said as she held a toy stethoscope to the Owen's chest. He was lying on the floor while James and Cody were shredding paper into the minipretend paper 'fire' from the other day.

"Well, time to wash up for dinner. We're having chili." She got up and backed from the room, the kids scrambling behind her, chattering about what toppings they had for the chili.

She sat in her normal seat beside Andy. "Owen, sit by me so I can help with your food."

The Soldier Gets His Girl

"Mandy, do you need help?"

"No, Daddy. I'm a big girl," she said, scrambling up onto the other end chair, opposite of Andy. Cindy's neck popped as she spun around to gape at Andy.

He shrugged sheepishly. "Remember how I said I wanted to talk about something too? This is the thing."

She was shocked. As she processed, she spooned the toppings Owen requested from the center of the table into his bowl before making her own.

Owen pouted, "I thought you didn't have a daddy, like me."

"We just found out while you were in the hospital, big guy. It was a surprise secret."

"Mama, I want a Daddy too!" Owen whined as she drank her water. She choked, nearly spurting it out of her nose. She wiped her mouth and took another coughing drink.

"It doesn't quite work like that Owen," Andy said with a smile. It was the first smile she'd seen since she'd arrived. It soothed her anxious heart. Her shoulders relaxed as she ate her chili.

"But Andy could be our Daddy too," James said. "He's good at putting up tents."

"Yeah, and playing soccer and making pancakes," Cody said between bites.

"No, he's my Daddy, not yours. I just got him, and I don't have to share. Gamma says I don't have to share new toys for a week. Tell them I don't have to share," Mandy said as she leaned forward on her knees in the chair and ate.

Cindy smiled and nodded, "That's right, sweetie. Boys, Mandy needs to get used to having a Daddy. Andy doesn't need four kids all at once. That's a lot to handle."

"But we'll be good!" James pleaded.

Andy laughed, "Let's just see how it goes, okay? Things can obviously change a lot in three days. We'll talk about it again in two weeks. Does that sound good?"

The boys all grumbled, making Cindy roll her eyes. Cindy asked about homework, but they denied having any over the weekend. After they finished eating, Cody rinsed and loaded the dishwasher while James walked to the bathroom to get ready for bed.

Mandy and Owen wanted to sleep in the tent, but Andy made them pick up the toys first.

"Is this going to be your room, Mandy? Are you going to decorate it?" Cindy asked.

Mandy raced over to the bedside table and opened the drawer, pulling out some paint swatches. "Uncle Mike said he'd help paint! I want it this one."

"That's beautiful! It's called lilac. The green bedspread will look really pretty in here with lilac walls."

They finished picking up their toys as Andy waved around the room. "Can you think of anything else she needs?"

She opened the door to the closet. "Probably would be helpful to have open shelves in here for her clothes. Or organizers. When the boys were younger, I printed out pictures of what to put in each cubby which helped a lot."

Andy typed up her tips on his phone.

"You might want some type of toy storage bin too," she chuckled as they finally put all the toys back into the cardboard boxes.

He grinned, turning as James came out of the bathroom. "Okay, you two. Time to go brush your teeth." He ushered them both into the bathroom and helped them with the toothpaste. They giggled and got as much on their shirts as they did in their mouths.

She looked through Mandy's boxes until she found a clean pair of pajamas. Then she helped her put them on as Cody got into the bathroom to get ready for bed. She made a pallet on the floor of the tent with a spare blanket, Mandy and Owen talking away the whole time.

Mandy helped convince Owen to take another dose of his other medicine to help him sleep through the night, then she kissed them goodnight and walked out, leaving the door cracked and the hall light on.

She walked into the other bedroom to see James reading in bed, and Cody on his phone. "Lights out in twenty minutes, boys."

They grunted. When she walked to the living room, Andy was in the recliner, so she flopped onto the couch. *This couch is so much better than mine*, she thought as she sighed and closed her eyes.

"You can go to bed if you want. You can sleep in the spare bed, mine, or the couch. Wherever you want," he murmured into the dim and quiet room. Soft giggles came from the opposite wall where Mandy and Owen were obviously still awake.

She smiled, then sighed. "If you're alright with it, I—I'd like to sleep in your room."

"Sure, I like the spare bed fine."

"No," she said with a deep breath. "I'd like to sleep in there with you."

The silence was oppressive. She opened her eyes and glanced at him. The shadows made it impossible to see his face. The weight on her chest deepened.

"I'd like that too, but tonight you need sleep. We'll talk tomorrow. Come on. Let's get you in bed before you fall asleep right there." With a mumbled reply, his voice thick and heavy with sleep, he shifted in the recliner and offered her a hand.

Their fingers intertwined, and tingles shot up her arm from his touch. She couldn't believe how much she wanted to be near him. This was so different from her past relationships. With the others, there were always doubts and hesitations, the feeling of not being enough. But with him, it all felt so natural and right, like coming home.

Her stomach twisted into knots about their talk tomorrow. Andy stopped by the boys' room to turn off the light as she brushed her teeth and changed. When she slid into the bed, her heart raced, but he turned to the bathroom. The sight of him made her heart flip.

She rolled onto her side to wait for him. Perhaps they could talk tonight. If it was dark and she couldn't see his face, maybe she'd be able to tell him the truth, of her love and her fears. She nodded off, never getting the chance.

Chapter Thirty-Nine

She jerked awake, sitting straight up in the bed and looking around. Andy was no where to be seen, but Owen was crying. As soon as she rolled out of bed, she hit the ground running, rushing to Owen even as Andy's deep voice vibrating down the hall.

She found them in the living room. Owen was curled up in Andy's lap with a sippie cup and a stuffed animal of Mandy's in the recliner. She slowed as Andy looked at her with a sleepy smile. He really looked happy to be exactly where he was. Her ex had never looked like that with the boys.

"Did he wake you?" She grabbed the bag by the door and found his medicine.

"No, I was already up. I wasn't sure what time school started, so I made pancakes. I probably woke him up."

"Here, baby. Take this. Do you want a pancake?"

Owen nodded but snuggled deeper into Andy. He squeezed gently, settling him on his good leg as he raised the footrest. "Just bring his plate. He can eat it right here. Would you like that, big guy?"

Owen nodded, never taking his mouth off his sippie cup. She glanced at the clock and calculated the time. She delivered the pancake before getting all the kids up, fed, and ready for school.

James and Owen fought over the bathroom. When Mandy got up, she did the potty dance all the way to the master bathroom, where Cindy helped her change into her school clothes.

"But I don't want to go to school without Owen," she whined.

"Owen is just going to sleep a lot today, but if you go to school, maybe we can ask your Daddy to get that paint for you? Then when you come home, we can start painting your room. How does that sound?"

She squealed and raced out of the bathroom, tugging her shirt down over her belly as she yelled for Owen. Owen's medicine had kicked in by that point, and he wanted to make the ride to school with them. She got all four kids in the SUV, Andy cajoling and making the kids smile. It was much different than her normal school drop-off, the boys happier and not as grumpy. They stopped at daycare last, and everyone wanted to see Owen and touch his cast, but he was already yawning.

Andy picked him up and carried him back out the door, leaving Mandy to talk about her new daddy and their big sleepover. Andy didn't seem to mind as he turned to talk to her over a rapidly fading Owen's head.

"Do we want to run into Denton and grab paint together? Will you at least drive with me?"

She shrugged as she buckled Owen back in. "I need to swing by the hospital to ask about overtime shifts this week or to see about a new schedule. But I brought his medicine, so we don't have to be back at the house immediately, no. Do you want me to drive?"

"That's fine. It's your SUV, after all, and there's not much traffic this time of day."

She pulled onto the road and headed out of town toward Denton as he routed his phone's GPS to the paint store. Owen was asleep in the back seat before they even hit the highway. She took a deep breath. Driving and keeping her eyes on the road made talking easier, and they had a lot of things to sort out.

"Andy, I'm sorry for what I said at the hospital. I was upset about being fired, worried about Owen, and took it all out on you."

"It's fine," he said, but she laughed and shook her head.

"It's not fine, Andy. You didn't deserve any of that, and I'm so sorry. I'm grateful for all your help this weekend. Even after I blew up at you, you still helped with the boys. Thank you, and I'm sorry."

He leaned over and ran a hand over her thigh. "Cindy, you're an amazing mother, and you were stressed. Don't worry about getting angry. We shake it off and move on, alright? I'll let it go if you will, and if we can work on our communication skills a little. But I don't want you to think you have to walk on eggshells or can't feel normal human emotions. That's not a healthy way to live."

She drove in silence for a while, the country song playing in the background. She'd lived like that for so long with her ex, she didn't realize it wasn't healthy until the divorce. By his own admission, Andy had never had a long-term relationship like that though, so how did he know so much about it?

She cleared her throat and glanced at him out of the

corner of her eye. "So tell me about Mandy. How'd you figure out she's yours?"

"Aunt Suzie and Uncle Mike came over Friday, right after I got home from the hospital. Do you remember me telling you about Sarah's roommate, Stella?"

"Your casual hookup? Oh!" she gasped.

He nodded and rubbed the back of his neck as he stared out the passenger side window. "Yeah, she apparently didn't want to tell me while I was deployed, then she passed in the car wreck. She had already made Sarah the backup legal guardian when Mandy was born. When Sarah was in the hospital, before she slipped into the coma, she told Suzie and Mike everything then signed for them to be guardians until I got back."

"Only you came back with the amputation."

"Exactly. They didn't want me to lose focus during the recovery. But now that I'm settled here, they said it was time to tell me."

"Wow, that's a lot of emotional stuff to take all in one day. First I yelled at you, then you found out you have a daughter. Is that why you drunk texted Maryanne about cake?"

He groaned, hunching his shoulders in an embarrassed shrug. "Yeah, I went to help build the float with Landry and Nick and—I don't know—it just all piled on, I guess."

It was concerning that his coping instinct was to get drunk, but maybe it was a social situation. She couldn't really fault him for it when she'd blown up at him as her own way to manage the stress. Guilt speared her, and she shook her head, focusing on the conversation at hand. "You seem to be pretty accepting of the change to dad hood."

"Accepting? I'm nervous and scared. I have this tiny

human that relies solely on me now. I found out on Friday and bam, she moved in on Sunday."

She laughed as they turned into Denton. "I shouldn't laugh, I know, but that's how I feel every single day! Being a mom is terrifying. Starting a relationship with you could end up hurting *them*. That's what makes me not want to do it, just so I can protect them, you know?"

He half-turned in the seat and moved his hand, massaging his leg. "Yeah, I get it, I really do, but I still think it's worth the risk, Cindy. I mean, what exactly are you afraid of?"

She pulled into the home improvement store and glanced in the rear-view mirror. "He's still asleep. Would you mind if I stayed out here while you run in?"

"Sure," he sighed. He hopped out and walked inside. She stared at his ass as he swaggered, knowing he was trying to cover up the limp. She wasn't even sure he realized he did it anymore.

What was she afraid of? She got out her phone and typed it out, hoping that would help her think.

Dad changed. Jerry changed. Didn't really know Cody's dad. He'd just been a crush from afar. What was love? Did it last?

Andy came back with a cart full of supplies. She popped the trunk, and he loaded it. The noise woke Owen up, who whimpered.

"Hey there, big guy," Andy said as he got inside. "How you feeling?"

"My robot arm needs help," he said, reaching for his sippie cup with his good hand.

"Want some snacks? We're going to go home and make some lunch," she said. She blinked. Had she just called his house home?

Andy talked with Owen, but she tuned them out as she navigated the city. To home? Was it really home?

Exhausted from the hospital, stress, and worry, she'd wanted to just curl up in his arms and not think about all this.

"Cindy?" Andy placed a hand on her arm. She blinked and glanced at him.

He smiled and the tightness around her heart eased. "You alright?"

She nodded slowly as Owen demanded her phone to play with. She handed it to him, then turned onto the highway. A few minutes later, Andy pulled out his phone and frowned.

"I think Owen texted me," he said. "What changed about your Dad?"

She groaned and rubbed her temples with one hand. "I—I didn't mean that to go to you. But you asked what I was afraid of so I made a list while you were in the store."

"Your dad and Jerry both changed. Was that change bad?"

"Definitely. Jerry, the ex, was a normal enough guy. We met on campus at school. He was probably using me to get into the prescription pads the entire time, but I didn't want to be alone. After a while, he... well, he squeezed a lot."

"He'd bruise you? Did he hit you?" he growled low, sending shivers up her spine. She didn't think Andy would ever hurt her, but if anyone crossed him, he'd stick up for himself.

"No, he never hit. But anywhere he could pinch or squeeze, he would, especially when I'd say or do something that he didn't agree with. I wasn't able to be myself and the longer we were together, the quieter I became, which just made him angry and verbally abusive."

"My mom was kind of like that. She'd call me names and belittle me all the time," he whispered. Her heart ached for the little boy he used to be. She'd done her best to shelter her boys from Jerry.

She took a deep breath and released it, as if exhaling all the pain. "It hurt, and I believed his lies it for a long time."

Andy put his hand back on her thigh and just left it there, not squeezing or stroking. It was a comfort, a gesture of not being alone that warmed her from the inside out.

He glanced back at Owen, who was still pre-occupied with her phone, then said, "So you're afraid that I'll what? Do the same thing? I told you I'd never hurt you."

"I know. And I believe you, but I moved in with him and was pregnant with James within six months. I didn't really have time to get to know him, not truly. You and I have moved so fast... that's what scares me. The moving fast and not knowing every little detail about each other."

Andy sighed and shifted on his seat, his hand leaving her leg again. "Cindy, we could live together for fifty years, and you'd still surprise me. We'll never know every little detail. The question isn't knowing everything but are you willing to try?"

She smiled as the tears came. She blinked them away and sucked in a big breath. Time to rip off all the band aids. "My dad was the best dad growing up. He was our softball coach, took us camping, all kinds of stuff when I was a kid. But about the time I hit puberty, he had a few deployments pretty close to each other... he just didn't come back as the same guy."

Andy stilled in his seat and looked over at her, his gaze heavy. "That happens a lot. I know I didn't come back as the same guy."

She gripped the steering wheel. "I know. It didn't make

it any easier to live with though. And I know that you're a civilian but still... If he can change like that after twenty years with my mom, could something like that happen with us in the future?"

As the silence passed, he wiped his hands on his jeans. "There are some things that are universal. People go through phases in their lives. Mid-life crisis is a real thing. They call them the golden years for a reason. That kind of thing. I think the key is to go through them *together*. Your dad, when he was deployed—well, your mom wasn't with him. She couldn't go through that stuff with him. But we can, because I'm not going anywhere."

She sighed as she turned into his driveway. When she pulled up in his drive, she stared at the house. His house wasn't home. *He* was.

"Is Mandy home?" Owen asked.

Andy unbuckled and opened his door as he said, "No, we're going to take this stuff inside, and make some lunch, then we'll go get her, okay, big guy?"

She helped Owen get out, and they all headed inside. Owen raced into Mandy's room, and Cindy walked to the fridge and took inventory. Andy came up behind her and wrapped his hands around her waist. She shut the refrigerator door and sighed, tilting her neck to the side so he could kiss it.

"Stay the week with me," he said softly. "You and the boys. Me and Mandy."

She shook her head and turned in his arms, wrapping hers around his waist and laying her head on his chest. His heartbeat was steady and calming as she sighed. "We can't, remember? Mandy needs alone time with you to get used to the idea of having a dad. But we can hang out here, eat dinners together most nights?"

He leaned back and looked down at her, his blue eyes piercing into her soul. "So you're willing to try? Make us an official thing?"

She felt her cheeks heat as she nodded, then cleared her throat and stepped away from him. She didn't want to get too attached. They needed baby steps.

They talked about the food for the week and made a grocery list. He made lunch and set out food to thaw for dinner while she called the hospital to ask about overtime.

"Mom!" Owen cried from Mandy's room. She canceled the call and ran to him. In the tent, he was grinning.

"Look! My tooth fell out!" He held his palm up to show his little bloody tooth. She laughed as she teared up.

"That's amazing! I'm so proud of you! Let's go rinse out your mouth and tell Andy!" She helped him scramble out of the tent and run to find Andy. She couldn't believe she'd been here for it. She could only remember a few times when she'd been home when the other's had lost their teeth. But she'd been there for Owen. She wiped a tear as they sat down to eat, Owen showing Andy his prized tooth.

Chapter Forty

The rest of the week flew by. They painted Mandy's room that afternoon, the kids making a bigger mess than needed. Then it was soccer practice to prepare for the tournament. Andy had to help build the float, so she kept Mandy with her.

They'd gone back to their apartment Monday night, but Cindy had tossed and turned all night... and the next night too. By Wednesday's massage with Holly, she was as tense and tired as she'd been last week.

She'd also found out that she hadn't gotten the job at the hospital that she'd interviewed for. They called her references and had been told about being let go. She didn't blame them but now her worry over money, Christmas, and paying the bills doubled.

She'd also picked up two overtime days at the hospital, but it wasn't enough to pay the bills, and she knew it. Worry was a constant knot in her stomach. Because she'd picked up the weekday overtime, she wasn't able to work Friday night like normal.

The kids were all excited about the Homecoming football game though. She picked up Owen and Mandy from school around lunch and drove over to Andy's house, the routine they'd fallen into that week.

Owen was glad to be back at school with Mandy. Mandy had a new part of her room done each day. Landry had come over and built some shelves perfect for little kids in the closet.

When she walked in the door, the kids ran to Mandy's room to play. Andy poked his head out of the master bedroom and smiled. She took a deep breath, her shoulders relaxing as she smiled and walked into his arms. He hugged her close, his mouth descending to hers.

His kiss was deep and slow, making her groan. "I missed you," he said.

She laughed, the soft movement raking her lips against his, making him crave her all the more. "I saw you last night!"

He pulled back, holding her securely in his arms. "I know, but I still missed you. Cindy, I want you here. I want you all here. Move in with me? We can start loading y'all's stuff today."

She laughed and pulled out of his arms. "You're crazy! We can't move in with you! We've only known each other for six weeks!"

"Time doesn't matter. They say when you know, you know. And Cindy, I know I love you."

She gasped, spinning back around to face him. Her eyes widened and her hand rose to cover her mouth. "Wh-what? Are you serious?"

"Absolutely," he said, stalking her through the bedroom until he'd pressed her up against the wall. "I have never felt like this before. You're the only one for me. You're my home, my family. Move in with me? Please?" He kissed her softly on the corners of her mouth as she ran her hands up his arms.

"I—I can't. Not yet," she gasped.

"Why not? You've been over here nearly every evening this week, and it's been perfect, except when you go back to the apartment."

"Life isn't perfect, Andy. It's too fast."

He pressed his forehead to hers, holding her gently in his arms against the wall. His erection pressed into her stomach, and the matching heat flooded between her legs. He rocked his hips forward softly, making her gasp.

"You like that?" he growled into her ear as he nipped it between his teeth. She moaned, squeezing his biceps and holding on as he rocked harder and harder, hitting her clit through her leggings every time.

Light exploded behind her eyes as she came with a gasp. Shudders raked her body as he slowed, taking her lips in a kiss that she felt down to her soul. It soothed the panic, the stress. It was like all the puzzle pieces finally fit into place.

When he released her, he stood awkwardly. "If you won't move in, at least spend the weekend with me?" Her brain whirled to remember their conversation.

"I have to work tomorrow and Sunday."

He sighed as he stepped towards the bedroom door. "Can I keep the boys? Mandy is less lonely when they're around."

"Mandy? Or you?" She followed him, cupping his ass through the jeans.

He glanced over his shoulder with a smirk as he replied, "Both."

She laughed. "Sure, we can even stay the night tonight,

The Soldier Gets His Girl

so they don't have to wake up when I have to go to work tomorrow morning."

She frowned as he picked up some kind of radio in the living room and took it to the recliner to tinker with. "Are you planning on taking them all to the Veteran's Day breakfast tomorrow? And the parade? And the Fall Festival?"

He nodded absently.

"I'll call Maryanne and Mom to see if they can help you keep an eye on the kids."

"Huh? Oh, that sounds good. I'm sure Suzie and Mike will be there too."

She pursed her lips and nodded as she texted about the plans tomorrow. She leaned down and kissed him on the cheek. He looked up as she ran a hand down his scruffy chin and smiled.

"I'm going to go grab some overnight stuff from my apartment. I'll be back in less than an hour. Owen is good to stay here?"

"Yep, if they get rowdy, I'll take them for a walk. No worries here."

She kissed him, running her tongue into his mouth. He sucked in a breath when she slid her hand up his cock. With a little squeeze and a smile, she turned and left.

Homecoming was loud. The kids were bouncing in the bleachers. She glanced nervously at Andy. His eyes were glazed and a light sheen of sweat coated his forehead. She reached over and squeezed his thigh.

He grabbed her hand and squeezed tightly. She winced. It wasn't a squeeze like Jerry, but it still hurt. She frowned. "You ready to go?"

He turned, but she didn't think he really saw her until he blinked a few times. "What?"

"The kids are getting tired. We're ready to head home."

He nodded woodenly and stood up. He didn't wait for them but just started walking down the bleachers.

"Come on, guys! We're going to head home," she said cheerily.

"Aww, but it's not even half-time yet!" Cody whined.

"Andy isn't feeling good, so we're going home."

James hopped up. "Oh, no! Is it scarlet fever? I was reading about it this week and—"

She laughed, "No, it's not scarlet fever. He'll be fine. He just needs to get away from the crowd."

She slung Mandy and Owen's snack bag over her shoulder and took their hands, leading them down the bleachers and to the SUV. Andy leaned against the passenger side door until she unlocked it. Then they all piled inside and headed home.

"Are you okay, Andy?" James asked. He always picked up on emotions.

"Yeah," Andy mumbled gruffly. "Just a migraine. It happens sometimes with big crowds. I'm already starting to feel better."

"I wanted nachos!" Owen whined. She'd promised him concession stand food tonight, but they had only been there an hour. She'd run into several former patients and friends who'd come over to chat while they'd sat in the bleachers, so she hadn't gotten him any.

"How about s'mores at home?" Andy asked.

"S'mores!" the kids all shouted.

Andy gripped his head with a low chuckle. "Oh, not so loud. This is the perfect season to make a fire pit."

"Can we make the fire? I've been wanting to go

camping for forever!" James practically bounced in his seat, but whispered his words.

"Fire! Fire! Fire!" Mandy and Owen chanted, also whispering, but then growing louder and louder.

"Enough, guys. You're getting too loud. If you want Andy's head to feel better so he can build a fire, you gotta calm down!" she said sternly as she pulled into the driveway. As soon as she turned off the engine, the kids were throwing open the doors and climbing out. Even Mandy had somehow unbuckled and hopped down with Cody's help.

They raced inside as Cindy rounded the front of her SUV and linked her fingers together with his. "Are you sure you're up to this?"

He smiled wanly, his lips white around the edges. "Yeah, I've wanted to do this since Halloween. I knew they'd get a big kick out of it. And later, after they're asleep, we can watch the stars from the hot tub?"

She grinned and slid her hand around his elbow as they walked. "Sounds like my kind of night, but only if you're feeling up to it."

"You could have these kinds of nights all the time if you'd move in." He shut the front door behind him.

She sighed, kicking off her shoes by the front door. "It's not that I don't want to, but you need time with Mandy, and I need time to know that this is real and lasting." The kids tumbled out of the kitchen holding the s'mores supplies up in victory.

"Where's the stick things to roast marshmallows on?" Cody asked.

James frowned, peering closely at Andy. "Maybe you should take some medicine. You look pale, like when Owen starts hurting."

"I'll take some while y'all get the roasting skewers from

the shed. Pretty sure I saw some in there," Andy said. Cody and James raced outside, Mandy and Owen hot on their heels. Cindy slipped on her shoes again while Andy grabbed some medicine, then they followed the kids. James had grabbed the lanterns from the tent where he'd left them earlier this week.

The kids stopped in front of the tent, Owen holding the metal sticks and the littles holding the s'mores supplies.

"Alright, to make a fire pit, first you have to make sure you're not directly under a tree. Why do you think that is?" Andy pointed to the trees and the tent.

"You said when we were putting up the tent that you didn't want it under a branch, in case it fell on the tent. That way no one would get hurt," James said.

Andy grabbed the shovel from the shed and they walked over to the tent. In front of it, out of the tree line, Andy scraped the grass to break up the ground.

"That's right. But with a fire, you don't want it to go up into the trees and catch the tree on fire."

"Oh," Mandy said, her eyes round with hero worship for her dad. Cindy rooted around in the shed, calling for Cody to come help her. She grabbed the folding camping chairs and handed them off. They each carried two over to where they were setting up the fire pit.

Half an hour later, she sat in a chair as the fire roared. Andy had shown each of the kids how to light a fire using cotton balls. He'd helped Owen and Mandy with theirs, and it had been so cute how patient he'd been. He really was a great dad. As time had passed, the tension around his mouth had eased and he'd smiled more, his shoulders lowering too.

They'd started off with three small fires in a circle. But

when they'd added the wood to it, it had become one big fire.

"We need rocks, right? To help it not spread to the grass?" James asked.

Andy nodded, stretching his leg out from where he sat in the camping chair. "Yeah, that's why we dug down a little and made a dirt lip. For now, it's safe enough. But a big fire safety thing is having a bucket of water ready in case you need to put it out quickly, or it gets out of control. Do you want to run to the house and grab a big bowl?"

"I'll do it!" Cody said, taking off at a jog.

"We'll go hiking Sunday after church and find some large rocks to make a circle around it. Should be some down in the creek." Andy said as he slid a giant marshmallow onto a skewer. He showed them how to spin the skewer slowly. Owen's first one fell into the fire. He cried, but Cindy helped him put on another one.

Mandy squealed when her marshmallow caught on fire, and she pulled it out so fast it went flying. The grass quickly caught fire.

With a quick jerk, she stumbled backward as her marshmallow flew through the air and landed in a patch of dry grass. The tiny flames grew rapidly, and Cindy turned to Cody with wide eyes. "The water!" she shouted, but Cody froze as Mandy continued to shriek and James and Owen joined in.

Andy sprang up and stomped on the fire as Cody finally regained his senses and doused it with water. Most of it hit Andy in the face, leaving him dripping wet. He just stood there speechless, his jaw hanging open in shock or from the cold water—she couldn't tell which.

Cindy held her breath. *This would be where he loses it*, she thought.

Andy shook his head, wiped the water off his face, chuckling at the chaos that had just unfolded. "Good shot. Why don't you roast a marshmallow? I'll go grab a towel and refill the bowl."

Cody was shifting from foot to foot with a frown, waiting to get in trouble. It broke Cindy's heart that he expected the yelling and screaming, a product of his former step-dad. Andy tousled Cody's hair and smiled. "Hey, no harm done. But while I'm gone, will you make sure that doesn't happen again? Keep an eye on things?"

Cody beamed and nodded, taking a seat and grabbing one of the sticks and a marshmallow.

"Mandy, honey, why don't you come sit with me, and we'll roast it together?" Cindy asked as Andy walked away. Mandy hopped onto her lap. This time, Cindy dragged it out of the fire slowly, blowing the flames off it.

Their soft voices rang out in the stillness of the night, and something shifted in her chest. Was she really done fighting all of this?

She loved being here just like this. Even the craziness of four kids was less stressful when Andy was involved. There was no denying she loved him.

She frowned. Why hadn't she told him yet? Why didn't she want to move in with him yet? He came back before she could figure it out. She smiled as he carried the bowl and set it behind them where it wouldn't get easily spilled.

He sat down in the camping chair beside her, Mandy slipping off her lap to crawl up onto his. Wiping the chocolate off her lips with the back of her hand, she snuggled into his arms.

Cindy's heart melted at the sight of him holding the little girl. She wanted this, wanted him. The boys talked on the other side of the fire, Owen trying to keep up with them. She glanced at Mandy, who was already asleep.

"Andy," she mumbled. "I... I... about earlier..."

Chapter Forty-One

She chickened out, swallowing hard and staring into his eyes as they glowed brightly in the fire light.

He smiled sadly, "I know. It's fine. It'll happen when it happens. I can wait. I know you might have felt put on the spot earlier when I said I loved you. While I mean it, you might not be there yet. Hell, you might never get there." He frowned, turning to gaze into the fire.

"It's not that," she drawled. "I do love you. I don't know why I didn't say it earlier, but I do."

He frowned at her, his brows raising. "You're saying that because I said it, aren't you? Don't do that, Cindy. Whatever you do, don't lie to me."

"I'm not lying. I love you," she whispered furiously.

He sighed as he stood up, turning and smiling as the boys looked at him. "I'm going to lay Mandy down. Do you want me to put Owen down too?"

She sighed in frustration. "Owen, time for bed. Andy's going to help you get ready and tuck you in, okay? I'll come kiss you when the fire is out." Owen came and kissed her before going inside.

James and Cody grew quiet, casting furtive glances at her and whispering to each other. Finally they moved around the fire to sit on either side of her.

"Y'all like it here, don't you?" She didn't need to ask. She already knew the answer. They nodded, telling her all about their favorite things. When they finished their s'mores, they fell silent. "All right, time for bed you two." They gave her kisses. She handed them the s'more leftovers to take inside.

Andy came back out and sat down, grabbing her hand and pulling her onto his lap. She laid her head on his shoulder and sighed. "You're a wonderful dad. Thanks for tucking them all in."

Gently, he placed a tender kiss on her forehead. "It's been an adjustment, but I think it's going well."

She gazed up at him with soft eyes, a hint of nervousness and vulnerability making her straighten his shirt. "Not just with Mandy, but with my boys too. They've never had a positive male figure in their lives before, and seeing you with them brings me so much joy. It warms my heart to see how they admire and look up to you."

A small smile tugged at the corners of his mouth. "Well, it's easy to love them. They're incredible kids."

Her hand found its way to his cheek and she whispered, almost shyly, "It's easy to love you too. I have for a while now, but I've been too afraid to say it. It feels easier in the darkness, where we can be honest and vulnerable."

He sighed, resting his forehead against hers. "Cindy, I've lived in fear my whole life. From when I first moved here as a kid to when I was first injured, I know how paralyzing fear can be. But *you* have to decide whether you're going to step out of it, let it go, and take a chance."

"I'm tired of giving in to the fear. I—I think I do want to move in. When I'm here, with you… It's like I can handle all the stress. I'm a better person when I'm with you. A better mom."

He took her hand from his cheek and kissed her palm. "You're an amazing mom, even without me. It's one of the things I love about you. Your patience with them helps me be patient with them too."

She sat back and looked at him, the firelight falling on his face. "It's not always going to be like that. I can get stressed and just want to retreat from the world. I can yell with the best of them. I've lost it a few times in the past year alone. You saw me last week at the hospital when I yelled."

He grinned and rolled his yes. "And you saw me earlier at the game. Sometimes things are just too hard to handle, and we have to step back and regroup. It doesn't mean we're surrendering the war. It means we're taking a breather before diving back into the fight."

She chuckled and laid her head on his chest, his arms coming around her to hold her tightly. She'd never felt so loved and cherished. "But love isn't supposed to be a fight."

His jaw moved against her head, and he stretched out his leg. "It won't be fighting each other. It'll be fighting *for* each other. Part of loving each other means being there when the other needs us. It means saying, 'Ya know what? You look like you need a break. Go take a bubble bath. I got dinner and the kids tonight.' Those days are going to happen, but as long as we go through them together, I think it'll all work out fine."

She thought about it as she listened to the sounds of the

surrounding woods. "How'd you get so wise about this stuff?"

He chuckled and kissed the top of her head. "Daily therapy for fifteen months will do that."

The coyotes began to howl in the distance, and she shivered, not from fear but from the cold as the fire started to die down.

He rubbed his hands up and down her back. "How about the week of Thanksgiving you guys move in? The boys won't have school that week, right? And then we can enjoy the holiday together."

She nodded as she yawned. "That's only a few weeks away. I don't know."

He tipped her chin up, his lips slowly descending to hers. His tongue lazily swept in, and she opened for him, the tightness in her chest at thinking of the move and major life step easing. She stopped thinking and simply enjoyed the moment.

"How about that hot tub?" he murmured as he flicked her nipple through her sweater. She gasped.

"Sounds wonderful," she moaned. He stood up with her still in his arms and let her slide down him, rubbing his cock against her before stepping back to extinguish the barely glowing wood from the fire.

When they turned to walk to the house, he linked their fingers. Breaking contact when they walked through the doors, her heart ached as she already missed his touch.

She checked on the kids then changed into her bikini. Maryanne had convinced her to buy it, even though she'd never thought to wear it in public.

But for Andy? She wanted him to love her, and if that meant doing things she wasn't comfortable with sometimes, she'd do it. And honestly, her thighs and stretch marks didn't look too bad in the dim light.

She grabbed a towel from the master bath and wrapped it around herself as she walked out the back door. He was placing two beers on the little table beside the hot tub. The cover was already off and the water bubbling, so she set the towel on a chair.

She smirked as his eyes raked up and down her body, taking in the little red scraps of fabric with ever widening eyes and lips.

"Like what you see?" she swaggered over to him. She slid her body past his, brushing her nipples against his bare chest and making him groan.

"Damn straight I do. You're my favorite wet dream every night, but to have you here?"

He gripped her ass as she walked past, making her laugh as she stepped up the stairs and slid down into the water.

"Oh, this is perfect!" she gasped as she sunk down and leaned her head back.

His prosthesis clicked as he unhooked it. "I could say the same thing about you."

She watched him set it against the table before he placed his hands on the side of the hot tub. He hopped up each step, sat down on the edge, and then swung his legs in before sinking down.

His biceps bulged as he controlled his body, every muscle popping in the soft light from above the grill on the opposite side of the deck. She licked her lips as he wiggled his brows. "You like what you see?"

She smiled as he turned her words against her. "Damn straight I do."

He chuckled as he leaned back in the opposite corner from her, stretching his legs out along the side. She asked about his therapy appointment that week. He told her how bored he was with it and how he didn't feel pushed or stretched or anything.

"I wish you were still my therapist." He sighed, picking up his beer.

She leaned her head back. "Me too. I like the consistency of PT, you know? At the hospital, you're always running around. It's chaotic sometimes and exciting. The PT used to be a good balance to that. I enjoyed meeting people in their homes too. It was fun."

"I'm sorry you got fired." He frowned, and she knew he really was sorry. He didn't think her career frivolous like Jerry had.

She shrugged and leaned her head back to close her eyes. "I'll figure it out. I met with the HR lady today too, to see if I could extend my hours at the hospital. For now, I'll work Saturday to Tuesday from seven pm to seven am. Those hours start on Monday though, so tomorrow and Sunday are still a forty-eight-hour shift."

"So what you're saying is that we need to make tonight count, because you won't be around much in the next few days?" he murmured into the darkness.

She opened her eyes as his hands moved up her thighs in the water. He was on his knees and pushed himself between her floating legs. His fingers played with the edge of her swimsuit, running along the crease of her leg.

Raising his other hand, he pulled the string at the base of her neck. He peeled the triangles down one by one, revealing her breasts. They bobbed in the water and the bubbles rolling on her nipples made her moan.

He dipped a finger under the band of her swimsuit as his other hand rolled her nipple and pulled. She gasped as his finger slid inside, first one then two fingers. Clenching around him, she spread her legs wider and untied the strings at her hips.

She flung her swimsuit over the edge of the hot tub, making wet slapping sounds on the deck. When she was naked before him, he growled as he sat back and stared. "My God, you're incredible. Beautiful is too tame a word for you."

He pumped in and out with his fingers, too slow for her. She raised her hips up to speed him along, gasping his name softly. The hand left her breast as he pulled down his trunks. He grabbed his cock and stroked it before lining up with her.

She arced her back as he filled her up, her gasp mingling with his groan as he grabbed her hips. The water made her buoyant, and she reached behind her to grab the edge of the hot tub. She held on as he pounded in and out, faster and harder than he ever had before.

She rose to the edge of an orgasm before he slowed down, her whimper of frustration making him chuckle. "Not so fast. I want to enjoy you. Turn around."

He pulled out, and she turned around on her knees on the seat in the hot tub. He moved her so that a jet hit her clit, and she jerked.

"Wha--?" she asked.

He leaned in behind her, moving her hips from side to side over the jet.

"I want to feel you come on my cock like this," he whispered in her ear. Pulling back, he lined his cock up with her, slamming inside in one thrust and moving her in the jet stream at the same time. She squealed as she jerked on his cock, clenching as she came.

He held still until her shudders eased. Then he moved her side to side, in and out of the jet's path slowly. Somehow he pulled out and slammed inside right as she slid over the jet.

But he couldn't hold the rhythm for long, especially when she leaned forward onto the jet, her breasts pushed against the side of the hot tub. Her back arched, and he pulled her roughly onto him. She squealed as she came again, longer and jerkier than before. Her body convulsed around his.

He stilled, panting in her ear as he pulled her off the jet. Her bones were putty in his hands. He pulled them both back to the seat, keeping his cock buried deep. Her back to his chest, he wrapped his hands around her font and spread her legs.

He placed her legs on the seat on either side of him, his knees between hers. His thighs were strong enough to support them both as he pushed deeper into her.

Then he slid one hand down to her sensitive clit and the other up to cup her breasts, holding tight as he thrust up.

His touch was like lightning. Where she'd been weightless before, the single touch now energized her.

She gripped the sides of the hot tub again and bounced up and down on his cock. He groaned softly into her ear, "Damn it, Cindy. You're going to make me come. Slow down."

She slowed but clenched, desperate to hear him gasp, before sliding off and turning to face him. She cupped his face in her hands as she slowly lowered herself onto him.

She leaned forward and kissed him, molding their lips together. He grabbed her hips and held her still, but she wouldn't stop rocking against him. She kissed him deeper, slamming her body down hard on his. She gasped as his pubic bone hit her clit perfectly from this angle.

It was heaven on earth. She could never go without this,

without him. She needed him like she needed air to breathe. With a squeal, she came again. He hit deeper as he thrust up, swelling as he joined her.

He pulsed inside as she jerked. Falling against his chest, he wrapped his arms around her.

"I love you," she gasped into his ear.

He squeezed her tighter, gruffly saying, "I love you too."

In this moment, all was right with her world and the worry about her job faded.

Chapter Forty-Two

Two weeks later, they were taking the last of their stuff over to the house. The boys had whooped for joy when she'd told them they were moving in. Even Mandy had been excited, forgetting all about not sharing her Daddy with them, excited to have Owen for a roommate. They'd stayed with Andy that Veteran's Day weekend, but Maryanne and her mom had helped wrangle kids at all the various events that day.

She'd been nervous, since he'd not handled the crowd well the night of Homecoming. But it had all worked out better than she'd expected. They'd stayed at his house a few nights since then, but this was the weekend before Thanksgiving. It was about to be official.

She pulled up to the house and frowned. She'd taken the kids to school and finished packing up the apartment while Andy was doing his PT appointment. An extra vehicle was in the driveway, and she debated turning around, thinking the PT appointment had run long.

The front door opened, and Andy stepped out. She

turned off the engine and got out. He kissed her hello, saying, "We'll get this stuff unloaded in a bit. Come inside first."

"Who's here? Was there a time mix-up with Monica again for PT?" He shook his head, looking uneasy.

"They came after Monica left," he opened the door.

'They' turned out to be Suzie and Maggie. She frowned as he led her to the dining room table and pulled a chair out for her. She sat, eyeing the two women with a tight smile. Her hands were tight fists in her lap, and her back was ramrod straight.

"Hello." She twisted her lips into a semblance of a smile, nodding at Suzie and then making eye contact with Maggie. She'd ignore Suzie for now.

Andy moved around behind her in the kitchen, but she needed him close.

"It's good to see you, my dear! How have you been?" Maggie's face was open and friendly.

"I've been alright. I picked up a four day, twelve-hour shift at the hospital, so I've been working." She didn't mention that it wasn't enough to pay her bills or that saving on the rent for the apartment was one of the contributing factors to pushing her to move in with Andy.

"That's good. I worried about you and feeding those boys," she said. Cindy stiffened at her words. She didn't want to be anyone's charity case.

"She's moving in this weekend, so she won't have to worry about groceries anymore." Andy handed her a cup of tea and sat. She sipped it slowly, taking a deep breath. She knew he didn't see her as a charity case either.

They'd bickered some about the groceries before having a sit-down meeting about money. They'd shared their budgets and decided who was going to do what. It had taken her a while to accept his help.

He'd spent a long time explaining how they were equals and how it could work, even though he clearly didn't have to worry about money. His disability pay alone was more than double what she had made with both her jobs combined. And he was getting more and more work from Nick with the radios every day too.

"I was also sorry to hear about Owen's elbow. How's he doing?" Maggie asked.

She nodded and blew on the tea cup. "He's doing better. All his classmates have signed his cast. Mandy's been a big help with him too, keeping him distracted from the things he can't do yet."

"He'll have the cast removed before Christmas though. He's looking forward to that," Andy said, placing his arm around the back of her chair.

An awkward silence descended as she drank her tea. The ladies glanced at each other before Maggie cleared her throat. Cindy glanced from Maggie to Suzie and back again over her cup as she sipped.

"Yes, well. I wanted to stop by and give you this." Maggie pulled a manila folder out of her bag and passed it to Cindy. She opened it and scanned the documents inside. She flipped through the pages with a frown.

"What is this?" she asked.

"It's making amends," Suzie said, staring down at her hands on the table with a frown. She glanced up and her blue eyes met Cindy's, the pain in them rolling off and making her own chest tighten.

"I shouldn't have gone to Maggie about your relationship with Andy. I get things in my head and tend to miss what's right in front of my nose. I saw y'all at the grocery store last week with Owen and Mandy."

Cindy's eyes widened as she glanced to Andy, who shrugged. Suzie sighed and wiped the corner of her eye.

"You were all one big happy family. I haven't seen that in you before, Andy. I... might have followed you around for a while after that. I watched at the park too."

Cindy's cheeks burned in—what? Embarrassment? Anger? She didn't know exactly.

Suzie met her gaze again again, her expression pleading. "I talked to Andy about the timeline of your relationship. Then I talked to some other church ladies and finally Maggie."

"Maggie asked me to come in last week to give a statement about what happened." Andy stroked her shoulder where his hand rested on the back of the chair.

"You can read it all there. The rough outline is that first page. It states that Andy pursued you before they assigned him as your patient, so you didn't violate any privacy laws with that. It also outlines that Andy pursued you while you were his patient but was adamant that nothing happened until after your last appointment with him. Suzie exaggerated the relationship, which is also stated."

Cindy frowned, reading through the first page as Maggie talked.

"Basically you didn't violate any procedures or policies of the company and the PT Association rules are rather vague. I confirmed it with them, and you won't have to go to the review board. They've dropped the case. You'll be on mandatory unpaid leave for sixty days."

"Leave only? I can come back?" Cindy asked, her head jerking up. Her heart raced at the news. "I'm not sure I want to come back. The past few weeks of only working one job has been good for me and my boys. I've been able to spend more time with them."

Andy reached over and stroked her thigh with his free hand, half turning his body to face her. "And you don't have to go back if you don't want to. I've told you before, your job is totally up to you."

Her anger flared at his reminder of their last argument a few days ago. "And I've told *you*, I won't be a stay-at-home mama," she said sternly, making him grin.

Suzie sighed and leaned back in her chair, smoothing her hands down her skirt. "That is exactly what I feared, Cindy. I thought you were after some baby daddy to mooch off of, but I was so very wrong. That's not you at all. Everyone in town has been telling me that."

"Uh oh, what have they been saying?" She tried to joke it off, but she shifted uncomfortably in her chair. Andy's hand held her steady, and she took comfort and strength from his presence.

"That you are always saying yes, even when you shouldn't. Like with the bake sale at the school. You had no time for that, but you did it anyway. You put others before yourself and always follow all the rules."

Maggie nodded, her glasses catching the light in the room. "That's true, which is why I was so surprised when Suzie first told me about your dating Andy."

"Except I wasn't dating him!" Cindy said, her voice low as her jaw tightened. Andy stood up and started massaging her shoulders. She breathed deeply and forced herself to relax.

Maggie leaned over and patted her arm. "I know that, dear. Andy's timeline proves it, as does Suzie's letter."

"You wrote a letter too?" Cindy glanced at Suzie.

Suzie twisted the napkin on the table, pulling it to her

lap. She sighed and frowned. "Yes, because of me being a drama queen, you lost your job. That wasn't right. I exaggerated a little and, honestly, I never intended to get you fired. I just wanted you to stop being Andy's PTA."

"But why? She's the best there is," Andy growled, his hands tightening on her shoulders. Cindy reached up a hand and touched his, drawing him back to the present.

Maggie chuckled and pushed her glasses up her nose. "That's true. This month has been a nightmare. We've had to hire two additional PTAs to handle Cindy's case load alone."

The comment made Cindy feel good, redeemed a little, but if the company didn't trust her to follow policies and procedures, she wasn't sure she wanted to be at that company.

Suzie looked away, then at Andy before landing on Cindy. "I did what I thought was best, but it turns out it wasn't. I'm a mama bear, not a wise owl, and I'm sorry."

Cindy leaned her head back against Andy's stomach and sighed, the anger and resentment lessening but not going away completely. "I appreciate the apology, Suzie, and Maggie—I'll think about coming back at the end of the sixty days. That'll be in January, and right now I'm just focused on Thanksgiving and Christmas."

Maggie sighed, shifting nervously on the chair and looking worried. "I was afraid you'd say that. I have a counter proposal. I'm ready to retire, Cindy. Would you be interested in taking over as the PT director of the home health branch?"

Andy's hands stilled on her shoulders as she caught her breath. "I'm not qualified to be the PT. I only have the assistant certification."

Maggie shrugged, her eyebrows raised. "You have sixty days anyway, so might as well study and take that test."

"What about hours and pay?" Andy asked. Cindy winced; leave it to a man to mention the hard things.

Maggie nodded, but didn't look at him, keeping her eyes on Cindy. "It's triple what you made as a PTA, at a minimum. You'd be working solid days in the office with a few main physical therapist duties going to people's houses to on board patients."

Cindy narrowed her eyes and crossed her arms. "I only want to work while the boys are in school. I want to be home in the evenings."

Maggie nodded and leaned forward, hand on the table. "Absolutely, I'll stay on for three to six months next year to train you and hand everything over. But after that, it'll be all yours, including the schedule."

Cindy was stunned. She hadn't expected this at all when she came home today. She glanced from Maggie to Suzie to Andy, who sat back down beside her. He linked their fingers together and smiled. "It's up to you. Whatever you want."

She squeezed and sighed, a huge weight coming off her shoulders as she turned to Maggie. "Let me think about it this weekend and look at that test. If I think I can do it, I'll let you know next week."

"Oh, that's Thanksgiving week. Just let me know before December 1st, alright? If I need to look for someone else, I need the time to do that," Maggie said, rising from her chair and gathering her big tote bag. "I have to be off now. I have some grandbabies to spoil this afternoon."

Andy walked her to the door and waved goodbye. Suzie and Cindy stared at each other across the table.

Suzie twisted the napkin and looked back down at the

table. "I really am sorry, you know. I didn't connect the dots on who you were, but I remember you growing up. Your grandma loved you dearly. If she had any idea of the trouble I caused you, I have no doubt she'd be haunting me right now."

Cindy laughed, the surprised sound high and sharp. "You... you're probably right. And thank you for speaking with Maggie," she said, her throat clogging with emotion.

Suzie raised her hands, putting the napkin back on the table. "I had nothing to do with that job offer. I just wanted to clear the air with Maggie, but mostly with you. I really am sorry. I've been talking with Mandy these past few weeks, and she's—well, she's excited to have a home with a Mommy and a Daddy." Suzie frowned, glancing from Andy to Cindy.

Cindy smiled softly and reached for his hand as he sat at the table. "I'm glad she's adjusting, but we all will take a while to get used to this. As for everything else? Everyone has talked about me my whole life. I'm the girl who rolled in with three kids, two fathers, and no husband. Of course there are assumptions."

"But there shouldn't be," Suzie said, her hand fisting on the table.

Cindy shrugged and reached for her her tea. "Doesn't mean it's not the truth." She sighed as Andy ran his hand along the back of her head before turning to put his elbows on the table.

"You two really are cute together. I can see the love there," Suzie said glancing between them.

They smiled at each other, then he looked at her cup. "It took a while to convince her to take a chance, but we're all in now, aren't we? Do you want more tea?" he asked.

She nodded, her cheeks heating. "No more tea, thanks,

but absolutely all in, yes. With that in mind... Suzie, what's your plan for Thanksgiving?"

Suzie shrugged, her shoulders lowering with her frown. "We used to do family dinners at my house, but since we've been in D.C. the past two holidays, we haven't done that lately. Why?"

Cindy looked at Andy, and he nodded at her to continue. They'd discussed this, and she's been prepared to meet with Suzie eventually. Andy had warned her that Suzie had wanted to apologize, so she'd had weeks to come to terms with it.

Plus Mandy talked about her Gamma all the time, and she knew the boys were craving more family.

She smiled at Suzie, the last of the bitterness fading away. "We're going to have a house warming Thanksgiving party on Thursday. Normally, we go to Mama's, but there's more room here. We'd love to have you and Mike join us."

Suzie perked up and smiled, her blond ponytail bouncing. "That sounds lovely! What can I bring? What time will it be?"

"I don't know yet. I've never done Thanksgiving and don't even know where to start."

"Andy, will you grab a notebook and a pen? We need to make a list!" Suzie said, practically bouncing in her seat.

Cindy laughed, seeing where Mandy got her enthusiasm and gestures. "I love a good list! Yes, that's exactly what we need." Andy brought over the supplies and glanced at his watch.

"I'm going to go get Mandy and Owen from school. I'll be back later. Will you be alright?" he asked, kissing her softly on the cheek. She smiled and nodded, watching him walk out, her heart nearly bursting with happiness.

Chapter Forty-Three

She woke up energized on Thanksgiving morning. For once, she beat Andy out of bed and jumped in the shower. Of course, he soon joined her.

It took her longer to get out than she expected but as she breathed deeply on his shoulder, her legs straddling him on the bench and coming down from her orgasm, she smiled. Totally worth it.

He handed her a clean towel and walked to his closet. They'd moved most of the boxes out this week, and her clothes took up one side of the closet now.

"Did you invite Nick and the Williams'?" she asked as she dried her hair and grinned at the joy of her new walk-in closet. She'd never had one before.

"Yeah, they're coming around noon. The Williams' Thanksgiving is at five, so they they'll be gone by four." He sat on the bed and pulled on his boxers then his pants.

"That's fine." She picked up her phone to text Suzie. This week, they'd gone back and forth about the plans for Thanksgiving. She'd talked to her Mom and Maryanne about it. They agreed she should forgive and move on, so she could focus on being happy with Andy.

And she truly was, she thought as she pulled on her jeans. He came back into the closet and fondled her breasts.

She laughed and swatted his hands away. "We're going to run out of time if you don't stop."

"What?" he asked mischievously. "I'm helping you put on the bra."

She laughed again, and he swung her up into his arms, her now covered breasts pressed to his. She dropped the bra and wrapped her legs around him.

"Andy, put me down! You'll hurt your leg!" she squealed in laughter. As he put her down, he kissed her hard, and her mind sighed in happiness. When he finally left her to dress in peace, her brain was in that mushy haze of desire.

He grinned in the doorway and slipped a t-shirt on. "You'll never be too much for me to carry, Cindy. I'll always want to wrap you up and keep you with me!"

Her heart melted. "Silly, we can't live like that."

He tilted his head and looked at her like she'd said the most ridiculous thing. "Cindy, every day I'm excited to come home because you'll be here. I might not be able to pick you up and take you with me in my pocket like I want, but I won't live in a world where we're not happy and together."

Her heart swelled with love and relief as she felt a weight lift from her shoulders. "I'm sorry, I just... I never imagined I could have this kind of happiness. It's scary to let someone in after being hurt so badly before. I don't know what to say when you talk like that."

He was always saying things like that, but it still made her heart flip with joy. He came back into the closet and pulled her into a hug. "Just say, 'You're the best, Andy. I love you so much, Andy. Your cock is the best in the world, Andy. Give me more babies, Andy."

She leaned back and laughed, swatting him on the arm and shaking her head. "Come on. We have to get started on all the bread or it won't be done in time." She bent to retrieve her bra as he stepped toward the doorway once more.

"Umm I can't. I have to run into town for a bit. Landry needs help with something this morning. Is that alright?" he asked over his shoulder as she slid on her shirt.

They walked down the hall past the still sleeping kids, and she waited to reply.

They walked into the kitchen to grab coffee and tea before she said, "That's fine. Suzie is going to come over here soon. Mama is helping Maryanne finish up some last minute orders at the bakery, but they'll be here by ten."

He put his coffee in a to-go mug and slipped his shoes on.

"Okay, I'll be back as soon as I can. Love you!" He kissed her, sweeping his tongue in quickly. When he left, she glanced at the clock. It was barely six in the morning. She wondered what Landry needed help with so early.

It didn't matter. It was time to make the bread. While the cinnamon rolls and regular rolls rose, she made the pumpkin and apple pies. She was stuffing the turkey when Suzie walked in.

"Happy Thanksgiving!" she turned back to the bird and rubbed olive oil and herbs all over the outside.

"Smells good in here!" Suzie put down her purse and pulled out a piece of fabric. She held it up as Cindy washed her hands.

"What's this?" Cindy asked, eying the pink and purple

apron with tiny black flowers all over it. A white lace edge ran along the hem and the pockets.

Suzie's eyes glazed over. "This was Sarah's. She loved to cook, and we had matching aprons made one year while she was in high school. I'd like you to have it."

Cindy shut off the water and wiped her hands on a towel. "Oh, Suzie. I don't think I can accept this. You should give it to Mandy."

"It's too big for Mandy. I had a kids' one made for her that's still at my house. When she gets old enough, I'll have a big one made for her too. This one... I need to give it to you. I need to let her go, and I don't want to give it to anyone but you."

"Suzie..." she teared up, then leaned forward and hugged her. Surprised, Suzie's hands wavered before she hugged Cindy back.

"I think by finally letting her go... I've lost one daughter but gained another. So thank you," Suzie squeezed back.

Cindy wiped her eyes and slipped the apron around her head. She tied it in the back as Suzie turned back to inspect what she'd done so far.

Hours later, people had arrived, but Andy still wasn't back. Cindy laughed with Holly and Lola as they set up two extra tables in the living room. Hunter and Gunner had brought the folding tables and chairs, on loan for a few hours from their mom.

The ladies decorated the table with white table cloths. She was quite proud of the centerpieces with faux leaves and mason jars full of fabric markers.

Parker had gone out to the camp site where the kids were playing. Landry had brought the little wooden Humvee from the float, now weatherproofed, and had set it up beside the tent for a kid's playground type thing. They called the kids and Parker inside to wash up, which he immediately turned into a competition for the cleanest hands.

Kendall arrived, and she welcomed him with a smile. He avoided Lola and hung out with the Williams boys at the other table in the living room. They talked about the town, the rain they would get later today, and the upcoming sheriff's election.

At five till noon, Cindy was fuming. Why would Andy leave her to entertain all these people in his house? If he didn't want a crowd, why had he suggested it? He was normally fine with a crowd of friends. It was big places he had trouble with.

"There he is!" Maryanne said from the door.

Landry pulled up behind Andy, and they both jumped out and walked up the steps to the house. Cindy waited for them outside, her arms crossed and her hip cocked out. Andy looked at her with a sheepish grin on his face as thunder rolled across the sky.

"Where were you? You said it'd only take an hour, not six!" she whispered furiously. He pulled her to the side of the door as Landry walked up and inside. She jerked her hand away and strode to the end of the porch, rubbing her temples.

"I'm sorry it took longer than I thought. Did you not get my texts?" he asked. She whirled around and faced him, her hands going wide.

"You think I've had time to check my phone? Between cooking and entertaining all our friends and family, I haven't even gotten to pee!" she sighed, glaring at him and trying to keep her voice down.

He grinned and grabbed her by the waist, swinging her

into his arms as he hummed a slow tune. "Sh, it's alright. It's going fine, isn't it?"

They danced on the porch as the rain fell. She melted into his arms. It wasn't even a conscious decision; her body just automatically molded to his now.

He kissed the side of her temple. "I'm sorry it took us so long. I had ordered a package that needed picked up in town, but it wasn't there. I had to go all the way to the Fort Worth location. I should've called or tried to reach Suzie or your mom. I'm sorry I made you worry." He drew circles on her lower back with his hand, his voice low, smooth, and calming.

"Why are we dancing? We have to go inside to eat. Everyone's been waiting for you," she murmured into his chest.

"My second weekend in town, I wanted to go dancing, because I wanted to feel alive again. I'd felt so cold, alone, and dead inside for months. Years really. But the crowd was too much. Too loud, too stinky, too many people. I was searching for something that night and ended up in the hospital. Remember that?"

She snorted, rubbing her face on the softness of his shirt. "Yeah, Holly still feels bad about hitting you."

He laughed softly and nuzzled her neck. "I realized later that you were what I had been searching for that night. When we met and I had the kidney stone... you weren't just my nurse. I felt it then, even in the haze of all the meds and pain."

"Felt what?" she asked, her heart starting to race at his words. Where was he going with this?

"You're more than just a nurse or a mom or someone to take care of me when I need it. You're my everything, Cindy. I love you more every day, and every day I think there's no way life can get better because it's already perfect with you in it."

Her eyes teared up with emotion as he pulled back to look down at her with those gorgeous blue eyes, eyes that had always seen the real her, flaws and all, and had accepted her anyway.

He smiled. "You are my family. You've taken away my loneliness, my fear of never being good enough for someone to love. You've accepted me just as I am, bum leg and all. I want to make a life with you, one full of laughter and kids—maybe even another baby or two."

Her heart skipped a beat at the thought of having his baby, and she froze. They stopped dancing, and he cupped her face, kissing her softly as he grinned. She ached for his tongue to meet hers, but he pulled back and dropped down onto one knee.

He pulled out a ring box from his pocket, and she gasped. Her hands covered her mouth as he opened it, the blue diamond matching the ice color of his eyes.

"I know you've only just moved in this past week, but I couldn't wait any longer. I had ordered this, but they didn't ship it to the Pharma in town in time. So I went to grab it from Fort Worth. The blue to match my eyes that you don't stop talking about."

She chuckled, but no sound came out, her voice frozen in surprise.

"It's gold because you're a warm and caring person whom I adore. And there are six sides because if you say yes, we'll be a family of six. I'm not just in this because I love you. I love those boys too, Cindy. Say you'll marry me. Say you'll make us a real family. Please, Cindy."

His blue eyes shone bright. The rain poured off the porch behind them, but for Cindy, time stood still. She memorized the lines of his face, the dark stubble on his jaw, the way his dark blue shirt clung to his pecs, the jacket bulging over his huge biceps.

Her vision swam as the tears filled them. She sucked in a ragged breath and cupped his face in her hands.

"Andy, I was scared for a long time, and I still am. I'm scared of being hurt, of being left, of change. But I think you're right. I think if we do this together, we'll be alright. I love you more than I've ever loved anyone in my entire life."

"So is that a yes?" he asked, taking her left hand and raising his brows.

This time, her laugh was full and loud. "Yes! Yes! Yes!" She was shrieking by the end, her hand shaking as she held it out for him to slip the ring onto her third finger.

He pushed himself up and swung her into his arms as the front door opened and almost everyone spilled out onto the porch. Tears rolled down Cindy's eyes as he kissed her swiftly and set her on her feet.

Her mom and sister pulled her in for hugs next, and Holly and Lola hovered around to pour over the beauty of her ring.

Andy walked inside where the guys slapped him on the back. When she finally walked inside, the kids stood together with Andy next to the window.

She heard him say, "So it's fine if I marry your mom? Can I be your dad too?"

James and Cody launched themselves into his arms, and he wrapped an arm around them both. Mandy and Owen latched onto his thighs, Mandy not even caring that the one she held was metal below the knee beneath his jeans.

Cindy practically floated over to them and joined the family hug as more tears streamed down her face.

December

"Damn girl, you're going to need to come in for a massage every day this week, okay?" Holly said as she kneaded her back. Cindy laid on the massage table and groaned.

"It should be a little less stressful now. I took my test yesterday, so I can focus on the wedding and Christmas."

Holly's hands dug into her shoulder. "Why are you even getting married so fast? I thought you wanted to wait and get to know him."

"I do want to get to know him more. I'm still scared that things could change in six months, or a year, or even five or ten years." Cindy sighed, her eyes closing. "But it's like I've known him my entire life instead of just three months. We don't hold anything back and talk about everything, Holly. And the sex? Oh my God. It's amazing! Is this what you had with your husband?"

Holly laughed, the tinkling sound reminding Cindy of music and the Tinkerbell movies Mandy was currently obsessed with. "Hmm, sounds like it. We used to sit up late at night and just talk, laughing over stupid cat videos and nothing in particular."

Cindy hummed before saying, "Did you know he helped me study for the test? He could probably go pass the test himself at this point. He's super smart."

"Kendall says he's always been like that. He stood out in Basic Training because he was so smart. Kendall likes to surround himself with those kinds of guys. Good, smart guys."

Cindy groaned as Holly dug into a particular knot.

"Yeah, sounds like Kendall. How's he doing without me at the hospital?"

"About the same. Grumbles and complains all the time, especially about Lola."

"What have they gotten into about now?" Cindy's muscles felt like liquid.

Holly told her the latest about the feud between the two before asking, "When's your wedding again? Saturday before Christmas? Why then?"

"We wanted to celebrate Christmas as a family, a real one. Then the kids will float between Suzie and Mom's while we go for our honeymoon for a week. We leave two days after Christmas for Cancun!"

"I miss the beach. Have you ever been? It's magical." Holly's voice was wistful.

"I haven't been in a long time. We used to go when I was a kid. When I lived in Houston—well, I didn't spend a lot of time on the beach there."

"Houston water isn't really oceany though," Holly whined, making Cindy laugh.

"I start the new job in January, so I didn't want to take a honeymoon next year with all that training going on. Plus, I didn't want Maryanne to feel bad about the baby bump in any wedding photos."

Holly gasped, her hands pausing. "My God, is she really pregnant? Did she admit it?"

Cindy sighed and shifted on the table. "No, she hasn't admitted it, but the signs are all there. I'm not going to push her about it though, because when I did that as kids, it blew up in my face. She'll tell me when she's ready."

"And the father?"

"She was talking about one of the insurance guys who

came to inspect her bakery when it flooded, but that's just my best guess."

"Well, that's still exciting." Cindy noted the wistfulness in Holly's voice. She sounded less sad than she had before when talking about babies.

Cindy cleared her throat and turned over as Holly held the sheet up. Groaning, she said, "Just keep it between you, me, and Lola. Once I find out for sure, I'll fill y'all in. If she is pregnant, are you going to be alright with a new baby in our group? How do you feel about it?"

Holly massaged her feet, and Cindy waited her out. Eventually, she said, "Frustrated. Sad. The new counselor at the middle school is doing evening therapy sessions. After you told me you thought she was pregnant, I've been seeing her twice a week to process it."

"Oh, Holly, that's so good of you! Andy is seeing her too. He says he actually likes having a vent session and missed it when he moved back. Weird, huh?"

Holly shrugged. "Not so weird. Sometimes it takes years to process out the trauma. I totally get it. He needs to keep seeing someone about losing his leg. You should probably go see her too. Everyone should, actually. She's amazing and will be at yoga Thursday too."

"I can't wait to meet her. Maybe once things settle down in the spring, I can schedule an appointment. I think Andy also talks about the adjustment to being a family of six. That's a pretty big change too. He's handled it well, but there are times we bicker. He has his PTSD moments and withdraws into himself."

Cindy's voice trailed off, thinking of the last time he had a moment. When Cindy got emotional, she yelled, like a firework, she exploded and then it was over. But with Andy, he tended to hide away and retreat, holding onto his feelings until he could express them sometimes days later.

"But it's worth it?" Holly asked, bringing her back to the moment.

"Oh yes, being with him is totally worth it. I can't wait for the wedding. He's going to look so good in the tux we picked out."

Holly laughed as they started talking about the wedding plans, and she finished the massage. Cindy was the most relaxed she'd been in years. As she got dressed, she smiled. She was also the happiest. Andy had shown her a side of herself she'd forgotten existed. Like the puzzle pieces finally clicked together, and she was finally whole.

Next in the Crimson Creek Series

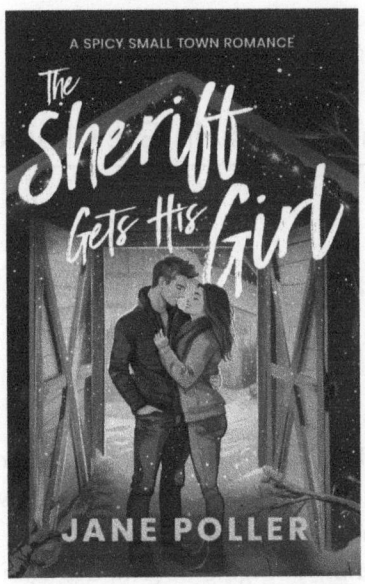

vinci-books.com/sheriff-gets-his-girl

Sometimes love comes with complications

Maryanne vowed to reclaim her carefree life—until a scorching night with Gunner, her disciplined childhood friend, leaves her pregnant. Can these friends-turned-lovers survive small-town gossip and clashing tempers, or will secrets extinguish their spark?

Turn the page for a free preview…

The Sheriff Gets His Girl: Chapter One

Beginning of October

When the bakery doorbell dinged at precisely 6:02am, Maryanne smiled, adjusted her bra to showcase the girls, pulled down her v-neck t-shirt to maximize cleavage, and walked through the swinging door to the front of the shop.

She sucked in a breath and almost fanned herself. Gunner never failed to disappoint. He was wearing the short sleeve uniform shirt today, which made his biceps bulge and strain against the thin material as he spun his cowboy hat in one hand.

The light from the floor to ceiling front windows shone on his light brown hair, making his natural golden highlights stand out. It was getting a little long, and her fingers itched to run through it.

Even when they were teens, he maintained that high and tight military haircut that she was so familiar with as an Army brat. He kept it longer on top now than he did back then. His jeans were pressed, and his black boots shone with military precision, not a speck of dirt on them.

Shaking herself out of her trance, she grinned. "Morning, Gunner. What can I get you?"

His strong jaw clenched before he smiled tightly and stepped up to the counter, setting his hat down and sending a shiver up her spine.

"Usual."

His growl made her heart skip a beat. His voice was rough and dark, just like all her deepest fantasies about him.

"I thought you might want to try something different this morning. Different could be fun," she sing-songed, waving a hand below her breasts before moving it over the goods under the glass. His eyes narrowed as she crossed her arms and leaned on the counter, pushing her double treats on display.

His eyes gleamed with a predatory heat. He didn't let it shine through very often. She let her shoulders dip a bit more, making him suck in a deep breath.

"Just the usual."

You'd think she'd be used to his rejection by now. He'd been shooting her down almost daily for two years. Still, she refused to give up on Gunner.

Pasting on a coy smile, she cooed, "Are you sure I couldn't tempt you into something else this morning?"

He shook his head, remaining silent, his face stony and expressionless, just like always. Even when they were kids and she'd come to Crimson Creek to visit her grandmother for the summer, he maintained that stoic expression. No matter how hard she tried, she couldn't shake him up.

She sighed and straightened, turning to grab a to-go bag and bending into the display case to fetch his order.

"Suit yourself. Maybe tomorrow. I'm experimenting with a pumpkin spice this month. You'll have to tell me what you think, alright? I'll throw in one of those, along with the apple one. But fair warning: next month, the normal bear claws will switch to cinnamon apple. You okay with that?"

She stood to place the box on the counter and caught his gaze zeroed in on her cleavage. His eyes shot to hers in surprise before he cleared his throat, shifted on his feet, and glanced away. The pink tinge on his tanned cheeks was the most adorable thing she'd ever seen.

"Yes."

Smiling wide, she arranged his treats in the small box. "Cool, let me grab the rest of these. How's everything over at the station?"

"Fine."

She tried a different tactic. "How's your mom and dad?"

"Good."

She rolled her eyes and sighed as she stepped to the cash register. "One of these days, Gunner, you're going to actually talk to me, and it's going to be amazing."

Catching his green hazel eyes, she saw them darken as he clenched his jaw. Then he blinked and relaxed his shoulders with a visible shrug.

"Nothing to talk about."

Turning to make his coffee, she sighed. "Darlin', if you ever want to work on your people skills, I'm here. I'll have you making small talk with the best of them."

"I saw you yesterday morning. Nothing has happened since then."

Her heart fluttered. "Wow. Two sentences in a row? That's a record."

She glanced over her shoulder and winked. His cheeks blushed again as he looked away.

Was he starting to thaw out? She wondered if he talked more at work. Or when he arrested someone. She could always try to get herself arrested so he'd have to recite her rights. It'd be worth it to hear his voice.

She finished his coffee and tried to pass it to him. He glanced at her outstretched hand but waved for her to put it on the counter as he pulled out his wallet.

Swallowing the knot of rejection in her throat, she rang up his total and grabbed the cash he'd tossed down as he picked up his breakfast and walked out.

It hadn't escaped her that he refused to touch her yet again. He'd kept well out of her reach since her first day back in town nearly two years ago. He'd pulled her over and their hands had met over her license.

She watched his ass as he crossed the street, and a dreamy sigh escaped her lips. She glanced out the front window at the rising sun, not realizing she'd crossed to the front of the store so she could watch him walk across the street and down the block to the police station.

The purples and pinks in the sky reminded her of when she'd escaped back home two years ago. Like today, it had soothed her confused and tired heart.

She'd always used her smile when she was a kid—and later, her generous curves—to get what she wanted. She'd smiled and things just fell into place. When she'd gone to Colorado for Culinary Arts school, her smile and curves had bitten her in the ass, though.

She'd opened an edible bakery with her then boyfriend. She shivered because two years later, he still gave her nightmares. She'd come home to lick her wounds and start over.

Her little red convertible had been packed so high with

her brightly colored suitcases and boxes that she couldn't even see out her side or rearview mirrors. That was when she'd seen the flashing lights in her driver's side mirror.

She gripped the steering wheel, knuckles turning white as she pulled over onto the side of the little two-lane highway, the anxiety climbed higher in her tense shoulders.

Shit. Her heart felt like it was going to race away when she remembered the pot stashed in her bags. Please, God, don't let them search the car.

She watched with wide eyes as the cop swaggered up to her window. There was something familiar about that walk, but with his cowboy hat, aviator sunglasses, uniform shirt, jeans, and boots, he could be anybody. Anybody who had bulging biceps and thighs, that is.

Shaking her head to free herself from staring at his body, she pushed the button to roll down her window.

"Ma'am. Do you know how fast you were going?"

"No, officer. Was I speeding?" *Her heart was definitely speeding at that deep, growly voice. It sent goosebumps along her arms.*

"Yes, ma'am. Speed limit through here is only fifty-five. You were doing seventy-one. License and registration, please."

She swallowed hard. "I'll need to unbuckle to reach the glove box. Probably need to shift my bag over too. Is that alright?"

"Sure."

He crossed his arms, making his biceps bulge and her eyes pop behind her sunglasses. The dude's massive muscles were barely contained in his uniform shirt. Her mouth watered as she caught sight of a piece of tattoo barely hidden by his shirt sleeve.

Slowly, she unbuckled and got on her knees to reach over her luggage set. She opened the glove box but could feel his eyes on her ass.

She wiggled a little extra as she found the paper and shut the glove box, then slid back to her seat. With any luck, her ass would get her out of the ticket.

"Here's the registration, Officer."

His fingers brushed against hers when he took the paper from her. The slight contact was like lightning up her arm. It left her breathless, and she snatched her arm back. It'd been years since she'd felt this zing.

Taking a deep breath, she reached for her purse and license. When she handed it over, she grazed his hand again, trying to replicate the effect. Would it work?

Hot damn, it did.

The lightning went straight to her core, making it pulse with need. She only reacted to one person like this. His hand jerked when she let go of the license, and he walked toward his vehicle.

Frowning, she leaned her head out the window. Was it him? She hadn't seen him in nearly a decade.

"Gunner? Is that you?"

He'd only gotten three steps when he turned halfway, his body in profile glowing in the setting sun. She'd always crushed on him when she'd stay with her grandma in the summers, but holy shit. He'd grown up and filled out that uniform perfectly.

Slowly, he reached up, making his biceps strain from the muscle, and took his sunglasses off. She could almost hear her vagina howling for him. The brightest hazel green eyes she'd ever seen flashed in the afternoon light, flecks of gold drawing her in like always.

Her heart spasmed with joy. It was Gunner, all right. The first boy she'd ever crushed on and her first kiss.

Well, maybe. She wasn't sure if it had happened or not, but in her heart, she counted it.

She whipped off her own sunglasses and grinned.

"It is you, all grown up now. What's it been? Ten years?"

"About that."

One side of his mouth tipped up, drawing her gaze to his lips. She licked hers, wanting a taste of him.

"That's too damn long. Being a cop suits you." *She gave her best*

flirty smile. "And that uniform... damn, Gunner. Not sure I've seen a sexier cop in my life."

Her laugh bubbled up when his cheeks turned pink, and he narrowed his eyes at her, putting his hands on his hips.

"Are you... flirting with me? To get out of a ticket?"

"Oh, am I getting a ticket?" She raised her eyebrows and flicked a hand to her chest in mock surprise. "No! Say it ain't so!"

He barked out a surprised laugh and shook his head.

"Let me run your license and see if you'll be getting that ticket. Hang tight."

She watched him walk away in her driver's side mirror. His ass in those jeans made her mouth go dry, so she reached for her soda.

He'd always acted cool and aloof when she was in town for the summers. She wasn't even in town yet, and she'd gotten him to laugh. That was new. Maybe he'd lightened up in the past few years.

When they were kids, he'd not paid any attention to her at all. He was always scowling and only laughed when his brothers were around. When they were all hanging out at summer barbecues or the city pool, he'd laugh and joke around with the group.

But by the time he was a senior in high school, it'd been painfully obvious—to her, at least—that he was keeping her at arm's length. And she had no idea why.

It hurt though, to think he'd laugh, joke, and talk with everyone else, but not her. What was wrong with her, anyway? Was she not interesting enough? Pretty enough?

She'd developed the traditional boobs and ass of her Latina heritage pretty early, but the more she tried to get him to notice, the more distance he put between them.

Then he'd started dating that Justine girl. Maryanne bit her nail as she watched him walk in the mirror. Justine had been the tall, blond cheerleader while he was captain of the football team. Maryanne had always felt inferior around girls like that.

She shook off the thoughts and leaned an elbow out the window as he squared up to it. "So, what's the verdict?"

"No ticket. Just a warning."

"Yes!" *She hit the steering wheel and bounced on the seat.* "Thank God! I cannot afford a ticket right now. Man, this is some welcome home."

He grinned, handing her license and registration back. She grabbed them slowly, holding his fingers for a few seconds longer than necessary. Her breath caught as she stared up at him, his hazel eyes burning a hole in the newly erected wall around her heart.

"No problem. Just slow down. Welcome home, Maryanne. It's good to see you." *His voice spoke straight to her core and made her quiver. A quick glance revealed no ring. Hallelujah, he wasn't married.*

He turned and quickly strode back to his SUV, lights still flashing.

The image from the past and present merged in her mind. Same uniform, jeans, boots, and cowboy hat. Same swagger and ass she just wanted to bite into.

The bakery door pushed open beside her, bringing her back to the present. She'd been staring aimlessly at the police station and hadn't even noticed Holly walking from the other direction.

"Morning, Maryanne. How's it going? Oh, I love your Halloween decorations! How'd you get the front window decorated so fast?"

Holly flicked her dyed silver braid over her shoulder. Holly had been in a car accident which caused a miscarriage and her husband's death two years ago. Last year, she'd moved to Crimson Creek, Texas, to join her brother and get a fresh start on life.

Holly's orange yoga shirt was loose over her black yoga pants, and she was sweaty from her morning session.

"Morning, Holly. I came in last night when I couldn't sleep. How was sunrise yoga? Did you have a big crowd?"

Maryanne asked as she bustled back behind the counter to make Holly's favorite fruit smoothie.

Maryanne didn't just have baked goods. She also had smoothies, milkshakes, cappuccinos, coffees, and more. She catered to her customers year-round. And with the addition of the CBD infused drinks and treats, business was booming.

Only a few years younger than Maryanne, Holly had moved to Crimson Creek with her brother last year. They both owned shops on Main Street and had quickly become friends.

"We had about half a dozen. Not bad for our second Saturday. What are you up to today?"

Maryanne handed over the smoothie and swiped her friend's card.

"Well, normally I'd be wrapping up about nine to take Cody to his soccer game, but Mom's taking all three of my nephews for the weekend."

Her sister, Cindy, worked at the hospital on the weekends, which meant Maryanne normally watched her nephews after closing early on Saturday.

"Wait, you have a free weekend? You're kidding me!"

"Nope. Want to have a girl's night? Unofficial, of course, since my sister is still working at the hospital. Maybe you and Lola can hang out? I need to dye my hair for the Halloween season."

"Tired of the purple highlights already? What are you going for next?"

"Orange," Maryanne said with a grin. She tightened her high ponytail and then leaned on the counter. Holly regularly came over to dye each other's hair: Holly's silver to match her grief, Maryanne's streaked with colors to match the holidays.

Holly had only been in town a year, but she and Lola were best friends already. Maryanne and Cindy grew up with Lola, always hanging out with her in the summers when they visited Crimson Creek.

"Why don't we go to the Electric Cowboy? Lola's been pushing me to get out and have some fun."

"Sure, that sounds great. I haven't been in years."

The Sheriff Gets His Girl: Chapter Two

October

"Wow, this place is packed! Is it always like this?" Maryanne asked Lola as she paid her cover charge and followed them into the bar on the outskirts of town. The L shape of the barn gave a view of both the bar and stage as she entered.

People mingled around on the dance floor in front of the stage. Orange Halloween lights draped the ceiling around the stage where a band was already playing. She couldn't see who it was, but they sounded good and she couldn't wait to dance.

Although the Electric Cowboy was legendary, Maryanne's busy schedule had kept her from the club over the last two years.

"Pretty much." Lola, the tallest of their group at six feet, glanced over the crowd and pointed to the side. "Let's grab some food first. Come on."

They walked past the bar and through the saloon doors into a back room. There were pool tables in the middle of the large space, with booths along the edges. The vibe was good here, relaxing and fun, and Maryanne instantly loved it.

They drew stares from the guys playing pool. Maryanne knew they were a striking group. Lola's dark auburn hair was pulled back in a ponytail. With her freckles and bright blue eyes, she was fresh-faced and all-natural. She wore her favorite plaid pearl snap shirt tied in a knot just above her belly button, tight jeans, and cowboy boots.

Holly was around five feet but with her dyed silver hair and blue eyes, she looked like a little fairy girl, ethereal, calm, smiling, and fragile in her petiteness.

She may have been a few years younger than Maryanne, but the tight purple dress and kitten heels definitely showed her as a woman in her twenties.

Maryanne was between the two on height, but she'd played up her other assets. Her orange sequined shirt was a deep v-cut nearly to her belly button, showing off her generous cleavage. Her favorite four-inch black heels did wonders for her legs and rounded ass.

They sauntered over to an empty booth and a waitress came and took their order. When she walked off, a loud, bushy-bearded man stumbled to their table, pool stick still in his hand.

"Hey, ladies. Wanna play a game of pool?" He smelled of cheap booze and cigarettes.

Maryanne flicked her black hair over her shoulder and smiled politely. "Maybe later, hot stuff. We need food first."

She turned to face her friends sitting on the opposite side of her as the man shrugged and wandered back to his game.

Holly laughed, covering her mouth with her hand. "You tell him, Maryanne."

Just then, the band in the main room started up a new song. The upbeat tempo seeped into her soul, making her body sway in her seat.

"Oh, I can't wait to get out on that dance floor." Lola tapped her fingers on the table in time to the muted music. "I really need to let loose a little. Mama's been driving me up the wall."

"Is she feeling any better?" Holly asked.

"Not really. Her cancer treatments are exhausting, but that's been going on for a while now."

Maryanne felt her heart constrict the more Lola talked about her mom.

The entire conversation reminded her of when her grandma passed away almost two years ago. She'd blown into town after her nasty breakup with nowhere to stay.

She'd moved in with 'Buela for a few weeks... only to find out that Hospice was already coming in to help. Mom and Cindy hadn't even known about Hospice.

She'd held on for another six months before passing away. It was hard to see her wither away slowly like that, and to hear that Lola's mom wasn't doing well...

The topic caused all three of them to fall silent until the waitress delivered their food and broke the tension.

"Perfect. Greasy food is just what I need on my weekend off." Maryanne popped a loaded French fry into her mouth. She needed to relax. Her CBD hadn't been as effective lately, and she didn't want to break out the last of her pot stash from Colorado. Maybe dancing would help.

"When are you going to hire someone to help at the bakery?" Lola asked as they ate.

Maryanne snorted. "Who says I need to?"

Lola rolled her eyes and dipped a fry into ketchup. "You haven't taken a day off all year, Maryanne, and it's the beginning of October. You're going to burn out if you don't get help."

"Nah, that's why we do girl's night on Thursdays, remember? To help us all meditate and de-stress and shit. Besides, I take off early on Saturdays for soccer games this time of year, and Sunday's we're closed."

"Taking off early isn't the same as taking a day off per week," Lola scolded. "And you still have all the church stuff to do on Sunday's, even if you're not in the bakery."

"Well, it's a good thing we're here tonight. I miss karaoke and dancing with my Colorado friends. Now, let's drain this pitcher of margaritas and hit that dance floor. The band is calling my name." Maryanne reached for her drink.

"It's the Williams' boys. They're pretty good, right? They play most weekends here. You should join them, Maryanne. Maybe you could do a duet with Gunner."

Maryanne nearly spit out her drink. "Wait, they're still playing? I thought they outgrew that years ago."

Lola grinned. "Nope. They're regulars here. Gunner says it helps keep the trouble away to have a cop as the lead singer at the bar. It's good, clean fun and none of that funny business you get at the bars down in Fort Worth or even over in Denton."

Maryanne drained her margarita, the strawberry tart on her tongue, and poured them all another round. She could feel the flush in her cheeks already, but hopefully her friends assumed it was alcohol related. Her thoughts naturally drifted to Gunner.

"I don't know that I've seen him out of uniform in the two years I've been back."

Holly tapped her chin. "I've seen him around the

grocery store a few times this year, but you're right. He's usually in uniform."

"And a mighty fine uniform it is, isn't it?" Maryanne sighed as she played with her straw.

"I love the short-sleeved one. I always want to push it up to see what that tattoo is." Lola wiggled her brows.

"But his biceps are so damn big, there's no way you could push his sleeve up even a little!" Holly smirked, making them all laugh.

"I never saw him as the tattoo type, but I guess the Marines changed him." Maryanne sipped her drink, wishing her mouth was wrapped around him.

"I didn't realize he was in the Marines. How long ago?" Holly ate the last fry and wiped her fingers on the napkin.

Lola shrugged, "A few years, right after high school. His girlfriend, Justine, wasn't happy that he'd enlisted, but he promised he'd stay faithful. Oh, I didn't tell y'all what happened did I? So, you know how Granny is friends with Mrs. Williams, right?"

Holly and Maryanne nodded, so Lola continued.

"Granny said that Mrs. Williams was so happy she was dancing in her kitchen last week because Justine moved back home."

"Because they're going to get back together?" Maryanne asked, a weight pressing on her chest.

Lola shook her head. "Nope, she was dancing because Justine and Gunner are officially over."

A lump formed in Maryanne's throat as she asked, "How does she know they're over?"

"Justine ran into Mrs. Williams with her new boyfriend and was so excited to move back home with him. Apparently, Justine didn't even realize that Gunner was waiting for her." Lola's brows waggled, and

Maryanne's heart ached for Gunner. He was probably devastated.

"Oh no, poor Gunner," Holly said. "He's such a good man. I hope he wins as sheriff."

Maryanne sat, dumbfounded as a new realization sank in. Perhaps Gunner had blown her off the past two years because of some misguided loyalty to his old ex-girlfriend. What did that mean now that he was free?

"Based on what Granny and Mrs. Williams said, I don't know if they were broken up, had expectations to get back together, or even if he's been faithful this whole time. Justine certainly hasn't, but I don't think Gunner's dated anyone, especially not since he moved home after the Marines." Lola's brows drew together as she reached for her drink.

Maryanne thought back to his visits to the shop the past few days. He wasn't keeping his eyes firmly on the floor or on the menu as much as last year. Her heart sped up at the thought that maybe she could finally win him over.

"We have to go dancing," Maryanne said, before chugging the last of her margarita.

Holly arched a brow. "Duh, that's why we're here."

"No, I mean right now. Come on!" Maryanne pulled them out of the seats and swaggered out the saloon doors onto the loud dance floor.

"Hey, I thought y'all were gonna play pool with us!" the older bearded man called.

Maryanne poked her head back in the door to say, "Maybe later. We want to dance!" Then she turned and headed toward the dance floor, with Holly and Lola trailing behind.

Grab your copy…
vinci-books.com/sheriff-gets-his-girl

About the Author

Jane Poller always wanted to write romance. After years of back and forth, she finally took the plunge and never looked back. She still teaches online and homeschools her teenagers full-time. But with a commercial pilot and Army veteran for a hubby, she has a lot of free time in between his trips to write whatever stories the characters demand of her. She lives in Texas in a small town on four acres with her family of four, plus their two dogs. When she's not doing all the family things, she's reading in the hammock by the pond, writing in the treehouse, quilting and crafting, or arguing with her characters who refuse to do what she wants.